Praise for Denzil Meyrick and the
D.C.I. Daley Thriller series:

'Touches of dark humour, multi-layered and compelli
Daily Record

'The right amount of authenticity . . . gritty writing .
most memorable'
The Herald

'Meyrick has the ability to give even the least important person in the plot character and the skill to tell a good tale'
Scots Magazine

'Following in the tradition of great Scottish crime writers, Denzil Meyrick has turned out a cracking, tenacious thriller of a read. If you favour the authentic and credible, you are in safe hands'
Lovereading

'Difficult to put down – it's definitely Scottish crime fiction at its best'
Scottish Home and Country

'Soon to be mentioned in the same breath as authors such as Alex Gray, Denise Mina and Stuart McBride . . . very impressive'
Ian Baillie, Lennox Herald

A note on the author

Denzil Meyrick was born in Glasgow and brought up in Campbeltown. After studying politics, he pursued a varied career including time spent as a police officer, freelance journalist, and director of several companies in the leisure, engineering and marketing sectors. Previous publications in the D.C.I. Daley thriller series are *Whisky from Small Glasses*, *The Last Witness* and *Dark Suits and Sad Songs*. He lives on Loch Lomond side with his wife Fiona.

THE RAT STONE SERENADE

THE RAT STONE SERENADE

A D.C.I. Daley Thriller

Denzil Meyrick

Polygon

First published in Great Britain in 2016 by Polygon, an imprint of Birlinn Ltd.

Birlinn Ltd
West Newington House
10 Newington Road
Edinburgh
EH9 1QS

www.polygonbooks.co.uk

ISBN 978 1 84697 340 6
eBook ISBN 978 0 85790 895 7

British Library Cataloguing-in-Publication Data
A catalogue record for this book is available on request from the British Library.

Typeset by Hewer Text UK Ltd, Edinburgh
Printed and bound in Great Britain by Clays Ltd, St Ives plc

At a fixed time of the year they assemble at a holy place in their territory.

Julius Caesar on the Druids

For my late grandfather, Cyril Pinkney, who drove the bus to 'Blaan' for many years.

Prologue

A hundred years ago. Blaan, near Kinloch

Torquil Dryesdale, lawyer and notary public from Kinloch, arrived on the back of Tam Murray's farm cart. The old farmer stuck out his hand, a knowing look on his face, as Dryesdale fumbled in his pocket and fished out a few coins with a sigh.

'Kindly wait here for me to conclude my business, Mr Murray.'

'Aye, that I will, sir. But you know fine, that'll mean mair coin.' He sniffed, then rubbed his nose along the length of a grubby sleeve.

'If you mean more than I've already given you, then yes, I'm well aware, Mr Murray. Just wait here.'

The lawyer brushed dirt and loose straw from his suit as he walked from the cart. He could hear a hammer clanging on metal in the distance, so followed the noise around the corner of the whitewashed house. Before him was a gravel yard, around which three open-ended buildings clustered. In the middle stood a massive Clydesdale horse, chewing on hay, as a large man bent over a plate-sized hoof, hammering in a new horseshoe.

'Mr Stuart!' shouted Dryesdale.

Though the blacksmith kept to his task, he raised a hand to show that he had heard. In a few moments, he stopped to examine the job, then stood stiffly, turning to face the lawyer.

'And jeest who are you?' he said, wiping his huge hands down the front of his greasy leather apron.

'I'm Torquil Dryesdale, of Perrit, Dryesdale and McCormack in Kinloch. We're the lawyers who sent you the letters you've been ignoring, Mr Stuart.' He held out his hand to shake Stuart's, but the big man didn't move.

'If this is anything tae dae with Archibald Shannon, I'm not interested.'

'It's nothing to do with whether you're interested or not,' replied Dryesdale, eyeing the hammer in Stuart's meaty fist. 'The law is the law: you sold this property to Mr Shannon over five years ago and now he wants to use the land for something else. You have to leave, Mr Stuart.' Dryesdale pulled at the tight collar of his shirt and swallowed, his mouth dry. He was much happier in court, or behind his desk in Kinloch. However, he'd drawn the short straw and the job of serving court papers to Nathaniel Stuart was his responsibility.

'This is from the Sheriff Court in Kinloch, Mr Stuart. You have exactly one calendar month from today to remove yourself from the premises. He reached into the inside pocket of his jacket and handed the big youthful blacksmith a folded document, fastened with a red wax seal.

Stuart looked down at the piece of paper and shrugged his broad shoulders, knots of muscle rippling in his thick arm as he lifted his hand to point into the distance.

'My people have lived here for hundreds of years, maybe thousands. We were here before the Lords of the Isles, who resided in the castle that used to sit at the top of that rock over there,' he said, pointing down the steep hill and along the beach to a distant promontory of land. 'Before Kinloch was a toon; before the red yins came o'er the sea and called oor country Scotland. Aye, an' I tell you something, right here's where we're going tae stay.'

'That's as may be, Mr Stuart. But you signed the deeds over to Mr Shannon. Surely you must remember doing this. The transaction was witnessed by my own office.'

'I remember fine. But Archie Shannon has reneged on his side o' the agreement.'

'There is nothing at all in the document signed by you and he that mentions anything that has not been taken into consideration by the court. This is a straightforward transaction, Mr Stuart. You sold the land to Mr Shannon and were given leave at his discretion to rent the property back, which you have done these past five years.'

'Aye, and should be able tae the next fifty years and then a further fifty, if those that come after me wanted tae,' growled Stuart, prompting Dryesdale to take a step back.

'No, Mr Stuart, that is most certainly not the case. As owner of the land, Mr Shannon has the right to ask you to leave this property after a notice period of one year has elapsed. That year is almost up.'

'He told me that we could live here for as long as we wanted – we shook hands on it. All he asked of me was tae pay the due rent, which I have done every quarter, jeest like he asked.'

Dryesdale shuffled his feet nervously. 'Whatever Mr Shannon may have said to you is not part of the written agreement, Mr Stuart. We've been through this in our communications. When Mr Shannon allegedly said this to you, who witnessed it?' Dryesdale's voice was croaky now because of his dry mouth.

'Me, I witnessed it!' shouted Stuart, his grip tightening around the handle of the hammer.

'Then I'm afraid that it is of no consequence. Frankly, Mr Stuart, I'm surprised that Mr Shannon has let you run your business from here for so long. Two blacksmiths in the one village can't be good for business.'

'Aye, well, we were here first. And forbye, he's no' a blacksmith. His faither and grandfaither, aye. Not him.'

'That's not important, Mr Stuart. He owns the business – and quite a few others in Kinloch, Glasgow and beyond. You have no choice. You have one month to take your leave or sheriff officers will remove you. Do you understand? Mr Shannon intends to build his new home here.' He gazed out at the scene below. 'And, I for one, don't blame him – despite the climb to get up here.'

Suddenly, Stuart lurched at the smaller man, catching him by the throat. 'Do you know who my people are, Mr Dryesdale?' he said, sending flecks of spittle over the lawyer's face.

'I've . . . I've heard it said you are of the Tinker community. I . . . I don't see what . . .'

'If I'm forced to leave this land, I will curse Archibald Shannon and all of his family, now and for ever more. Every fifty years, to mark the promise broken tae me, calamity will befall his family, aye, until the end o' time. Dae you understand?' He pushed Dryesdale onto the ground and stood over him. 'Go back tae Kinloch an' tell Archibald Shannon that.'

Dryesdale scrambled up and ran back around the corner and onto Murray's cart. 'Move, Mr Murray, and don't spare the whip!'

'C'mon, auld girl,' shouted Murray, calmly lifting the reins. 'As for the whip, well, that'd be a lot mair coin,' he added, as the cart moved slowly off, the large figure of Nathaniel Stuart watching it go.

The beach at Blaan, near Kinloch

He loved this beach, even though it was always winter, always cold, when he was here. He watched a gull riding the wind above the green storm-tossed sea – as though dangling from a string like the model planes on the ceiling of his bedroom in London.

Sometimes he could see ships on the horizon, but not today. The sky was slate-grey. At the far end of the stretch of fine yellow sand, the promontory thrust out into the sea like a rocky finger. He always imagined it had the head of a lion, big and bold. His father had told him stories of the castle that had once sat on the clifftop, facing the cold depths fearlessly from its tall perch. The boy was bewitched by thoughts of the olden days; to think that his ancestors had once lived there, on the high rock, in a time when men had swords and fought battles. Now, there were only a few stones left, an earthly reminder of times past.

When he had asked how many men their ancestor had in his castle – conjuring up in his mind the kings and princes he had read about in books and seen on trips to the big cinema in Kensington – his father had smiled indulgently.

'We weren't rich then, Archie. We fought for the clan chief, but we were strong and fierce.'

When Archie looked towards the other end of the beach, up to the high cliff on which the great house stood solid and indomitable, he couldn't imagine his family having ever been anything else but rich. He'd seen some children begging in the streets near home, just before Christmas. His mother told him they were poor. He'd studied one miserable little boy with a dripping nose and in ragged clothes and decided that he never wanted to be poor.

Up at the big house, he could see his mother on the terrace from time to time; no doubt checking that he hadn't strayed too near the sea. Like him, she was wrapped up against the cold.

He wanted to play a trick on her. He looked around. There, between two dunes, a small burn trickled over soft sand. As he followed its course backwards, away from the sea, he could no longer see the cliff, the house, or his mother.

His young mother shivered as she looked out from the terrace and to the beach below. She breathed deeply. The cool moist air was so fresh, so different from London. Glancing at her watch and deciding it was time that both she and the boy were out of the cold, she looked for her son.

She had seen Archie what seemed only moments before as he skipped and played on the sand, but she was dismayed to note that, so engrossed had she been in her novel, more than twenty minutes had now elapsed since she had last checked on him. Now, there was no sign.

She rushed to the balcony railing, a slight dizziness making her aware of the sheer drop on the other side. Leaning out as far as she dared, she could see nothing of her son on the beach, or the steep path that snaked up the cliff towards the mansion that loomed behind her.

'Archie! Archie!' she called, her heart pounding, face stinging against the cold. Some primeval instinct was pricking her. She craned her neck out further, terrified that she would see her son struggling in the crashing surf. But there was no one there and the cold green sea went about its relentless business.

The boy stopped in his tracks. When he looked back, he could still see the beach between the cleft of the large dunes, but as he made his way along the burn, the grey light seemed to darken and the sound of the waves grew muffled, as though he had his woollen bobble hat pulled over his ears. The smells were different, too; the salty tang of the sea gave way to something earthier, a rotting smell, like on his father's compost heap. He wrinkled his nose. This was the stench of something old, something decaying.

Startled by a faint rustling noise, he looked ahead.

'Hello?' he called, his voice dampened by the rough clumps of machair that clung to the sides of the dunes. 'Oh!'

There, only a few feet in front of him, stood a figure, still and silent, dressed like the monks he had seen on holiday in Italy. The hood of the man's dirty white cloak covered his bowed head.

'Hello. I'm Archie Shannon,' the boy said, accustomed to meeting strangers and raised to be polite. He turned around, wishing he could see the cliff, the big house and, most of all, his mother. Was this one of the boys from the village he'd played with on holidays? It was too big. But there was something intriguing about the hooded figure, something that compelled him to take a few steps closer . . .

1

The present day, Kinloch

The little boy was on the couch, only feet away from Daley.

'Come on, James,' he encouraged. 'Say "Dada".'

James Daley smiled at his father, gurgling.

Daley gave him an exaggeratedly eager look, leaning further towards him, grinning broadly. 'Dada,' he repeated.

The little boy appeared to think about this, gurgled and then burped, laughing. Reflections of the fairy lights on the large Christmas tree twinkled in his bright eyes.

Daley picked him up and stood at the window of the bungalow high on the hill above Kinloch, looking out across the bay. Trees swayed in the strong wind, and despite being sheltered from the storm-tossed sound by the island at its head, the loch simmered with white-tipped waves.

As he bounced his son in his arms, he realised that he would miss this place and its people. He had made friends here, good ones. And there was something cheering about waking up to the beautiful view every day, seeing the seasons change, the mood of the landscape altering to suit the weather. A vista that was cold and forbidding could be transformed by a sudden beam of winter sun shining bright through the clouds, turning this far-flung part of the west coast of Scotland into a scene reminiscent of an expansive Alpine lake.

He sighed as his gaze caught the line of white crosses that paraded, straight and true, along the hillside opposite. The dead of war were as they had been in life, in rank and file, shining bright above Kinloch's cemetery despite the gloom of the day. He saw the faces of those he had known, the fallen from his own time, but his sudden melancholy was fleeting, as he looked back into the eyes of his son, the image of his mother's, cornflower blue under sleepy, slanting lids.

He was still jiggling the boy on his knee, telling him a meandering tale of kings and princes, when he heard a car crackle on the stone chips of the driveway and stop near the house. He did not bother getting up, he didn't want to. He knew who was coming to call.

The door to the lounge swung open, revealing Liz, brushing away a loose strand of hair from her brow, her hands white with the flour she was baking with – her latest obsession.

'Didn't you hear the door, darling? Honestly. This is Chief Superintendent Symington. You knew she was coming.'

From behind Liz, a shorter woman appeared, resplendent in full uniform, the gold braid on her hat catching the lights in the room and glowing in response.

'Good morning, DCI Daley, I'm sorry to disturb your time off. As I said on the phone, I wanted to introduce myself away from the office. I'm sure you understand,' she said. Though short in stature, even at this brief exposure she exuded self-assurance. Liz grabbed James Daley junior, made her excuses and left them to it.

Daley studied his new, if very temporary, boss as she sat on the chair opposite. She had removed her hat to reveal short, dark hair. A sallow complexion framed her keen dark eyes, thin nose and full mouth. Despite her Mediterranean looks, she spoke with a soft English accent, which, though he didn't know why, surprised him. She was slim, straight-backed and immaculately turned out, in a uniform that spoke more of Hugo Boss than it did of the police service's tailor. Daley reckoned that she was probably in her mid thirties, though he had always found it difficult to put an age on policewomen in uniform, strange for one who had spent so much time around them. There was something about a uniform that aged people – especially the fairer sex, in his opinion. He reasoned though, given her exalted position, she could hardly be any younger.

'I trust you had a nice Christmas,' she said, sitting forwards in her chair.

'Yes, yes I did, thanks,' Daley replied, suddenly conscious of the fact that he hadn't said anything so far. He stood and held out his hand, which she shook, her grip surprisingly strong.

Daley sat back down. 'The wee man's first Christmas – always special.'

'Yes, I'm sure. Not something I know much about.'

Daley could hear Brian Scott's 'married tae the job' maxim echo in his head.

'Well, you know why I'm here, DCI Daley, I won't try to dress it up.'

'No point.'

'Indeed. You have, what, three weeks of your notice left to work, am I right?'

'Correct. Well, twenty-three days, to be exact.'

'I must tell you that our senior executive officers are still most unhappy with your decision to quit the job. In fact, the chief constable himself has urged me to personally ask you to stay. That's why I'm here, in fact.'

'Really?' Daley thought for a moment. 'But, what do you think?'

She paused and pursed her lips. 'In all honesty, from a personal point of view, I'm of the opinion that if an officer becomes so disenchanted with the police service that he or she contemplates taking early retirement, with all that entails, it's unlikely that they have the correct mindset to contribute effectively. However, I know that this is not an opinion shared by my superiors.'

'Thank you for your candour,' he said, noticing her take a quick look at her watch. She'd done what she came to do, now she wanted to be on to the next job.

'Do you have anything lined up? For the future, I mean.'

It was his turn to hesitate. He and Liz had argued long and hard about the future. She couldn't understand why her husband, having attained a reasonably high rank with prospects of further promotion, had decided to quit his job. For his part, despite being convinced that life as a police officer was no longer for him, he was at a loss to think of anything else he wanted – or was qualified – to do, save the usual options of security consultant or suchlike. In any event, the best and most lucrative of these roles were normally the preserve of retirees from the top of the tree, not its middle branches.

'Oh, I have a few irons in the fire,' he replied, less than convincingly.

'I would have thought that a man who has just started a

family, albeit late in life, would have been looking for security of employment. But there you are, nowt so funny as folks,' she continued, revealing more of her accent, probably from Yorkshire, Daley surmised. 'All this aside, however, it is my task to inform you that you would be in line for a permanent appointment as sub-divisional commander should you decide to stay. No immediate advancement in rank, but certainly a greater prospect of such in the very near future.'

Despite the offer, Daley had the feeling that Chief Superintendent Symington was merely going through the motions.

'Are you Donald's direct replacement?'

'If you are referring to the late Chief Superintendent John Donald then yes, I am.'

'Congratulations.'

'Thank you.' She looked about the room. 'Your wife has good taste.'

'How do you know I'm not responsible for the décor?'

'I've read your file DCI Daley, that's how I know. Anyway, I've imparted the information as requested. I'll leave you to the rest of your festivities. You're back at work tomorrow, I'm right in saying?'

'Yes, Hogmanay.'

'Good. I'll see you then.'

Symington shook his hand again as he showed her out of the front door. She didn't look back as she got into her waiting car, which took her back down Daley's drive towards Kinloch.

'Darling, I so wish you would change your mind,' said Liz, her son on her hip.

'So, you were listening?'

'Of course,' she replied, handing him the child. 'We'd better hope I get better at this baking lark – looks like I might end up doing it full time.' She looked down, then smoothed the front of her jeans. Daley's heart sank as thoughts of another woman filled his head.

2

Blaan

The Reverend Ignatius More puffed his way up the hill. He could see his church, small, neat and well maintained, nestled in the valley below and, despite himself, his heart soared with pride. The road from here back to his roots in the Australian Outback was a long one. From rough stockman to a man of the cloth, a minister in the Church of Scotland; it was something he could never have imagined.

His wife – as usual – was much further up the hill than he, at the top of the rise, almost. It was at times like this that the twenty years between them told. Mind you, he reasoned, she kept herself so fit it was unlikely he'd have kept up with her even if their ages coincided.

Soon they were both standing at the peak of the hill, looking down over a glade of oak trees and out across the sea, the loom of the island of Ireland a grey shadow in the distance. The festive season was his busiest time of the year and he appreciated the opportunity to get away from preaching and sermon writing to commune with God in the way he preferred – out, under the heavens, bathing in the glory of all before him.

‘Shall we turn back, or do you fancy going down to the woods?’ she asked, her Irish accent lilting on the breeze.

He looked at his watch. ‘Yes, I have loads of time before I have to get ready for tonight’s service. Why not?’

This was the second-last day of the old year, the day before Hogmanay, and being a Sunday, his flock would be expecting their evening service. He had to admit, he’d been surprised how pagan parts of the Christmas holiday had clung on here, not only in the village and its surrounding farms, but also in Kinloch, the town only ten miles or so away. It was strange to think that easily within living memory, the people of south Kintyre had worked as normal on Christmas Day, then had their holiday and exchanged gifts on Ne’er Day, as they called the first day of a new year. When he’d first come to the UK from Australia, he’d been fearful that he would be somewhat out of place in this modern, up-to-the-minute society. He’d detected something else though, especially in the more remote parts of Scotland; something old, something unseen and unspoken, but ever-present, nonetheless. People were still reluctant to let red-haired folk cross their threshold in the first hours of the new year; folk memory from a long time ago, when the sight of red-haired people in this part of the world meant death and destruction. It was strange how the tradition had persisted.

‘As long as you don’t tell my church elders I’ve been down at the Rat Stone,’ he said to her with a smile.

‘I wouldn’t dare. Sure, wouldn’t they be astonished that we’d made it back alive?’

‘I should imagine they would. Mind you, so would most of my parishioners.’

'I'm sure we'll be fine. Come on, time's not for waiting.' She heaved the straps of her rucksack higher onto her shoulders and set off down towards the oaken glade with the ancient stone at its heart. Strath na Draoidh – the Vale of the Druids.

There followed the familiar traipse through boggy ground that sucked at his walking boots, leaving cloying mud on his gaiters, then up onto the little plateau with its circle of trees.

He'd been here a handful of times before and on each occasion had felt strangely disconcerted as he set foot amongst the old gnarled oaks. It was the opposite feeling to being in a holy place, where the silence soothed and spoke of goodness and peace. Here, though there was quiet, there was no peace; the silence seemed to threaten.

He stopped in his tracks. The wind was getting up and with it a wail, a moan almost, whistled through the ancient grove. The Rat Stone Serenade, the old song of the trees. Local tradition had it that the trees were wailing for the past, for older, darker days and all those that inhabited them. He shivered, wishing they had opted to cut their walk short at the top of the hill.

'Ignatius, quickly!' His wife's shout was short and anxious. As the whine through the trees became louder, he hurried towards her. He tripped and fell over the knotted root of an old tree that twisted from the ground like the curls of a serpent.

'Iggy!'

He got back up and half limped, half ran towards her – anxious now, hearing panic in her voice.

'Look!' she said, almost in tears as she pointed to a flat slab of granite, an oblong about the length of a tall man, but twice as broad.

'Oh my . . .' Fear constricted his throat.

There, arranged in perfect anatomical order, lay a skeleton, the bleached white bones stark against the black stone; by their size, the remains of a child.

Having spoken to his new boss already that day, Daley hadn't expected to hear her voice on the other end of the line when he picked up the phone. Now he was in a rickety old Land Rover with Superintendent Symington and a young DC as they made their way across a rutted field. As the vehicle jolted them along, the farmer it belonged to, Charlie Galbraith, at the wheel, Daley reflected on yet another day off spoiled by a recall to work. Not for much longer, he reassured himself.

'Am I right in thinkin' you're English?' asked Galbraith, turning in his seat to look at Symington.

'And that's important, why?' she replied, staring straight ahead.

'Och, you know how it is with us Scots, missus. Rightly or wrongly, we don't always see eye tae eye with Sassenachs. That's all I'm saying, mind.'

'We're not far away now, are we, Charlie? Daley asked, trying to shut the elderly man up. 'Bloody dark already.'

'Aye, dark in mair ways than one, Mr Daley. This land has been in oor family for generations. I grew up here, aye, an' I spent my life right here on this farm. But I'll tell you something; I've only been amongst they auld oak trees a handful of times.'

'Really, in your whole life?' enquired Symington, suddenly interested in what he had to say.

'Aye, and it's many years since I was last there, tae.'

'Oh well, this'll be a nice change for you,' she replied, not without a hint of sarcasm.

'No, not for me,' he said, bringing the Land Rover to a halt. 'I would rather cut oot my ain eyes than go up there tae the stone. This is as far as I'm going.' He folded his arms across his chest.

'You aren't being serious?'

'I am indeed, madam. In any event, there's no way this auld thing would make it up the rise. From here you're on foot. Aye, and on your own, tae.'

Daley shone the heavy torch along the ground in front of him, anxious to avoid tripping over the tree roots that thrust from the terrain like the gnarled fingers of an old woman. He heard Symington curse as she tripped, and turned to see her being hauled up by up the large and more than capable figure of DC Wilkinson.

Daley was used to death; its cloying stench had followed him throughout his years as a police officer. From the pensioner lying dead of cold in a Glasgow multi-storey to the gangster, face down in a pool of his own blood, he had seen it all. But rather than become inured to it, each time he looked into the glazed eyes of a corpse he pictured them shining bright with the vitality that had been taken away. These were people robbed of something more important than all the wealth in the world – their own existence. Yet another melancholy thought he hoped would disappear with his police ID.

'What a bloody racket!' shouted Symington above the whine of the wind through the trees. 'I hope we haven't got much further to go.'

There was indeed an eerie moan; high-pitched, it echoed through the trees.

'No, nearly there,' replied Daley, seeing the flash of a torch up ahead.

Soon, they reached a clearing, where three figures stood, huddled into their coats.

'Hello, sir. Sorry to drag you out, but I thought you'd better see this right away,' said Pollock, the middle-aged, thickset constable whose rural beat covered Blaan and who had been first to respond to the call. 'It's like nothing I've ever seen before, sir,' he continued, his salt-and-pepper moustache bristling.

Daley stepped closer to the couple who were entwined in an embrace, their breath rising in clouds. The man was tall, but only slightly more so than the woman, who was wide-eyed and upset, her head leaning on his shoulder. By the lines on his face, Daley saw that he was older than his female companion. He'd heard of Ignatius More, the minister at Blaan church, though he hadn't met him. He remembered the rumour and innuendo in Kinloch when he had taken a new – and much younger – wife. Recollections of a young woman, nervously pressing the front of her skirt, flashed through his mind again. He banished the thought.

'Reverend More, I'm Jim Daley. Sorry to have kept you here, I came as quick as I could.' In fact, thought Daley, he was surprised that Pollock hadn't sent the couple home out of the cold once he had arrived at the scene.

'Hello, Mr Daley, I've heard about you – all good, of course,' said More, his Australian accent strong. 'This is my wife, Veronica.'

Daley shook the woman's gloved hand. 'Pleased to meet you, though I wish the circumstances were different, Mrs More. Let's have a look at what you've found.'

'Oh, it's horrible, Mr Daley,' she said. 'Just horrible.'

Daley shone his torch down to the dark slab at their feet. It was only knee high, but long, approximately rectangular in shape. The bright white bones stood out on its black surface, all in order, as he'd been told. The neat little skull was on his left, the thin bones of the feet to the right.

'Let's get you back out of the cold and we can talk,' said Daley, seeing Mrs More shiver.

'May I enquire why you left these good people out here to freeze in the first place, constable?' asked Symington.

Pollock shifted from one foot to the other. 'Aye, well, ma'am. I wasn't just sure how you would like to proceed. I mean, it's not every day we come across something like this.'

'Oh, please don't blame the constable,' said Reverend More. 'We weren't about to leave him here alone.' As he spoke, the wind whined louder through the trees. 'Not the kind of place anyone should be alone, I reckon.'

As Symington and the Mores picked their way by torchlight through the glade of oaks, back to the Land Rover, Daley took the chance to speak to PC Pollock.

'I'll leave DC Wilkinson with you until SOCO and the rest of the troops arrive. I want to interview the minister and his wife at home. You know the score, maintain the integrity of the locus etc. I'll be back to see how the team are getting on.' Daley hesitated. 'Are you OK, Willie?'

'Aye,' he paused. 'As you know, sir, I'm not one for romancing. None o' this bloody fanciful stuff – a spade is a spade as far as I'm concerned. But I'm not ashamed to say, well, there's something about this place . . .'

'C'mon, Willie, I expect that kind of thing from old Charlie Galbraith, not you.'

'Aye, easy to say, not so easy to dae, sir.' He looked down at the small skeleton. 'Who's going to tell the Shannons about this?'

'The Shannons? What do they have to do with it?'

'You'll recall, sir, that every year the Shannon family hold their AGM up at Kersivay House. Remember you had me detailed there over Hogmanay last year? You know, at the gate, sir?'

'Ah yes, the Superintendent's idea, not mine, if I remember rightly,' replied Daley, recalling Donald's obsession at getting everything 'just right' as far as the Shannon family were concerned. Was that really only a year ago? So much had changed.

'You might remember that they suffered a family tragedy, back in the sixties, sir.'

'Vaguely. I think I've read something about that, now you mention it.'

'Aye, a wee boy, about six when he disappeared. Never saw hide nor hair of him again, apart from his left shoe lying on the beach.' He shone his torch down on the black stone. 'I'm no pathologist, but that's the skeleton of a child, sir. And the way the bones are bleached, well, they look old – in my book, anyway.'

Daley stared at the little skull. He knew something of the Shannon family case, knew that they were a very rich family and that Pollock was right, as far-fetched as it may seem, to flag up a possible connection between the bones laid out in front of them and the family who visited the clifftop mansion once a year. It looked as though the last few weeks of his police career were not destined to be as calm as he'd hoped.

3

The manse stood at the edge of the village, on the road back to Kinloch. Having been driven back across the field by the indelicate farmer Galbraith in his Land Rover, Symington and the Mores had swapped vehicles; Symington's exceptionally clean police car, complete with driver, was now parked on the gravel driveway outside the solid Georgian house.

Daley raised a hand in farewell as Galbraith reversed back down the driveway. He chapped at the large brass knocker and the Reverend More opened the door.

'DCI Daley, do come in out of the cold,' he said, ushering the detective into the warm hallway. Daley noted the paintings of local beauty spots jostling for space with photographs on the walls as he walked into the wood-panelled lounge, a blazing fire at its heart. Veronica stood elegantly, her back to the flames, while Superintendent Symington perched on the edge of a Chesterfield couch.

After the usual pleasantries – and the offer of a glass of whisky that Daley regretfully declined – More made his apologies and left the room to change, in readiness for the evening service. He would, he reassured Symington, only be a few minutes, following which he would be able to answer any questions she and Daley might have for him.

Left alone with Symington and Daley, Veronica launched into conversation. It turned out that she and her husband walked most days, taking in the beautiful scenery around Blaan, as well as helping the new Mrs More meet her husband's flock outwith the confines of the church.

'I've come to realise that the life of a minister's wife is much more involved than I had expected, Mr Daley,' she said, nursing a glass of wine. 'I've never been involved with so many groups and societies. All great fun, though. And the people here are just lovely.'

'So you haven't come across any resentment?' asked Symington, rather brusquely, Daley thought. 'I mean, you are clearly a few years younger than your husband. I know how difficult certain elements of small rural communities can be about that sort of thing. I'm from one myself.' Daley wondered if his new boss had inadvertently given something of herself away by that remark. Certainly, he detected a momentary look of regret on her face.

'Oh, you and me both, superintendent,' replied Veronica. 'This place isn't all that different to the village in Ireland where I grew up – the same obsession with gossip, for one. But sure, don't we all have our own faults? In the main, people are nice and kind. Iggy works hard and I think folk appreciate that.'

'Iggy?' asked Daley with a smile.

'I know. Iggy, short for Ignatius. I love the man but not his name, Mr Daley. Of course, I daren't call him that in front of the parishioners. It would cause nothing short of a riot. They'd probably take me down to the Rat Stone and . . .'

'What do you know about this Rat Stone?' asked Daley.

'Just what I've been told, mainly by the older members of our congregation. It's ancient, I know that. The Vale of the Druids, if you please. Old Jock would be able to tell you more. He's a retired writer, lived here for most of his life and loves the history of Blaan. It was him that first took me to see the stone.'

The lounge door swung open. 'One of the very few local people who will go anywhere near the place,' said More, now decked out in his vestments. 'Lovely guy. There's nothing about Blaan he doesn't know.' He stood beside his wife, putting his arm around her waist. 'Strange how traditions maintain in this country. I found it so odd when I first came here. In Australia, we've all kind of lost touch with our roots. Leave all that ancestor stuff to the Aborigines. Not that there's anything wrong with that, you know,' he added hurriedly, after a look from his wife.

'What traditions are you talking about?' asked Daley.

'Oh, you know, all that ancient magic stuff, paganism, a certain way of doing things. Fascinating if you study it, dates back to the sun worship of prehistory. Little quirks still persist, like never clockwise, always anti-clockwise – widdershins, they call it.'

'Fascinating, I'm sure,' observed Symington.

'Yeah, it is. Do you know, they don't come to church here, they still "go to the stone"?'

'I thought nobody went there?' said Daley, momentarily confused.

'Oh, it's to the church they come, but that's what they say. It's an echo of what used to happen. Clearly, the Rat Stone was the centre of worship here, long before Christianity was even heard of.'

Veronica's face darkened. 'Though I'm not sure that worship is the right way to describe it. Evil – pure evil – went on there. Human sacrifice, that's what the druids were all about.'

'Oh, don't listen to her. The druids were devoted to learning, healing, protecting the environment,' said More. 'My wife finds it hard to leave her old profession behind, sometimes.'

'I'm sure no one is interested in that,' she said, glaring at the minister.

'Why not?' said Symington.

Veronica raised her eyes to the ceiling. 'Once upon a time, I was a nun. I spent eight years of my life locked away from the world. It was a long time ago but, as you can see, I saw the light and decided to carry on God's work out in the open. In the community rather than hidden from it. The druids might have been the first eco-warriors my husband describes, but if you crossed them, or formed part of their rituals, well, you weren't in a good place. We know that much.'

'But old habits die hard, is that not right, my dear?'

'Ha ha,' she replied, her smile thin. 'Seriously though, there's something about that stone, it draws you in. It's like the feeling you get when you stand too near to the edge of a cliff. You feel that you want to jump.' She looked straight at Daley. 'There's no good there, no good at all. I – everyone – can feel it. It pulls at you.'

'And you, Reverend More. You are a long way from home. Why choose to be a minister here?' asked Daley.

'Oh, I love it – dream come true, in fact. Mind you, if I were to stand here and bore you with all the twists and turns my life's taken, I'd miss the service tonight – and probably the one after that, too.'

'So you didn't enjoy your pastoral work in Australia?' asked Symington.

'Oh, yeah, I mean, for the short time I was there. I only worked as a man of the cloth at home for a couple of years. Spent my earlier life drifting, you know. I've been a stock man, sheep shearer, tour guide – you name it.'

'So why the church?' asked Daley.

More smiled. 'I had an epiphany, if you like. No heavenly trumpets, choirs, or golden visions, but I woke up one morning after a night on the grog. We'd been taking a thousand head of cattle over to new grazing in the Northern Territory. It was hot, dusty work, so we all enjoyed a coldie of an evening. Me more than most.' He grimaced. 'I'll never forget it. I woke up under a blanket, just as it was getting light, the sun was rising, but the stars . . . billions of them still in the part of the sky that was black.' He paused, looking up as though he could still see them glinting. 'I watched as the sun slowly washed those stars out and I could feel its warmth on my face. Something happened, I don't know what. Suddenly I just knew that there was something else – something bigger, you know what I mean?' He looked to Daley and Symington with a smile.

'And you ended up here. Happy?' asked Daley.

'Yup, and never regretted it. I had a pretty rough time as a kid. My father was handy with his fists, especially when he'd had a tinny or two, which was most nights.'

'Is that not something you have in common with him? Enjoying a drink, I mean?' asked Symington.

'No, not at all.' More's tone was pleasant, though Daley recognised a flash of irritation on the minister's face. 'Back in my stockman days, yes, everyone drank. I like a glass or two but that's where the similarity ends. In any case, my father and I didn't share any genetics, superintendent. I was adopted as a youngster.'

'What about your real parents?' asked Symington.

'My father refused to say and my mother was too scared to disagree.' He shrugged his shoulders.

'Have you ever tried other channels?' Symington persisted.

'Yeah, I did – half-heartedly, I suppose. Though much good it did me back then. Thousands of orphaned kids found themselves adopted by families who used them as slave labour – nothing else. I was no different.'

'If you'd approached the authorities, could they have checked back for you?' asked Daley.

'No questions asked in that part of the world back then, Mr Daley.'

'A lot of unwanted children from Ireland were shipped down under, and from the UK, too,' interjected Veronica. 'As my husband says, treated like cattle – little more than unpaid help until they reached an age that they could do something about it and leave. I'm right, aren't I, darling?'

'Yep, pretty much. But a bad start to life doesn't mean that the rest of it will be the same – I know that.'

Daley thought of some of the children he had come across in the course of his career, many of whom had not been as lucky as the Reverend More – a bad start leading to a worse middle and pitiful end to life.

He asked the Mores some further questions then made his excuses, anxious to find out if the forensic team had arrived to examine the skeleton found on the Rat Stone.

Outside, he was just about to radio in to request that the police Land Rover pick him up when the manse's front door opened again and Symington walked out.

'I want you to come with me to Kersivay House, DCI Daley.'

'If you say so, ma'am.'

'I want to present a united front. From what I can glean from the files in Kinloch, these Shannons can be bloody difficult. They're real players, the company is still family owned and it's one of the biggest private enterprises in the world.' She looked at Daley. 'And in my experience, the more money people have, the more demanding and difficult they can become.'

4

Ailsa Shannon sat by the window of her top-floor room in Kersivay House. The only light came from the gibbous moon, which hung low over the sea, casting a pale thread upon the rippling water.

She loved the view from this window, high in the big mansion on its towering cliff, dark and immovable. It felt as though both the house and the sheer granite upon which it perched had been hewn by the forces of time and nature.

In her eightieth year, she mused on how important this place had been in her life. Faces passed before her mind's eye: some youthful, now grown old; some for ever young, frozen for eternity where time had left them. Memories, both good and bad.

A Mozart symphony soared in the large room; a suite really, with a separate bedroom and sitting area. To dispense with the long climb, she had ordered a lift be installed for her convenience, though for those of more tender years, fleet of foot and heart, the dizzying spiral staircase still corkscrewed down to the ground floor.

She felt this mansion was part of her, solid and ever present, always in the back of her mind – a hundred years old, nearly. Kersivay House had been the dream of Archibald

Shannon, a dream made real in stone and glass, facing boldly out to sea from the cliff that shared its name. No wind was too strong, no sea too wild to breach its tough façade; a symbol of the family that made it. A hundred years ago it had been a portent of the success that was to come, the success that saw the Shannon family, the descendants of a humble Blaan blacksmith, rise to dominate the world of business and commerce.

In the shadows cast by the pale moonlight she noticed that a dark crack had appeared in the high ceiling, splintering down to the top of the wide window frame. As the music faded, the old house creaked and groaned in the quiet cold of the midwinter evening. She thought of her husband, now long dead, the feckless son who now frustrated her so, and the little boy, lost to her long ago. She pictured her in-laws, nieces, nephews, their children, spouses, friends, lovers; her granddaughter, so beautiful, so sensitive, but so troubled. They were all here for another New Year, but for how many more?

She stared down onto the terrace balcony, which overlooked a stretch of sand upon which the tide lapped cold and dark. In her mind, under a long-ago grey sky, she could still see the little boy with his bobble hat and coat, buttoned up to its velvet collar to keep out the cold.

A knock at the door broke the spell.

'Come in,' she called. The solid oak door creaked open and an old man stepped into the dark room.

'Sorry to disturb you,' he said politely, though his low voice was laced with insincerity and irritation. 'We have visitors.'

'We have lots of visitors, Percy. To whom in particular do you refer?'

'The constabulary are here, they want to speak to you.'

'Oh well, please put on some lights, then show them up, if you don't mind.'

Percy mumbled under his breath as he hobbled around the room, switching on various lights. 'Why are you sitting in the dark?' he asked, the question more like an accusation.

'Because that's what I want to do. I'm sorry that it doesn't meet with your approval.' She watched him, the room now bright in the lamplight. He was thinner than ever, stooped, the wrinkles on his face highlighted by the white of his hair and sparse goatee beard.

Percy was the old family retainer, a throwback to days long gone. He and his plump wife lived in a small cottage in the grounds, one of the few buildings left standing after the old blacksmiths had been demolished to make way for the mansion. He had been caretaker for more than sixty years. She remembered him when he was young and fit, dark haired with a lantern jaw, able to turn his hand to anything; irascible, but with a kind of guileless charm. He had made Kersivay House his life; as caretaker he had taken his role seriously and performed it well. Accustomed to having the place to themselves, he and his wife had become less and less happy with the annual influx of Shannons as the years went on – but then again, so had Ailsa.

'How old are you now, Percy? I always forget.'

'Not in my dotage, as your nephew thinks,' he replied testily, careful not to reveal his age. He had taken a cloth from his pocket and was rubbing at the brass surround of a light switch. 'Honestly, I don't know what people are doing with their hands these days. Finger marks all over the place. I was brought up to wash my hands and not plaster them across everything.'

Ailsa smiled as he mumbled on, his attention now taken up by the angle of a lampshade. 'I'm sure the police officers won't mind about that. Please go and fetch them – and take the bloody lift! Climbing that staircase in your mid eighties is bordering on the suicidal.'

'I'm in my early eighties,' he replied, less than convincingly. 'Anyhow, the policeman doesn't look as though he'd make it to the first floor, great gut hanging over his trousers. And as for the little bitch he has with him, well, by the sound of it, she's English. Adorned with buttons and braid like the old king, if you please – just a wee lassie, too. What good would she be in a fight? I don't understand why they bother with policewomen.'

'Off you go – and try to keep your archaic prejudices to yourself,' Ailsa chided as he mumbled his way out of the door.

In the lamplight, the crack above the window frame looked longer and deeper. She stared at it then picked up the business magazine lying at her side.

There he was, her nephew, Maxwell Shannon, under the bold headline: THE RISE OF THE HEIR APPARENT.

She scanned the article once more: *After running Shannon International's North American banking operation, Maxwell Shannon's stellar rise in global business seems without limit as he is poised to take control of the world's largest private company from his ailing father.*

I want to begin the process of forming Shannon International for the twenty-second century, never mind the twenty-first, he was quoted as saying. *My vision will see us continue to challenge the largest multinationals and our dominance in areas of finance, mineral extraction and technology go from strength to strength.* There was an accompanying picture of Maxwell smiling sickeningly from behind his large desk in the Shard, the lighting angled strategically to minimise the lines around his eyes.

She took a deep breath and thought of her own son, Bruce. Were it not for his father's premature death, it would have been he and not his cousin Maxwell being interviewed, struggling behind the scenes to wrest control of the company from the hands of the board.

But the two cousins were on opposite poles. Maxwell was ruthlessly focused, Bruce dissolute and self-indulgent. While Maxwell would sell his soul to succeed, her son was more likely to turn over in bed to sleep on, to hell with business and its exigencies. There was one thing, though, that she was sure of: Bruce had a good heart. Maxwell was cruel, manipulative and vindictive – a living embodiment of the very worst qualities of the Shannon family she had been part of for so many years.

She gazed at that face again, smiling triumphantly from the glossy pages of the magazine. 'You haven't won yet, nephew.'

She put the magazine down and stared at her reflection in the black window, waiting for her visitors to arrive.

Hidden from Ailsa's view, on the beach below, a dark figure emerged from a cleft between the dunes and looked up at the mansion on the cliff, a deep hood obscuring their face.

The sea splashed onto the shore, hissing over the shingle on its retreat. A cloud of breath rose from the cloaked figure, illuminated only by the moon. Light flashed off cold steel, held out in front of the hooded face. A soft chant was carried on the light breeze, up from the beach, across the fields and, gaining strength, through the trees that guarded the Rat Stone.

Brian Scott started the car in his driveway in Kirkintilloch, turning the heater on full blast to melt the ice that obscured his windscreen.

He rubbed his hands together and cursed. The night before Hogmanay and here he was, just about to embark on the drive to Kinloch; a journey which was long and arduous enough on a bright summer's day, never mind on a night like this, as the temperature plummeted in tandem with his resolve.

Scott was a man with a mission: he had been tasked – by the Chief Constable, no less – with persuading his long-time colleague and best friend Jim Daley to withdraw his resignation.

He mentally replayed the conversation with his boss of bosses.

'With the greatest respect, sir. When oor Jimmy – I mean DCI Daley – has made up his mind, there bugger a' . . . there's not much you can dae to change it.'

'Nonsense, DS Scott. If there is one man that Daley listens to, it's you. I've read your files – both of them,' he added, staring at Scott from over his narrow spectacles.

'That cannae have made pleasant reading,' mumbled Scott, not intending his superior to hear.

'Indeed it did not,' observed the Chief Constable, opening a file on his desk. 'I find here that you've been arrested

– *arrested*, mark you – on no less than four occasions since joining up.'

'Aye, well, sir, you'll see that these arrests were proven tae be in error,' said Scott, nervously clearing his throat. 'I wasn't guilty of any crimes, so tae speak.'

'Apart from the assault on Inspector Galloway at your office party in Paisley three years ago, I think I'm right in saying.'

'Och, I mean, passions was running high, sir. And you'll note that bas— that the Inspector dropped the complaint no' long after.'

'Not before the late Superintendent John Donald, upon whom we shall not dwell, metaphorically forced his arm up his back to do so, reading between the lines of this report, at least.'

Scott grimaced then looked at the floor. 'Aye, eh, whatever you say, sir.'

'I also note that you are in receipt of ten commendations and the Queen's Police Medal for bravery, DS Scott. As well as having been shot twice in the line of duty.'

'Aye, well, feast and famine wae me, sir, if you know what I mean.'

'This is a new force, Brian. And as you know, all has not been plain sailing since the formation of Police Scotland.' He removed his glasses and stared at Scott. 'I am relying on experienced, talented, clever detectives like you and DCI Daley to be the backbone of this new organisation. I want you to help bring on the next generation of police officers, in the way that the previous generation nurtured you.'

Scott gulped.

'You look surprised, Brian.'

'No, it's no' that. I just cannae mind much nurturing goin' on.'

'Well, times have changed and they'll change more and more. I need the likes of you and Daley to be the core of this new force as we establish ourselves as the best crime fighting institution in the UK. I cannot afford to lose someone like Daley, and I want you to make sure that I don't – understood?'

Scott watched the ice slip down the windscreen as the heater did its work. 'Easy tae say, not easy tae dae,' he muttered, as he flicked on the windscreen wipers, then jumped as someone knocked on the window.

'Are you trying to gie me a heart attack, woman!' he shouted above the noise of the engine.

'Typical. No "thanks for remembering my sandwiches, or, cheerio, dear, I'll miss you"', said his wife, Ella, resplendent in a fake leopard-skin onesie.

'Oh, aye, thanks,' replied Scott, as she handed the plastic box of sandwiches through the window. 'Get yourself back in the hoose.'

'Don't worry. A blast of cold air won't dae me any harm.'

'I'm no' thinking aboot that. I'm no' wanting the neighbours tae see you parading aboot like Catwoman gone tae seed. Why oor Tracy bought you that for Christmas, I'll never know.'

'You drive safely, you grumpy bastard,' she said, leaning through the window to kiss him on the cheek. 'And don't be hitting the bevy as soon as you get doon there. You've done really well o'er Christmas. Just a couple o' beers wae your dinner. Try and stick tae that.'

'Aye, well, I'll try and keep it doon tae a dull roar. It's not so easy, sitting all by yourself in a pokey wee hotel room, night after night, wae nobody tae talk tae.'

'You? You wae nobody tae talk tae! Aye, and I'm the Pope.'

'You'll have tae hand back your season ticket at Ibrox in that case.' He smiled.

Ella hurried back indoors as he edged the car out of the drive. 'Bloody Kinloch, here I come,' he sighed, turning up the car stereo in the hope that Pink Floyd would make the next few hours pass more quickly.

5

'Well, I don't know quite what to say,' said Ailsa, clearly upset. 'One tries to keep the past in its place – especially when we all congregate here every year. This has brought it back as though it all happened yesterday, not fifty years ago.'

'Yes, it must be so hard,' replied Symington. 'That's why we came to tell you now, instead of leaving it until morning. Sad to say, connections are bound to made locally.'

'Not much doubt about that,' Daley added.

'And this – these remains – how likely do you think it's . . .'

'A forensic team is at the site now, Mrs Shannon. The skeleton will have to be taken to the lab in Glasgow. If we can make any kind of identification – and that is by no means guaranteed – we'll inform you as soon as we have the details.' Symington reached across to hold the old woman's hand. 'This may be some sick prank, or completely unconnected to the disappearance of your son. I'm sorry that you have to go through this.'

Daley, admiring the way his new superintendent was handling the awkward situation, was quietly observing Ailsa. Though he knew her age, he found it hard to believe she was an octogenarian. She had grey hair, cut and styled in a modern fashion, though not out of keeping with her age. She was tanned, slim and fit, her clothes understated yet elegant and, despite news of the gruesome discovery, she remained composed, her bright green eyes focused on Symington, taking in every detail. He tried to imagine how she must feel, the loss of her son brought back in such an unpleasant way.

'I will inform the rest of the family tonight. As you say, there is little point trying to keep anything like this quiet in Blaan. We bring in extra staff, most of them local, at this time of year, to help with numbers. I imagine the village – and Kinloch, come to that – will be abuzz with this news already.'

'Will there be a lot of people about?' asked Daley. 'I had imagined that your meetings here were relatively small family affairs.'

'Oh, the family – the board – are the focus of events. But nowadays, when you add on wives, children, grandchildren, personal staff, accountants, advisors, lawyers, etc., well, the whole thing has become rather a three-ringed circus.'

'So it wasn't like this fifty years ago?' asked Symington.

'No, no. The family was so much smaller then. And, of course, Percy and his wife were much younger, so apart from a couple of maids whom we brought with us, he and his wife coped with our requirements. So much better, in many ways. But as I'm sure you know, Superintendent, times change, and rarely for the better, in my opinion.'

'Is Percy the older gentleman who showed us up?' asked Daley.

'Yes. He's become an irascible old bugger.' She smiled. 'He and his wife should have retired years ago, but they don't want to, and since they've become such an institution as far as the family is concerned, I daresay there'd be a wholesale revolt if they tried to.'

'So, was this Percy – sorry, I don't know his surname – were he and his wife here when your son went missing?' asked Symington, revealing some of the bluntness Daley had spotted earlier in the day.

'Percy and Morag Williamson – and most certainly they were here then. In fact, they've been here since Percy was in his twenties. In the past he was responsible for maintaining the house and gardens, while her preserve was cooking and housekeeping. Over time we've had to force them to wind down a bit. Now he mainly potters about, fixing things here and there or riding about on the little lawnmower tractor we bought him. He's more of an odd-job man now. If anything of any consequence needs attention, we bring in contractors from Kinloch.' Ailsa inadvertently cast her eyes up to the large crack above the window as she said this. 'They live in the old cottage in the grounds. It's been their home for more years than I care to remember. Makes me feel my age.'

'So, basically, the house is only occupied for a few days each year around this time?' asked Daley.

'Well, yes and no, chief inspector. The house is available to be used by family and friends throughout the year. But they all have such busy lives now and are more likely to spend their holidays in the Bahamas rather than Blaan. One or two still come up in the summer. I try to visit each June, that's a lovely time of year here. And the bloody Bahamas are too hot for me.'

'So how many people will be in the house this New Year?'

'As many as sixty, perhaps more. We have the house itself and the annexe that my husband built,' she said.

'So a considerable number. Quite an undertaking, I would imagine,' said Symington.

'Yes, superintendent. Of course there are some of my family who would much rather that this little tradition was dispensed with entirely.'

'Times change, I suppose,' said Daley. 'Your husband died quite young, I believe, Mrs Shannon.'

'Yes, in his late thirties, I'm sad to say. He never got over the loss of our son, Archie. We had another child, but he never came to terms with whatever happened to his first born.' She looked at Daley sadly. 'He started drinking heavily. I suppose the grief along with running the business was just too much to bear. I couldn't get close to him, latterly.'

'So he was in charge?' asked Symington.

'Oh, yes, very much so. In many ways, despite his premature death, what he put in place were the foundations of what the company has now become. He was far-seeing in terms of investment and new opportunities. We made a move into minerals and oil at the right time, when prices were cheap. He was a clever man.'

'So who runs the show now?' said Daley.

'Well, we all have a say. After my husband's death, his younger brother took over as managing director. As the business became much more complex, we had to bring in expertise from the wider business community. Though my brother-in-law is still alive, he has been incapacitated for many years with dementia. His son – my nephew Maxwell – runs the business with a chief executive.'

Daley noticed the look of disgust that crossed her face and raised his brows.

'Goodness,' said Ailsa, noticing his reaction. 'Are my inner thoughts so transparent? Well,' she laughed, 'though my son and I still have a significant shareholding, we have been rather marginalised. Of course, much of the problem lies with him. Though Bruce – my son – has a keen business brain, like his father, he shares the same demons.'

'Meaning?'

'He assuages his frustrations with drink and goodness knows what else, Mr Daley. He should be here now, but he's still in London. It's the curse of getting old: one's family becomes more and more troublesome and disappointing as the years go by, or so it would appear.'

As if on cue, the door burst open to reveal a young woman, her bowed head shaded from the lights in the room. She looked to be in her late teens or early twenties, with dark, almost black hair, cut into a bob with a heavy fringe. She lifted her face to look at Ailsa and the police officers, then started to moan; a quiet, low keening.

'Nadia, dear,' said Ailsa, rising from her chair and hurrying over to the girl. 'Hush now, there's nothing to worry about.'

Seconds later, a woman wearing a plain blue dress arrived and gently took the girl by the arm. 'I apologise, Mrs Shannon. Nadia is really unsettled tonight for some reason. I turned my back for a second . . .'

'Quite all right, Mrs Watkins. I'll come and see you shortly, Nadia,' she called as the girl was led away. 'I must apologise. That was my granddaughter Nadia.' Ailsa looked upset.

'I hope she hasn't heard the news,' said Daley.

'Oh, it's possible. She is perfectly intelligent, but sadly she suffers from a condition which affects the frontal lobe of her brain.'

'How does that affect her?' asked Symington.

'She sees and hears things that aren't there, superintendent.'

*

The two men crouched amongst the ferns, shivering with cold as they watched the policemen in white overalls working under the lights in the glade.

The smaller man squinted at the scene. 'How close do you have to be to get a decent image, Brockie?' he whispered to the man beside him, who was looking through a camera with a long lens, poking through the shrubbery.

'To get any definition, I need a few more yards.'

His companion slowly crawled forwards, a narrow-beamed torch pointing low to the ground so that those ahead couldn't see its light. He signalled to the photographer to follow him.

After a few steps he heard a dull thud, followed by a gasping sound. 'Fuck's sake, Brockie, you clumsy bastard,' he said, flicking his torch at the man behind him. 'And get down, these buggers'll see you!'

Brockie had dropped his camera and was now standing to his full height, staring straight ahead.

'Get down!' This was a shouted whisper from the man in front, who shaded his torch with a gloved hand and directed the diminished beam towards Brockie. Dark blood oozed from the photographer's mouth as he fell forwards, his full length crashing heavily onto his companion.

As the journalist tried to wriggle free from under the dead photographer's weight, his call for help was stopped in his throat.

6

Daley sat in the back of the large police car with Symington as they made their way down the steep, well-lit driveway that led from Kersivay House and turned onto the narrow single-track roadway leading back into the village. They had spent some time interviewing Percy and various family members already gathered in the house after speaking with Ailsa Shannon.

'I bloody hope I'm as sharp when I'm eighty,' said Symington.

'Yes, just shows what pots of money can do for your longevity,' replied Daley, whose own mother had died in her sixties, the cancer that killed her left undiagnosed until it was too late.

'Very cynical, if you don't mind me saying. Some folk are just lucky, DCI Daley. Evidently, she's had her fair share of tragedy.'

Daley was about to reply when his mobile phone buzzed in his pocket.

I'm in the County. Mine's a ginger beer and lime ☹ B

Daley smiled. 'Have you met DS Brian Scott yet, ma'am?'

'No, not face to face, but I feel as though I have after reading so much about him.'

'Well, once seen, never forgotten, I . . .'

Before Daley could finish what he was saying, the car sloughed sideways and came suddenly to a halt, propelling the police officers forwards in their seatbelts with a screech of brakes.

'What is it, Paul?' Daley shouted to the young constable who was driving.

'Something lying in the road, sir. I think I managed to miss it.' All three unbuckled their seatbelts and got out of the car, walking back the few yards to the black shape huddled under the moonlight. Daley took his torch from his pocket and shivered. To his left over the sea wall, dark waves broke on the beach.

'It's a body!' said Symington, squinting into the beam cast by Daley's torch.

'I need to find out if he's still alive. Here, son, hold this,' said Daley, handing his torch to the constable.

'I didn't hit him, sir. I'm sure of it. You know yourself, we would have heard the thump.'

Daley gently rolled the man onto his back, but before he could search for a pulse he recoiled. The man's eyes had been gouged out and his ears roughly hacked off. His mouth appeared to be a gaping black hole, devoid, Daley saw, of tongue or teeth. He felt the bile rise in his throat.

'Superintendent Symington, here,' he heard behind him. 'I don't know how far on SOCO are with the skeleton but I want them and all available officers on the roadway at Kersivay House in Blaan, as soon as. Body at this locus, foul play strongly suspected. Rouse the Force Doctor, too.' She ended the call. 'Do we know who this is?'

'With the mutilation it's too hard to say, ma'am,' said Daley, still swallowing back the bile in his throat. 'Hold on.'

He reached into the inside pocket of the blood-soaked jacket and found what he was looking for. 'Whoever did this, they weren't trying to conceal the identity of the victim,' he said, flourishing a leather wallet. 'Give me the torch.'

The wallet contained the usual array of bank cards, loose coins and notes. Daley fished a pink plastic card out of its holder.

'Bloody hell, I know him,' he said, studying the driving licence under the torchlight. 'Ian Brockie, he used to be a snapper for the *Glasgow News*. He's been freelance for the last few years, paparazzi work, that kind of stuff. What the fuck is he doing here?'

'The Shannons?' asked Symington. 'When it comes to the business community, they're as high profile as it gets.'

Daley stared back down at the corpse, then at Symington, who was still looking at it intently. One thing he knew for sure about his new boss: she had a stronger stomach than he did.

As Scott jumped back behind the wheel of his car in the County Hotel car park, he reflected on the various merits and demerits of staying sober. Normally, after the long drive to Kinloch, he'd have sunk into a bottle of whisky and been neither fit to drive nor recall himself to duty.

'Lucky me,' he said to himself, as he watched the first fat flakes of snow fall under the streetlights.

He'd been surprised at how easy it had been to stop drinking – well, after the first few days, that was, when he thought his world was coming to an end. He had been doped up with some not-strictly-prescription medication and his wife's homemade broth to take away the pain. It hadn't worked. As the first week passed though, things got easier, and soon he managed to regain some of his old cheer.

He had been left with a couple of problems, though: a nagging anxiety that gnawed at him every second of the day and, worse still, strange flashes, visions, call them what you will. For seconds at a time, he would see faces, shapes, movement in the darkness. Rather than have this on his medical record, he'd visited the Glasgow mortuary, where his old friend, pathologist Andy Crichton, had given it to him straight.

'Delirium tremens, Brian. More commonly known as the DTs,' declared Crichton in the same matter-of-fact way he spoke when dissecting a body. 'The way you were drinking, it's lucky that's all you have. With a bit of luck this will pass if you stay off the bottle. Go back on it, though, and who knows where you'll bloody well end up. We've all seen those gibbering wrecks that hang around the streets of this city; buggered, everyone of them. And if it's not the booze, it's drugs. You've stopped imbibing in the nick of time, old boy.'

These words had echoed around Scott's head ever since. He hated the feeling of imminent calamity, the shadow that moved at the corner of his eye as he was lying in the darkness trying to get to sleep. He hadn't told his wife and he certainly hadn't informed anyone at work – including Daley.

As he drove out of Kinloch and took the road to Blaan, Crichton's words reverberated in his head again.

'I hate to tell you, but before these things get better, they can often get worse. So, if the hallucinations become more real, or you start to feel more anxious, my advice is to visit your GP, regardless of the consequences. Fingers crossed you'll be fine, though,' he said, ending his dire warning on a bright note.

'Aye, fine. Nae bother tae me, Andy,' Scott said under his breath, keeping his eyes on the road as the snow became heavier. 'Here's me off tae stare at another poor deid bastard.'

The pub in Notting Hill Gate was busy with revellers who had just about got over Christmas and were now getting warmed up for New Year's Eve.

Amidst the smart suits and party frocks, the laughter, song and high spirits, sat a man at a table on his own, swilling the last drops of an expensive whisky in a small glass. He checked the time on his watch then sighed, looking up towards the side door of the hostelry.

He felt the phone vibrate in the pocket of his jacket.

Dad, please call me – something has happened. We need to talk!

He put the phone back, shaking his head. 'Not now, darling,' he said beneath his breath, lifting his glass towards the barman who acknowledged his request for another drink with a smile and nod.

As he scanned the room once more, he marvelled at how sophisticated young women looked these days compared to his youth in the eighties. They even appeared to be physically different; tall, thin and elegant, not the bustling girls with the big hair he had been used to then. Maybe it was just his age and the realisation that he could no longer turn the heads of beautiful young women – unless they knew how much money he had, that was. He was entering middle age kicking, screaming and hating every minute of it.

He was momentarily mesmerised by the shapely behind of a dark-haired beauty as she bent forwards to pick up the bag at her feet, but his thoughts soon reverted back to the real reason he was here: the meeting with the man who could change his life.

He gave the barman another twenty-pound note and told him to keep the change. Just as he was taking his first sip of Springbank malt whisky, the face he had been looking for appeared through the huddle of drinkers.

'Where have you been, you bugger?' he said, standing to greet his visitor, raising his voice in order to be heard over the din of the pub.

'Traffic in this city,' replied the newcomer. 'Makes Boston look like a village. So this is your favourite watering hole? Nice,' he said, looking around the crowded bar and smiling at the dark-haired girl, who smiled back magnificently, showing a full set of snow-white teeth and fetching dimples.

That was the trouble with being an aging womaniser, thought Bruce. Eventually the day comes when the come-to-bed eyes flutter at someone else. In this case, that someone else was Trenton Casely.

'Time for that later, Trenton, baby. I want to know how much money you're going to make me, first.'

'Well, as to that, it all depends how much Shannon International holdings you can get me, buddy.'

'Oh, I think it's fair to say that we'll be looking at a controlling share.'

'You're talking fifty-one per cent?'

'Got it in one, Trent. As you long as you keep to your side of the bargain with my cousin, we're home and dry.'

'That's one of the reasons I wanted to meet you tonight in person, Bruce,' said Casely. 'I want you to realise that once this ball starts rolling and we put in place what we've discussed, there is no way back.' He lowered his voice, moving closer to Bruce. 'This thing happens, or we stop happening – do you get me?' He paused for a heartbeat, looking straight into Shannon's eyes as he nodded in agreement. 'Good – good. Just let me make a call, OK?'

'Be my guest. In the meantime I'll get us a couple of bottles of champagne and we'll see if we can't catch a few of the pretty fish in this little pool.'

'That would be a most welcome diversion,' replied Casely, eyeing the dark-haired girl again. I'm sure the champagne corks will be popping in New York too, once I've passed on the news.'

Bruce watched him weave his way back towards the door, making time to brush against the girl, who beamed at him.

'Prick,' muttered Bruce. Go on, you get the girl, he thought. Perform all the bedroom gymnastics you desire – been there, done that, many, many times, my friend. Just make sure you can deliver on your side of the bargain.

Bruce sat back in his chair and signalled to the barman again. Soon he would be a billionaire in his own right. He could do as he pleased and not have to listen to his patronising cousin, or hang on the petticoat tails of his overbearing mother. And he would never have to visit that bloody house on the cliff again.

'Yeah, shag that bint to your heart's content, Trent, my boy. See if I give a toss,' he whispered to himself, then let more of the fine malt whisky do its job.

7

'Pleased to meet you, ma'am,' Scott said hesitantly, as he shook the hand of his new superior.

'You too, DS Scott. As I said to DCI Daley, I feel as though I know you already.'

'Eh, aye, well, it doesnae dae to be putting too much faith in they files, ma'am. A lot of that stuff was written by your predecessor, if you know what I mean.'

'We'll draw a line under that, shall we,' replied Symington with a weak smile.

Daley was busy directing uniformed cops as they sealed the roadway on either side of the corpse, now being lifted into the back of a private ambulance by the forensic team. Snow already covered the scene, cloaking the officers and road alike as they worked in the beams of police car headlights.

'This is all we need,' muttered Scott, as he brushed more snow from the sleeve of his jacket. 'I've never seen snow here before.'

'Really?' remarked Symington. 'I thought Scotland was snow central – well, as far as the UK is concerned.'

'No' here, apparently. Something tae dae with the Gulf Stream and it being a peninsula, ma'am.

'Quite the meteorologist!'

'No, not me, ma'am,' said Scott, looking heavenward. 'Cannae say I know much about they meteors an' asteroids an' that.'

'No, meteorologist, as in the weather,' she replied. She was about to expand upon this when Daley reappeared in a flurry of snow.

'That's everything secured and the remains in the SOCO ambulance, ma'am. I've detailed three constables to stay here. Two of them will draw firearms from Kinloch. We'll have our rural boys patrol the village tonight until we can get something more substantial organised tomorrow. I'll need to call on reinforcements from division, ma'am.'

'Quite the baptism of fire for me,' observed Symington, raising her brow. 'Two bodies in one night. I have to say, I didn't expect this.'

'At least I'm no' on a boat,' said Scott.

'I agree with the steps you've taken, DCI Daley, but I'd like someone with a bit of clout up at the house tonight. You'll have your hands full getting things moving at the office.' She looked at Scott. 'I want you to stay at Kersivay House tonight, DS Scott. Everything has to be kid gloves as far as this is concerned. I've already had the ACC on the phone.'

'Like you said ma'am, where there's wealth, there are any number of potential problems,' said Daley.

'Yes, though I hadn't envisaged anything of this magnitude.'

'Don't let anything surprise you doon here, ma'am,' said Scott. 'Fortunately, I never got the chance tae take my case oot the back o' the car in Kinloch, so I'm good tae go.'

'Good. I'll get back up there and tell the Shannons what's been going on. You come with me, DS Scott. I'll see you back in Kinloch, DCI Daley.'

'No' another pompous bastard,' said Scott as he watched her walking towards her car.

'Don't think so, Bri,' replied Daley. 'She's got something about her.'

'Aye, a crown on her shoulder and a gold band on her bunnet. That place up on the hill gies me the creeps. I wisnae fixing on spending the night there wae the Addams family!'

'All part of life's rich tapestry, Brian. I'd better go and get things moving down the road.'

Scott watched Daley walk away into the snow and shivered. Right now, he thought, I would give my left bollock for a dram. He sighed and followed his new superintendent.

Veronica More woke with a start, her chest tight with anxiety from the nightmare.

Her husband wasn't in their bed, so she squinted at the bedside alarm clock, which read *03:22* in bold red letters. She stretched and decided that she needed a cup of chamomile tea to calm her nerves – not that the nightmare was new to her. She had the same one almost every night.

She slid out of bed and wriggled her feet into her slippers, wondering where her husband was. Probably in his study, she reasoned, working on his Hogmanay sermon, or writing his book about the history of Blaan – his pet project. He was a night owl, so his not being in bed at this time was not unusual.

As she padded down the stairs she noticed light escaping from under the door of the study. She was about to go in and ask Iggy if he would like a cup of tea when she heard him speaking in low tones, his familiar voice deep and resonant. She stood for a moment, listening, then walked into the kitchen, a frown on her face.

When she returned to bed, despite the chamomile tea, she couldn't get back to sleep. Veronica tugged at the little crucifix at her neck and stared into the darkness.

Maxwell Shannon was dressed in a casual suit with an open-necked shirt. He had a floppy quiff of flaxen hair that, though he was now in his mid forties, made him seem younger – and a patronising attitude that belonged in another century.

'I have two points to make, Sergeant Scott. Firstly, I should have been informed of this bloody skeleton's appearance before my elderly aunt. Secondly, though I welcome the presence of your men in and around the grounds of the house, there is no need for you to spend the night on the premises. We have very able security people here with us. Isn't that right, Neville?' he said, nodding to a large man sitting in the chair behind him.

'That is absolutely correct, sir,' replied the man in a distinct Cockney accent. 'There is no chance of anyone getting near Mr Shannon or the rest of the family, I can assure you, sergeant.'

Scott hesitated for a moment, contemplating calling Daley and letting him know that the Shannon family had brought its own muscle, but decided against it at the last moment.

'I have my orders, Mr Shannon. So, if you don't mind, I'd just as rather you find me somewhere to lay my head,' he said looking around the large ballroom they were in. 'In a place this size, there cannae be a lack o' space.'

'It would surprise you, sergeant. There are a lot of people here for the meeting already, who all have to be catered for. However, I suppose it's too late to change your orders at this time of night.' He turned to the burly man behind him. 'Neville, take the detective here to Percy, tell him he needs a corner for the night.'

As Scott followed the large man from the room, Shannon called back to him. 'You didn't tell me why I wasn't informed about the discovery of these remains – before my aunt, I mean.'

Scott stopped and turned around. 'I wasn't here, sir. But it seems tae me – if I understand things correctly – this incident may have a connection to Mrs Shannon's son who disappeared fifty years ago. Am I right?'

'Yes.'

'Well, I would hope that answers your question, sir.' Without another word, Scott turned on his heel.

Daley looked out from his glass box within the CID suite at Kinloch Police Office.

One search on the web had produced all he could ever want to know about the Shannons and their business. From humble beginnings in Blaan to the largest private company on the planet, it was a tale of success piled upon success.

He happened upon some old newspaper reports about the abduction of Archie Shannon in the sixties. An inset picture showed the young boy with his mother – an attractive woman whom Daley recognised immediately. Ailsa had retained her elegance in old age, but had been a real looker when she was young.

The story was a tragic one, ending in the death of her husband a few years after the disappearance of her son.

As he wound his way through the search results he came upon details about the company's massive mineral contracts in China and Russia. These contracts had insulated the company against the recent global financial meltdown; in fact, they had profited from it, managing to eat up some vulnerable blue chip companies as well as buying up large portions of international banks desperate for cash. All in all, it was a story of unmitigated, almost unprecedented, business success.

He looked at a picture of Maxwell Shannon, interim boss while his father suffered from crippling ill-health. Even the image of him in the still photograph exuded an arrogant confidence.

He found little about Ailsa, apart from a cookbook she had written in the seventies, no doubt contrived as a sop to keep her occupied while the Shannon men got down to the real business in hand. For some reason, Daley found this hard to reconcile with the woman he had met. He doubted that it had been easy to keep Ailsa Shannon in a box over the years.

He looked through the window to the room beyond. The process he'd witnessed too many times was gearing up once more. Up went the clear-boards with photographs of the dead and the places they'd been found; the same spidery writing in red pen clinically labelling these gruesome images; the same buzz as detectives and uniformed cops began to analyse the death of another poor soul.

For an instant, Daley thought about trying to work out the body count of the dead he'd had to deal with since becoming a policeman, but quickly decided against it. The simple answer was that it was far too many.

Hopefully – most probably, in fact – this would be his last murder inquiry. And then what? It saddened him that he was worried about leaving this parade of corpses, for want of something else to do. Surely he was worth more than this? Surely he could do something that didn't involve dealing with the very worst humanity could dish up? The questions echoed in his mind until a knock at his door thrust him back into the present.

'May I come in, sir?' asked DC Mary Dunn.

'Yes, yes, of course,' he replied, sitting up straighter and pulling in his stomach. Since Liz and James Daley Junior had moved back to Kinloch, his working relationship with his young DC and ex-lover had been strained. He had done his best to be as professional as possible, treating her like any other officer under his command. There was no doubt, however, that losing her from his life had cast a shadow he had not expected. He had been so devoted to Liz, and for so long, that he found the ache of missing another as strange as it was heart-wrenching. Though he was loath to admit it, it was one of the reasons he had refused to reconsider his resignation.

'I know this is a bad time, sir,' she said, now sitting across the desk from Daley.

'I think you'll find that when it comes to our job, it's always a bad time.' He gave her a neutral smile.

'I need some time off.'

'How long?'

'Just a couple of days, sir. I know that I have a few left from my allocation.'

Daley suddenly remembered the trip to Paris with the young doctor she'd been seeing since they split up. He also remembered his insane jealousy and how hard it had been to hide it from Liz.

'It's not a good time, you know, considering what's just happened. I have a new boss, I have to keep things straight.'

'I have a hospital appointment,' she said, staring at him with a detached expression.

'Oh, yes, right. Well, not a problem. When do you want to go?'

'It's in Glasgow, so if I could have the fifth and sixth off, that should be fine.'

'OK,' said Daley, making a note of her request. 'How are you, anyway? I'm sorry I haven't had a chance to . . .'

'I'm fine,' she replied, as she got up and walked towards the door. 'How's James? And Mrs Daley, of course?' Without waiting for an answer, she left, closing the door behind her.

'This is the only room available,' said Percy, somewhat petulantly. 'Just a box room, really, but all we have.'

'Aye, thanks, mate,' replied Scott, peering into the little room once Percy had switched on the light. 'Mr Shannon wasn't keen I was given a room at all.'

'That English bastard! Honestly, I don't know what's happened to this family,' he continued. 'Bloody dandies and public schoolboys. Nothing like the way things used to be, you know.'

'So you've been here for a long time?'

'I've devoted my life to this shit,' spat the old man. 'No thanks, piss-poor wages, while they get richer and richer. I tell you, I'm not surprised things are coming home to roost.'

'What do you mean?'

'Just what I say. Poor wee Archie, he was a nice little boy.'

Scott studied the old man. His face was creased with wrinkles; thin glasses perched on a nose tinged purple, which, along with the smell of fresh whisky, marked out Percy as a heavy drinker.

Doesnae make you a bad person, thought Scott. 'What's the scoop wae the door over there?' he asked, pointing to the room opposite, which was adorned with a wreath of red roses.

'Ah, that's the boy's bedroom. Puts a wreath there every year. She's kept it the same for fifty years, not moved as much as a lamp. We keep it clean and aired, of course. Bloody shame,' said Percy. 'I was fond of him.'

'Would you mind if I had a look? Bearing in mind what's been going on and all,' asked Scott.

'Eh, well, I suppose it won't do any harm. If the bones they've found are his, well, things will change.'

'Fifty years is a long time tae be wondering,' said Scott, as he watched the old caretaker fiddle with a set of keys.

'A least you've got a good Scot's tongue in your head,' said Percy, opening the door.

Scott was taken aback; he felt as though he'd stepped straight back into his own childhood. An old-fashioned basket-weave lampshade hung above a bed covered in a cream candlewick bedspread. The wallpaper pictured knights on horseback and men in armour with swords. On a small chair, a pair of jeans with a yellow and black snake belt sat neatly folded under a couple of knitted jumpers. A pile of old comics lay on the bedside table, their pages yellowed with age. Scott recognised the *Eagle* and *The Beano*. In short, it was a child's room from fifty years before, perfectly frozen in time, almost like a museum display.

'Fuck me,' said Scott. 'I always wanted a pair o' denims wae one o' they snake belts. Harped on at my faither for months.'

'Did you get it?'

'Naw. Ended up wae moleskin trousers held up wae my sister's skipping rope. Bloody great in the winter, but you ended up wae right sweaty bollocks in the summer, I'll tell you. Aye, an' we had tae dae wae second-hand comics, too, half o' the pages missing, or stuck the gether wae snot.'

'Trust me, my childhood was worse.'

'Aye, those were the days.'

'He was the last hope for the family, you know,' said Percy.

'What dae you mean?'

'Young Archie, the boy that went missing. There is another, but he's a waste of space. A lush like his father,' continued Percy, almost to himself.

Pot calling the kettle black, thought Scott, as the old man locked the door and they bid each other goodnight.

8

Daley stretched before he put on his jacket. It was almost two a.m. and he had to get some sleep. Tomorrow promised to be a challenging day. He left his glass box and said good-night to the detectives manning the nightshift. Outside the CID Suite the corridors of Kinloch Police Office were eerie in the subdued night lights.

He was about to leave via the backdoor into the car park when he heard footsteps behind him.

'I'm sorry, Jim – sir. I didn't mean to be so abrupt earlier on,' said Dunn, appearing from the shadows, nervously smoothing unseen creases in her trousers.

'Don't worry. My fault, not yours. I'm just sorry things . . . Well, you know,' replied Daley sadly.

'I really hope it all works out – with Liz and the baby, I mean.'

'Thanks. It's all going to be very different when I don't have a job to go to.'

'I hope that's nothing to do with me. I had applied for a transfer, but then, well, Angus and I . . .'

'No, don't worry, nothing to do with you,' Daley lied. 'I wonder if I should ever have been in this job in the first place. I'd certainly be a different person now if I hadn't had to look at all the horror and misery I've seen over the last few years, I can tell you that for nothing.'

'Well, anyway, I'd better get back to it.' She smiled wanly.

'Mary, I miss you, I—'

'Please don't. I'm with someone and so are you. Goodnight.' She turned on her heel and ran back down the corridor.

Daley sighed as he sat in his car. He felt his throat tighten and his eyes started to sting. The empty feeling in his chest was one he was well accustomed to, even though the cause of it was new. Slowly, he pulled out of the car park and onto the road; the road back home, to his wife and child. The song on the radio spoke of lost love under the lights that shone. He turned it off.

Scott turned over in bed again. His bedtime reading had been the files and photographs on the Shannon family, sent from the police office to his smartphone. He was comfortable, warm and certainly tired enough after his drive to Kinloch. Despite this, he found sleep hard to find. There was something about the house he didn't like; it was cold and austere. A house that wasn't a home. He wondered if anyone had ever really thought of it as that.

He thought back to a visit to his great aunt on the Isle of Mull. His mother had been unwell – 'women's problems' his father had said. To temporarily remove the strain of bringing up two small boys, he and his brother were farmed out to reluctant relatives for the long summer holiday. With family unwilling to put up with two boisterous boys, he and his brother were split up. Charlie went to an uncle in Troon, while he, being the oldest, was put on the train from Glasgow to Oban, where an old woman met him. He'd never seen her before in his life, but she did have a distant resemblance to his mother – her niece.

'Aye, your faither looking straight oot of you,' she'd said.

He'd never really been on a boat before. He'd seen them ply their trade up and down the Clyde under the tall shipyard cranes, but he'd never been out to sea. It was an assault on the senses: the motion of the vessel and the tang of salt mixed with fumes from the large funnels made him miserably sick for the whole hour or so it took to reach the Isle of Mull.

A rickety bus took him and his aunt on a journey that never seemed to end. Eventually, they alighted at the end of a bumpy farm road.

'A mile or so and we'll be there,' said his great aunt, taking him by the hand. They walked over a small hill then along a rutted path. On top of another rise, Scott was able to look down onto a small valley, in the midst of which sat a low black cottage.

It was blacker inside than out, lit by gas lamps and the huge fire that his aunt kept burning in the grate, despite the time of year. He spent a miserable few weeks with only the old woman for company, willing the long summer nights to last around the clock. The dark hours of night, though mercifully short, were the darkest he'd ever known. Unless the sky was clear – which it never seemed to be – and the moon shone, the whole house was black. He remembered thinking that this was what it would be like to be blind. The creaks and inexplicable noises of the night terrified him.

At home, he might be at risk of a clip around the ear from his father, or a bleaching from the big MacDougall boy down the street, but the young Brian Scott could cope with these things.

What he couldn't cope with was the long highland summer where he could only sleep when the short night was over.

Lying in his bed in Kersivay House, he felt the same way.

Twice, he'd used his radio to check in on the cops patrolling the grounds of the mansion. On both occasions, there'd been nothing to report.

He knew he had to get some sleep, that he would be exhausted the next day otherwise. This was the way it had been since he stopped drinking, but this house made it worse somehow.

'Bloody misery,' he whispered to himself.

He had started to doze, on the edge of sleep, when something roused him. He sat up in bed and listened; nothing at first, but, just as he was about to lie down he heard it again. Footsteps, light and quick like a child's running up and down the corridor outside his room.

'Typical, bloody weans.' He was wearing a pair of shorts and a T-shirt, and shivered as he levered himself out of the bed and away from the warmth of the duvet.

He padded across the thick carpet then opened the door and stepped out into the dim corridor. The cold almost took his breath away as he squinted into the gloom. 'Looks like your central heating's burst, Percy,' he mumbled.

He was stepping back into his room when he heard it, the soft tinkle of a child's laughter. He spun round. 'Right, you wee bugger, where are you?'

As his eyes adjusted to the darkness, he noticed, with surprise, that the door opposite, the one with the wreath of red roses, was lying open.

'Ach, you stupid old bugger, you've no' locked the thing right.' He crossed the corridor, grabbing the handle of the door to pull it shut. As he did so, he heard the heard the child's laugh again, this time coming from behind the door.

'Got you!' Scott swung the door open and fumbled for the light switch, cursing when he pressed it and nothing happened. Then, in the darkness, something caught his eye. Sitting on the chair on top of the folded denims and jumpers was a tiny figure, a young boy, staring straight at him.

The breath caught in Scott's throat. He wanted to walk towards the child and remove him from the cold room, but he couldn't. Trying to speak, he watched as the boy stood up and walked slowly towards him.

'Hello. My name's Archie Shannon.'

The boy reached out to him, but in that same instant was gone, leaving Scott alone in the cold, empty room with his heart thudding in his ears, struggling for breath.

Driving along Kinloch's Main Street, Daley noticed a figure walking slowly, huddled against the cold wind. Recognising the man, he stopped and wound down the passenger window.

'Hamish, bloody hell, you must be freezing. Come on, jump in.' The old man slid onto the passenger seat, bringing a blast of bitterly cold air into the warm car.

'What are you doing out on a night like this – it's bloody freezing,' said Daley.

'Och, this time of year. I hate it. Never have liked the festive season.'

Daley stared at him. 'Anything else wrong? You've got a face like a wet weekend.'

'Just a feeling. Aye, and it won't go away. I had tae get oot o' the hoose tonight – jeest tae break the spell, you understand.'

'What kind of feeling?'

'I don't know. Like something's no' right with the world. I daresay you get it yourself fae time tae time. No rhyme or reason tae it at all.'

'I get feelings like that all the time, Hamish. But then again, I don't have your second sight.' Daley laughed, hoping the old man would join in. He didn't.

Daley pulled the car up by Hamish's cottage on the outskirts of the town, by the side of the loch, with its island guardian looming in the darkness. The street lights far behind, he stared into the darkness.

'Hey, wait. Your front door's lying open, Hamish.' He jumped out of the car and walked up the narrow path.

As he stepped inside and started groping for a light switch, he heard sudden movement from inside the room. Before he could swing round, something crashed into him, forcing his head hard against the wall. The blow stunned him, but the agony in his scalp was worse, tiny needles thrusting into his head. He cried, desperately trying to shake off his attacker.

'Hamish, help!' he yelled. He felt pain in the back of his neck; something sharp was piercing the skin.

'Here, you daft bastard.' Suddenly the room filled with light and with a blood-curdling screech the attack stopped, leaving Daley breathing hard, trying to take in what had just happened. He felt something running down his face and, patting at it, saw that his hand covered in blood.

'Bloody hell, Hamish. What the fuck.' He looked around the room, now lit by a single bare bulb hanging from an old flex. Hamish's home had been trashed. The old man stood in front of Daley, keeping a huge striped cat at bay with a walking stick.

'Jeest you stay where you are, Hamish. There's nothing tae worry aboot noo, son,' he said to the cat, which was still squatting in an attack pose, ears flat against its head, hissing loudly.

Scott shivered in his bed. He'd toyed with the idea of asking one of the cops on duty in the grounds of Kersivay House to come to his room, but thought the better of it. He then considered heading out into the grounds himself to meet one of his colleagues, but couldn't face walking out into the cold corridor again.

He couldn't keep his limbs still; with trembling hands he reached for his mobile, managing to steady the device enough to switch it on. Thankfully he had signal. He scrolled down his contact list until he came to the name Crichton. Awkwardly he touched the screen and held the phone to his ear with both hands.

Just as he was about to hang up, the call was answered. 'Brian Scott. What on earth is going on? It's just after four in the morning, man.'

'Listen, Wattie, you've got to help me.' Scott quickly blurted out the details of what he had seen in the child's room.

'As I thought,' replied Crichton testily. 'It's the DTs, they're reaching the psychotic stage. No bloody wonder after all the booze you've flung down your neck. How real did this all seem?'

'Bloody real. I . . . I saw a boy. He fucking spoke tae me, Wattie.'

'Listen to me. I want you to calm down, take deep breaths, think of something calming: Rangers winning the treble, for instance.'

'Steady on, Wattie, I'm no' that far gone yet. I've had enough hallucinations fir one night.'

'There, see. You're calming down already. Take your time, Brian, deep breaths.'

Crichton continued to speak to Scott in quiet tones as, slowly, the detective regained some of his composure.

'Now, listen to me, Brian. You're going to have to get medical help. You need something to calm you down, to stop these, well, experiences. You need to see a doctor.'

'I'm in bloody Kinloch – well, near there, anyway. In the middle of fucking nowhere, in fact.'

'It doesn't matter. This won't go away by itself. In fact, without treatment, it'll likely get worse. See a bloody doctor!'

Scott apologised for waking his friend then ended the call. He felt much calmer now, but still reckoned he'd wait until daylight before venturing out of his room. He propped himself up against some pillows and closed his eyes, willing sleep to come.

Daley helped Hamish make the best of tidying his house. 'I jeest canna understand it, Mr Daley. Who would want tae dae a thing like this? It's no' as though I've got anything worth stealing.'

'No,' agreed Daley. 'But I don't think this was your usual burglary.'

'Well, whoot were they after?'

'Look, see this box of photographs, and the one in your bedroom, scattered as though they've been looked through. If your aim is to steal something of value, you're not going to sit down and go through the family albums before you do it, Hamish.'

'Aye, right enough. I hadn't thought o' that. But they're jeest old pictures. Some o' them belonged tae my mother.'

Daley answered the door to a young detective and a uniformed cop. 'I want you to fingerprint the usual surfaces and see if you can pick up anything from these photos. There's more in the bedroom.'

'Thanks for all your help, Mr Daley,' said Hamish. 'I canna get my heid around this at all.'

'Looks like your premonition of something being wrong was spot on. Once the boys are finished in your bedroom, try and get some sleep. I'll make sure there's a cop at the door until we can make some kind of sense of this. In the morning I want you to go through the photos and see if any are missing. And keep Hamish the cat under control, he could have had my eye out.'

'Och, he was jeest feart. It's his wild instincts coming oot. He likely got a fright when they burglars were in. He's quite highly strung, you know.'

'Yes, I've got the teeth marks in the back of my neck to prove it. Anyway, I want you to concentrate on what's missing, if anything.'

'Aye, nae bother, Mr Daley. But I can tell you right noo aboot one that's been stolen.'

'How do you know?'

He pointed above the mantelpiece to a rectangular patch of wallpaper, a lighter shade than the rest of the walls.

'What was the picture of, Hamish?'

'My mother.' A look of sadness passed over Hamish's wrinkled face. 'She was jeest young when it was taken. Och, a few years before I was born, I reckon.'

'And who else was in the picture?'

'Jeest her an' a few o' her workmates, as well as some o' the folk fae the big hoose.'

'What big house?'

'Where she worked in they days, Mr Daley. She was in service at Kersivay Hoose, in Blaan. Och, I'm sure you know it fine, up there on the cliff. Great big rambling place.'

'Oh, yes. I know it.'

'I'm telling you,' Hamish sighed. 'The world's far from right tonight, and that's a fact.'

Daley walked to his car pondering once more on Hamish's gift of prescience, as he watched the snow fall over Kinloch.

9

Colin Grant was cold very cold. His whole body shook as he came to on the damp floor. Bound in a sitting position, his hands were tied to his ankles. His teeth chattered as the dim moonlight illuminated the space in a cold, thin light. He could hear the sound of waves crashing on a beach; the smell of the sea was strong, but overlaid by a dank, earthy smell.

He tried to swallow, his tongue sticking to the roof of his dry mouth. Then the memory of seeing the steel point appear through the neck of his colleague Brockie came back to him. He started to scream, trying to shuffle forwards to the mouth of the cave, but he was manacled to something at his back and any movement was impossible.

'For fuck's sake help me!' he shouted. At his feet, moonlight glinted on puddles of ice on the floor of the freezing cave.

Gulls squealed and the sound of the sea grew louder in his ears, but Colin Grant's screams did not summon help. Eventually, only a croak emanated from his ruined throat, giving way to sobs.

As he was about to lose all hope, he heard the crunch of footsteps on the pebbled beach. With all the force he could muster, he cried out again.

A shadow loomed across the mouth of the cave. He tried to squint at the figure, but the bright sunlight obscured all features.

'Please help me,' he said, straining at his bonds. 'I have money . . . you can have anything. Please, please . . .' His pleas were cut short as something stung his chest, making him writhe in pain.

Scott asked the officers who had patrolled the grounds of Kersivay House through the night to come to his room to make their reports. Nothing out of the ordinary had happened, but he made sure they accompanied him out of his room and down the corridor to the stairs. He hadn't dared leave the room by himself, though he was careful not to let his colleagues see his nervousness, cracking jokes as he walked past the door with the red wreath. Despite the presence of two constables, a shiver went up his spine.

They were shown to a large dining room, where a long table had been set for breakfast.

'Help yourselves,' said a plump old woman, directing them to a table laden with an array of fruits, breakfast cereals and pots of tea and coffee. 'If yous would like a cooked breakfast, it'll be another few minutes.'

'Oh aye,' said Scott, suddenly ravenous. 'The full Scottish for me, dear.'

As the policemen took their seats at the table, Maxwell appeared in the doorway. He was wearing sweatpants and a white T-shirt and was mopping his brow with the corner of a towel that lay draped across his shoulders. His large minder eyed the police officers with a look of distaste.

'Ah, Sergeant Scott. As predicted, nothing untoward happened last night.'

'Well, no . . . nothing of any significance, anyhow,' replied Scott.

'Good. When can we expect the results of the tests on the skeleton?'

'I don't have that information, sir. I'm sure someone will be in touch with Mrs Shannon later today.'

'As I said last night, I'm in charge here. I want to be the first to know of any developments. He poured himself a cup of coffee, but didn't sit at the table with the police officers. 'On second thought, don't worry about it. I'll call your superior later this morning. I'm sure he'll see the sense in what I'm saying.'

'I wouldn't be too sure of that,' Scott mumbled under his breath.

Before Maxwell could reply, a young woman walked into the room. She looked to be in her late teens, pale, her hair cut into a bob. An older woman in a plain blue dress accompanied her.

'Well, well,' said Maxwell. 'May I introduce my cousin's daughter, Nadia.'

She smiled nervously at the policemen.

'I hope you've calmed down after last night's little episode,' said Maxwell.

'If you don't mind, sir, Nadia just wants to have a quiet breakfast,' said the woman in blue.

'Come and sit wae us, dear,' said Scott, pulling the seat beside him back.

Maxwell smiled patronisingly as Nadia took a seat. 'Well, I must get on, I have a busy day ahead of me. If any of you gentlemen fancy a workout, there's a fully equipped gym in the basement. A little exercise wouldn't go amiss.' He looked pointedly at Scott, then leaned down towards Nadia. He leaned on her shoulder and whispered into her ear, loud enough though for everyone to hear what he was saying. 'No histrionics today, my dear. We have a lot of important guests.' He sneered at the young girl's obvious discomfort. 'Mrs Watkins, make sure to keep her out of the way today.'

'Yes, Mr Shannon,' she replied through gritted teeth.

With his minder in tow, Maxwell strode out of the room without another word.

'He might have been tae one of those public schools, but charm sure wasn't on the curriculum,' observed Scott.

'He's the boss,' said Mrs Watkins. 'Please don't let him put you off your breakfast.'

'Och, don't worry aboot that,' replied Scott. 'It'll take a wee bit mair that Maxwell tae put me off my scran this morning.'

Nadia turned to Scott, her brown eyes sad. 'You see things, don't you?'

'Eh . . . sorry, lassie. See what?' said Scott, taken aback.

'You saw my uncle. You saw Archie Shannon. I see him too.'

Suddenly, Scott's appetite had gone.

Maxwell sat behind the desk in his room, phone in hand. 'I don't care whether they're Scotch or Hindustani, I want them off my back. The whole thing is ridiculous. We have a perfectly adequate security team here, we don't need these Jock plods all over the bloody place. Just attend to it, or you'll have to survive on your wages from the Met and with your lifestyle I reckon that would be nothing short of a disaster.' He slammed the phone down, breathing heavily. Nothing, not even the bones of his long-dead cousin, was going to ruin this. It was his time. In a few days he would be in full control of one of the largest companies on earth – one of the largest business enterprises in the history of humanity.

He picked up the phone back up again. 'Is everything in place – for the meeting, I mean?' He listened to the brief reply. 'Just make sure that it goes the way we want.'

Daley barely slept through the short hour's rest available to him. He thought of the Shannons, of the missing boy from so long ago, of the white bones on the dark stone, of the disfigured face of the photographer. Here he was again, being flung headfirst into a pool of mayhem, murder and horror. It was as though the fates were pulling out all the stops to make his last few weeks in the job as difficult as possible.

Thoughts of the future plagued him too. He had slept in the spare room to avoid waking his wife and baby son. How was he going to support them? How was he going to pay the bills? How was he going to spend the rest of his working life? What was going to replace the police force?

Then there was Symington: neat, efficient and focused, but not without a sense of humour. She was so different from John Donald. There was something about her that reminded Daley of himself; a reticence, almost intangible, but there just the same. What manner of ghosts kept her awake at night, he wondered.

And Mary. He could see her soulful face, her pleading blue eyes. He knew the sadness he had brought into her life, because he felt it too.

He looked at his alarm clock, dragged himself out of bed and padded to the shower. His career as a detective wasn't over quite yet.

Suddenly Colin Grant was awake. He was naked, kneeling, his hands tied above his head to some kind of frame. He shivered in the rising sun, with fear as well as cold. He was facing out to sea, his knees firmly planted in the pebbles of a beach. A few feet in front of him, a gull pecked at the shale, undisturbed by his plight.

'For fuck's sake, what is this?' he yelled. 'What are you doing to me?' He had the sense that someone – something – was behind him, out of sight. As the wind buffeted him and blew in his ears, he was sure he could hear breathing.

He searched the sea for a help. No vessel was to be seen on the grey ocean. To his left was a white hill, covered with snow, as were boulders on the beach, just within his line of sight. He cried out again, before he heard footsteps on the pebbles behind him.

'Who are you? What the fuck are you trying—'

His words were cut short by a sudden, blinding agony. Something was sliding down his back; something was slicing him open.

Daley was surprised to find Scott sitting in his glass box when he arrived for work.

'Everything OK, Brian? You look pale.'

Aye, aye, Jim, just fine. We're just back fae the hoose of horrors there. By fuck the road's bad wae snow. It's not as bad here in the toon, but at Blaan it's deep.'

Daley looked out at the sky from the window in the CID suite. It had the pale grey look that presaged heavy snow. 'It could still be a problem.' He turned to look back into the busy office, noting a few strange faces; clearly Superintendent Symington had already drawn down help from division.

'Have you met Maxwell Shannon yet?' asked Scott.

'No, he wasn't there when the boss and I turned up. What's he like?'

'Piece of shit, Jimmy. Arrogant bastard. He's no' happy that you went to see his aunt and no' him. Demands tae be the first tae hear any news about the remains found on that stone.'

'Aye, well, wanting and getting are two different things, Bri. I read a file on him yesterday. Looks like the typical spoiled rich kid – you know, secret societies at university, trashing restaurants and pubs. Allegation of sexual assault when he was eighteen, but nothing came of it in the end.'

'Aye, don't tell me, the lassie withdrew her complaint.'

'Bang on, buddy. Unlike his cousin Bruce, he doesn't drink now.'

'Good for him,' replied Scott, the thought of a large glass of whisky passing through his mind.

'Nothing on that stone yet?'

'What? Oh, the bones. They should have news by mid morning according tae one of the nightshift boys. We've got something else tae worry aboot, though.'

'What, as well as a child's remains and the body of a mutilated press photographer?'

'Aye, Brockie was working freelance for one o' the tabloids wae a journalist. Colin Grant, the guy's name is. They were trying tae get as much shit on this Shannon family as they could.'

'Let me guess. The guy's disappeared and he's not answering his phone.'

'Got it in one, big man.'

'Brilliant.'

Daley was about to ask more about Grant when the door to his glass box swung open.

'Just to let you know, sir. Reports of four housebreakings last night,' said Sergeant Shaw. 'Mostly in Kinloch, one near Blaan.'

'What, including Hamish's?'

'No, sir. He's number five.'

'Bugger me, Jim. We've got a crime wave. This on top o' everything else.'

'Yes, strange, isn't it. Just when all this is going on. Try and find out what, if anything, has been taken during these break-ins, sergeant. Oh, and ask particularly about pictures or photographs.'

Scott looked puzzled.

'I'll explain in a minute,' said Daley, thinking about the blank space above Hamish's mantelpiece.

10

Bruce Shannon yawned as the company jet flew north, leaving the sprawl of London behind. This was the means by which most of those attending the Shannon AGM travelled; a special flight from London to Machrie airport and back again – as soon as possible, he hoped.

Normally, the meeting took a few hours, though if complex issues were on the agenda, adjournments – favoured by older members of the board – could see the family and its senior business managers marooned at Kersivay House for days on end. He shivered at the thought.

Kersivay House had always been straight out of his worst nightmares. His older brother had disappeared from the place, so, unsurprisingly, his mother had kept him a virtual prisoner when he visited Blaan as a child, terrified she would lose another son to the mansion on the cliff. Now, while there, he always felt as though his head was about to burst. Nothing to do: no fun, no sex, with only the local hostelry and dubious delights of Kinloch as any kind of diversion.

His head hurt. He had drunk too much whisky the night before, though he had been sensible enough not to attend the party his American friend had organised after the pub in Notting Hill closed. Now that he was reaching his middle years, he disliked nothing more than watching younger men play the game of chase, capture and reward he'd excelled at during his halcyon days. It wasn't mere jealousy, it was seeing it all done so badly, so clumsily, that annoyed him most. In his teens, twenties and thirties, it was all he had lived for. The most depressing aspect of it all was the realisation that, apart from drinking, it was all he was really good at. He was like an old sports car; still plenty miles in the engine, but the bodywork was crumbling, dated by the shiny curves of newer, sleeker models.

He looked around the cabin. He was one of twenty-five passengers, mostly lawyers and accountants and including the Swedish Global CEO Lars Bergner and his subordinates Matthew Lynton, Chief Operating Officer and Charles Brady, Finance Director.

Bruce despised Bergner. They were the same age, but the years hadn't ravaged the Swede the way they'd ruined him. No sign of a paunch, bags under the eyes, or even wrinkles. Bergner was the classic example of Scandinavian manhood: tall, fit and blonde; effortlessly elegant. If this wasn't enough, he was intelligent, bordering on brilliant, with a hefty dollop of ruthlessness thrown in. In short, he was the perfect leader in the dog-eat-dog corporate world. He and Maxwell – interim chairman, though de facto boss – made an interesting pair. Bruce often wondered how two men so similar could operate as a team at the head of a multinational organisation. Somehow, though, they did.

The real company workhorse was Matthew Lynton. An Oxford-educated former City banker, he was in his early sixties. Everything that happened within the organisation passed across his desk. He wore his power lightly, in a self-effacing way that almost bordered on subservience. He was neat, efficient and quiet. A grey man in a grey suit. He left the cut and thrust of business to Bergner and Maxwell while he made sure everything hung together.

Charles Brady was the only one of these three men whom Bruce liked. In fact, he supposed, Brady was one his dwindling number of close friends. A tough-talking New Yorker, Brady had the responsibility of controlling the company finances. With a turnover outstripping many small countries, this was no mean task, but Brady's burdens did not weigh him down. He liked women, drink and gambling and this alone commended him to Bruce. His cousin Maxwell hated him, but such were the complexities of Shannon International's financial affairs that he was forced to tolerate the thickset accountant in his mid-fifties. Brady, Bruce and Ailsa formed a power block on the board. But that was going to change.

'A large G and T, please,' he said to a uniformed flight attendant as she passed. He was depressed to note that she stopped and whispered into Bergner's ear before heading back to the galley to fix his drink. It was obvious that the responsibilities of the CEO included how much alcohol he was permitted to consume.

He was looking out at grey clouds when the waitress returned.

'Get me another,' he demanded.

'Sorry, sir? This is your usual double measure. I . . .'

'Get me another!' he snapped, drawing the attention of his fellow passengers. 'And this time, do me a favour, don't OK it with Mr Bergner first. Remember, I'm a Shannon, not him. I hope you've got that.'

He felt vaguely sorry for the girl as she headed back to the galley, but he wouldn't be told what he could and couldn't do by some Swedish automaton.

After gulping down both drinks in a fit of childish petulance, he felt tired and closed his eyes. But his doze was shortly disturbed by the captain.

'Ladies and gentlemen, we'll be landing at Machrie airport in about five minutes, please ensure that you return to your seats and fasten your belts. It's a bit snowy down there, so please wrap up before you leave the aircraft.'

'You,' he called to another flight attendant. 'Get me another drink. Quickly.'

Bergner returned his smile with a blank stare.

'Fuck you,' Bruce whispered under his breath. We're nearly there, he thought. I need all the help I can get.

Veronica More watched as her husband traipsed back home through the snow. Her own boots lay beside the large kitchen range, steam slowly rising from them. The sky outside was a luminous white and everything was still. It was as though their little part of the world lay asleep under its white blanket. A small bird flitted from branch to branch, flicking powdery snow as it went.

'Out walking early today, darling,' she said, as he arrived in the large kitchen.

'Oh, yes. I couldn't sleep for thinking about that skeleton. And it was such a beautiful morning, I just wanted to get out and see the place in the snow. You don't get a lot of the white stuff where I come from, dear,' replied the Reverend More, his cheeks red from the cold.

'You didn't take the camera?'

'Oh, no.' He seemed suddenly unsure. 'I never bloody thought. What an idiot.'

Veronica poured a little hot water into a large brown teapot and left it to warm. For her, making tea was an art, a blessed routine that took her back to her childhood in Ireland. Warm the pot, infuse the tea, then pour; she loved the whole process. It was calming and familiar, like an act of devotion. She tipped four heaped spoonfuls of dark tea into the pot, followed by hot water.

'What variety of tea are having now?' he asked.

'Oh, just plain old English breakfast. Give it a few minutes.' She thought for a moment. 'Where did you go?'

'Just around. Didn't want to go too far in case I got stranded. Big drifts up past Achenbrie Farm. I had a trot about, took in the scenery. The place looks spectacular. Did you know, a guy I worked with as a stockman – Ted, his name was; big rough bloke – that was his one ambition in life.'

'What was?'

'To stand knee-deep in snow. Never got his wish, poor bugger.'

'Why was that?'

'Got crushed to death by a Mallee bull. He was a good mate.'

She watched as her husband sat in front of the range and bent to take off his walking boots. 'So did you see anyone?'

'No, not especially. Old Jock at a distance – he was walking across the low field. Gave me a big wave. That was all, really.'

'Oh,' she said quietly, looking out of the window at the footprints her husband had left in the snow.

*

Bruce gazed out the window as the jet circled the long runway at Machrie then began its descent. The aircraft landed awkwardly and then began to taxi towards the small terminal building.

He was unbuckling his seatbelt when he felt a tap on his shoulder.

'You all right, Bruce? You look pale. That landing a bit too tasty for you?' asked Brady in his low New York drawl.

'Bit of a head, you know.'

'Bit of a fucking hangover, you mean. Listen, I need to tell you something.' He sat in the seat beside Shannon and spoke conspiratorially into his ear. 'They found bones up on some old stone relic yesterday.'

'What kind of bones?'

'A child's skeleton. You know what I mean? I wasn't sure whether you knew. I know our big Viking over there wouldn't mention it.'

'No, I didn't. What – I mean, do they have any idea who it is?' replied Shannon, remembering the missed calls and texts he'd had from his daughter Nadia the previous evening.

'Still running tests. The skeleton of a child, though, buddy.' He looked at Shannon with raised brows. 'The cops are all over it. And they found a mutilated body on the road under the house.'

'What? Shit, what are we walking into here, a bloody war zone? Who was it?'

'Some paparazzo, down there to aim his lens at us. Listen, I'll talk to you when we get to the ranch.'

Bruce watched as Brady walked down the aisle of the plane towards his very attractive blonde wife. He felt guilty about what he was about to do, but it was all for the greater good.

An image of his older brother, taken only days before he disappeared, flashed into his mind. The little boy with the dark hair and rosy cheeks was holding the model train he had just received as a Christmas present up to the camera. There he was again, frozen in time and into Bruce's heart.

'Oh damn!' shouted Veronica Moore, as she watched the large plastic milk container burst on the stone floor of the kitchen. 'Honestly, I'm so clumsy.'

'You can say that again, dear. I'll get the mop and clean it up, don't worry.'

'You're a darling. Listen that's all the milk we had. I'll take a walk along to the shop and get more. What with this snow and all, sure we better stock up in case we get cut off from Kinloch.'

'Wouldn't worry too much, dear. With all the dairy farms around here, I don't think we'll run out of milk too readily.'

'Ah, but pasteurised is best now,' she replied, smiling back at her husband.

She quickly put on her walking boots and got ready to leave, just as her husband emerged with a mop and bucket.

'Are you sure you don't want me to go?'

'What, and stay here and mop the floor? No chance,' she laughed.

The air was cold and the snow crumpled under her boots as she walked down the path. When she turned to look back at the house, there was no face at the window. Instead of turning left for the village, she followed her husband's footprints across the field.

*

They were waved through the terminal at Machrie Airport; no security checks necessary for these VIP visitors. Outside, a mismatched assortment of local taxis were scattered around the car park, waiting to take the Shannon International party to Kersivay House. The family could have provided a much grander fleet of vehicles for the journey to Blaan but Ailsa had insisted that it was good for public relations to be seen to help local businesses and no one had seen fit to gainsay her.

Bruce shivered as he walked along the narrow ribbon of cleared pathway towards the nearest vehicle. He had seen a few light dustings of snow here over the years, but when he looked out across the fields towards Kinloch it was clear that this was no mere covering.

As the driver took his bag, he watched Bergner cross the snowy car park towards him.

'Bruce, it's good you could make it,' he said in his sing-song Scandinavian accent.

'Why wouldn't I? This is a habit of a bloody lifetime for me, let me assure you. Apart from the unnecessary welcome, what do you want?'

'I know you are aware that there have been slight difficulties in Blaan over the last twenty-four hours – some unpleasantness.'

'Rather more than that, I would have said.'

'Yes. Well, let us not stray into the realm of speculation. As you know, I only like to deal in fact.'

'Really? How refreshing to hear that. When I was reading the last accounts, I could have sworn they were a work of fantasy.'

'Perhaps an inability to grasp a balance sheet correctly,' replied Bergner with a sneer. 'If you would like me to have someone with greater understanding go through things with you, please just let me know.'

'If you've just come over to take cheap shots, then please fuck off, burger boy.'

'No, what I have to say to you before we get to Blaan is very serious. About your daughter, in fact.'

Bruce felt a chill run down his spine. 'Is she OK?'

'Well, as far as her physical well-being is concerned, yes. As you are more than aware, her mental state is less so.'

'Be careful, old boy. Don't cross the line. Not unless you want to celebrate the new year in Kinloch hospital, that is.'

'I am only talking to you out of concern for the girl. I am informed that the events of the last few hours have disturbed her greatly. Remember, she is as aware of what took place here fifty years ago as you are.'

'I don't need any advice about my own daughter,' replied Bruce, wondering if now was the right time to tell Bergner about the alleged exploits of his own teenage daughter.

'No, indeed. Though I must tell you that, as a board, we feel it would be better if you took her back to London. This AGM promises be the most important in the history of the company. We cannot be distracted by Nadia's histrionics.'

'You mean that's what you and my cousin Maxwell think,' said Bruce, his breath billowing in the cold air. 'Nadia is a shareholder in Shannon International – a Shannon herself. As far as I'm concerned, she has more right to attend the AGM than you. Now fuck off.'

Bruce cursed as he settled himself into the back seat of the taxi. Why was he so stubborn? He'd just spurned a free pass out of this awful place. Then he remembered: he had things to do at Kersivay House – important things. This would be the most important meeting in the history of the company. But not in the way that arsehole Burger thought. He smiled to himself as the taxi pulled slowly away.

The tracks stopped by the burn at the end of the low field. Veronica scanned the scene before her but all she could see was virgin snow.

Where did you go? she asked herself. She felt her chest tighten. Why am I so worried? What can I possibly think my husband has been doing? 'Stop being so stupid,' she whispered to herself, then walked back in the direction of the village to buy milk.

11

Snow was now falling heavily in Kinloch. Daley watched it pile up on Main Street, where a crowd of people had gathered. In most places he'd been, people cursed this weather; not so in Kinloch. Because of the Atlantic Drift from the warm waters of the Gulf Stream, snow was a rare commodity in this part of Scotland. The town's populace revelled in it.

The lights in the office dimmed for a split second before returning to normal. The door of his glass box burst open, revealing Superintendent Symington, brushing snow from her thick uniform jacket.

'Good morning, DCI Daley. If this continues, it will complicate things tremendously.'

'Yes, ma'am. If there's one thing we're not set up for here, it's the white stuff. I can give you an update on things if you'd like.'

'Yes, that's why I'm here. I've decided to stay on for a couple of days. Until we get this Shannon International meeting over with, at any rate. You'll still be in charge of enquiries, of course.'

Daley smiled as he offered her a seat. 'Not a problem, ma'am. Your late predecessor was a great man for taking an *overview*, but never missed a chance to grab the helm when he thought things were favourable enough.'

'I'm not like that, I assure you,' she replied. 'You didn't like him, did you?'

'Honestly? No, I didn't like him at all.'

'Yet – I've read the files – you and he worked together for years, in one way or another.'

'Well, in my case, familiarity definitely led to contempt.' Daley opened up an image on his computer, leaving the conversation about John Donald behind. 'This is the journalist accompanying our dead photographer, Brockie,' he said, turning the screen to face his superior. A dark-haired man in his late thirties stared back at them. 'He started off in a regional paper in Aberdeenshire then did a bit of radio. Moved to the tabloids five years ago; after that, freelance. Our rural patrol found their vehicle parked at the side of the road just outside Blaan. Nothing much to report about it, other than it was located just across the field from where our skeleton was discovered.'

'How could they know about that?'

'The way this force is now, ma'am, every bugger and their friend seem to be leaking stuff to the press. I'd rather find the whereabouts of this Grant guy than worry about who's telling what to whom. That's the job of the top brass. I'm just concerned about criminals out of uniform. I've had enough of the other kind.'

'Point taken, DCI Daley.'

'In addition to this, there were a number of break-ins last night in and around Kinloch.'

'Not unusual these days.'

'It is here, ma'am. Everyone knows everybody else. Miscreants soon discover the error of their ways – real community policing in action.'

'Yes, I'm sure,' she said, looking doubtfully at Daley. 'So, any theories about any of this?'

'As far as Grant and Brockie are concerned, not really. We have teams of officers out looking. The snow isn't making life easier on that front. I'll need to draw down more manpower from division, ma'am.'

'OK, I'll deal with that. And the break-ins?'

'Nothing solid, but I'll let you know. I think we'll have to be very careful with our friends at Kersivay House, ma'am.'

'Oh, don't worry about that. I have a detachment of the Support Unit on their way. They'll take over duties guarding the house and free up your personnel. The Shannons have friends in high places.'

'I've no doubts about that. It's their enemies I'm worried about.'

Moments after Daley spoke, the lights in Kinloch Police Office flickered and went out. After a few seconds power was restored, but this time from the station's emergency generators.

Daley called the emergency number he had for the electricity supplier. It soon became clear that the whole of south Kintyre was without power.

Scott shivered as he left the County Hotel. He'd had a shower and change of clothes and felt more like himself. The cellar man had been cleaning the hotel's beer lines, filling the lobby with the glorious smell of alcohol, making his longing for a drink even more acute.

He remembered the young boy from the night before; he had been so real, so terrifying. Surely, if everyone knew the real dangers of boozing, no one would drink at all. The very thought of it, though, seduced him like an old lover. The calming, cosseting effect of a drink was a hard one to replace. He sighed.

Across the road, he noticed the lights in a shop flicker out. As he looked down Main Street he saw that every emporium was now in darkness.

'That'll be the power off, sergeant,' said a burly local in a boiler suit. 'The last time we had a bad snow like this it was oot for near two weeks. The toon was fair starving.'

'Aye, I'm sure you all got by.'

'You would be surprised. They had tae put big vans oot in the street. You know, serving pie an' beans and the like. Hoor o' a cauld it was.'

'Did they run oot o' drink?'

'Well, things were bad, but that would have jeest been tragic. See ye later.' The man plodded on through the snow.

'Aye, tragic right enough,' said Scott.

He heard his name and turned around. Annie was standing in the doorway of the hotel.

'Brian! Can I have a wee word wae you?'

'Aye, what is it, dear,' he replied, trudging back on the snowy pavement.

'I've jeest had a message fae my cousin Jessie. She runs the Black Wherry in Blaan.'

'Och aye, that wee hotel. I passed it this morning on the way back tae the toon.'

'Aye, well, she's jeest had a message fae Blaan Taxis. They canna get up Durie Hill cos o' the snow.'

'Ach, tell them tae send another taxi tae tow it up.'

'Noo, that's no' as easy as you'd think, seein' as there only is the one Blaan taxi. I think Big Johnnie calls it Blaan Taxis tae sound mair important. You know fine how conceited folk can be.' She stopped as the phone rang in her pocket. 'Hello, County Hotel, the general manager speaking,' she said, in affected tones.

'What were you sayin' aboot conceited?'

She waved her hand to shut him up, listened for a few minutes, then ended the call. 'That was her again. There no way anyone's getting up that hill until the snowplough's been through.'

'I wish them luck, but I've got mair things on my mind today, Annie.'

'Oh, I daresay. But you know they Shannons, they'll no' take too kindly aboot being stuck in the snow.'

'Sir, I have Constable Pollock on the phone from Blaan,' said Sergeant Shaw, speaking on Daley's internal line.

'Oh, if it's about the road, tell him that DS Scott has just told me,' replied Daley, watching Scott, wet with melted snow, drying his hair with a towel.

'No, sir. I think it's something else. He sounds quite shaken up to be honest.'

Daley asked Shaw to put the call through; presently he heard the wind gusting on the other end of the line.

'Willie, it's Jim Daley, what's up?'

'You better get here as quickly as possible, sir. I think I've found our missing journalist and it's not a pretty sight.'

'Dead, I take it, Willie?'

'Oh, aye, sir. As dead as dead can be.'

Bruce pulled himself out of the taxi and looked up the steep hill. His car was in the middle of the convoy heading for

Kersivay House. Near the prow of the hill, he could see a taxi sloughed sideways in the road, a number of individuals trying to push the vehicle back out of a drift. They were having little luck, by the look of things, as plumes of freezing breath faded into the grey sky.

He looked back down the hill to the flat plain beyond. To his left, the grey sea was dull beneath a sky hanging heavy with snow. To his right, darker clouds were unburdening themselves over Kinloch.

He thought of his daughter; beautiful, but so sad, so vulnerable. He remembered her screams when she was a child. The doctors had assured him that she was merely troubled by nightmares, which would pass. They rolled out the old maxims: don't let her eat cheese before bed; don't tell her scary stories, or let her watch anything that may unsettle her on television; don't let her have sugary drinks, or anything containing caffeine.

They had been wrong. He knew it when he watched her stare blankly into space, fully awake, then start screaming at the top of her voice – this was no nightmare. In her hysteria, she scratched his face and bit her tongue. Slowly, as he held her, she would begin to calm, sobbing quietly into his shoulder.

Eventually she had been diagnosed with frontal lobe disorder, a disorder of the brain that caused hallucinations. These visions were often dark, violent and terrifying, but seemed mercifully short in their duration. Drugs and counselling had helped; but every time that look of terror passed across the face of his little girl, his heart broke.

Then, when she was eight, her mother, his wife, died.

Some people said it was as a result of a broken heart; others that the stress of seeing a child so afflicted by this vile condition was too much for her to take and she had just lost the will to live.

The Shannon PR machine had roared into action, ensuring that the press, or anyone outside the family, would never know that the cause of Hermione Shannon's death had been a pint of vodka and two bottles of sleeping pills.

He cursed himself for his inability to cope. In the main, unable to handle his feelings and her condition, he had left the upbringing of his troubled daughter to her nanny and his mother. In effect, his little girl had lost two parents: her mother to the embrace of death; her father to women, booze, designer drugs and parties.

He felt the shame and guilt wash over him. He had failed his daughter, his mother and his dead father.

It was time for redemption. It was time for Bruce to put things right.

12

Daley had to think quickly. There had a been another murder in Blaan, but with the road blocked by snow he faced the problem of how to get to the locus of the death as quickly as possible.

A snowplough had been despatched to Durie Hill, followed by DS Scott in a Land Rover to ease the passage of the Shannon party once the road was clear. After the events of the last few hours, it was clear that Blaan had become an increasingly dangerous place to be. Scott and two constables were to be responsible for the Shannons' safety until the party reached the relative sanctuary of Kersivay House.

Daley tried in vain to conjure up the police helicopter before being forced to consider another option. He called James Newell, who told him that he would be glad to take investigating officers round Paterson's Point by sea in his large RIB, currently the only way to get to Blaan.

Daley walked out into the busy CID office. 'Who can be spared from the Brockie murder team?' He was surprised to hear a familiar voice reply.

'Me, sir. I've been checking Brockie's personal records. I'm stuck until the phone company get back to us,' said DC Dunn.

'Yes, well, OK, then,' replied Daley. 'We'll have to take Newell's RIB to the locus.'

'Don't worry, sir. It's snowing, but I think the sea's quite calm. I'm sure I'll be fine. I don't expect to have to fight for my life every time I go out in a boat.'

'OK, point taken. I'll be with you in five minutes.' Daley returned to his glass box where Symington was still seated, reading a file about the murdered photographer on a laptop.

'Do you think that's wise, DCI Daley?'

'Sorry, ma'am, is what wise?' Daley was searching his desk for his mobile phone.

'I know you saved DC Dunn's life during a previous sea journey.'

'Oh, yes. Well, the prospect of going back out doesn't seem to worry her.'

'I also know about your relationship with her.'

Daley stopped what he was doing. 'Ma'am, I don't know what you've read or been told about that. Our "relationship", as you call it, has been over for some time. As you know, I'm back with my wife and working my notice.'

'In other words, butt out.'

'In other words, yes.'

'I'd like to come too.'

'Ma'am?'

'Don't worry DCI Daley, I'm not going to tread on your toes. I want to be at Kersivay House. I can see we're going to be in for a difficult time.' She looked at her watch. 'And we all have our orders,' she said, without further explanation.

Though the convoy of taxis carrying the Shannon International party was only five miles out of Kinloch, it took the police officers in their Land Rover almost an hour to reach Durie Hill, following the large yellow snowplough as it worked its way through the drifting snow.

Scott watched as other vehicles edged into the side of the road in order to let the large machine past and get on with its job. They sat well back, waiting until things got moving.

'Your man fae the council tells me that once we're over this hill it should be plain sailing tae Blaan,' said Scott, shivering in the vehicle alongside three uniformed cops. 'I want a couple of you tae go up and tell that lot what's happening.'

'Would it not be better if you went, sergeant?' asked a fresh-faced constable.

'Aye, it might be, right enough. But mind, I've done my fair share o' standing out in the pissing wet and freezing cold over the years. It's your turn – get on wae it!'

He watched as the two cops, clad in thick uniform ski jackets, walked up the hill, slipping and sliding on the snow.

'Here, son,' he said to the young PC at the wheel of the Land Rover. 'Dae you want a smoke?'

'Eh, sergeant, smoking is prohibited in all of our vehicles now.'

'I'll take that as a no, then,' replied Scott, lighting his cigarette. 'Let me tell you something, son. See if you want tae survive in this job, learn tae bend the rules once in a while. Otherwise, trust me, you'll go aff your napper.' He took a long draw of the cigarette, his remaining guilty pleasure.

Veronica returned to the manse in Blaan to discover a note from her husband, pinned to the fridge with a magnet.

Gone out to help clear snow from the church drive. Stay here until I get back. Weather's looking dreadful.

She thought for a moment, then trudged out of the kitchen and along the hall, still in her soaking boots. The door to the Reverend More's study was closed and she was surprised to find, when she turned the handle, that it was locked. She stood at the door for a moment, her head resting against the polished oak. She closed her eyes and breathed deeply. Suddenly she was falling, dropping through the air as though she had just jumped off a cliff. She slid down the door, barely able to breath. Now on the floor, she curled up into a ball, praying, desperate for the sensation to pass.

As quickly as it had arrived, it was gone. She uncurled and sat on the floor, her back against the stout door. She held her hand out in front of her face. It trembled uncontrollably.

She stayed there for a few minutes, breathing deeply, then got to her feet. Instead of making the cup of sweet tea her body yearned for, she changed into another thick jacket and left the manse by the front door.

'Do you mind if I take a wander up and help the lads?' said the young cop at the wheel of the Land Rover. His nose was curled against the smell of Scott's cigarette.

'You're a' powder puff, these days. See when I was your age, we had tae sit in polis boxes for hours on end wae three other guys smoking their lungs black. Och, you don't know you're living, man,' said Scott, waving his colleague out of the van. He shook his head as he watched him take tentative, faltering steps up the hill towards the jam of vehicles.

He wound down his window and flicked the butt of his fag out into the snow, watching it glow then fizzle out.

As he was winding up the window, he felt suddenly breathless. It was as though something heavy had landed on his chest, hindering his breathing. He heard himself wheeze, then tried to cough it away. As he fought to regain his composure, a high-pitched whine modulated in his ears. He could feel his heart thumping in his chest and, despite the chill, felt beads of perspiration on his brow.

As he struggled for breath, the taxis, yellow snowplough and distant figures on the glistening hill before him seemed to melt away. The world was white and still. He felt loneliness and fear grip his soul. He thrust his head into both hands in an attempt to banish the episode.

'Why are you so sad?' It was a child's voice.

'What the . . .' gasped Scott, turning to look in the back of the vehicle. There, sitting behind him, was a little boy. He looked pale, but his cheeks were rosy, as though from the cold. Scott felt his head swim. He reached for the door handle, desperate to escape.

'My name's Archie Shannon,' said the little boy, just as Scott fumbled open the door and fell out onto the soft snow. Only his lack of breath prevented him from screaming. The whining in his head was so loud it was making his eyes water. Scott wasn't sure if the tears that were freezing on his face were caused by pain or fear.

Panic was taking hold of him now. He grabbed at his tie, loosening it, trying desperately to breathe. He gulped at the freezing air, but nothing happened. I'm dying. The words echoed around his head.

Through his pain and terror he heard footsteps coming towards him, getting louder than the whining noise in his head. He wanted to run, to escape. At that moment, even the thought of death seemed better than this hell he was experiencing. He was frozen to this spot – but by fear, not the powdery snow.

The scene at sea was cold but magnificent. Despite the survival suits they were wearing, the three police officers shivered as the powerful RIB left the loch and entered the sound. Daley watched Mary brace herself in her seat as the vessel's trim altered. The bow rose into the air and, as they passed the large island at the head of the loch, Newell eased the throttle forwards.

The sky had the colour and luminosity of pearls as they forged through the slow swell of the sea. To their right, the land lay like a white ribbon; hills, cliffs and promontories softened by the thick carapace of snow. It was a scene he knew well but didn't recognise. Even the smells and sounds were different: the tang of ocean was there, but somehow diluted. Though the gulls still soared through a pale, seemingly infinite sky, their cries were muted, no longer echoing from the high sea cliffs under their white blanket.

Daley felt the cold sting at his eyes. Symington looked straight and confident in her yellow survival suit. Her sallow skin reflected the red of her lifejacket as she turned her head to and fro, taking in all before her. Beside her, Mary hunched into her seat. For an instant, he saw vividly a vision of he and Scott making desperate attempts to grab her flailing hand as she disappeared under the tumult at Corryvreckan. Her auburn hair was tied into a ponytail, which swayed in time with the motion of the boat. Daley sighed, remembering her long hair brushing his face as she eased herself onto him when they made love.

'Another fifteen minutes!' shouted Newell through the vessel's loud intercom. Daley looked at the sea and sky, at a buoy they were passing, bright red against a white backdrop; at anything, in fact, other than Mary.

Soon, he recognised the long sweep around Paterson's point; they were nearing Blaan. Newell slowed the RIB's progress, the hull easing back into the slick ocean as he turned the vessel towards the white loom of the coast.

'That's the beach we're after,' he called, pointing towards a thin stretch of dull sand and rocky shore.

Daley squinted into the distance. Already, his senses were pricking; his experience, his feel for the job that had been such a huge part of his life, told him something was wrong. Something was very, very wrong.

'Sergeant, Sergeant Scott, are you OK?' He saw the face of the cop who had driven him here. Suddenly he could breathe again, the noise faded and he felt the chill of the snow all around him.

'Aye, aye, son.' He was gulping down air now. 'I tried tae get oot o' the bloody Land Rover and slipped – I've winded myself, that's all.'

'You're soaking, Sergeant,' said the constable, brushing snow from his colleague's jacket. 'Here, take my hand, we better get you up out of this.'

Scott felt himself being dragged, unsteadily, to his feet. He was cold and wet, but he was still alive. 'I'm fine, son. These bloody shoes. Nae use for this weather.'

'There's a problem up ahead, Sergeant.'

'What kind o' problem?'

'The snowplough is making good progress and the first

taxi is back on the road. We wanted to get the convoy moving but one of the Shannon party is missing.'

'What the fuck dae you mean?'

'Nobody can find him. His wife's going frantic. He went to help push the cab out of the ditch and he's vanished.

'Who, who's vanished?'

'His name is Bergner, I think. He's some kind of boss. Everything's quite confused up there, Sergeant.'

'Come on,' said Scott, already slipping and sliding up the hill. 'We better find oot what's going on.'

13

Daley paddled, ankle deep, through the freezing water, having jumped from Newell's RIB. Constable Pollock and another uniformed officer were standing on the beach a few yards from him, their backs turned away from the grisly scene behind them.

The dead man was in a kneeling position, his arms spread wide, each hand tied to posts driven deep into the sand. Daley walked closer, slowly, narrowing his eyes, trying to take in the bare minimum visual information required in order to make any kind of assessment. The sounds and smells he normally associated with being on or near the sea were obscured by the sickening smell of fresh blood. This stretch of beach, bordered by snow-covered hills and trees, looked like a Christmas card but smelled like a butcher's shop.

'You don't want to get too close, sir,' said Pollock, now at Daley's side.

The man's ribs, cut away from his spine, stuck out behind him like the wings of a bird. Over each shoulder, two dark lumps still oozed dark blood, though most of it had congealed, black in the sand. Daley realised these were the victim's lungs.

'Fuck,' he said, already recoiling from the sight of this

latest horror. He turned. 'Superintendent Symington, DC Dunn, stay back!'

'Blood-eagled, sir. I've read about this in books, I never thought I'd come face to face with anything like it,' said Pollock. 'If the sick bastard who did this was being authentic, this poor soul will still have been conscious while it was being done.'

'What? You aren't serious.'

'Yes, sir. It's an old method of execution. Favoured by the Vikings and, some say, the druids. Horrific torture, agony then death, reserved for only their worst enemies.' Pollock paused for a second. 'Old Mr McLachlan, who has Leadie Farm over the hill, heard screams. Thought it was one of his cattle in trouble. By the time he got here, this was all there was to be found. The force doctor and SOCO have been informed. I just thought you'd like to be here first.'

'Nobody move.' The voice was calm and authoritative. 'I want everyone to look back at their own footsteps before they walk anywhere. The prints of whoever is responsible for this monstrosity must be here on the beach, or in the snow up there,' said Symington, seemingly unperturbed by the ruined figure in front of them.

Daley looked back at the corpse. He should have given that order, made sure procedure was being properly adhered to. The dead man's bloodied hair hung down above the pool of congealed blood, obscuring his features. But he was certain; they had found their missing journalist.

A neat man of medium height met DS Scott behind the queue of taxis on the snowy hill. Blue exhaust fumes filled the cold air and the metallic rattle of diesel engines jarred.

'Are you in charge?'

'Aye, well, for the time being. Detective Sergeant Scott. I understand one of your party is missing?'

'Yes, our Chief Executive is nowhere to be found. I'm Matthew Lynton, Chief Operating Officer of the company.'

'A lot o' chiefs where you come fae, Mr Lynton.'

A tall, attractive woman ran towards them. 'My husband, I saw him about ten minutes ago. He had to take a call of nature, so went over there,' she said, pointing to a dry-stone wall at the side of the road.

She walked through the snow, Scott and Lynton in tow, following a set of footprints Scott assumed were her husband's. The man had reasonably large feet, so his tread was distinctive and easy to follow.

The prints ended at the wall. Snow had clearly been disturbed where the missing man had climbed over it in an attempt to gain some privacy to answer his call of nature. Scott stared out at the field beyond; virgin snow, no sign of any footprints leading away from the road and none leading back from the wall to where the taxis were still idling. A fringe of frozen mud snaked down the hill, in the lea of the dyke, unaffected by the drifts. On the hard dirt, there was no chance of finding any footprints.

'Where is he?' asked the woman, in a foreign accent. 'Where can he be?'

Scott turned to the uniformed cop behind him. 'I want you to go to each car and ask them if they have seen the missing man – sorry, what's his name?'

'Bergner, Lars Bergner,' replied Lynton. Despite the situation, he appeared unruffled.

Most of the Shannon party had retreated to the vehicles, ready to be driven to Blaan, but Scott could see another middle-aged man approaching. He was tall, his brown hair shot with grey. Though his face was lined, he was still handsome, in a lived-in kind of way. Scott recognised the face of someone who, like himself, was no stranger to the joys of alcohol. There was also something strangely familiar about him.

'What's up, Matthew?' he asked, putting his arm around Mrs Bergner, who had started to cry.

'Lars has disappeared.'

'Your name is?' asked Scott.

'Bruce Shannon. If you're a policeman, you'll no doubt have made the acquaintance of my cousin, Maxwell, in the last twenty-four hours or so. Lucky you.'

Scott realised why he found this man so familiar. He bore a striking resemblance to his odious relative, though with a different hair colour and less well-groomed mien – and with softer, more kindly features. He was also a few years his senior, Scott thought.

'First of all, I want tae get these taxis moving, sir. Get you all over tae Blaan before this snow starts again.' Scott thought for a second. 'Obviously, I'll get some men up here as quickly as possible to try and locate the whereabouts of Mr Bergner, but if some of you gentlemen would care tae stay behind and help us in the search, I'll make sure more suitable clothing is brought for you from Kinloch.'

Shannon nodded. 'Yes, count me in. It's not as though I've got anything better to do.'

'I really must get to Kersivay House,' remarked Lynton. 'There is so much to do. I really don't know what's going to happen if we can't find Lars. This is unbelievable!'

Scott looked up at the sky. The clouds were dark, but with

a luminous quality that foretold more snow. He took the phone from his pocket and pressed the screen.

Daley admired the no-nonsense way that Symington had dealt with the horrific scene before them. Overhead, he could see a yellow helicopter circling, looking for a place to land. Finally, help was on the way. Soon SOCO officers would be able to do their job and the ruined corpse of Colin Grant would be afforded some dignity.

'Sir, can I have a word?' It was DC Dunn, her normally pale features rosy in the cold. 'I've had a message from the station. One of the Shannon party has gone missing.' She related the details of Lars Bergner's disappearance to Daley, who listened intently, then let out a long sigh.

'Ma'am. We have another problem.'

As he told Superintendent Symington of this latest woe, the buzzing from the helicopter grew in volume as it came in to land behind the beach.

'OK, DCI Daley,' said Symington. 'You take the chopper back to Kinloch. I'll liaise with SOCO, then base myself at Kersivay House. I'm going to have to get HQ onto this. What the fuck is going on?'

Daley looked back at Grant's body. 'I wish I knew, ma'am. I think we'll have to lock the place down once those taxis arrive, until we can try and make some kind of sense of what we're facing.' He looked across the small bay. Tiny flakes of snow were starting to fall again, settling in the matted hair of Colin Grant.

'I agree. DC Dunn, you stay with me. The murders and this missing man will be your priority, DCI Daley. I'll make sure everything at Kersivay House is secured.'

'What about the press, ma'am? They're on this already because of Brockie and Grant. When they discover the details of this little horror, things will erupt.

'We'll just have to worry about that when it happens. To think, I thought coming here from Leeds would be a walk in the park.'

'I know what you mean,' replied Daley. 'Trust me.'

Two men in white suits were making their way across the snow and down onto the beach. Daley followed their tracks back up the hill and was soon in the yellow helicopter, being whisked back to Kinloch. Despite the death and horror that was again enveloping him, he thought about Mary, wrapped up against the cold, only feet away from Grant's mutilated body: beauty side by side with visceral ugliness.

It was chilling how seemingly tiny choices, decisions taken without a moment's thought, could shape one's life, or hasten its end. When Colin Grant embarked upon his trip to spy on the Shannon family, could he have ever imagined that he would lose his life in such pain?

Daley had seen this all-too often; the sudden, violent termination of existence, springing from the mundane. He had never really been comfortable flying. Large planes were the easiest; smaller aircraft, particularly helicopters made him feel very uneasy.

Not for the first time, DCI Jim Daley wondered how and when his own end would come.

The hut, tucked in a cleft in the rolling hills that overlooked Blaan, was small and stank of damp and age. He stared out over the village, towards the cliff from which Kersivay House glared at the ocean beyond.

Snow covered everything: thorn bushes, fences and walls bore a white coat, softening them, blurring the lines and boundaries of the fields he knew so well. A small burn trickled nearby, following the tilt of the glen down to the sea. He had played here with his brothers, so many years ago. They whittled little boats from pieces of wood and watched to see whose would sink first, the melting spring snow swelling the burn into a torrent of white water.

But spring was far away today. He decided to make his way back down the path to his cottage in the village before it got any deeper. He was cold, but that cold made him feel alive. His body was beginning to fail now – whose didn't at nearly eighty-five – but his mind was still sharp. As he took one last look down the glen, on this, the last day of the old year, words formed in his head. The habits of a lifetime spent writing hadn't disappeared with retirement. Still the prose came, words to make sense of what was before him, the urge to put pen to paper – or in his case, fingers to the stiff keys of the old typewriter that sat in his study at home. For the last eight years he had ignored these mental promptings and tried to settle down to retirement.

He thought of his wife; the way she used to bustle about the kitchen, fussing over the old stove, baking, cooking, making endless cups of tea, making him smile, making the house that he now lived in a home. He supposed that in the modern world her tasks would seem those of a time long past. But then, he was from a time long ago, when life was easier, happier and more rewarding.

For what shall it profit a man, if he shall gain the whole world and lose his own soul? The words from the scriptures ran through his head, where they had been ringing since he was a child, standing at his father's side at the Old Kirk in Blaan.

He had gained much in his lifetime: praise for his writing, a nice home, a fine golf handicap (which he often cursed), a good life and a decent bank balance. But he had lost her.

'Oh, Cathy,' he whispered to himself, as he rose stiffly and made his way down the white glen.

He paused. Though he was old, his hearing was still remarkably sharp, no doubt the benefit of years spent in the peace and quiet of Blaan and an aversion to loud music. He looked across the field to his right. Something was moving. Jock Munro strayed from the path and went to investigate.

14

Trenton Casely was rudely awoken by a knock at the door of his upmarket, central London hotel room. The dark-haired women beside him stirred and mumbled in her sleep.

He shrugged on his robe and padded across to the door, opening it to find a hotel porter bearing an envelope.

'This was left at reception for you a few minutes ago, sir. The gentleman said it was urgent and should be brought straight up.'

'Oh, I see. This guy, what was he like, did he leave a name?'

'I don't know, sir. I can ask at reception if you want. I was just handed the note to take up to you,' said the porter in a heavy Eastern European accent.

As Casely crossed the room to retrieve his wallet, he saw his female companion sit up in bed, her large breasts displaying magnificently above the duvet cover.

'Here, thank you. Much appreciated,' he said handing a twenty-pound note to the porter. Tearing open the envelope, he smiled as he read the message inside. He looked at his watch – they wanted to meet him in two hours. He had time to spare.

Casely walked over to the bed and took off his robe. The woman smiled as he climbed in beside her. 'You've got a busy day, judging by what you told me last night. Don't you ever get tired, Trenton,' she said in her clipped Home Counties accent.

'Only when I'm dead, honey, only when I'm dead,' he replied, for a brief second wondering exactly what he had told her the previous night. Banishing this thought, he grabbed her by the shoulders and turned her over in the bed, making her squeal. It took him a few heartbeats to find what he was looking for, but soon he was thrusting hard, making her gasp into the white linen pillowcase.

The phone on Daley's desk buzzed into life. 'DI Gunn at HQ, sir,' said Shaw from the front desk.

'Put him through,' replied Daley, anxious to find out when reinforcements were likely to arrive. Gunn was in charge of logistics, responsible for moving officers about the division when required. The large area this covered made for a difficult job, but Daley liked him and always found him accommodating.

'Hi, John, when can you get me those men?' he asked.

'Sorry, Jim. You're going to have to manage with what you have at the moment. The road is blocked in two places because of the white stuff.'

'What? Bloody hell. Can we do anything else? I have two murders and now a missing chief executive, John. It's getting pretty desperate here.'

'We know the position, Jim. But this snow is right across the country. We're already down on personnel with guys not able to make it into work because of the state of the roads. I'm trying everything I can, I promise. If the worst comes to the worst and I can pull together any numbers, I'll send them down by air. I'm warning you though, it's looking pretty unlikely at the moment.'

'OK. I know you're doing your best,' said Daley, then put the phone down with a clatter. Since his arrival in Kinloch, he had been forced to draw down manpower from division on quite a few occasions. He had never really considered that the weather could play such a pivotal role. Why did nothing happen in isolation? Was he indeed facing the perfect storm?

He walked through to the front office, where Sergeant Shaw looked harassed, dealing with an increasing number of calls from the local populace who were marooned in the more rural spots around the sub-division or having accidents on the treacherous roads.

'We'll need everybody in, Bill. I'll need you to cancel all leave and rest days. Can you get round everyone and see who we can muster?'

'A general recall to duty, boss?'

'Yes. I know lots of the guys will be away for the festive season, but we'll bring in the off-duty shifts and see if we can find any stragglers. I'll get a cop to help you here.'

Daley was just walking back to his glass box when the phone rang again. 'Sir, it's the *Mail* for you. Not just the usual stuff – it's the editor, he says it's *very* important. Something that may help our enquiries, sir.'

Daley walked back to his office and sighed as he picked up the phone and took the call. The last thing he needed was to be deluged by the press but he couldn't knock back the offer of help – certainly not from a newspaper editor.

'Jim Daley, can I help you?'

'DCI Daley, Ian Ward. I know you're literally snowed under at the moment, but I have some information for you.

I've just come from the press conference in Pitt Street regarding Grant and Brockie.'

'Ah, yes. I'm afraid the news doesn't get any better on that front,' said Daley, realising that the news about Grant's death was yet to be released.

'I know he was murdered. I know it wasn't a pretty sight, either.'

'May I ask how you came by this knowledge, Mr Ward?'

'Never mind that just now, DCI Daley. I noticed that your PR officer got something very wrong earlier.'

'What, exactly?'

'About the nature of their business in Blaan. Grant and Brockie weren't in your area to dig up dirt on the Shannons.'

'No? No doubt they were here studying new crop rotation methods,' replied Daley.

'Nothing of the kind. They were following up reports of some kind of cult.'

'What?' It took Daley a few moments to assimilate what Ward had just said. 'What do you mean by cult?'

'Oh, you know, dodgy rituals, group sex, that kind of thing. We had a tip off some time ago.'

Ward went on to tell Daley that the paper had been sent some grainy images from someone who signed himself or herself merely as 'a concerned Christian'. Brockie and Grant had been despatched to Blaan to cover the story. Now they were both dead.

'I'll email these images to you. I just thought that it was important that you knew the facts. I really want you to catch the bastards that did this, Chief Inspector. You have the full backing of the paper – of the entire journalistic community, I shouldn't wonder. We are a dwindling band, but not without clout, as I'm sure you realise.

We'd have gone with the images as they were, but we were worried that it was all some elaborate hoax. I sent the boys down – they needed the work and I knew them both so well. Bloody hard for freelancers these days.' Daley could hear the tinge of regret in his voice.

'Thank you, Mr Ward. Perhaps you could also tell me how you found out about the death of Colin Grant?'

'Now, Mr Daley, you know the red lines as well as I do. I just think there's something strange about this.'

'In what way?'

'Apparently Colin Grant had been splashing the cash, lately. We're not bad payers, you understand, but this wasn't going to make him rich. Freelancers have to be fiscally prudent. Anyhow, I'm sending the email now. Please don't hesitate to call if you think we can help.'

Daley rubbed his chin. He had envisaged a slow wind down in his last few weeks in the job. It now looked as though he was destined to be assailed by one last flourish of horror and death before he could return to any kind of normality.

His email pinged and he brought the message Ward had sent him up on his computer screen.

There were three images, monochrome, apparently taken with the aid of an infrared camera. Whoever had tipped off Ward's newspaper had access to decent equipment. A group of figures – Daley counted eight – were standing with their heads bowed. They looked to be wearing hoods; dressed like monks, Daley thought. The second image was slightly clearer. Daley realised that he knew the location where these pictures had been taken – the Rat Stone was easily identifiable now. He could make out the figure of a woman on her hands and knees on the stone, facing away from the camera. One of the hooded figures had grabbed her long hair and was clearly joined with her in the act of copulation. The third image was less clear, though Daley spotted something held behind the back of one of those standing around the stone. He enlarged the screen in order to try and identify it. He flinched when he realised that he was looking at a long, thin blade. He remembered Brockie's mutilated face and Grant's horribly ruined body.

'Shit,' he said to himself as stared again at the grainy images in front of him.

Trenton Casely knew the place well; it was in a little lane just off Great Portland Street in central London. He was always amazed how well preserved these old pubs were; it was like walking back in time as he stepped into the oak panelled room. Despite being one of the largest, most modern cities on the planet, London's famous past shouted from every nook and cranny.

He bought a drink and picked up a copy of the *Financial Times* from a rack of newspapers on the bar. He sat down at a quiet table and spread the paper before him, taking the opportunity keep in touch with what was happening in the business world.

As he sipped his pint of London Pride, he reflected on the last twenty-four hours. He had arrived in London, a city he loved, made a deal that would change his life and bedded one of the most beautiful women he had ever met. Not bad for a guy who had started life on the wrong side of the tracks in the Boston projects. He decided that, with the proceeds of the Shannon deal, he would buy an apartment in this city. There was something about the UK, London especially, that he adored. He liked to think it was something to do with the fact that a distant ancestor had left this place for New England at the time of Samuel Pepys. He smiled at the thought; like many Americans, he was fascinated by his antecedents in the old world.

The phone chimed in his pocket.

Running late. Make yourself comfortable. Be with you soon.

Typical. Still, the beer was refreshing, he was feeling mellow and he was pleased to read that a business belonging to a guy he had hated while at Harvard was failing spectacularly. Life was good.

Being New Year's Eve, the pub was quiet. People were saving themselves for the festivities later that evening. A few people milled about at the bar, as the English were wont to do. He was mildly irritated by a model of Santa Claus that shouted 'ho ho ho' at intervals and by a woman whose high-pitched laugh grated.

He walked through to the toilet, the usual British standard, low, gloomy and stinking of piss. As he relieved himself, the slight sting he felt reminded him of the sex he'd had earlier. In his opinion, there was nothing better than fucking an upper-class English woman; watching that dam of cool restraint give way to screaming passion.

Casely returned to his table and flicked the page of the large newspaper. Profits from oil fracking were reinvigorating the US economy. It was good to know.

He took a long gulp of his beer, still trying to slake the thirst left over by the booze he had consumed the previous evening.

As he turned another page he began to feel strange. His heart began to thump in his chest, pounding in his ears, and he felt his throat constrict. He clutched at his neck, struggling for breath. Just as he felt a wave of nausea wash over him, he was enveloped by darkness. He slumped forwards on the table, sending his pint glass crashing to the floor, where it smashed into tiny pieces. A thin stream of blood trickled from his nose and onto the newspaper, obscuring the article about US futures.

The woman's grating laugh turned to a high-pitched scream, but now it didn't bother Trenton Casely in the slightest.

Daley had done all he could. With the help of local volunteers, particularly from the RNLI, coastguard and fire brigade, he'd managed to initiate a full search for Shannon Chief Executive Bergner. As the time passed though, things looked more desperate. Though it couldn't land, the force helicopter had joined in the search, using its thermal imaging camera to try and pick up the signature warmth of life in the snow.

Symington and Dunn had their hands full at Kersivay House, while Scott had been detailed to remain in Blaan with some uniformed cops, just in case the council's best efforts to keep the road open failed. Fortunately, the contingent of Support Unit officers had arrived by boat and were now guarding the mansion on the cliff.

Across the country, the sheer amount of snow was causing the new police force, Police Scotland, huge problems. As Daley had discovered, just getting officers from their homes to their place of work was proving immensely difficult.

Despite the pressure, he had to think methodically, follow the little guide book in his head, the instructions laid down by the great detectives he'd worked with when the job was new to him.

He had three main problems, all connected in some way with the Shannons, or Blaan, at least: two murders, a high-profile missing businessman and the break-ins across the sub-division.

There was a small chink of light though. In one of the homes broken into, an old man had spotted the thieves – just a glimpse, but better than nothing. Mr McGuiness lived in a housing scheme in Kinloch, so Daley decided to pay him a visit. Despite everything, he had a gut feeling about these robberies. He tried to picture the photograph stolen from Hamish's home. Black and white, turning brown with age; old-fashioned photography displaying a glimpse of the past.

Jim Daley felt that there was something about these images that could help solve the rest of his woes. But, as was so often the case, he couldn't explain why he thought this.

He zipped up his ski jacket as he left the office and took to his car. The main roads in the town were being kept clear by hard-working council staff. He wondered how long they would be able to keep it up. Already, some of the more remote communities on the peninsula had been cut off. He knew that a special effort was being made to keep the road to Blaan open.

As he drove through the snow, the street lights flickered then dulled, their last phosphorescence fading. The power cut earlier in the day had lasted for two hours; he hoped this one would be more brief. As fat snowflakes landed on his windscreen, he decided not to hold out too much hope.

15

Bruce Shannon was shivering as he was finally deposited at Kersivay House. Despite spending almost three hours looking for Bergner in the snowy fields, they had seen neither hide nor hair of the chief executive.

He looked at his phone. Thankfully, due to pressure his family had placed on the phone company, the mobile signal in Blaan was good. He had no messages, missed calls or emails. He wasn't sure if this was a good sign or not and wondered about Bergner's disappearance. He had made sure that the deal he had struck insured that nobody – not even the Swede – would be hurt.

He flicked down his contact list and clicked on the name Trenton Casely. Bruce let it ring for longer than he would normally before he clicked the phone off.

'Get off the bint and back on the fucking job,' he whispered to himself, as he stood at the lift doors and pressed the up button. It was time to face his mother.

John McGuiness's home was dark, lit only by candles, but surprisingly warm – in the lounge at least – thanks to a portable gas fire, which gave the room a welcoming red glow.

McGuiness was lean and fit for his age, with a chiselled face and a square jaw, which jutted out as he spoke. His flattened nose marked him out as a pugilist; by the way he carried himself, not an unsuccessful one, thought Daley, though his peak must have been more than half a century before. An old dog panted beside the fire. McGuiness patted it as Daley looked on.

'If I had jeest been a wee bit quicker doon they stairs, Mr Daley, I tell you, I'd have given that big bastard a surprise.'

'Big, you say – so you caught sight of him?'

'Oh aye, he must have heard the dog barking and me moving up the stairs. By the time I got doon, he had shifted oot the door. But I saw him disappear behind the big hedge at the front. It was dark, you understand, but he was a big bloke, dressed in black – dark claithes, at any rate. I didna see his coupon, unfortunately.'

'What woke you?'

'Och, the auld boy, here,' he said, scratching the dog's head. 'He's a' the company I've got since my wife passed away. Sleeps in his basket beside the bed, noo. Bessie wid have a fit, she didna let him upstairs at a'.' He smiled down at the animal. 'Bit like mysel' these days – both past oor best. Aye, but I tell you, we're no' done yet.'

Daley looked around the room. Pictures and old photographs danced in the shadows cast by the flaming candles; a row of trophies glittered on the mantelpiece. 'You've won a few prizes in your time. I hope none of them were stolen.'

'No, well, no' that I can see, anyway. He went through all the drawers in my sideboard, mind, but he left my wee collection of boxing awards alone. Och, they're no' worth a toss noo, no' in money, at least. But they're important tae me.' He stared along the row of small cups, shields and tiny fighters set on plinths, tight packed above the fireplace. 'Started boxing in the army and found oot I had a talent for it. Different in they days, Mr Daley – none o' the fuss and corruption that you see noo. Two men, straight up and doon, Queensberry Rules, an' may the best man win, as my auld drill instructor used tae say.'

'When did you pack it in?'

'Noo, let me think. I was a pro for five years – light featherweight – fighting oot o' a gym in Paisley. Good days, but bugger me, it was hard tae make ends meet. By the time I was in my mid thirties I knew fine the game was up, so I came back hame, way back in the sixties.'

'So you're from Kinloch?'

'Aye. Well, sort of. I was brought up in Blaan. Been in the toon for fifty-odd years, mind.'

'I know that the power's off and everything, but if you could give me a call tomorrow and let me know what, if anything, is missing, I would be most obliged.'

'Aye, nae bother. But I can tell you aboot one missing item noo.'

'Oh, what's that?'

'Jeest one thing, as I can make oot,' he said. 'Strangest thing, an auld photo my daughter had blown up for me. It used tae sit in a frame on the wall, jeest o'er there.'

'Can you describe it for me?'

'I can dae better than that, officer.' He fished out a faded yellow folder, filled with photographs, most of which were to be in black and white. 'Noo, let me see . . .'

Daley looked on for a few moments as he searched amongst the old images, peering through the gloom with a pair of spectacles balanced on the end of his nose.

'Ah, here we are, Mr Daley.' McGuiness handed the detective a small photograph. Even in the poor light, it looked faded, sepia rather than monochrome, curling at the edges with age. 'That's the very picture.'

Daley studied it: a big man was standing straight-backed, dressed in a suit and a button-down collared shirt. He was broad shouldered, with a gut, but looked powerful and, a bit like John McGuiness himself, gave the impression of strength despite his declining years. He had a long, drooping moustache. In his arms was a small girl, her hair in a bow, no more than a couple of years old. Beside him, a young boy stared out from the photograph with a disgruntled scowl. He was wearing very long shorts, one sock pulled up to his knee, the other down at his ankle.

'Is that you as a boy, Mr McGuiness?'

'No, no' me. The man wae the 'tache is my great-uncle Nat Stuart. This photo was taken just before he left Blaan.'

'What did he do?'

'Och, he was a blacksmith, way back, when folk still had horses and carts. An unfortunate man in many ways, but a bit o' a legend in oor family.'

'Oh, why so?'

'We were a family o' tinkers, some wid say, though my mother widna hear that name in the hoose. He was like the head o' the clan, the main man. He had his lands stolen fae him – aye, stolen fae us all.'

'What land?'

'Long time ago noo, Mr Daley, but my uncle used tae own the land where the big hoose is built in Blaan. You know, on the cliff. He had his blacksmith's shop there. The place had been in oor family hunners o' years. Aye, maybees longer.'

'Who are the kids?'

'That's two o' his grandchildren,' replied McGuiness with a sigh. 'See the wee lassie?'

'Yes, what about her?'

'Her mother – his daughter – died in childbirth when she was being born.'

'Oh, that's sad.'

'Och, some folk said the woman wisna in her right mind. The tale is that she was in and oot o' an asylum maist o' her adult life. Even worse when her man buggered off and left her on her ain. No' easy in they days, Mr Daley, whoot wae nae social security or the like. Wid have been hell tae pay if the big man had got a hold o' him, right enough. He didna suffer fools gladly, so they say. Looks it too, wid you no' agree?'

'Yes, I wouldn't pick a fight with him,' replied Daley with a smile. 'What happened to the children?'

'Auld Nat brought them up like his ain. Took them with him when he left. I never seen my wee pal again.'

'Oh, did you know them?'

'Aye, me an' the wee boy, Lachie, wee used tae run aboot Blaan when we were weans. Bad tempered wee bugger he was, tae. Always ready for a scrap. But he was my buddy. That's how I got the photograph enlarged. I tell you, Mr Daley, see when you get tae my age, you get fair nostalgic.'

'Would you mind if I took this with me? I'll bring it back, I just want to make a copy so we know what we're looking for if we come across this thief.'

'Aye, be my guest. Mind if you don't bring it back, me an' the auld fella here'll come lookin' for you,' said McGuiness, patting the old dog again.

The animal looked up at Daley, who was studying the photograph intently and stroking his chin. He took the phone from his pocket and snapped a quick image.

Scott was shivering as they pulled up in the car park of the Black Wherry Inn. The small hotel was near the centre of Blaan, on the main road, between a small estate of five private bungalows on one side and a row of cottages on the other. After nearly four hours in the freezing snow searching for Lars Bergner, Superintendent Symington had arrived and taken charge. Because Kersivay House was now bursting at the seams, she had made a forward operational base at the small hotel, where Scott was now to spend the night. Apparently, apart from a bemused honeymoon couple who had thought spending a quiet time on the idyllic west coast of Scotland over New Year was a good idea, the hotel was empty.

That'll be a honeymoon tae remember, thought Scott, as he watched a dozen freezing police officers pile into the establishment to get dry, warm and fed before being transported back to Kinloch. He was thankful, though, that this meant he wouldn't have to spend another night in Kersivay House. For a second the small boy's face passed through his mind but, as he was enveloped in the warmth of the hotel bar, these thoughts soon passed.

A small woman with grey hair was fussing around her new visitors. 'Jeest get they wet claithes off, gentlemen. There'll be hot food on the go in aboot an hour. Nae menu, yous'll have tae take whoot's on offer. Jeest lucky we've got the generator, or it wid be cans o' soup heated o'er the fire.'

Like Kinloch, Blaan and the rest of south Kintyre was without power.

'Which one o' yous is Brian Scott?' she called.

Once he'd left his jacket steaming on a radiator, he walked over to introduce himself. 'You'll be Jessie, then.'

'Aye, and you're the famous Detective Sergeant Scott,' she said, winking at the policeman. 'I've heard a lot aboot you.'

'A' good I hope,' mumbled Scott, starting to feel slightly uncomfortable under the scrutiny of yet another formidable hotel chatelaine.

'Och, I thought you might be a bit taller. But she's right enough, you're no' an affront tae the eye.'

'Cheers, I'm sure. I take it you mean Annie?'

'Who else?' she replied, a large grin spread across her face. 'I know all aboot you an' her an' all those cosy wee nights at the County. I've been telt tae gie you oor best room – honoured, right enough. Come wae me.'

Jessie led Scott along a narrow passageway and up a creaking staircase. The hotel looked old, with its wood panelling and red carpet, but, unlike the fading grandeur of the County, the Black Wherry was newly painted, neat and well maintained. Scott was surprised to see his case sitting on one of the beds in the bright twin room. The room contained the usual chest of drawers, wardrobe and assortment of brochures detailing the delights of the area, but had a fresh, new smell.

'We've jeest had a refurb, Brian, so make yoursel' at hame. Because o' this power cut, we'll be putting off the electricity in the night. Since it's Hogmanay, I widna think that'll be too early, mind you.'

'Aye, thanks. What's wae the name, by the way?'

'Jessie? Och, my granny was called Jessie – and her granny, if you get my drift. Used tae be the name my family gied tae the first born grandchild, boy or lassie.'

'I'm sure the lads were chuffed tae ten wae that.'

'We stopped that when my uncle Jessie tried tae droon his mother because o' it. But, as my ain Granny Jessie used tae say, "don't affront the name and the name'll no' affront you." '

'Aye, right.' Scott hesitated. 'I was actually meaning the name of the hotel, tae be honest.'

'Oh, the Black Wherry? Right. That was the name gied tae the vessels o' the night, if you know what I mean – smugglers. They were rife here, och, a long time ago noo. The story goes that when Aeneas Ronald got too auld tae see in the dark tae cross the North Channel, he built this place tae stick two fingers up at the law. In a manner o' speaking,' she said, with a tinge of embarrassment, suddenly remembering Scott's profession.

'A nice wee place, anyhow.'

'We dae oor best. An' I tell you something else – as long as you an' the boys are guests in this hotel, yous needna worry aboot any awkward questions, or the like.'

'Well, that would be very good, thank you, it's much appreciated.'

Jessie sidled up to the policeman. 'Mind you, it widna dae any harm tae let me know jeest whoot's happening. We're hearing terrible stories in the village aboot a' these goings-on. Auld Mrs McLachlan was too feart tae take in her washing the day. Frozen stiff on the line apparently, covered in snow. Her Sunday drawers and everything.' Jessie shook her head, tutting. 'If you can gie me an idea o' the right o' things, well, I can make sure these gossips' tales are nipped in the bud,' she declared, looking up at Scott hopefully.

'You probably know as much as me. Noo, is any o' that grub you were talking about on the go? I'm fair famished,' said Scott, anxious to change the subject.

'Aye, of course,' replied Jessie with a sniff. 'If you want tae freshen up, I'll have something for you in the bar in twenty minutes.'

No' another one, thought Scott with a smile. But, for the first time since his arrival in Blaan, he felt almost normal.

16

Bruce watched his cousin Maxwell fidgeting in his chair. Despite her age and marginalised position within the company, Ailsa could make life uncomfortable for the most confident interlocutor. Bruce knew it would be his turn next.

'I must say, I had expected some nasty surprises at this year's AGM, but the disappearance of Mr Bergner and all this death and brutality, not to mention the connection with Archie, has all come as a bit of shock.'

'Nothing to worry you, Aunt Ailsa. In fact, the police tell me that the deaths of the two journalists may be totally unconnected with the family.'

'And what about the skeleton? Just a coincidence, Maxie?'

Maxwell raised his eyebrows at the contraction of his name, but decided not to make the point. 'You know how some people see us, Ailsa. Folk here, well, we're of them but not part of them any more. Must be a bit galling to see what this family has become.' He stole a look at Bruce, one eyebrow raised. 'Mostly, we're a resounding success. Regarding these bones, they still haven't managed to get DNA evidence and may not be able to at all; they've been bleached in some chemical or other. My guess is that this is just a sick prank. Let's face it, everyone in this sorry hole knows about that stupid bloody curse.'

'And Lars decided to pop out for an impromptu hike in the snow, I don't doubt.' His mother's response made Bruce snigger.

Undaunted, Maxwell sat forwards on his chair. 'This is the most important meeting in the history of this organisation. We simply cannot let anything affect the way we take this company forward. I'm sure there is a reasonable explanation for Lars's disappearance.' The phone buzzing in his pocket distracted him. 'I have to go. We can talk about this at the meeting proper tomorrow,' he said, getting up to leave, a sudden look of concern across his face.

'Problem, Maxie?' goaded Bruce.

'Nothing I can't handle, cousin. You stick to what you're best at and let me handle the important stuff.' He excused himself and left Ailsa's apartment, high in Kersivay House.

'Arrogant prick,' said Bruce, reaching for the glass of whisky on the small table before him.

'Clever prick,' added his mother. 'Please go easy on the bloody sauce this year, darling. You made a complete arse of yourself at the last meeting. It really doesn't help our cause.'

He stared at his glass, taking a few moments to consider what she'd said. 'He's not as clever as you think, mother. And as far as "our cause" is concerned, if we are to continue along the usual path of soft power and persuasion, we'll get to where we always end up – nowhere.'

'Maxwell isn't the boss yet.'

'Oh, come on!' Not for the first time, Bruce was riled by his mother's opinion. 'My uncle is a demented old man, slavering into a bib and shitting in a potty. Do you really believe for one second that he'll ever regain his senses?'

'Please, Bruce, less profanity. Of course he'll never recover, but while he's alive, Maxwell cannot get his hands fully on the reins of power.'

'It's only a matter of time until the old boy croaks.'

Ailsa looked levelly at her son. 'And I suppose you think the same about me.'

'Please don't, Mum. Must every conversation we have be this way? No wonder I drink. I'm bloody sick of it. I'm taking steps of my own this year, if you must know.' As quickly as he said it, he regretted it.

'Wonderful, Bruce. Another of your pathetic little plots that invariably come to nothing and make you look even more inadequate than you actually are.'

'Oh, bugger this!' He slammed his glass into the table and got to his feet, his face red with fury. 'When will you get it into your head that this bloody pantomime we attend every year is just that. The real decisions are made in Zurich or New York or in Maxie's new office in the fucking Shard. Blaan, this bloody house, it's all just a relic of the past. Give it up, Mother!'

'This company's true wealth will always be based on the mineral contracts in Russia and the Far East, negotiated in the fifties and sixties. Your cousin forgets that.'

'Oh, great, another wander into the past. It's the same as this bloody place.'

'You've always hated it here.'

'Do you wonder why? Living with the ghost of my dead brother for company every year. I sincerely hope that skeleton is his, then maybe we can move on with our lives. Surely fifty years in mourning is enough?'

She placed her china teacup back on its delicate saucer and sighed wearily. 'Let's imagine that we leave the dead where they are. What then? What about the living? It's clear to me that you have as little regard for them.'

'Mother, I see you when I can. You wouldn't want me hanging about like a bad smell all the time. I love you, you know that.'

'No, not me!' For the first time in the conversation, Ailsa raised her voice. 'What about your poor daughter? Have you even spoken to her since you arrived, or were you too keen to get your face in a glass as soon as you walked through the door? You're a disgrace!'

He took a deep breath. No, he hadn't seen his daughter. Yes, the first thing he'd done when he arrived was pour a large measure of malt whisky. A disgrace? Yes, he probably was. Yet again, Bruce's mother had succeeded in making his feelings of self-loathing even more pronounced. Yet again, the guilt he felt over his daughter almost made him cry out with the pain he felt in his heart. Did this ever change? Did these feelings alter from year to year?

He drained his glass and left the room, with only the familiar feelings of deflation, defeat and shame for company; his oldest friends.

Snow covered just about everything. Gnarled roots poked from the snow like beckoning, blackened fingers; a silent come-hither from the realm beneath. Heavy fir branches drooped, bowed under their chilling blanket, as though weeping at the burden. The sharp, craggy lines of a large boulder, left behind by an ancient glacier, were cloaked once more in white, a fleeting return to the frozen world of long ago.

On the Rat Stone, however, not a single flake had settled. Its black eminence glowered; harsh, unforgiving, irresistible.

It lay darker than the dark night as the last hours of the old year seeped away. Neither the winter moon nor stars glinted across its surface, as though terrified their distant twinkling light might be sucked in, consumed in a dance with time itself.

The man ducked under the line of yellow police tape, stretched between two metal posts. An unseen animal rushed through the undergrowth; snow cascaded from an overburdened branch. He watched it spring back to life in the beam of his large torch, the pine needles green and sharp in a soft, white world.

He mumbled under his breath, the words old and barely perceptible. Then, in a louder voice, in the common tongue, he spoke: 'Light of the sun, radiance of the moon, depth of the sea, splendour of the fire, stability of the earth; today I return.'

He sank to his knees, the snow halfway up his thighs, and pulled back the sleeve of his jacket. His flesh was as white as the snow; the steel of the short dagger he held glittered in the torchlight. The calluses on his hand were at odds with the a neat manicure that left the tip of his fingernails white and even. He ran the sharp blade down the length of his thumb. The thin line of blood soon became a rivulet; he leaned forwards and rubbed it along the length of the stone.

'Be still now.' The woman's voice was quiet but insistent. She pulled his head back, revealing his pale throat. The beam cast by the torch revealed his face as an echo of the skull that lay beneath. His eye sockets were dark and lifeless, his cheekbones threatened almost to pierce his skin.

'Your life in my hands; your soul is my gift; your blood is your beginning and end.' She held the blade close to his throat, the tiny pressure sending another stream of red along its length. 'Will you give yourself to me this night?'

'Aye.'

She hesitated for a minute, feeling the power of life and death course through her, balancing need with want, existence and oblivion. 'So be it.'

The knife moved gently in the darkness, as the wind began to whip through the trees. The old song would be sung again. The serenade had begun.

Lynton, Brady and Maxwell stared at the bank of blinking screens in the old outbuilding that had been converted into a large communications facility at Kersivay House. With a wealth of modern technology at their fingertips, the Shannon family were no longer isolated when they paid their annual visit to their clifftop retreat. Even the local power cut didn't pose a problem, due to the state-of-the art back-up generators the Shannon family had installed. Maxwell enjoyed the fact that from this place where horses had once been stabled, one of the world's most successful companies, its tendrils reaching out to every continent, could be managed.

He felt little joy now, as rows of numbers flashed and changed colour, mostly to red.

'What is this? I mean, how is it even possible?' croaked Maxwell, the sight in front of him making his throat constrict. 'We're losing money across all of our ghosts in the USA. How is this fucking happening!'

'Please don't refer to them as "ghosts"', said Lynton, peering through his small spectacles at another red line on the screen. 'These are diversified public holding companies.'

'Yeah, that nobody knows about but us,' added Brady. 'At first, I thought this was a blip, but it can't be. If this was a general run on the market it would be bad enough, but it only involves organisations in which we have our "shareholding". We're being deliberately shorted on every front.'

Shannon thumped the desk in front of him with a clenched fist. 'Not only is this virtually impossible to do in such a coordinated way, who the fuck knows about the connection other than us?'

'Do I really need to answer that?' sighed Lynton. 'Only four of us have knowledge of the complete picture. Others are aware of our discreet PLC operations, but we four are the only ones who know how it all fits together.'

'And there's no elephant in the room, guys, if you get my drift,' said Brady, looking between both men, his hand, in which he held a glass of bourbon, shaking slightly.

'That is a fucking ridiculous notion, Charles,' said Maxwell. 'Are you seriously saying that Lars Bergner disappeared into the snow this afternoon in order to cause a run on our company's assets around the world? Come on.'

'Are you kidding me, Maxwell!' Brady stood, flinging his glass onto the carpeted floor, where it bounced rather than smashed. 'We own controlling shares in one hundred multinational PLCs. Remember, spread the risk across many jurisdictions, too big to fail? Only me, you, Lynton and Lars know about every one and the full extent of our exposure. So Lars takes a walk in the fucking snow and a few hours later the bottom is falling out of every one of those organisations. Every fucking one! Even your dumb niece would be able to work this out!'

'Don't patronise me, you prick. Your job is to keep an eye on this. How come this is the first I've heard about it?'

'Only started happening in New York about three hours ago,' replied Lynton. 'There lies the good news, though.'

'How can you possibly extrapolate good news from this?' asked Maxwell.

Lynton looked at his wristwatch. 'Trading stops on Wall Street soon. The markets don't start up again until the day after tomorrow because of the New Year break. We have to source what's happening and fix it before then. Or . . .'

'Or we have to go to the rest of the board and tell them they've gone from being one of the richest families on the planet to paupers overnight,' said Brady. 'I've just worked out how much we've lost in the last ninety minutes, or so.'

'Well, do tell,' insisted Maxwell.

'The thick end of a billion dollars. If this spreads around the world after the holidays, well, I don't need to tell you guys.'

'No, you don't. And may I remind you gentlemen that we have the AGM of that board tomorrow. The consequences for us would be much worse than mere bankruptcy. Collectively, we've broken almost every company law and protocol that exists. We'd make those chaps from Enron look like the backstreet gang that robbed the corner store.' Lynton took off his thin glasses and rubbed them with his handkerchief. 'Regardless of the jurisdiction, they'd throw away the key.'

'Fucking cool hand, over here,' remarked Brady. 'I don't need reminding that we're stuck up in this eyrie with the world collapsing around our ears. Shit, even the power has failed. I sure hope that old man can keep the generators going.'

'It's not his job. We have contractors,' said Maxwell. 'Don't worry about anything else but this. We have to work this problem and work it quick.'

'And what of Lars?' asked Lynton.

'Lars is on his fucking own.' Maxwell stared at the screen as yet more numbers turned red.

'And what if someone else gets wind there's something up? All this is well disguised as far as we're concerned, but it's already causing ripples around the business world. Some of the PLCs will be beyond the point of no return soon. I'm thinking mainly of your aunt, Maxwell. She's no fool, plus she retains a merry band of most able advisors.' Lynton placed his spectacles firmly back on his nose.

'They can't be that sharp, we've not been discovered so far,' said Brady.

'Nothing like this has happened before.'

'Shut up, both of you,' said Maxwell. 'We turn our current location to our advantage. We can limit internet access and cut the power when required. In short, we keep everyone that matters cooped up here until we sort this out. Lars's disappearing act gives us the perfect excuse.'

'Happy New Year.' Brady grimaced at the thought.

17

Scott was now in the Black Wherry. To his left, drinks were being served across a busy counter, while to his right a few men stood around a pool table. At the back of the room a small group of locals looked on as a man, hand poised in front of his face, aimed at a dart board, one eye closed in concentration. An old man with wavy grey hair sat on his own at a table, staring at a folded newspaper through old-fashioned reading glasses.

The subdued atmosphere surprised Scott. Though it was early evening, it was Hogmanay, but Scott detected none of the exuberance or high spirits normally associated with New Year's Eve in Scotland.

He ordered a coffee from the barmaid who told him to take a seat and that the beverage would be brought to him.

He sidled up to the old man reading the newspaper and asked if he minded sharing his table. The man nodded and smiled so Scott sat down, pleased to take the weight off his feet and be out of the snow. He had agonised about leaving his room and putting himself in the way of temptation in the public bar, but he needed company. Sitting alone upstairs, the face of the little boy had begun to encroach on his thoughts.

'It's no' real,' he kept whispering to himself. 'Just get over this and you'll be back to normal, Brian boy.' He repeated these words over and over again like a mantra. Secretly, though, he found it hard to be convinced of their veracity. The child had seemed so real. He cursed himself for being so stupid and allowing abuse of alcohol to burden his life in such a way.

At least here, despite the subdued atmosphere, he was amongst other folk. Yes, he would love to be waiting for a large whisky to land on his table rather than a black coffee, but he was determined to beat the urge.

'Quiet in here, eh?' he said to the old man, who peered at him over the rim of his glasses.

'Aye, it is now, won't be later on, mind.'

'So everyone's just saving themselves for tonight, then? Oh, well. I'm Brian Scott, by the way, pleased to meet you.'

'Jock Munro, at your service, Brian.' He took Scott's hand in a firm grip. 'You're a police officer, if I'm not mistaken?'

'Is it that obvious?'

'Well, we don't get too many visitors at this time of year. And bearing in mind the rumours in the village, it wasn't too hard to put two and two together.' Jock had a deep, resonant voice and spoke slowly, with just a hint of a local accent. 'And don't worry, I'll not be fishing for information. I spent too many years doing that for a living to be worried about such things now.'

'How do you mean?'

'I was a member of the fourth estate for more years than was wise, Brian. A hack, in other words. I worked on the dailies in Glasgow for twenty years until I saw the light and started writing for myself.'

'What kind of stuff do you write?' asked Scott, warming to the old man.

'Oh, I had a pretty eclectic portfolio. Latterly biography, but children's books, history, sci-fi, even a bit of crime. I retired a few years ago, so I prefer reading to writing now.' He noted Scott's slight sigh as his coffee was placed on the table by a young waitress. 'Are you on duty?'

'What? Oh, aye – well, sort of,' said Scott. 'You'll know yourself, a policeman's work is never done and all that.'

'Goodness me, things must have changed. I remember sharing a bottle of whisky or two in the old Press Bar in Glasgow with a lot of cops who weren't particularly concerned whether they were on duty or not. Different days, I daresay.'

'Oh, aye. You can say that again. Anything stronger than a wine gum noo and you're doon tae the supermarket looking for a job as a security guard. So, when will things liven up here, Jock?'

'Och, no' until the folks here have been to the kirk. We're an old farming community here, Brian. Most of the lads here will head off to church and sing a couple of hymns and listen to our minister before they get in the mood for the bells. Strange, we normally see a Shannon or two in the bar before now on Hogmanay.'

'They're feart tae step oot o' Kersivay Hoose, Jock,' shouted one of the pool players. 'Last I heard, they were a' cooped up in the big ballroom wae half o' the SAS for company.'

'I heard a Chinook was on the way tae ferry the whole lot o' them back tae London, jeest in case the the old yins get the rest o' them. Is that no' right, officer?' shouted a thin man holding a pool cue.

'You all know fine I canna say anything about such things. Get on wae your game an' stop gossiping like a parcel o' auld women.'

'Who are these "auld yins"?' he asked Jock, in a much quieter voice.

The old man leaned forwards. 'They have a lot o' names, Brian. The healers, the magicians, the Society of the Golden Bough, even the wise men from the Good Book itself. You would probably call them druids.'

'What, seriously? The only druids I've seen prance aboot Stonehenge wae white sheets on their heids and they funny hats.'

'There's lot that would say the same. But, as I said, old traditions run deep in places like this. Traditions, stories, folklore – the ghosts of the past, Mr Scott. There's a thin veil between our world and the place beyond, of that I've no doubt.'

Scott looked at his coffee cup, deep in thought. 'I don't think a family like the Shannons will give two hoots about druids, or the like,' he said eventually, forcing a smile, his thoughts transported to the terrifying experience he'd had at Kersivay House.

'They might say that, but I wonder if it's true,' replied Jock. 'That old house is built on the site of an ancient tinker's encampment. You can think what you like about the tinkers, but they have some of the oldest human DNA on the planet. In every sense, they are the old people, likely on these islands for millennia before the Scots or anyone else got here. People think of them as travellers, but their name refers to their skill with metal – tin in the old days. The family of tinkers in Blaan, the Stuarts, have lived here for hundreds of years, aye, maybe thousands. A tinker's curse is not a thing to be taken lightly and the Shannons were cursed with one a long time ago. A hundred years, to be exact.'

'I wouldn't have though a man like you would believe in such things.'

'When I was your age, Brian – aye, and long before – there was nobody more sceptical than me. But I tell you, as the years go on and the little notions you have in your head get more pronounced, well, the less of a sceptic you become. The druids were guardians of their world, making medicines from plants, caring for man and creature alike. Though they had another side.'

'Don't tell me, they liked a good party and a few bevies.'

'No. You just have to read Julius Caesar to find out that he thought them to be the most formidable force Rome had faced. There were many cruelties: execution, torture, barbarity beyond belief.'

'Bit schizophrenic, is it no'? One minute you're making them sound like a cross between Mother Theresa and James Herriot, the next like Hannibal Lecter.'

'They would do anything to defend their land. Caesar had them massacred on their sacred island, Ynys Môn – Anglesey, as we know it. But he just pushed the power base north.'

'You talk like it was all yesterday, Jock.'

'By our measure it's a long time ago. But ask the old hill or the stone about time and you'll get a different response.'

'Aye, right,' replied Scott. Suddenly he didn't feel as content again.

Daley was driving down Main Street in Kinloch when he spotted Mary trudging through the snow. He stopped his car and wound down the window.

'When did you get back to the town?'

'Oh, about half an hour ago. Superintendent Symington said I could take the rest of the night off. She's still in Blaan with the Support Unit. I got back to the station with the backshift guys.'

'Jump in, I'll give you a lift. Where are you off to?'

She hesitated then jumped into the car. 'I'm going to Angus's parents' house to take in the New Year,' she said with a forced smile.

Daley smiled back, though his heart sank. He tried his best to keep any contact with Mary to a minimum: work only. With Kinloch being so small in size, when Dunn had began her relationship with the young doctor they had bumped into each other in the town's bars and restaurants. Over time, Daley had learned to cope with seeing her with her new boyfriend. But the sight of her now, at such close quarters in his car, made his heart leap.

He was about to drive away when his phone rang. He answered it, a look of surprise growing on his face.

'What's up?' asked Dunn, as he ended the call.

'Seems the late Colin Grant had quite a bit of money in his bank account.'

'Oh. How much is quite a bit?'

'Nearly half a million pounds.'

'Wow! Really? But I thought he was just a freelance hack.'

'Didn't we all. More than that, most of this money came from one source.'

'Who?'

'The big payments into his account all come from Shannon International, through an account registered to one of their subsidiaries on Switzerland.' Daley thought for a moment.

'Listen, I'll drop you off, then I better take a trip back to Blaan. Time I had a word with Maxwell Shannon.'

'So he wasn't on the trail of some cult then? Listen, don't bother dropping me off,' replied Dunn. 'I'll come with you.'

'What about Angus and his folks?'

'Oh, don't worry,' she smiled. 'I've never liked Hogmanay, anyway.'

Veronica fussed around a vase of flowers on a small table beneath the pulpit. She could hear the clunk of the old pipes as the ancient oil-fired heating system stuttered into life. With no electricity, the church was bedecked in candles, giving the old white walls and rows of wooden pews an otherworldly feel. It would be a struggle to keep warm in the old kirk at Blaan this Hogmanay.

She watched her husband as he prepared for the last service of the old year. He had a long black overcoat on over his vestments and was thumbing through the pages of tonight's sermon with gloved hands. He looked up at her and smiled.

'Bloody cold in here, love,' he said, stamping his feet on the floor to aid his circulation. 'Hope the punters have had a dram or two before they arrive. They'll need it.'

'Not too many, though. Do you remember old Mr Hunter last year?' She laughed. 'Snored the whole way through. I hope your sermon will be short, Iggy. You know there's not a great collective attention span at this time of year.'

'Oh, no worries. Short, sweet, with the promise of salvation and a joke at the end. What more could any congregation want on Hogmanay?' His smile faded. 'Though not everyone's going to be full of the joys, considering what's been going on and all.'

'It's your job to raise spirits, my love. I'm sure you'll be equal to the task.'

'Make them forget about old bones and dead bodies, you mean? It's all that anyone in the village can talk about. Just lucky the weather's like it is or we'd be all over the news.'

'No doubt they'll be here soon enough. Have you heard from the Shannons?'

'No, not a whisper. Don't think we'll be seeing them this year. Staying put up on the cliff, so I heard. They've got the police and security up there. With one of their top guys going missing this afternoon, as well as everything else, it's no wonder they're a bit jumpy.'

'Shame, though, it would be nice to see as many souls as possible.'

'We'll miss the hefty donation, you mean.'

'No, I did not mean that,' she said, mocking hurt pride. 'Though you must admit the money comes in handy when we're trying to keep this place going.'

'Yeah, but that's all you get from them, isn't it? Money. No bloody soul, that lot.'

'Why do you dislike them so much?'

'I don't dislike them, more what they stand for, the way they earn that wealth. You show me a global company and I'll show you money made off the back of the poor and exploited. It's a fact, love.'

She raised her eyebrows and carried on arranging the flowers in the large vase. She'd often noticed her husband's antipathy towards the Shannon family. He was a kind man who normally saw good in everyone, or at least tried to. His attitude towards the folk who did so much financially to keep the old church going seemed at odds with this. But, she pondered, who really knew anyone, even those closest to them? What fires in the heart were hidden beneath a smile, only hinted at by a chance remark or unguarded expression?

She studied her husband again. Everyone had fires in their heart.

Daley drove carefully along the road to Blaan. He had asked the council to try and keep the route clear and was pleased to see a large yellow gritting lorry out spreading salt on the highway, orange lights flashing. Large walls of white snow stood sentry on each side of the road, luminous in the moonlight.

He and Dunn hadn't spoken much since leaving Kinloch, just a few comments about the weather and how, for the time being at least, the snow had abated. The clouds had indeed parted, allowing the moon to cast a blue light over the hills, trees and fields of south Kintyre. Here and there, candles flickered in the windows of farmhouse cottages on the way to Blaan. According to the electricity company, there was no chance that the supply would be restored until the next day, and only then if no more snow fell. The whole country had been affected, stretching the emergency services all over Scotland to the limit.

'It's really beautiful,' said Mary, looking out on the moonlit scene.

'Yes, it is. Pity we're up to our ears in blood and gore, as usual.'

'Please don't resign, Jim. Don't leave the job . . .'

'Eh, sorry. Wow, I don't know what to say.'

'You don't need to say anything. I'm sure there's time for you to reconsider.'

'Yes, there is. But what's the point?'

'The point is that you're a good detective and a good man. The police force needs more people like you, not fewer.' She looked at him and touched his arm. 'And I'll miss you.'

Daley could feel tears welling up in his eyes and he swallowed back the lump in his throat. He'd become used to wondering where his wife was or what she was doing over the years. In the last few months, however, and despite his best efforts, he had found it impossible to get the picture of Mary from his mind. He could feel her, touch her, even smell her, as he remembered their nights making love, the breeze moving the light curtains, wafting the scents of summer into the small bedroom of her cottage. Then, as had happened with his wife, darker visions plagued him. This girl, this beautiful woman, being wholly possessed, consumed, taken by another. Someone else's hands on her smooth flesh, another tasting the sweetness on her lips as her body arched with pleasure.

Now, here they were, alone together for the first time in months and she was telling him that she would miss him. This joy he felt was unexpected and bittersweet. 'And what if I did stay? What then?'

'You'd be doing a job you're brilliant at, a job that needs to be done.'

'And stopping you from missing me.'

'Yes, that too.'

'Listen, Mary, I started thinking about leaving the police when Brian was lying in the hospital at death's door. What's happened since has done nothing to change my mind. I'm afraid that making sure that you won't miss me is not a good enough reason to carry on. I'm sorry.'

'Oh,' she said after a few moments. 'I'm sorry I said anything.'

'Don't be like this!' snapped Daley in frustration. 'You must know how I feel about you. Surely you realise what it's like for me.'

'And what do you think it's like for me? I see you all the time and I know you've been with her. I can sometimes even smell her on you.'

'Oh, don't be ridiculous,' he replied, realising even as he spoke that he experienced exactly the same feelings in reverse. 'You see, that's one of the reasons I need to go.'

'This is all totally fucked up. Do you really believe that I love Angus?'

'Well, I assumed . . .'

'To assume is to make an ass of you and me. That's what DS Scott says.'

'Oh, I know what DS Scott says.'

'Please, not here, not now, but soon, can we talk? Properly, I mean?'

'What the fuck is that?' asked Daley, slowing the car. Up ahead, on top of a hill, red and yellow flames stood out in the pale landscape.

Scott and a string of locals trooped through the snow to the Old Kirk. It stood at the edge of the village, silhouetted against the snow and moonlight and surrounded by dark trees. Scott stared out across the bay; he could just make out the old promontory that thrust into the sea, where once a castle had stood. He had enjoyed talking to Jock about the history of the village; many a battle and much blood had been spilt in and around the fortress. It was being spilt again, thought Scott.

Despite his age and the conditions underfoot, Jock kept up a smart pace. He was tall and his long legs ate away the yards, leaving Scott breathing heavily.

'You're fair pecking, Brian,' said Jock with a chuckle.

'I must admit tae being a wee bit oot of condition. I'm going tae fix it though.'

'I walk three miles every morning and play a round of golf in the afternoon. I've been doing it for years; nothing like it for a healthy constitution. Look at that lot,' he said, jerking his thumb at the group of young men behind. 'All got great guts and pudding faces. Half of them sit behind desks all week, while the other half lean against a wall watching cattle being milked by a machine. They all guzzle more beer than is good for them and eat like plough horses.'

'Oh, aye,' Scott replied. 'Ever thought of the church as a second career? You've got the right voice for it. I can just see you haranguing the odd sinner from the pulpit.'

'Funny you should say that. My late father was a man of the cloth. Och, different days they were, altogether.'

They walked along the road, a dark ribbon in the snow. All was quiet, save for the chatter behind them and the crunch of their boots on the newly gritted roads.

'Bugger me, but it's cold,' declared Scott.

'Och, away with you. Bracing, that's what it is. A few hymns and a prayer or two will soon warm you up.'

'It's a long time since I've been in a church.'

'The Lord loves no one more than a sinner that repents.'

Before long, they spotted candlelight flickering through the arched windows of the church and made their way down the gravel drive and out of the snow.

Daley had parked the car in a lay-by and was staring up the hill at the fire. He knew that people in this area celebrated the coming of the New Year in many strange ways, many dating back hundreds of years. But there was something about the fire he didn't like, something that set his instincts on edge.

'How far away do you think that is?' he asked Dunn.

'I don't know. A couple of miles or so, maybe a bit more? You're surely not thinking of hiking up there to investigate?'

'No, I'm not that keen,' he laughed. 'We'd get lost in the dark or end up stuck in a drift. I just think it's strange, that's all. When we get to Blaan I'll get a hold of Willie Pollock, see if he can throw any light on it.'

He turned to walk back to the car, but she stood still in front of him, staring up at his face.

'Can you hold me? Just for a second?'

For the briefest second, Daley hesitated, before reaching out to embrace her. He felt her shiver and rubbed his hand up and down her back to warm her.

'Please stay, sir.'

The church was warmer than outside, but not much. The light from the many candles shimmered, casting shadows on the good folk of Kinloch as they prepared to say goodbye to the old year and greet the next. Scott was surprised at the number of people who streamed in; from old, stooped men and women to young children, it was clear that the kirk was still popular in Blaan.

'A good turnout,' said Jock, in what Scott assumed was intended as a whisper, but still resonated in the cold air. 'That's the minister's bonny wife in the red dress.

'Oh, right,' said Scott, remembering that she and her husband had found the small skeleton on the Rat Stone the day before.

'Aye, bonny and young, Jock,' said an old man, turning to address them from the pew in front. 'No wonder the minister has a smile on his face every time I see him.'

The woman beside lifted a mitted hand and slapped him on the back of the head. 'Peter, did I no' tell you not tae say a word aboot this, before we left the hoose? You're obsessed wae that poor lassie. What the minister does is his ain affair.'

'See "poor lassie",' he replied. 'I don't hear you referring tae Gertie or Peggy o'er there as lassies.'

'That's cos they're no'. You're jeest jealous o' the man. I can see it a mile off. If a younger woman wid take you on, you'd be off like a shot. Is that no' right, Jock?'

'All I'll say, Kathleen, is that the good Lord is first to take the righteous to his breast. So I think you'll be keeping a hold of Peter here for a good while yet.'

'Mair's the pity,' she said, as the pair settled back.

Scott watched a line of men and one woman walk onto the dais below the pulpit. 'What are they all aboot, Jock?'

'That's the kirk elders. We'll be in business shortly.'

The music from the old organ swelled and presently the Reverend Ignatius More appeared from the vestry door, dressed in dog collar and white surplice and clutching a large Bible. He climbed the short stairs to the pulpit, placed the

Bible on the lectern in front of him and looked out over his large congregation.

'Welcome, one and all on this last night of the old year. It's my privilege to be before you tonight in this house, as always.' He smiled, then started to cough. 'Excuse me,' he said, reaching under the lectern. 'Bit of a frog in the old throat.' He put a mug of water to his lips then started to splutter. 'Oh, shit!' he shouted, his Australian accent suddenly pronounced, as he began to retch.

The old man in front of Scott turned around in his pew. 'Canna say I've heard any minister say that before, eh, Jock? It's jeest an affront. Odds on the man's fair knackered keeping his wife at bay. Bound tae tell on a man o' his age. He's only a couple o' years younger than me.'

'If he's only a couple of years younger than you, you'd better get up there an' have a drink o' whootever he's having,' said his wife.

Veronica rushed to her husband's side. His face was red, in stark contrast to his grey hair.

Scott excused himself as he pushed his way along the pew. 'I'm a police officer,' he said, rushing up the aisle towards the pulpit, the eyes of the congregation upon him.

'There was something in my drink,' spluttered More, regaining some of his composure,

'What, poison?' asked Scott, looking for the receptacle.

'Oh, for all that's holy!' Veronica fished an object out of the mug. She screamed and let it slip from her fingers to bounce down the short row of pulpit steps and land at Scott's feet.

He picked it up, then recoiled. It was now clear why the Reverend More had choked. Scott held a finger, pulped at the end where it had been severed from the rest of the hand, bearing a complex and distinctive gold ring.

'I don't suppose anyone's missing a finger?' he said, holding up the item as a murmur of disgust spread around the Old Kirk at Blaan.

18

'I see you've hurt your own hand,' said Daley. The church was empty now save for himself, Scott, the Mores, DC Dunn and Roy Simpson, an elderly farmer and church officer.

'Oh, this?' said the Reverend More, holding up his bandaged hand. 'The perils of DIY, Mr Daley. I was trying to fix my bloody snow shovel, as it goes.'

Mr Simpson clucked at the oath.

'Sorry, Roy, still a bit off me stride, mate. It's not every day you nearly swallow someone's finger.'

Daley looked at the severed digit, now sealed up in a polythene evidence bag. The ring looked expensive, the design unusual. 'Take some pictures of this with your phone, please, DC Dunn.'

'Are you going tae put it on your wall, Jimmy?' asked Scott.

'No. I'm going up to Kersivay House. When it comes to expensive designer jewellery, they're most likely to fit the bill, wouldn't you say?' He watched as Dunn took a couple of shots on her camera. 'Give it to the next cop going back to Kinloch and get it through the books and up to Glasgow at the first opportunity. I know that could be some time, given the weather conditions.'

Veronica looked on quietly. The bandage on her husband's arm had been roughly applied, probably by himself. Why he hadn't asked for her help? She had wondered why he had been wearing gloves as they prepared for the service. Obviously it hadn't been all about the biting cold.

'Och, it's a terrible thing. The last time anything like this afflicted this kirk would be way back at the time o' the Covenanters,' said Mr Simpson, shaking his head. 'Back then, the minister had a rare taste for blood. He couldna see the McDonalds spill enough o' the stuff. It's terrible, jeest terrible. Auld Mrs Beaton fainted away when she seen that awful thing. You have my sympathies, Reverend More.'

'What aboot the guy that's lost his finger?' asked Scott. 'I daresay he's no' feeling too chipper, either.'

'Who put the mug of water there?' asked Daley.

'That would be me, officer,' replied Simpson. 'It's my job tae make sure that the minister is catered for – help him on with his vestments, make sure the church is in order, put oot the hymn books. All that sort of thing.'

'So when you filled the mug there was definitely nothing in it?'

'Funny, I've been thinking aboot that. I jeest picked the mug off the shelf in the kitchen, filled it and took it through tae the kirk. I canna remember looking in it at all.'

'Surely you'd have noticed a finger floating about?' said Scott.

'How wid you? Dae you stare intae your mug o' tea every time you pour it? I certainly don't.'

'Remind me never tae come tae your hoose for dinner.'

'OK,' said Daley. 'To your knowledge, who has had access to the church since you opened it this evening?'

'Ah, now there's a thing, Mr Daley,' replied the Reverend More. 'We don't open the church, as such.'

'Meaning?'

'Meaning it's a proper kirk, a place o' worship, jeest like it should be. The door tae the Lord's hoose is never closed tae them that's looking for salvation,' said Simpson. 'I'm no' even sure if the locks on the big doors turn. That's the way it is in Blaan.'

'There wouldn't be one nail left in the place, if it was where I come fae,' said Scott. 'Never mind pews and the like. I think it's time you reviewed your security policy tae fit in the realities o' life in the twenty-first century.'

'Oh, is that a fact? Tae be like the folks up in Glasgow, no doubt? Well, no thanks,' said Simpson. 'We've got half o' the polis force here and there's folk getting butchered all over the village. My auld faither is likely turning in his grave.'

'Around here, I wouldn't be surprised if he was up dancing aboot,' replied Scott. He turned red when he realised that everybody was staring at him. 'Just an expression, if you know what I mean.'

'I don't suppose you saw anything, Mrs More?' asked Daley, taking his eyes off his flustered DS.

Veronica burst into tears. 'I'm sorry, it's all just too horrible,' she sobbed, lowering herself into a pew, her head in her hands.

More sat down beside his wife and held her. 'I'm sorry, Mr Daley. First that skeleton then all the rest of the trouble that's happened in the last day or so. My wife is quite fragile, I'm afraid.'

Daley looked on as Veronica shrugged out of her husband's embrace and ran out of the church.

'You'll excuse me,' said More, rushing after her.

'What's all that aboot?' asked Scott, looking puzzled.

'Not to worry, Brian. She's probably off to have a word with some of these dancing corpses you were talking about.'

'Aye, a slip o' the tongue, Jimmy. Sorry.'

'Och, she's a delicate flower, right enough,' said Simpson. 'Had a hard time in the nunnery, by all accounts. The nuns fair bullied her, so I'm told.'

'Aye, they nuns can be right bastards. We're never done lifting them for brawling in the street and harassing decent folk,' said Scott, as Dunn stifled a laugh.

'You may jest, but I'll tell you something for nothing. That poor lassie had a terrible time wae them. That's how she left.'

'Lost the habit,' said Scott, much to Daley's distaste.

19

The snow glowed in the moonlight as the men looked to the far end of the bay and Kersivay House on its precipitous cliff. Lights shone from almost every window – unlike the majority of homes in the village, where only feeble candles guttered.

The men were dressed in black, eyes shining through balaclava masks. One of them was listening intently to his mobile phone as the other three scanned the scene below. Behind them, hidden in the trees, were three tents, almost invisible in the darkness of the ancient wood.

The man ended his call and walked towards his companions. 'Right, let's get changed. We all know what to do.'

'We wait,' said the man closest to him.

'Yes, we wait,' he looked at his watch. 'Only a couple of hours until midnight. We wait until everyone is relaxed, then we'll get the word to move.'

'I hope your contact in the house knows what they're about,' said the largest man.

'Oh, trust me. We are very well informed.' He lifted a pair of night-vision binoculars to his eyes and searched along the hillside. Just over a prow there was a glow in the sky, blotting out the night-vision view in a flash of white. 'Some bastard's started a fire over there.'

'Don't worry, boss. One of the local yokels. You know how the Jocks love New Year.'

'I can think of a few Jocks who won't be enjoying it much – not by the time we're done.'

Bruce Shannon was uneasy for two reasons. He found the sight of his mother deep in conversation with Maxwell's burly bodyguard strange and disconcerting. When he had arrived unannounced in her suite in Kersivay House, she had smiled and looked relaxed, but he could have sworn that the guard looked flustered, almost furtive.

His mother dismissed this casually. 'The security detail is here to protect us all, not just your cousin. He was briefing me on the latest developments in the search for poor Lars Bergner. His wife is beside herself and no wonder. The search is suspended overnight because of the conditions. Poor man.'

He stared at his phone, his second cause for concern. Try as he might, he had failed to raise Trenton Casely. He hoped that his 'little plan', as his mother would have called it, wasn't going awry. Casely had assured him that the people he was working with were serious and experienced. He'd asked to meet them, but the American had warned him that, because of the nature of their trade, these individuals remained firmly in the shadows. 'If you see them, you probably won't see anything else – ever,' he had said, with typical American overstatement. At least, Bruce thought, he hoped it was overstatement.

He watched the smoke from his cigarette thread through the night air. The stars he remembered so well from his childhood were out now, twinkling in the clear sky. Living in London you almost forgot they existed, he realised.

He watched his daughter and her 'companion' as they walked out of the bright doorway onto the steps.

'Are you sure this is a good idea?' asked Mrs Watkins.

'Don't worry, Murren. I have plenty of friends in the village. And it's New Year for fuck's sake. Aren't you coming too?'

'Oh . . . I didn't think I was invited,' she said.

'Go and get your frock on, it's party time. And don't worry, one of Maxie's goons is coming with us, just in case anyone tries to disappear us like Lars.'

'And you trust them?'

'Good point. But, we can't sit cooped up here for the duration. Drives me mad.'

'What do you think, Nadia?' he watched his daughter as she gazed out across the landscape. Her face was blank, her eyes clear under the straight fringe of her hair.

'Yes. Yes, Daddy. I'd like you to come, Murren. I should have asked you. I didn't think.'

'You think too much, darling,' said Bruce looking at his watch. 'Where's that bloody car?'

Symington was out of uniform when Daley arrived in the small room she had been given in Kersivay House. She looked entirely different in her casual jeans and thick, patterned jumper – younger and less authoritative. DC Dunn had been sent to locate Lars Bergner's wife.

'I thought we'd bring her here, ma'am,' said Daley.

'So you're confident that the finger belongs to him?'

'Well, it would seem obvious. Worth a shot, anyhow. Goodness knows when we'll be able to get it analysed in Glasgow if this weather holds up.'

'Let's say you're right, DCI Daley. Why put the finger in the minister's mug? Where's the ransom demand? I assume that's what this is all about.'

'Yes, I wondered that, too. Either we have a cold, calculating perpetrator, who murdered Grant and Brockie then deposited this digit in the church to build up the tension and give us proof of their intentions, or it's a complete nut job.'

'Whichever it is, we're on our own. I've just been on the phone to HQ. It's blizzard conditions up there now. The main road is blocked by snow and two jack-knifed lorries, plus the airport is shut down. Nothing's moving.'

'At least the road between here and Kinloch is clear and we've managed to rustle up some support. We should count our blessings, ma'am.'

'Oh, please. Less of the ma'am when it's just you and I.'

'Yes, oh, of course,' said Daley. 'Sorry, I don't know your first name.'

'Carrie,' she replied. 'My mother was a fan of horror films. Don't ask.'

A knock sounded at the door and Daley stepped across the room to open it. DC Dunn was standing beside a tall, flaxen-haired woman. Lars Bergner's wife was beautiful, but looked drained. She was wearing a long black dress that accentuated her height, blue eyes shining above high cheekbones.

'Please tell me that you have good news,' she said.

Daley invited her into the room and pulled over a chair, onto which she slumped, obviously fearing the worst. Dunn pulled her mobile phone from the pocket of her ski jacket.

'I would like you to look at this picture,' said Daley.

Ursula Bergner gasped as she looked at the image of the severed finger. 'Oh my, oh . . .' She burst into tears. 'That's Lars's ring. I bought it for his fortieth birthday.'

'Listen,' said Daley, kneeling in front of the woman and taking her hand. 'I know this is horrible, but in a way it's good news.'

'How could this possibly be good?' she sobbed.

'We now know that someone has taken your husband. But why would they do this unless they wanted us to know that they have him captive?'

'So you think he's been kidnapped?'

'Yes, I think that's the most likely reason for his disappearance. And if someone is kidnapped there is always a reason – usually money. We're just waiting to hear what they want.'

'Don't you think he'll end up like those other men, the journalists?'

'No. I think they've taken your husband for a reason, most likely financial gain. What happened to the other men was horrible. But it may be a warning, their perverse way of showing us that they're serious. A man in your husband's position is worth a lot to them.'

'So, what now? What can we do?'

'We wait,' said Daley, realising he wasn't being much of much comfort to the distraught woman.

At his own request, Daley was taken to see Maxwell, who was standing on the terrace in the snow wearing a large overcoat. He held a large glass of whisky in his hand and was staring out across the moonlit bay.

'DCI Daley, at last. Superintendent Symington tells me that you're in charge of this fiasco you call an investigation. I have a number of points I wish to raise with you, so be a good man and stand there and listen until I'm finished.'

Daley moved closer to Maxwell, until they were almost toe to toe, and stared down at the slightly shorter man.

'What the bloody hell do you think you're doing!'

Silently, Daley reached into his pocket for his phone. 'Read this,' he said, handing the mobile to Maxwell.

Reluctantly Maxwell peered at the illuminated screen, scrolling down with his thumb. 'Where did you get this information?'

'That's none of your business, Mr Shannon,' replied Daley, staring unblinkingly at the interim Shannon International boss. 'I have two murdered men, the unidentified remains of a child and a missing chief executive to think about. What you want is of absolutely no interest too me. I hope I make myself clear.'

'You realise that I'll go straight to that pretty little superintendent of yours – and beyond, if I have to.'

'I don't give a fuck what you do, Mr Shannon. Now, tell me why Colin Grant had almost half a million pounds in his bank account from your company?'

'I'm chairman of a multinational global enterprise. It may surprise you to know that I don't sign every cheque my company issues. I will make enquiries, of course, but I see that these payments were made by our Swiss division, who, like the rest of the civilised world, are on holiday until after New Year. Conversation over, I think.'

'So you have nothing to say about this, no knowledge whatsoever?'

'No. You must realise, chief inspector, half a million might sound like a lot of money to you, but it doesn't to me. I'm sure that there is an absolutely reasonable explanation as to why this payment was made. Now, I think it's time for you to answer some of my questions.'

Daley said nothing as he grabbed the mobile phone out of Maxwell's hand. 'Take a look at this.'

'Must we play this little game all night?' Maxwell smirked. 'How tiresome.' With an exasperated sigh he took the phone again and stared at the screen. 'What in hell's name . . .' He took a gulp of his whisky and rubbed his mouth on his sleeve, a look of disgust on his face. 'What do you mean by showing me that? I'm interested only in what's happening here and now. Got it?'

'That picture was taken this morning. You might even know the victim.'

'What do you mean? How could I know this . . . monstrosity?'

'It's the mutilated body of Colin Grant. The same man your company paid almost half a million quid to over the last few months. Does that ring any bells now?' Daley could tell by Maxwell's look of horror that he knew exactly who the dead man was and why he'd been paid so well. 'If you want to talk, my good man, I'm easy to find,' said Daley, walking from the terrace and back into the warmth of Kersivay House.

More had managed to calm his wife down after the ordeal with the severed finger and they'd arranged to walk over to the Black Wherry Inn to take in the New Year with the rest of the village.

As he waited for her to get ready, he swilled the brandy around his balloon glass and felt his own mood change for the better. The log fire was the only light in the room because of the power cut, but somehow it augmented the fug the spirit was producing in his head. He was relaxed and content.

The chime of the old clock demanded his attention; it was eleven, only an hour to go. He placed his glass on the coffee table, grabbed the big torch, got up, stretched and stifled a yawn. Couple of beers and some good company and I'll be right, he thought as he walked out of the warm lounge and bounded up the stairs. He knocked on the bathroom door. 'Come on, love. If we don't get a move on we'll miss the bells.'

Silence.

He knocked again and called her name, still nothing. He tried the handle and, to his surprise, the door opened. Normally his wife, tired of him running in to pee as she had a relaxing soak, locked the bathroom door. The old oil lantern was burning on the windowsill but the room was empty, no water in the bath and no steam on the mirrors.

'Bugger,' he said, walking across the landing to their bedroom, expecting to see her asleep on the bed. But there was no sign of her. He looked in the spare bedroom and the box room – nothing.

As he ran down the stairs he called her name again, then checked the kitchen and the downstairs toilet. 'Listen, love, if you're trying to scare me, you're doing a good job. You've had your little game, now come out!' He stood stock-still in the dark hall, the only sound the ticking of the old clock.

'Veronica!' he shouted as he opened the back door. The moon was bright and he could see that she wasn't in the manse garden.

He pulled his mobile phone from his pocket and dialled her number. When she didn't answer, he dialled another. 'It's me, I've got a problem. It's Veronica, she's gone.'

*

The flames of the huge bonfire leapt and sparked as the ring of eight people, holding hands, circled anticlockwise – widdershins – around it. The deep hoods of their robes covered their faces as they chanted. With the heat of the fire and the tread of their feet, the snow had melted into a slushy circle and each step splashed mud onto the hems of their long cloaks.

Their movement slowed in time with the chant until they came to a stop, heads bowed, hands still linked.

A man's voice sounded above the crackle of the flames. 'Spirit of the fire, might of the sea, majesty of the sky, we are here joined as one, with the one. Under this night sky, beside the cleansing flames of this fire, we bring you our tribute.'

They dropped their hands and two figures left the circle; the others began a low resonating hum.

The voice called out again. 'Our stone, we are removed from you, but we still make our tribute. This fire is our beacon, our light, as we seek your strength.' The two hooded figures returned, this time dragging a man, his head lolling as he was half carried, half dragged through the mud and snow. Something was placed under his nose and he coughed and spluttered, slowly regaining consciousness.

He raised his head and called out in a foreign tongue. The hooded figures either side held him tight as his sobs broke in the night air.

As the low humming gained intensity another figure broke the circle. Standing between the stricken man and the fire, she let her crimson cloak fall to the ground to reveal her naked flesh, orange in the flames. Light and shadow danced across her body as she walked towards the man, her arms held out straight before her. In her hands she clutched a polished, sleek blade that flashed in the light.

‘We are the old people, we protect and nurture our world,’ she shouted above the moaning hum and the sobs of the captive man. ‘We are the magicians, the wise ones. We give this to the earth, the sea, the sky and the stone.’ With one fluid movement she stepped forwards and slashed at the throat of the captive. His screams were cut short, now a strangulated gurgle. ‘Now give me life and the strength to prevail.’

She ran her hands down the neck and body of the dying man as his heart pumped the last of his dark blood from the severed artery of his throat, gushing over her hands and up her arms.

20

The Black Wherry, as Jock Munro had predicted, had livened up considerably when Scott returned from the kirk. The bar was packed and the pool table had been pushed into the corner of the room to make way for an accordionist who was rattling through his repertoire of jaunty reels and jigs. Older men and women sat at chairs and tables, keeping time, while younger revellers danced an impromptu eightsome reel to much whooping and cheering. In an effort to conserve the fuel used by the hotel's generator, most of the lights had been turned off; the room was lit by a blazing fire and oil lamps, giving proceedings a cosy, nostalgic feel.

As Scott followed Jock to a table that seemed to have been reserved for the old writer, he felt more at home than he had done in the church. Though one thing was missing; he looked on as glasses of whisky, beer and wine were tipped back by those determined to see in the New Year with insobriety.

'Something for you, or are you still on duty?' asked Jock, about to head for the crowded bar.

'Och, a wee ginger beer and lime,' replied Scott, sincerely wishing that it was something much stronger.

'As you wish, Sergeant Scott, as you wish.' The big man plodded to the bar, where he was soon being attended to. It was clear that Jock Munro was well liked and respected in the village of Blaan.

Scott was surprised by a tap on the shoulder. 'I hope you're behaving yourself. I'll hear all aboot it if you're no.'

'Annie, what are you doing here?'

'Och, I couldna let you have all the fun,' she said, taking a seat. 'The hotel closes at ten on Hogmanay. Thought it would make a nice wee change tae come o'er here. I managed tae bring another friend with me.' She opened her handbag to reveal a bottle of malt whisky. 'Buggered if I'm paying Jessie's prices for a good dram. You lean forwards between me and the bar and I'll pour us a couple.'

Before he knew it, Scott was nursing a good-sized dram in the small glass that Annie had produced from her handbag. He looked at the deep golden spirit as he swilled it around.

'Whoot are you, a connoisseur or something? Neck it the noo and we'll get a few in before the bells,' she said, knocking back a large measure in one.

As the whisky touched his lips, Scott could feel his senses enliven. The alcohol made his tongue tingle and warmed his throat and chest as it slipped down. Almost instantly, the world seemed like a better, happier, kinder, more interesting place. The ancient mantra of the recalcitrant drinker echoed through his thoughts: 'och, one or two won't do any harm.' It drowned out the tiny voice screaming no.

'I'm sorry. I have to stay with this,' said Daley into his mobile phone. Liz had called, wondering why he wasn't at home to bring in the New Year. 'It's the last time this will happen, darling.'

'Is she there?' the question was brief but accusatory.

'Do we have to do this every time? I'm at work, Liz.'

'Is she?'

'Yes . . . We're working. It's all very difficult here and I've got to keep on top of it.'

'Huh. I don't have to think for long to imagine what else you'll be on top of.'

'Liz, please stop this. I only have a few more weeks of this and then we can do anything you want. Liz . . .' The line was dead.

Daley sighed as he walked along the corridor, adorned with old black-and-white photographs. He looked distractedly at them as he pondered yet again on the state of his marriage. He had completely forgotten about the time – the fact it was Hogmanay, even. This house, the Shannons, the tiny skeleton, the dead journalists and the missing man crowded in. For the first time since coming to the area, its isolation bore down on him; the snow had all but cut them off.

He was used to Liz being difficult. She had been that way for the greater part of their marriage. He tolerated it, hardly even thought about it, he reasoned. This time, because of the pressure of the investigation, because of the snow, maybe even because this was his last case, he was angry about her slamming down the phone – furious, in fact. He felt his face growing hot as he picked the phone back out of his pocket.

'Don't bother apologising,' she said on answer. 'I'm not interested.'

'I wasn't apologising. I was just wondering why you are such a self-centred, rude woman and how I've managed to put up with you all this time. I've bent over backwards to keep you happy, tolerated your fucking affairs and flirting with just about any man with a pulse. I'm fucking sick of it.'

'Affairs! Well, that's rich coming from you, off spending New Year with that tart. Don't you know she's only fucking you to get a promotion? Why on earth would she find you attractive otherwise?'

'Listen to me.' He lowered his voice as a policeman approached him down the long corridor. 'I do not have time for this right now. Just don't put the fucking phone down on me again!' He ended the call.

The cop nodded and smiled as he passed. Daley stopped at an old image; two figures standing in front of some scaffolding. The photograph was brown, discoloured with age. It reminded him of the picture he'd seen at McGuiness's home earlier that evening, even though the people in the image were different. A well-dressed man in a bowler hat stood beside a young woman. He had a watch chain spread across his waistcoat and his bowler hat was at a jaunty angle. He oozed self-confidence and assuredness. Daley squinted at the tiny writing under the image: *Mr and Mrs Archibald Shannon at the laying of the foundation stone of Kersivay House.* Daley stared at the man again and realised that it could have been Maxwell, the resemblance between the two was extraordinary.

For some reason he couldn't fathom, the face of the young policeman he had just seen crossed his mind. The cop needed a shave. When Daley had been a constable in uniform, an outraged shift sergeant would have chased him the length of Stewart Street Police Office if he he'd turned up for duty like that. He turned around, but there was no sign of the constable in the long corridor. One of the Support Unit guys, he thought. Things are slipping. He made a mental note to bring the subject up with the unit sergeant. It was a small point, he knew, but sometimes small things were important. He didn't know why, but suddenly his stomach lurched and he felt a tightness in his chest. He put it down to the acrimonious phone call with his wife.

He looked back down the corridor and stroked his chin.

Bruce craned his neck over the crowds in the Black Wherry, looking for a table for himself, his daughter, Mrs Watkins and their minder. He handed the tall, wiry security man a small wad of notes and sent him to the bar. 'Open a tab with this, will you. We'll find a seat somewhere. Get a waitress to come over when she's ready.'

He spotted a table. The imposing figure of Jock Munro was sitting beside two others. He'd known Jock since he was a child, when he'd been given the writer's books to read and thoroughly enjoyed them. They were full of derring-do and, in the main, set in and around Blaan. His favourite, a children's novel, had been the one about the massacre at the castle. He'd made the mistake of letting his daughter read it when she was younger. Nadia had been so upset by it that she hadn't slept for days afterwards. He remembered his wife's face as she had tended to the stricken girl. Why was it that the ghosts of one's past refused to lie down and die?

He made his way over to Jock's table, suddenly recognising the detective who'd been coordinating the search for Bergner earlier in the day. He gave him a nod of recognition.

'Mind if we take a seat, Jock?' he said, above the din of the accordion and the excited revellers, many of whom were staring at him. 'Not long until Big Ben chimes in the New Year!'

'Be my guest.'

The Shannon party took their seats as a waitress appeared at the table.

'Get my friends here whatever makes them happy. In fact, buy the whole bar a drink and put it on my tab. Happy New Year!' He took a twenty pound note from his pocket and handed it to the smiling waitress. 'That's for you. Keep 'em coming,' he said, winking at the girl.

'Cheers, Mr Shannon,' said the detective, holding up his glass. His face was flushed and Bruce could see he'd already had a few. Lucky him, he thought.

'My pleasure, sergeant,' he replied.

'Och, less o' the sergeant. My name's Brian. This is my mate Annie from the magnificent County Hotel in Kinloch.'

Bruce shook the woman's hand and she beamed in response. For the first time since he'd arrived in Blaan, he felt relaxed.

He looked at his daughter. She was gazing from beneath her fringe at a group of young people dancing a reel, as fascinated by them as though they had sprung from another planet.

'Here, Mr Shannon,' said the woman, pushing a glass brimfull with whisky across the table. 'This'll keep you goin' until the lassie gets back wae yours.'

'Cheers, much obliged.' It was time to forget about his troubles, if only for a while.

Ignatius More was walking along the road on the outskirts of Blaan, a large torch illuminating his path between the manse and the Old Kirk. The air was cold, the snow on either side of the road deep. The eerie stillness made the search for his wife an anxious one.

He was about to turn onto the long gravel driveway that led towards the church when movement to his left made him stop in his tracks. 'Hello?' he called, but there was no reply. He stood listening for a few moments then walked on. As he reached the church a flicker of light through a long arched window caught his eye. He climbed the three low steps and turned the big brass handle of the kirk's oaken door, wincing as it squeaked in protest.

'Roy, is that you mate?' he said, hoping that his church officer had returned to the building for some reason. There was no reply. Distantly, he could hear something dripping, a steady tap, unnaturally loud as it echoed around the old building. He shone his torch along pews and aisles. A single candle flickered on the solid communion table, directly below the pulpit; its flame guttered at an angle, shying from some draught.

The dripping sound grew louder and, in the beam of his torch, he noticed that the vestry door was lying open. Normally, as it contained the Minister's personal papers and the church silver, it was the only part of the church to be locked. More could have sworn he'd locked it before leaving the kirk earlier that evening. 'Roy, Mr Simpson, are you there?'

The only response was the metronomic drip, drip, drip. The Reverend More edged through the door and into his vestry.

21

Everyone looked to the television behind the bar at the Black Wherry Inn. Thanks to the hotel's generator and satellite television, its customers could see images from around the country of the Hogmanay festivities. The picture switched between images of Big Ben and Princes Street in Edinburgh, which was thronged with revellers anxious to begin the party the city had become famous for.

'Three . . . two . . . one! Happy New Year!' As the chimes of Big Ben rang out, celebrations began across the country. The customers in the Black Wherry embraced, kissed and heartily shook each other's hands, all to the clink of glasses and the swirl of the accordion. As the first bars of 'Auld Lang Syne' rang out, the good people of Blaan linked arms and greeted the New Year in the traditional manner.

When the singing ended, Jessie, somewhat unsteadily, climbed onto a table and addressed her customers. 'Right, everybody. Even though we're oxter-deep in the snow, yous will be pleased tae hear that we've managed tae salvage the bonfire and the fireworks. So get your coats on an' follow me!'

'What's going on?' asked Scott.

'We always go out the back for a bonfire,' said Jock. 'We've been doing it for years, long before those buggers in

Edinburgh and London started to copy us. The field is where we hold the Blaan Highland Games, but it's got an older history than that.'

'Aye, it has that,' said Annie, shrugging on her coat.

'Well, don't keep me in suspense,' said Scott, warmed now by a few whiskies and thoroughly enjoying himself.

'It's called the Bloody Glebe. It's where the government soldiers executed every man from the castle. Struck off their heads, as the minister shouted for the blood of his own parishioners. A dreadful day, indeed.'

'That's a wee bit extreme, is it no'?' said Scott, draining his glass.

'The Red Preacher, they called him. He's remembered and reviled here, to this day. We burn his effigy on the bonfire every New Year, a bit like yon Guy Fawkes, though we did it first.'

'Hell mend you if you didna go tae church in they days, eh?' observed Scott.

'The worst of it was he was a local man. He made sure that men he'd grown up with were butchered by the king's soldiers. The killing only stopped when the commanding officer himself could take no more. Still the Red Preacher called for more death, as the blood lapped at his very ankles, so they say. He and his family bear the shame to this day.'

'What was his name, Jock?'

'The Red Preacher? Thomas Shannon.'

More shone his torch around the vestry. A long sideboard holding the parish silver, only used for special occasions like christenings and communion, stood beside a tall wardrobe where his vestments were stored, the old devotional threads covered by modern suit carriers. The contrast had always amused him. In the far corner of the room he shone the beam of his torch on a deep Belfast sink into which a tap was dripping, the sound echoing from the vestry and amplified in the body of the empty kirk.

He turned the tap off and, taking one last look around the room, noticed that the door to the wardrobe was slightly ajar. He felt a strange sensation in his chest as he stared at it, something between fear and excitement.

Scott admired how the people of Blaan had not been discouraged from celebrating New Year in their usual way, despite the deep snow and the horrors being perpetrated in their small community. Part of the field had been cleared to make way for an enormous pile of wood, on top of which he could make out a still figure, no doubt the effigy of the Red Preacher, Thomas Shannon.

He wondered how Bruce Shannon felt about this, but the middle-aged businessman was all smiles, flirting with two young woman swaddled in thick coats, scarves and gloves. Scott kept an eye on him as Jessie, now assisted by her cousin Annie and a group of thickset farmers, placed fireworks in buckets of sand.

Scott reckoned there were about three hundred people in the crowded field; it was clear that a good proportion of the village's population had turned out, despite the inclement weather.

He walked closer to the pile of wood which would soon be the blazing bonfire. The smell of petrol was strong. The effigy looked realistic, dressed in the black clothes of a man of the cloth and sporting an improvised dog collar. The only thing that spoiled the effect was the bag that served as the dummy's head. It was white and looked as though it had been filled with cloth to bulk it into the shape of a man's skull.

'You could have at least have drawn a face on that poor bloke,' Scott said to Jessie, now at side.

'Never mind that. C'mon, you, and take part in the competition. There's a bottle of whisky as first prize. I jeest hope Mecky Deans doesna win again. Five years in a row, noo.'

'What's the competition?'

'Flingin' the bale, of course. I'm hopin' the cauld this year will rob him o' his grip. That's him o'er there.'

Scott looked across the field, bright with the light of various lamps and torches held by the crowd. He was just about the biggest man Scott had ever seen; tall and broad with it. The bail in question was of straw, about a foot square, bound together with thick twine and tied to a sturdy rope. As the man held it in his big hands it looked small and light, but Scott knew that it was just an illusion caused by the man's sheer size.

'Never let it be said that a Scott wisna up for a challenge.'

'That's the spirit,' said Jessie, as Annie looked on doubtfully. 'They've been tossing the bale here for years. Some say it represents a severed head, like the yins they used tae fling fae the walls o' the castle – prisoner's heids.' She smiled with what Scott thought was slightly too much relish. 'Aye, but Mecky Deans is a champion tosser – his faither was the same. Great family o' tossers, all the gither.'

'I know a few families like that, myself,' said Scott.

'I must say, I wasn't expecting you to call and wish me a Happy New Year, DCI Daley. But the very best to you and yours.' Local solicitor and coxswain of the Kinloch lifeboat

John Campbell's voice was slurred. 'We're all in the dark here. Any idea how long this power cut will last?'

'None, I'm afraid to say,' replied Daley. He'd agonised about making the call, but reckoned that, despite the festivities, he needed to find out more about what had happened in the lead-up to the building of Kersivay House. 'I need to pick your brains, John.'

'Wish I hadn't stowed as much Ardbeg on board, but I'll do my best.'

'I think your firm dealt with the land sale prior to the construction of Kersivay House, am I right?'

'My goodness, a blast from the past, indeed. Yes, it was our firm. Well, the firm as it was then. My grandfather didn't become a partner until the twenties, but he remembered old Dryesdale who was mainly responsible for the case. He told me many a tale about him. Miserable bugger, by all accounts. Came to a tragic end, mark you.'

'How so?'

'Well, his career was rather framed by the whole experience. Of course, he behaved in an exemplary manner as far as the law was concerned. Unfortunately, Nathaniel Stuart didn't think so, held it against him for the rest of his life. Cursed the poor old bugger, as I recall.'

'I'm pleased you know so much about this,' said Daley.

'Oh, yes, one of the great old tales of the firm. We are a small-town solicitors, Mr Daley. Our association with the Shannons has been one of the high points in our history.'

Daley heard whispering, the chink of a bottle on glass and the glug of the pouring spirit.

'Just about everything has been passed down. Apart from their business, I'm sad to say.'

'So you no longer do work for the family?'

'No, unfortunately not. The Shannons have always been difficult to deal with. After the death of old Torquil, Archibald Shannon withdrew his favour. He was a rum old cove by all accounts.'

'Meaning?'

'Oh, the list is endless. Suffice it to say he didn't found the empire on goodness of heart or charity. I must admit, I have sympathy with Nathaniel Stuart. I don't think the firm behaved very well throughout the Kersivay House debacle, if you want me to be absolutely frank.'

'So you think there was some kind of injustice?'

'Well, not strictly speaking, not as far as the written account would have you believe.'

'And the unwritten account?'

'Well, I suppose I can give an opinion as it's almost eighty years since we worked for the family. It was pretty clear that Archibald Shannon entered into a verbal contract with Stuart, ensuring that he would have at least a hundred years tenancy of the ground upon which Kersivay House now stands. Stuart sold the property in good faith. Money was tight and with two blacksmiths in Blaan and the motor car on the way, things weren't set to improve. Who wanted to make the climb up to Stuart's business when Shannon's blacksmith shop was at the heart of the village? I daresay old Nathaniel thought that cutting the deal with a man he had known all his life would ensure the land stayed in his family, as it had done for centuries. He was wrong.'

'Sharp practice, then?'

'Off the record?'

'Of course.'

'Absolutely it was. Please don't quote me, Mr Daley. The existing Shannons are every bit as vindictive as their illustrious forebear, trust me. I certainly wouldn't want to fall foul of them.' Campbell hiccoughed at the end of the sentence.

'So it's fair to say that the Stuarts were justifiably pissed off.'

'Putting it mildly. So much so, in fact, that Nathaniel's descendants were questioned by your colleagues when young Archie Shannon went missing fifty years ago.'

'Do you know anything about them?'

'Old Nathaniel left this area sometime in the thirties, I believe. He'd worked on farms, lived in a tied cottage somewhere. He decided to move away, couldn't bear looking up at Kersivay House, so they say. As to what happened to the family thereafter, I'm not sure. I could try and find out.'

'Yes, if you could. Thank you, John, this is most informative. What happened to Mr Dryesdale? You said he had a tragic end.'

'Oh, indeed. He was found dead. His throat was cut.'

'In Kinloch?'

'No. Not far from where you are now, in fact. Nobody was ever brought to book, of course. His body was found at the Rat Stone in Blaan.'

22

Reverend More closed the door of the vestry and pulled the handle to make sure the lock had clicked into place. He shivered as he shone his torch around the empty church. Then something he hadn't noticed before caught his eye.

Underneath the pulpit, on the altar, sat the large silver goblet usually reserved for communion. He definitely hadn't seen it before entering the vestry. A shiver shot down the length of his spine.

Edging towards the table, he almost jumped out of his skin as the phone in his pocket bleeped.

'You almost gave me a heart attack,' he said as he answered the call. 'I still don't know where she is. I'm worried. You'll have to give me more time. I have to find her . . .' Before he could finish the sentence, movement from above distracted him. Quickly, he directed the torch beam at the source of the sound. There, above him in the pulpit, a figure dressed in white, face covered in a shroud, stood, arms outstretched, head raised to the heavens.

The Old Kirk at Blaan resounded to the echoing screams of Ignatius More, minister of the church.

Scott swung the bale backwards and forwards on the rope, like a pendulum, trying to gain momentum.

'We've no' got all night!' shouted someone from the crowd, just as Scott let go. He watched it arc through the moonlit sky, well under the bar he had to get over to qualify for the next round.

'Bugger,' he swore to himself, rubbing his freezing hands together.

'Aye, good try, Brian,' shouted Annie. 'You've got another two shots, mind, so don't gie up!'

'Would this not be better done in the summer? I can't feel my bloody hands.'

Next came the huge farmer, Mecky Deans. He grabbed the rope and swung it much more energetically than Scott had managed. Despite the cold, he'd taken off his coat and thick jumper; the detective could see the muscles bulging under his T-shirt.

'I hope there's no low-flying aircraft aboot,' said Scott. 'This big bugger's bound tae wallop one, by the looks of it.'

Eventually, Deans let go and the bale soared high over the bar, clearing it with plenty room to spare. 'What happens now?' Scott asked Jessie.

'We'll, noo we raise the bar. You've got two lives left, so it wid be good if you could get it over this time. It'll get higher yet, if I know Mecky Deans.'

'Likely. What's the prize, by the way?'

'Oh, a bottle o' malt whisky and the honour o' lighting the bonfire.'

'A great honour, indeed,' said Jock, handing Scott a hip flask. 'You'll go down in the annals of the village.' He smiled wryly.

'And forbye,' said Jessie. 'Only one polisman has ever had the honour and that was back in fifty-six. Maurice McGinn, now he was a real good tosser. The Deans were fair scunnered.'

'Plenty o' big tossers tae choose from now in the polis. But me representing the force? Now there's a first. Don't go telling the bosses, I'm quite sure they'd have put somebody else up as the poster boy – just about anybody bar me, I shouldna wonder,' he said, stamping his feet in the snow, getting ready for his next turn.

'If anybody can gie it a good tossing, you're the man,' shouted Annie.

'Heartfelt, cousin. Heartfelt,' said Jessie with a smile.

Daley stood on the terrace of Kersivay House. The view below was stark but magnificent. To his left he could see the village; the field behind the Black Wherry was dotted with lights from torches and lanterns. Distant shouting and laughter echoed up through the night air.

The great French windows behind him swung open and the chatter and music from the ballroom inside drowned out the noises of the revellers in the village below.

'I thought you would manage one, just to bring in the New Year, sir,' said DC Dunn as she handed Daley a crystal glass containing a small measure of whisky. 'What a brilliant view. I'm always amazed that Ireland is so close.'

As Daley looked ahead, the great loom of the Emerald Isle across the short stretch of the North Channel seemed almost close enough to touch. A shaft of moonlight shone along the still water like a silver pathway.

'Yes, the place looks magic, with the snow and everything.' He took the glass from her and smiled. 'Happy New Year, Mary,' he said, as they chinked their glasses together.

Mary was wearing a thick coat and a bobble hat, the fringe of her auburn hair sticking out below it. She smiled. 'Happy New Year, sir – Jim.' They looked at each other for a moment, then embraced. Daley gently lifted her chin with one hand and found her lips with his. He could feel her shiver as they kissed.

Before he knew it, he said, 'I love you, Mary,' holding her close on the terrace high above Blaan.

Far below, on the dark side of the mansion, a policeman gasped for breath as he wrestled with a man who had sprung out of the shadows. In a heartbeat, his body went limp. In the darkness, the attacker bent over the police officer, calmly removed the radio from his lapel and pulled him into the darkness.

More pulled at the large door at the back of the kirk. 'Help me,' he shouted, realising that it was locked. He let his torch fall to the floor as he tugged frantically at the handle with both hands.

He heard the soft padding of feet behind him and turned to face it. The figure walking slowly towards him was cloaked in shadows.

'Please, who are you? What is happening? Take what you want, just leave me alone.' He fell to the floor, his back against the door.

The dark figure continued its slow progress up the narrow aisle.

Ailsa Shannon stamped the snow from her boots and rubbed her hands together as Percy closed the back door of Kersivay House. She thanked the large minder who had accompanied her and turned to the old family retainer, who was mumbling under his breath about the clods of snow now lying in the dark passageway.

'This stuff doesn't clean itself, you know,' he said, helping her off with her jacket. 'Why on earth you wanted to go out on a night like this, I'll never know. And if you wanted company you should have taken me, not that great lump.'

'As you know, Percy, we have to be mindful of security. There's still no sign of poor Lars Bergner. It's awful. And I just had to get out for a while. You know how I feel, well, when the bells ring out.' She grabbed his hand and embraced him. 'Happy New Year, Percy.' They looked at each other levelly for a few heartbeats.

'Not sure how many more I'll muster – or you, come to that.'

'Charming.'

'At our age the lights can go out at any time, you know. Aye, and for no reason, either. Just going about your drudgery one minute, then gone the next.'

'Sounds as though it will be a blessed relief for you, Percy. Why worry?'

'I'm telling you, none of us know what's in front of us. Not even you, Ailsa *Shannon*.' He placed an emphasis on her surname that made her smile. 'Look at this, bloody mud as well as snow. More work for me.'

'Why don't you join us in the ballroom, Percy? I'm sure the party is well underway.'

He turned to face her, a look of disgust on his face. 'I don't understand you. All this mayhem and you still find time to have a party. Well, it's not my style, I tell you.'

'What do you suggest? That we all sit in our rooms and lament the night away?'

'Och, I'm not interested in that foreigner, Bergner. As aloof and condescending as that idiot nephew of yours.' He grabbed her hand and looked into her eyes. 'What about wee Archie? Does nothing touch you any more?'

She sighed sadly and squeezed his hand. 'Those bones are most likely a horrid game somebody is trying to play to put us off our stride. Half the world knows about that ridiculous curse. What better way to get back at our family?'

'I'm not a bloody Shannon,' said Percy, suddenly raising his voice.

'But you're part of this family. Been here longer than all of us.'

'Not quite,' he said, staring at her.

'Listen, Percy,' she said, grasping his hand in hers. 'Stop worrying about all of this, about Archie, anything that's happened. There's nothing for you to be upset about. Please trust me.'

'And what about the Rat Stone,' he replied, a dark shadow crossing his face.

As Ignatius More lay huddled at the door of the Old Kirk, his head buried in his hands, eyes closed tight against the horror, he was suddenly aware that all was silent. The slow pacing of the footsteps coming towards him had stopped. He felt his chest rise and fall with his heavy breath, felt the constriction in his throat, his heart beating in his ears. Every fibre of his body was tingling, on edge, waiting for the cold slice of steel or the hammer blow that would take away his life. He whispered a silent prayer too himself over and over again.

Than he heard it; quietly at first, then gaining intensity as it echoed around the Kirk. Someone was sobbing.

He tried to steady his own nerves. The wailing seemed to come from everywhere, all around him, a piercing lament. Then came a tiny voice: 'Help me, please, help me. Please make them go away!'

He recognised it instantly. Slowly uncoiling from the huddle he had made of himself at the old oak door, he looked through the shadows of the church. A shaft of moonlight illuminated the woman lying prone in the middle of the aisle.

'Iggy, please, help me.' Through the sobs, Veronica's voice was unmistakable.

Bruce watched as the detective failed in his second attempt to heave the bale over the bar. He was feeling mellow now, glad to be away from his family, glad to be having a drink, glad that he wasn't standing in the ballroom at Kersivay House, desperately trying to make polite conversation and console Lars Bergner's wife. Even though he hated the man, he felt sympathy for her and their children. To him, it just confirmed what he'd always thought about the old house: it was cursed, the last place in the world he wanted to be.

He took the phone from his pocket and dialled Trenton Casely. Again, the call went straight to voicemail and instead of leaving yet another message he clicked the call off. He looked at his watch; things should be happening by now. Through a haze of alcohol he fretted as to why he couldn't get in contact with the young American. Though he'd done his bit and, as arranged, had made sure he wasn't at Kersivay House.

He tried to picture his cousin's face when what was about to happen became clear. That self-satisfied, arrogant shit deserved all that was in store. Bruce revelled in the thought of him removing his belongings in boxes from the Shannon International office in the Shard, the way redundant bankers had been forced to do when the global financial crisis hit. He took another swig of his hip flask in silent celebration.

Despite himself, he also imagined his mother's reaction. She'd be surprised that he'd pulled off such a coup, but would she be proud? He wasn't the boy who disappeared on the beach half a century before. He could never be.

He smiled at a blonde-haired woman standing nearby. He'd been at a party at her house on Hogmanay a few years before. As her husband slept off his festive over-indulgence, he'd had her on the kitchen floor of the two-up, two-down council house. He'd been surprised how loud she'd been; when he asked if she thought her spouse might be awoken by her moans of pleasure, she had just smiled and showed him a small bottle of sleeping pills. She'd crushed three into his beer.

Time for a repeat performance, he thought. If one thing turned him on, it was the thought of a woman who would go to any lengths in order to cheat on her other half. He was about to walk over and talk to her when a lonely figure standing beside the pile of timber caught his eye. The young woman was stock-still, staring up at the unlit pyre in the moonlight; very much on the periphery of the crowd, rather than part of it. As everyone laughed and joked, as the bale flew through the freezing air, she looked very alone – but then again, she always did.

He felt a deep pang of guilt and, instead of walking over to chat up the blonde woman, pushed his way through the villagers to be with his daughter.

'Nadia, where's Mrs Watkins?' She didn't reply. 'Nadia, did you hear me?'

He hugged her close and followed her eye line to the top of the unlit bonfire where the Blaan guy sat, its white head slumped forwards.

'Why didn't they give him a face?' she said, still gazing up at the effigy of her ancestor.

'Oh, come on, darling. No point staring up at that bloody thing, it's just a bundle of old rags and straw. Let's join the party. We'll find out where the hell Mrs Watkins has got to.' Bruce looked around the snowy field to try and locate his daughter's nurse.

'He has no face, but he has a smile.'

'What?' he replied distractedly. 'Enough of this, come on.' He pulled at her sleeve, glancing up to give the bag of rags one last look.

He wasn't sure why he hadn't noticed it before; a thin red smile seemed to be slathered across the effigy's white face. He gaped as he watched this flat smile slowly turn into a broad grin.

23

Percy searched the large cupboard in the laundry room at Kersivay House. He knew he had spare salt and grit to spread on the paths around the building, but for the life of him couldn't remember where he'd put it. He cursed his age and forgetfulness.

'Bloody losing it,' he muttered to himself as he closed the cupboard door. The old outhouse was the only other option he could think of. It, as well as the cottage he and his wife had shared for all these years, was one of the few original buildings that had stood on the land before the big mansion had been built. He'd often wondered what the place would have looked like. He'd heard stories of Nathaniel Stuart, heard about the man's power, his ferocious temper and the depth of hatred that he bore for the Shannon family after being conned out of the land that had been in his family since the dark days, when only stories told stood as a reminder of deeds done.

Percy looked along the row of keys, mostly of the modern variety, until he came to the big black mortise key, tarnished with age but so familiar. He'd been using that key for most of his life and every time he remembered the blacksmith who had used the old outhouse to store the tools of his trade.

Though the key had lost its lustre, there was still a patch of shiny brass on the fob, worn to a gleam by time spent on the belt of Nathaniel Stuart – or so Percy imagined.

He opened the large back door and stepped carefully out into the snow. The beam from his old torch was weak, casting a golden beam along the glistening white pathway. He cursed himself again for not remembering to replace the batteries.

The old buildings sat at angles to each other, though the courtyard they once lined was long gone. He could see candles flickering in his cottage, which was not supplied with the emergency power enjoyed by the office block and certain parts of the house. His wife was still up, probably peering at a book in the dim light. 'Bloody books,' he murmured, as he shivered in the cold.

He rounded the large holly bush, its red berries poking through the snow like tiny rubies. On his left was the outhouse, to his right the former stable, which was now an office block used by Maxwell and the rest of the board when in residence. He was surprised to see bright electric light spilling from behind the blinds, an extreme contrast to the gloom he had to endure in his own home. 'Wasteful bastards,' he grumbled. 'If we run out of diesel for the generator, the whole bloody place will be in darkness.'

He crunched through the frozen snow and stood on his tiptoes to look through a chink in the blinds. Having expected the large office to be empty, he jumped back when a dark figure passed between him and the glowing computer screens inside.

He collected himself, stomping to the door and banging hard with his fist. 'Mr Shannon, just what is going on? They'll be running out of diesel in Kinloch, you know. And bugger knows when they'll get another delivery if it snows again. Mr Shannon!'

As he heard footsteps on the other side of the door, he reversed. A blow to his back sent him tumbling to the ground.

Brian Scott was just about to have another go at tossing the bale over the bar when he heard the scream. He looked across the field, white snow and shadows in the light of lanterns and torches. Bruce was trying to pull his daughter away from the unlit bonfire, shouting for help as he did so.

People running, more screams. Scott was breathing heavily. He heard the distant whine in his ears and shook his head to try and rid himself of the sound that he had first heard in the dark room at Kersivay House and then on the road from Kinloch to Blaan.

'No, fuck me, not now,' he whispered to himself, beginning to feel strange, hot and disoriented, everything around him slipping away.

The scene before him changed; the screams were louder, more visceral. There was no snow and a grey light shone on a sickening scene. Ahead of him steel flashed, slicing through frail skin and thudding into hard bone with a roaring agony. Red blood, muck and gore was spattered across his shoes. He tried to banish the whine as it rose to a scream, tightening his chest.

Another blade swung before him, connecting with a man's shoulder. He was kneeling on the ground, his long hair matted across his face. Scott saw blood pump from the wound as the stricken man struggled to regain his feet.

A tall figure emerged, hooded by a dark cloak. He stood with his head bowed, hands clasped, then kicked the injured man in the back, sending him crashing face down onto the gory soil. The hooded figure walked calmly towards the victim and slammed his foot onto the dying man's back, forcing him into the sodden ground.

Scott was rooted to the spot as he watched the man struggle to get his head out of the bloody mire in a desperate attempt for breath. Red bubbled for a heartbeat as he managed to wrench his head up to look at the light one last time.

The man held out his hand, begging Scott to help, pleading through the blood-slathered hair that plastered his face. Scott felt as though his head was going to burst with the screeching in his ears, his chest seemingly constricted by metal bands.

He watched the man's lips move, but couldn't hear what he was trying to say.

He felt, but did not hear, himself scream as the hooded figure reached behind his back and with both hands swung a long sword up high.

It was then that he recognised the man being butchered to death in this hellish field. Only for a second did he think of Jim Daley, then his vision began to clear and he was back, lying in the snow.

Two men in police uniforms dragged Percy's body into the bright office. One of them tied the old man's hands and feet and left him propped up in the corner of the room.

'Who the fuck is that?' asked a thickset man.

'He's the old caretaker,' shrugged one of the others, his face a spray of acne. 'Light as a feather. Skin and bone, the poor bastard. Do you want me to slot him, Paddy?'

‘Leave him where he is just now. I want Maxwell in here as soon as you can get him. And stop using my fucking name! We have the upper hand here, but these bastards don’t mess about. When we’ve finished, they’ll be looking for us. So keep your pig hats on when you go into the house.’

Percy started to moan in the corner and was soon silenced by another blow. ‘We’ll have to do something more permanent with this old geezer.’

‘Give him a jab,’ replied Paddy. ‘And hope to fuck he doesn’t die.’ He reached into a stainless steel briefcase and removed a syringe. ‘This’ll keep the old bugger quiet. Hope he’s got a strong heart.’

‘Will we go and get Shannon now?’

‘Yeah, tell him there’s been a development. Meet our man, he’ll pass this on so that bloody inspector doesn’t get wind. I’ll send him a message.’

The two men made sure that the peaks of their police hats were down low over their faces as they left the bright office and stepped back into the yard, Kersivay House looming above them.

‘Brian, Brian! Are you OK?’ shouted Annie as she tried to rouse the detective, who was slumped face down in the snow.

He jolted back into consciousness, gasping for breath. ‘Jim, Jim – what the hell?’

‘Eh? What do you mean Jim? He’s back up at the house, is he no’? Maybe you’ve had wan too many, Brian,’ she said, helping him to his feet. ‘You’ve been knocking them back since afore the bells.’

‘Quickly, please. I think somebody needs to take a look at the minister on the bonfire,’ shouted Bruce, his sobbing daughter at his side.

'What on earth do you mean?' asked Jessie. 'He's just a pile o' auld rags stuffed intae John McEachran's boiler suit.'

'If that's the case, his face is bleeding,' replied Bruce.

'Come on, Brian,' said Annie. 'You need tae get yourself the gither and take a look at this.'

Scott stood, still stunned and breathing heavily as Annie did her best to brush the loose snow from his clothes. He was shaking from head to toe, desperately trying to compose himself. Bruce walked towards him, his daughter now being comforted by her nurse.

'You'd better get over there, sergeant.'

'Why, dae you reckon it's a stolen boiler suit?' replied Scott, doing his best to sound normal though he felt anything but.

'No, but I don't reckon it's filled with old rags, either.'

Scott was trembling. That latest episode was the worst yet. It all felt so real, like being flung headlong into another world while being slowly choked and deafened by that awful whine.

The stench of petrol was strong as he stared up at the effigy on top of the bonfire. With most of the villagers gathered round with their torches and lanterns, it was much easier to see that the white bag that served as a head was now stained a dark crimson colour.

'Right, I'll need tae get up there and have a look,' said Scott, his voice throaty and unsteady. 'Can someone come up and gie me a hand?'

'I'll help you,' said Mecky Deans.

'Right, fine man. Come on.'

The pair slowly scaled the mound of old wood and general rubbish that the bonfire was constructed of. Scott's foot slipped through a rotten plank to a gasp from the crowd, but

Deans, coughing at the stench of petrol, soon pulled him free, and in no time both men were perched, somewhat precariously, at the top of the pyre.

As soon as Scott touched the sleeve of the old boiler suit, he knew it wasn't filled with old rags. He took a deep breath and gently pulled up the white bag, now almost entirely stained a deep red.

He recoiled in horror as a frantic murmur, then screams, spread through the crowd. Scott stared at the face before him, almost unrecognisable as a human, thick blood oozing from a dark wound that appeared to have been hastily stitched up with rough twine.

A strand of pale hair not soaked in gore caught the light. Then Scott heard a deep thud, a puff of sound. There was a crackle, then a roar and suddenly the bonfire burst into life, blue flames devouring the petrol-soaked pyre.

24

Daley and Mary were in a small room, hidden down a long corridor that led away from the large ballroom in Kersivay House. She had taken him by the hand and led him through the first door she had found unlocked.

They kissed passionately, then she slid her body down his and onto her knees. His fingertips grazed her hair as she worked slowly backwards and forwards, his legs trembling as he leaned against the wall of the dark room. He looked down as a narrow beam of moonlight illuminated her auburn hair and desperately resisted the urge to pull her closer.

'No, stop,' he moaned, pulling her to her feet, stroking her face.

'I don't want to,' she whispered throatily as she undid the button of her jeans with one hand, caressing him with the other.

Instinctively, desperately, he lifted her up by the thighs and turned so that her back was against the wall. She curled her arms around his neck and wrapped her legs around his back as he gently eased himself into her. Slowly at first, then frantically, they made love.

He could feel her heart beating in her chest as their passion climaxed then subsided; they held onto each other, breathing in time, the smell of her hair and her perfume filling his senses.

'I so, so love you, Jim Daley,' she whispered, nuzzling into his neck.

His phone rang, buzzing loudly against the floor where his trousers lay. He let her down gently, then pulled them up, searching in the pocket for the mobile.

'Where are you, DCI Daley?' He recognised Superintendent Symington's voice instantly; he also noted the urgency in her tone. 'We have to get down to the hotel. There's a car at the front door. It's DS Scott – he's in trouble.'

Maxwell stared from one man to the other, then back to the large computer screens in front of him.

'If you think I'm going to be blackmailed in this way, you can fuck off,' he said, his voice slightly slurred from the whisky he'd drunk. 'Nothing in the world will make me do this.'

The large man in the dark uniform of a police officer got to his feet. 'You're not understanding the situation, Mr Shannon. I'm here to help you,' he said, his Irish accent strong.

'You sound like a fucking double-glazing salesman. I'll say it again – fuck off!'

The big Irishman stepped forwards towards Maxwell, who was squirming uncomfortably on a swivel chair. 'You've spent your life thinking the world should do what you want it to, haven't you, Maxie, boy.' He lunged forwards, grabbing Maxwell's chin in his large hand and angling his head up so their faces were only inches apart. 'You can't be happy seeing your wee *subsidiaries* doing so badly, can you?'

'How do you . . . What are you talking about?' replied Shannon, cursing his mistake.

'I would have expected better from a man like yourself, Maxie, I really would. The question is, why is it happening?'

'Because you're trying to paint me into a fucking corner so that I give you control of my company. Well, it won't work. We have assets to burn; I already have a team of people working this problem. When they discover who's behind it, you'll find out what it means to be bullied.' He tried to stand, but was pushed back into his seat by the big man.

'That's where you're very wrong, Mr Shannon. Of course, my friends would love you to give us control of your organisation. Who wouldn't want their hand on the tiller of the biggest private company in the world and everything that comes from that, eh? Aye, we had a nice plan – still have it, in fact – a plan to make you desperate to help us. But things have changed.'

'In what way?'

'We're here to help you with the collapse of your *associates,* let's call them. In fact, we want to be your new partners. So, would you not say that it's time me and you tried to work together? Because I tell you, if you don't do something quickly, there'll be no such company as Shannon International by this time next week and you and your friends on the board will be behind bars for the biggest fraud in corporate history. How does that sit with you, Mr Shannon?'

Maxwell's face lost all colour as he sat back in the chair. He looked at the Irishman, his companions, then the huddle on the floor that was the family caretaker, Percy. 'Is he dead?'

'No, he's not dead, just having a nap, so he is.'

'Pity, he's an irascible old bastard. He used to boot me in the arse when I was a boy. Do us all a favour and make him disappear, then we'll talk.'

The big man smiled at his captive. 'You're a real charmer, eh? Kill an old man because he kicked you in the backside when you were a sprog – a boot you no doubt deserved. Well, this is one wish that won't come true for you, Maxwell. That old man seems to have friends in very unexpected places.' Without warning, he swung his fist and caught Maxwell squarely on the jaw. 'That's for having no respect for your elders. And in any event, you've no idea how long I've wanted to do that to you. Now, you get cleaned up and get back to your party. And remember, one word to the boys in blue and you'll be taking in the next New Year – and many, many thereafter – behind bars, my friend.'

'And what will I say to the rest of the board, to my senior execs? I take it you have Lars Bergner?'

'Oh, I'm sure you'll think of something to say to those good old boys. That's your strong suit – talking, cajoling, making folk do things they don't really want to. And no, we have as little idea where Mr Bergner is as you do, nor are we responsible for everything else that's happened in this village over the last wee while. It would appear that you've got enemies coming out of the woodwork. Trust no one, Maxie, do you get me?'

'So I just do what you tell me to? I'm at a disadvantage here, but believe me, I'll make sure you, and whoever is behind this, pays.'

'You believe just what you want, Maxie. But I'll tell you this: with the help of my friends, you can be one of the richest men in the world in your own right. No waiting for your old father to peg out or your hatchet-faced auntie tae give you the thumbs up before you can make a move. We're going to move you along a bit more smartly. I think it looks as though we're the only friends you have.'

As the police car drove into the village, Daley could see flames leaping from the large bonfire in the field behind the hotel. People milled about, some being comforted by their fellow villagers.

His chest was tight; that familiar feeling, like an old friend, or perhaps his worst enemy, always there when those close to him were in peril.

The car skidded to a halt in the car park of the Black Wherry Inn. He jumped from the vehicle and raced towards the dancing flames of the bonfire, forcing his way through the crowd of people, many of them looking tearful and stunned.

His heart lurched in his chest as he walked towards the smouldering remains of a man lying on the ground, covered by a singed overcoat. The weight at his core was impossible to resist as he sank to his knees on the hard snow.

'I'm so sorry,' said Jessie, putting her hand on his shoulder. 'We called you as soon as we could. Tried tae get the fire oot but we couldna get enough water ontae it. Turned oot there was a big hole in oor hose.'

'What . . . I mean, how did this happen? Couldn't some-one have tried to pull him down? Tried anything?'

'We'd put too much petrol ontae the wood. Wherever that stray spark came fae, a kid's sparkler or whootever, the whole thing jeest went up – boom!' She raised her hands to emphasise the event. 'If it's any comfort, we know he didna suffer, the poor bugger.'

'How on earth do you know that?' asked Daley, looking blankly at the smouldering remains under the old coat.

'By all accounts he was in some state before the fire caught. He wiz well out of it before he started tae burn, probably deid. A blessing, poor man.'

Daley looked again at the corpse, a mound under a heap of singed rags. Again, the cruel nature of fate clawed at him. The stench of burning flesh was strong. He wrinkled his nose. 'How did he manage to get into such a state? I only saw him a few hours ago.'

'Oh, I didna know that,' said Jessie, looking surprised. 'Well, he was sitting at the top o' the bonfire wae John McEachran's auld boiler suit on and his heid in a hessian bag the last time I saw him.'

'He was what?' Daley stared at the woman in disbelief. 'Why wasn't I told about this? I was up at Kersivay House when all this was going on!' Daley turned to the woman, his eyes flashing with anger. 'This isn't just anyone; though for anyone to have died like this would have been a tragedy. What the fuck is wrong with you all?'

Daley was breathing heavily, the world spinning before him. Superintendent Symington reached out to place her hand on his shoulder. Behind them, people moved aside to let a man with a blackened face, shoulders covered by an old blanket, through to where the corpse lay.

'Aye, no' a pretty sight, right enough,' he said, before starting to cough.

Daley turned to face him then jumped to his feet, eyes wide in disbelief. His mouth was moving but no sound came out.

Symington, standing at his side, decided to break the

silence. 'I had a call to say that DS Scott had been set alight on a bonfire and to get here as quickly as possible. My colleague,' she said, nodding at Daley, 'obviously came to the same conclusion as me.'

'Oh, right, said Jessie. 'Och, it was one o' the boys in the hotel that called you. Chinese whispers in this bloody place. But, right enough, he was up on the bonfire when it went up, but big Mecky Deans pulled him doon. The pair o' them jumped clean through the flames. We couldna get this poor soul doon, mind you. Had tae wait until Erchie got here wae his earth mover an' we kinda scooped him aff the top an' doused him wae water.'

'You thought it was me under that coat,' said Scott. 'Nae wonder you look like you seen a ghost!' Despite the obvious tragedy, Scott stifled a laugh.

'Since this clearly isn't the last mortal remains of DS Scott, just who is it?' asked Symington.

'I think I know the answer to that, Superintendent,' replied a well-spoken man. 'He was pretty mangled when I saw him before the fire, looked as though he'd been hit by a train, but I'd swear that the man lying there is Lars Bergner,' said Bruce.

25

More looked down at his wife as she slept on the couch by the roaring fire. He stroked his chin and sighed, reaching once more for the phone in front of him. He had covered her with a blanket and now stared, deep in thought, as her long dark lashes flitted in the light of the flames.

The whisky he was drinking was straight, the undiluted spirit stinging his throat as he gulped another mouthful. Why did I agree to this, he thought, as he passed his hand through his greying hair, tugging at it in desperation. 'You fucking fool,' he whispered under his breath.

He answered the phone almost as it rang, anxious not to wake her, but even more concerned to speak to the caller.

'Are you alone?' the man on the other end asked in a low voice.

'Yes. Well, my wife is here but she's asleep.'

'Listen very carefully. The situation has changed. You will have to do what we talked about.'

'But how? The place is crawling with police now – the whole village is.'

'The cops are stretched. They can't get more manpower to the area because of the weather. We've taken a few extra steps to keep them off our back and it's about to snow again.'

'Shit, mate. So me and the guys are stuck here with no way out?'

'Come now, that's not the kind of stuff I expect from a man of the cloth. There's always a way out, trust me.'

'Yeah, sure, but maybe not the way I want to go.'

'Relax, Reverend More. Take another few glasses of whisky, but be ready for a call tomorrow. We can do this, but you've got to play your part.' The call ended.

'Shit,' snapped More, making his wife stir again in her sleep. He put down the phone, picked up his glass and walked over to her. 'I'm doing this for us, honey,' he said quietly, stroking her hair. The whisky burned his throat as he drained the glass.

Scott was in the passenger seat of a police Land Rover, Pollock at the wheel. Daley had demanded he go for a check up at the hospital in Kinloch after his brush with incineration. He was deep in thought as he stared through the window, watching large flakes of snow settling on the glass only to be brushed away by the windscreen wipers.

The brief euphoria of being rescued from the flames of the Blaan bonfire had receded rapidly when the old coat had been removed from the charred body that Daley had thought was him. It had been surreal watching his friend begin the process of mourning his death – humorous, even. But then, as the adrenalin and whisky in his system had started to fade, the cold reality dawned that one day the man burned to a cinder or shot dead on the beach would indeed be him.

'Penny for them,' said Pollock.

'Och, ever get the feeling that it was time you moved on? How long have you been in this job – about the same as me, likely?'

'Aye, I would say so. Not long till we both get tae retire, though.'

'If we make it, that is,' replied Scott with a shake of his head.

'I'm surprised. Everybody tells me that you're the joker in the pack. You're no' sounding too funny the night, Brian.'

Scott gazed out into the darkness. 'Some days it just doesn't seem right tae be laughing.'

They drove past tall banks of snow forced to the side of the road by the snowploughs. The Land Rover skidded slightly on the slick road. Snow, then ice, then more snow – it was a lethal combination. Pollock managed to keep the vehicle on the road, slowing down even further.

'Bugger, we'd be able tae walk quicker. The bloody road's in some state. If this is going tae be another heavy fall, I can't see them being able to keep it open,' said Pollock.

'Don't say that. If we cannae get to and from Blaan by road, the bastards will have me aboard a boat before you know it.' He sighed deeply and fished in his pocket. 'Mind if I have a fag? I hope you're no' one of these delicate flowers like the lads that brought me here earlier. You'd have thought I'd asked if I could piss o'er his heid when I went tae light up.'

'As long as you gie me one as well, we'll be fine.'

'Good man,' said Scott. Once the cigarettes were lit and sweet, blue tobacco smoke filled the cab. 'How long have you been on the rural patrol doon here, Willie?'

'Just a month off fifteen years. Tae be honest, I wouldnae be anywhere else. When I'm out here in the Land Rover, I'm away fae any trouble with the boys in braid, if you know what I mean?'

'Aye, you can bet your bottom dollar I know what you mean,' replied Scott. 'What the fuck's going on in Blaan? I've never seen the like.'

'Well, tae put it in perspective, do you know how many arrests I made last year?'

'Tell me.'

'Four,' said Pollock. 'Aye, and that includes the same man twice for being drunk and incapable. They wanted tae gie me a service promotion tae sergeant and stick me in the office at Kinloch. Why would you want that?'

'I hear you, pal, I hear you. How far tae go?'

'Another five miles, we're just aboot halfway there,' replied Pollock, peering into the gloom.

Daley felt Superintendent Symington's gaze on him as he and Dunn took statements at the Black Wherry Inn. He wondered if she guessed what he and his young DC had been up to before the dash to rescue Scott.

As the last villager left, the police officers sat at a table with a large pot of steaming coffee. Jessie and Annie busied themselves cleaning tables, washing down the bar and polishing glasses. At another table sat Jock Munro, savouring the last few mouthfuls of his whisky. It was after four in the morning and Daley's eyelids felt heavy. He sipped the strong coffee and hoped it would get to work quickly.

'There's something here that doesn't make sense,' said Symington, breaking the silence. 'We must consider this to be a sustained campaign against the Shannon family, planned well in advance and being executed by professionals. But they couldn't have known how the weather would behave with this snow. Under normal circumstances, at the first sign of danger the Shannon party would just have shipped out en masse. There's no way anyone could have planned for them being marooned here.'

'Maxwell Shannon has no intentions of leaving, regardless of the circumstances,' said Daley.

'Not even if we discover that charred corpse is Lars Bergner?'

'He says the family won't be intimidated. Adamant that they're staying put until they get this AGM over, at least.'

'Well, DCI Daley, he can be as adamant as he likes. If a weather window opens up long enough to get them out of here, out of here they'll bloody well go,' she exclaimed, her voice raised.

Looking at her steely expression, Daley had no doubt about her determination. Here was somebody who was used to having an opinion and getting her own way, he thought.

'They've been the same down the generations,' boomed Jock Munro, standing and zipping up his jacket. 'Sorry, I couldn't help hearing what you said, madam. The Shannon family are stubborn bastards. Aye, and now they're collectively as rich as Croesus, there's not much can be done to gainsay them.'

'Well, we'll see. We don't have to be billionaires to change the course of events.'

'In any case,' said Jock. 'I don't think you're about to get your weather window.'

'Not good,' said Daley. 'I think we're stuck with the Shannons for the duration, ma'am.'

'I meant to say this to your Sergeant Scott,' said Jock, leaning his large hand on the back of DC Dunn's chair. 'I was up the Breachory Glen early yesterday. Would you believe that there's someone camping up there?'

'What, in this weather?' asked Dunn.

'Aye, my thoughts exactly, my dear,' said Jock. 'They didn't see me but I saw them. A man, well built, purposeful, if you know what I mean?'

'Purposeful?' asked Daley.

'Och, maybe I've spent too long being a writer, observing the way people behave. I daresay you've done a fair bit of that in your time, Mr Daley. Like poor Robert Louis Stevenson when he was a boy, confined to his bed for days on end with asthma. He could tell who was who and what they were up to by the sound of their footsteps: *"the steps fell light and oddly, with a certain swing.'* He was a fine, fine writer. But these steps weren't light at all. This man meant business.'

'And who would have business in a tent in Blaan in the middle of a snowstorm?' said Daley.

They were about two miles outside Kinloch now, their progress slower still. The snow was falling so heavily now that Pollock was forced to turn the windscreen wipers to their highest speed. He leaned forwards as he carefully edged the Land Rover along.

'This road will be closed again within the hour if they don't get the ploughs out soon,' he said to Scott, who was nervously smoking his third cigarette of the journey.

'Are we going to make it, Willie? I don't fancy getting snowed up in this jalopy.'

'Aye, we'll make it. But if we'd left a few minutes later than we did, we'd have had no chance. We're on the home stretch now.'

Scott wound down the passenger window slightly and cursed as a flurry of cold snow hit him in the face while he was trying to dispose of his cigarette butt. As he wound it closed, he suddenly felt his chest tighten.

'You OK?' asked Pollock

'Aye. Aye, fine,' said Scott, feeling anything but. He stared through the windscreen, willing the journey to come to an end. It was low and soft, but the whine in his ears was unmistakable. He tried to grit his teeth against the sound but it grew in intensity as he began to struggle for breath.

It was then he saw the grey figure in the road ahead, standing stock-still in the heavy snow, illuminated by the headlights. Now gasping for breath, he lurched forwards and grabbed the steering wheel, pulling it out of Pollock's grasp. The Land Rover sloughed one way then the other, jolting Scott's chest painfully against his seatbelt. Brakes squealed and Pollock yelled, then – for a few heartbeats – everything was quiet. It was as though they were flying. The whine in his ears was replaced by the beating of his own heart. The world was in slow motion until Pollock screamed again and they came to a stop with a sickening thud and jolt.

26

As Daley, Symington and Dunn walked back through the large front door of Kersivay House, they were greeted by Aitcheson, the inspector in charge of the armed Support Unit officers who were guarding the perimeter of the mansion. His pale face and worried expression were enough to set off the alarm bells in Daley's head.

'What's up, DI Aitcheson?'

'One of my men, Constable Booth, is missing. He missed our last rendezvous and he isn't answering his radio.'

'When did you discover this, inspector?' asked Symington.

'About an hour ago. We checked in with him by radio at two. The reception was poor, but he sounded OK. But now I'm beginning to wonder if that was him at all.'

Daley hurriedly arranged a search of the building and grounds. He called Glasgow in search of assistance, but the weather there was even worse than in Blaan and he was left in no doubt that the officers he had were the only ones he would see until the snow had abated. His superior in Glasgow promised to send the police helicopter as soon as it became available; however, it had been grounded for the last few hours because of the weather and looked likely to remain so.

'I think we all need to draw weapons, DCI Daley,' said Symington. 'I don't want to spread alarm amongst the lads, but up until now, anyone who's gone missing has turned up dead – if the man on the bonfire proves to be Bergner, that is.

'I agree,' replied Daley. 'We're rapidly getting out of our depth here, ma'am. I'll get a hold of Brian, he'll be back in Kinloch and have been checked out in the hospital by now. I'll have him round up as many men as we can spare and bring them here with firearms.'

Daley called the office in Kinloch, only to be told that Scott and Pollock had yet to arrive. He asked the desk sergeant to contact Kinloch hospital and have Scott call him as soon as possible. Don't tell me there's actually something wrong with him, he thought, then worried that his friend might have already sunk into a bottle of whisky.

It was after six, but still there was no sign of morning in the dark sky, laden with snow clouds that were now discharging themselves over Blaan and the rest of the country.

He watched Dunn, who was busy studying footage from Kersivay House's CCTV system. She looked so young and beautiful that he felt stricken with guilt that he was about to ruin her life. In his heart, he now knew his marriage was over – had been over for a long time, if he was honest with himself. But how long could he keep hold of a woman so much younger than himself? How long would it take before the person she saw before her turned into an old man?

'How are you doing with that?' he asked.

'Not that well, sir.' She smiled thinly. 'There are only three cameras: one on the bottom gate, one on the drive and the other covering the front of the house. I haven't come across anything unusual yet.'

‘Keep trying . . .’ He was cut short by his mobile ringing in the pocket of his thick ski jacket. ‘Daley, yes, have you located him?’ He listened for a few moments, a look of concern spreading across his face. ‘I want you to send out somebody in a four-wheel drive to have a look. They left here nearly three hours ago.’ He ended the call and looked up at Dunn.

‘Trouble, sir?’

‘Brian and Pollock haven’t arrived back in Kinloch. Well, if they have, they’re certainly not where they should be.’ Quietly, he cursed the lack of faith he now had in his DS, his friend. Then he remembered Brockie’s eye sockets, the disgusting mutilation of his colleague Colin Grant and the smouldering body lying in the snow.

When Scott came to he was cold – very cold. He couldn’t see anything in the darkness apart from a red warning light on the dashboard of the Land Rover. The vehicle had landed on its side and his head was hard against the passenger window. He could feel the cold of the snow through the glass.

‘Willie! Willie!’ he shouted, reaching up towards the driver’s side of the car for his colleague. The seat was empty.

He struggled to take off his seat belt then, with great difficulty, managed to wrestle his mobile phone from the inside pocket of his jacket. He pressed buttons in the darkness until the screen illuminated. He swore loudly when he noticed that he had no signal and, in any case, his battery was about to fail.

Scott had often heard Jim Daley ruminate upon how his life would end. While Daley was thoughtful – often morose, in fact – Scott tried to avoid the close analysis of life and its inevitable finality. However, after being shot in two separate incidents involving his job, he often imagined the dark, cold hand of fate hovering above his head. He always pictured his father's face, silhouetted by the white linen of the pillow as cancer drained his life away; his mother gasping for breath as that very same disease slowly choked her to death.

He struggled up to the driver's door, now above his head. 'I don't want tae die,' he pleaded, reaching out in the darkness.

The Reverend More sat in his kitchen and prayed. He was almost sure that what he was about to do was the right thing, but he still had nagging doubts. People like the Shannons were a cancer that fed on those who worked and struggled hard just to keep bread on the table and a roof over their heads. What did he owe them?

He reached for the bottle of whisky on the large kitchen table, then thought the better of it. His head was already swimming and he needed to be ready to act quickly if called upon in a few hours. Tired, he rubbed his forehead with his hand as he took deep breaths.

The doctor, from a private practice far from Blaan, had said his wife's 'episodes' should improve as the prescribed medication took hold. More wasn't convinced – if anything, they seemed to be getting worse. Not long after he'd first met the former nun, he'd been astonished to find her in his bed, dressed in only a pair of black stockings and suspenders, her face made up gaudily with bright lip gloss and dark eye shadow. At first this aroused him, but soon he realised that the woman before him bore no resemblance to the person he had met, like someone under the influence of strong drugs, or alcohol. He had talked to her quietly and soon she'd slept.

In the morning, when she was shocked to find herself dressed in such a manner, he knew she had a problem. Her stories of how her fellow nuns had tormented her fell into place; either her behaviour had been so extreme they were forced to let her go or her problems had been magnified at the hands of the order.

Despite his better judgement, he reached again for the bottle and poured a large measure of whisky into the small crystal glass.

Through the crack in the kitchen door, Veronica watched her husband silently.

Daley was in a Land Rover with the old farmer Charlie Murray and a uniformed cop. Symington was coordinating the search for the missing member of the Support Unit, but he had to try and find Scott.

They had travelled no more than a mile when Murray slowed the old vehicle to a stop.

'We have to turn round, Mr Daley, we've nae choice.' The snow piled against the windscreen, making the wipers whine in protest as they struggled to clear it. 'They might be able tae get a snowplough in from Kinloch but there's no way we're getting through this. If we try, aye, we'll be as marooned as your sergeant likely is.'

Daley stared at the huge flakes as they sprang out of the darkness. 'Yes, you're right,' he said, the regret in his voice plain. 'We'd better turn back, Mr Murray. Thank you for trying.'

'The worst fall of snow we've had here since '63. I was a young man then, but it was like living through a white hell. We lost so many sheep – aye and folk, tae. Arthur Lays from

Ballybeg farm went oot tae rescue some tups and we didna find him until it thawed about two weeks later. Aye, a terrible thing, the snow. I could gie these stupid bastards that call it pretty a good kick up the arse,' he said, struggling with the steering wheel as he turned the Land Rover back towards Blaan. 'Still, tae die in the cauld is the kindest death o' all, they say. Och, you jeest sleep away. No' a bad way tae go if you ask me.'

'Honestly, Charlie, you aren't helping.'

'I'd gamble my dear wife on the fact your man will be jeest fine. He's likely sitting in some steading wae a bumper dram, waiting for the boys tae arrive fae Kinloch wae the snowplough.'

'I wish I shared your optimism,' said Daley. 'I really do.'

As Scott struggled to pull himself up he was surprised to find that the driver's door was partially open. 'Willie? Are you there?' He managed to lever himself up from his seat to grab the steering wheel, pushing with his other arm against the heavy door. A flurry of snow hit him at almost the same time as he was dazzled by a bright light shining directly into his face.

'What the fuck!' he shouted, as strong arms lifted him clear of the stricken vehicle and out into the cold.

27

Daley was still fretting about Scott's whereabouts as he joined other officers in search of the missing Constable Booth from the Support Unit. The hunt took them all over Kersivay House, which was even larger and more luxurious than he had first imagined.

As he stared from a window in the rear of the house, a thin, pale line against the horizon marked the dawn of the first day of the new year. To his left, he saw the long modern building that was the new accommodation block, built to contain the overflow of the Shannon International AGM. Across a narrow strip of land, where a rough pathway had been dug through the snow, sat two further buildings, at right angles to each other. One of them had clearly been modernised, while the smaller construction looked old, most probably in its original form. Taken together, they looked out of place with the rest of the house.

Daley heard someone walking towards him and turned to see Nadia Shannon, dressed in a thick jumper and jeans, her blood-red lipstick in contrast with her pale face. He wondered just how the girl was coping with the events of the previous night.

'Hello, Mr Daley,' she said quietly. 'I hear you have a missing police officer.'

'Yes, we're searching for him now. What are those two buildings?'

'Oh, the small cottage is where Percy and his wife live. Next to it is the office and communications building. It used to be a stable, but Maxwell had it converted a few years ago. All very hi-tech, apparently.'

'Thanks,' he said, smiling at the dark-haired girl. 'We'll get down there and tick them off our list.'

'I'm sorry about my family, Chief Inspector. It seems that everywhere we go, misery and tragedy follow. I've not been able to sleep, I rarely can when we're here.'

'You don't like Kersivay House?'

'I hate it. I can't think of anyone who likes being imprisoned here every year, not even Maxwell. Perhaps my grandmother, but that's all.'

'Yes, she mentioned that she liked it here. Maybe it's easier for an older person to enjoy being in a place like this, rather than someone your age.'

'My family would turn the nicest place in the world into somewhere I didn't want to be,' she said. 'Good luck finding your colleague. I had better report back before they send out a search party for me.'

He watched her wend her way back along the long passageway. A young woman with the world on her shoulders, he thought.

He made his way wearily down the stairs. He had to find Inspector Aitcheson and search those outbuildings.

Scott shivered, watching the thin line of dull light spread through the sky over Kinloch. He was standing in the yard of a farmhouse, knee-deep in snow, smoking a cigarette. He heard the back door open and watched as Constable Pollock waded his way towards him, an impromptu bandage wrapped around his head, covering the cut he'd sustained when their Land Rover left the road.

'The landline's down and there's no mobile signal unless we scale that hill o'er there, according to Mr Moyes. I'm afraid I don't have my crampons with me so we'll just have to keep oor eyes on the road and hope that the snowplough is trying to get through.'

'Listen, Willie,' said Scott, shuffling his feet in the snow. 'I'm sorry, I just thought I saw someone in the road. Do you know what I mean?'

Pollock thrust his bottom lip out and sighed. 'Jessie telt me that you had some kind of fit at the bonfire. Aye, and one o' the boys told me he found you lying in the snow fair ranting when the road was blocked.'

'I slipped, man. And as far as the Black Wherry is concerned, I just fell over wae the drink.'

'An auld cop I used tae work with once gave me advice I've never forgotten.'

'Aye?'

'He telt me never tae be afraid tae shout for help, no matter what the situation was.' He looked Scott straight in the eye. 'I've seen good men go doon tae the bevy, Brian. Don't be one of them. There's nothing tae be ashamed of. If you're at the stage where you're seeing stuff, well, you need help, my friend.'

'Listen. Thanks for pulling me oot that Land Rover and getting us here. And as I says, I'm sorry for, well, the accident. But dae me a favour, don't listen tae any gossip aboot me, Willie. The only thing I can see right noo is a warm bed, aye, wae me in it.'

'As you wish, Sergeant Scott, as you wish. I'll put our wee skid off the road down tae the conditions, so there'll be no repercussions, you can trust me on that. And remember, if you need tae talk about anything, I've a listening ear.' And with that, Pollock turned and trudged back through the snow towards the farmhouse.

Daley stood at the door of the communications office with two armed members of the Support Unit, Inspector Aitcheson and a worried but irritable Maxwell Shannon.

'I don't know why you need to see in here. The place is locked up and has been since the early hours of this morning. I turned the lock myself and I can assure you that there were no missing police officers to be seen,' said Maxwell, glaring at Daley.

'We have to make sure this location is as secure as it can be, Mr Shannon. I don't have time to argue with you about this. Unlock the door or I'll instruct my men to force it open.'

Reluctantly, Maxwell fumbled with a bunch of keys, selecting one and opening the heavy door. He flicked on a switch and stood, wide eyed, for a few heartbeats.

'You look surprised,' said Daley, studying the businessman carefully. Maxwell had now composed himself, but the detective had seen the bewildered expression on his face as the panel lighting hummed and flickered to life, illuminating the large room.

Daley looked around. The space was not unlike a modern CID room – all large screens and computer keyboards, with a projector screen at the far end of the room. Expensive paintings, polished wood floorboards and deep, comfortable chairs, however, marked it out as something altogether more luxurious.

'Not at all, just stunned to be back in here at this hour. I have a very important meeting this afternoon. I had hoped to get some sleep, not chase about after police officers in places they couldn't possible be.'

'What happened to your chin?'

'I was playing with the children last night. Got caught with a toy truck, if you must know.'

'Nasty colour,' observed Daley, certain that Maxwell was lying. He walked around the room, moving from desk to desk, studying the large bank of screens. 'So this is where you run the company from when you're here?'

'Yes. Nowadays, a business can be run from just about anywhere in the world. Not my first choice of HQ, mind you.'

'You were the last in here, then?'

'Yes. Switched off the lights and hoped to go and get some sleep, as I said.'

'Muddy boots, I see,' said Daley, looking at the dirty marks on the floor.

'With all this snow and slush about, is that a surprise?'

Daley sniffed the air. 'Someone's been smoking in here, too. You're not a smoker are you, Mr Shannon?'

'No, just the occasional cigar. I had one earlier – to celebrate the New Year.'

Daley bent down and lifted something from the floor, tucked behind the corner of one of the large desks. 'But you don't smoke these,' he said, holding up a cigarette butt.

Maxwell shook his head, shrugging off the question. Daley moved closer to the company boss, looming over him.

'If I discover that you know something about what's been happening here and haven't seen fit to pass this information on to me, all the money in the world won't save you.'

'Interesting, Mr Daley,' Maxwell replied with a sneer. 'What could you possibly do to me, as a retired police officer, washed up, overweight and unemployed? Your job is to catch whoever is perpetrating these awful crimes against my family. By placing the focus of your investigation on me, you are giving the real culprits a free hand – a mistake that I will be informing your Chief Constable of as soon as I can raise him today.' With that, Maxwell walked out of the room.

'I want someone following him – subtly – from now on,' said Daley to Aitcheson. 'I'm going to head up the glen and check out whatever it is that Jock Munro's seen.' He took one last look around the room before leaving, catching sight of a mark low down on the wall beside the door. He kneeled down to take a closer look. 'Blood, wouldn't you say, Inspector?'

28

Scott was lying in a private room in Kinloch hospital, having been delivered back to town, with PC Pollock, by a snowplough. Though a paramedic had examined him, the busy nursing sister wanted him checked over by a doctor prior his being discharged.

He had dozed, but this fitful sleep had been populated by bad dreams, the face of the boy haunting him.

As he stared at the ceiling, he wondered whether or not this was the time to confess to the hallucinations and his struggle with alcohol. Time to end the hell he was going through and get help with the problem before it consumed him wholly.

But then what would he do with the rest of his life? Would this new, shiny police force want anything to do with a foot soldier who was capable of putting his own and other people's lives at risk? He wasn't like Jim Daley; he wasn't willing to abandon the only career he'd ever had just because he liked a drink or two too many. He'd known a battalion of police officers in his time who had fought similar battles with booze and won, surviving to spend happy days in retirement in Spain on a pension provided by a grateful nation. Mind you, he'd known many others who had succumbed, their reward a hospital bed to lie in and wait as their livers faltered then failed in tandem with the death of their brain cells.

He didn't need to put his future in jeopardy just because he was experiencing this temporary crisis in his life. Ride out the storm, his father had told him years before. Hang on until the wind changed – it always did.

The phone on his bedside table rang and he answered without checking who the caller was.

'Brian, where the hell have you been?' Daley's voice was loud in his ear.

'Stuck in a snow drift, Jimmy. Me and Willie Pollock put the Land Rover off the road. Aye, lucky tae walk oot o' it,' he said, hoping that his colleague would stick to his promise and put the accident down to the weather conditions.

'Where are you? I called the station and said you were going to the hospital.'

'I'm here noo. Waiting for a doctor tae gie me the all clear. I was having a wee doss when you phoned, Jim,' he lied, hoping Daley wouldn't question him about his insobriety the previous evening.

'One of the SU guys is missing and I'm sure Maxwell Shannon has an idea what's going on. He knows something anyway. We're just heading up to have a look at some kind of encampment old Jock Munro spotted up the glen.'

'Well, you be careful, Jim. I tell you, I cannae see how they'll manage tae clear that road any time soon, even wae a whole army of snowploughs. We were lucky they got as far as us, and that was just a mile or two outside Kinloch.'

'We've got a few bodies here, so we should be OK. When they give you the all clear, I want you to dig up John Campbell, you know, the lawyer from the lifeboat. He has information from years back about the history of the Shannons. I'd like you to get your hands on it, as soon as.'

'Will do,' said Scott, but Daley had already ended the call. 'Oh, I'm feeling fine, how are you?' he muttered to himself, as a youthful doctor, accompanied by an equally young nurse, knocked on the door and entered the room.

'Now, Sergeant Scott, I hear you've been in the wars. Nearly went up in flames then in a car crash, I believe.'

'Aye, happy New Year, son. If it carries on like this, I'll no' make February.'

He winced as the doctor placed a cold stethoscope on his bare chest, asking him to breathe deeply.

'Now, since these incidents, have you experienced anything odd – confusion, feeling that all's not well? You know what I mean.'

'No, son, nothing like that. I've got too much on my plate tae have time tae get confused. And as for feeling that all is not well, I've been experiencing that since the day I joined the polis.'

Today was not the day that Brian Scott would introduce his demons to the world.

Bruce sat at the traditional early breakfast, taking in the scene at Kersivay House. There was no sign of Lars Bergner's wife or children; they were still waiting for the body pulled from the bonfire at the Black Wherry to be formally identified. His mother was there and his daughter, Mrs Watkins in tow to keep her on an even keel. A host of nieces, nephews, cousins, aunts and uncles, plus lawyers, accountants and the senior executives of the company all orbited around the main power bases, namely Ailsa Shannon and her nephew Maxwell, locked in the struggle for control of the company.

As was tradition, breakfast would begin with a few words and a prayer. This was normally conducted by the company chaplain but he had recently retired, so the Reverend Ignatius More had been tasked with the job. He was looking nervously about the large ballroom, stripped down after the festivities by a team of hired help from the village.

Ailsa stood up from her seat and moved round the table towards Bruce, who steeled himself for yet another dressing down. He was surprised when she held his hand and looked worriedly into his eyes.

'Mum, what's wrong?'

'Oh, Maxwell has just told me that Percy is unwell; confined to his bed, apparently. He seemed fine when I talked to him last night.'

'I wouldn't spend too long worrying about Percy, he's as tough as old boots. More likely he had too much whisky last night and needs to sleep it off. He still tries to drink like a twenty year old. Daft old bugger.'

'You're probably right, Bruce. I'll pay him a visit once this little charade is over.'

It was Bruce's turn to look concerned. He had heard nothing from Trenton Casely and feared that his attempt to wrest power from Maxwell would come to nothing, despite his plotting. As though she had read his mind, his mother caught him by the sleeve of his jacket and leaned in closer.

'You must promise me that you'll let events here take their own course, Bruce. This isn't the time for you to tilt at another windmill. I want you to have a word with Charles, he may want your help when it comes to voting.'

'He's a good guy, Mum, but don't you think we'd be in a better position now if he had any real influence over Maxie?'

'Maxwell is greatly disadvantaged by Lars Bergner's absence. An awful situation, but it has worked to our advantage.'

'Why is Maxwell going ahead? I mean, Lars's disappearance is the perfect excuse to postpone. Aren't you concerned?'

'We'll see,' replied his mother, regaining some of her poise. 'Maxwell thinks that it's just a matter of time until his father dies, so we should all tread water and watch the rise of the new regime. He's very confident.'

There was something about the look on her face that troubled Bruce. In fact, she was more serene than he had seen her for years. She and her brother-in-law had navigated a steady, if unspectacular, path to greater success, based on the foundations laid by her late husband. But since her nephew had inherited his position, a silent battle had raged. Maxwell plotted and schemed, waiting for the day his father would die and the real power would be his and his alone.

At the moment, he ran the company as a weakened regent, with Ailsa, supported by other family members, able to veto plans as they chose. The pall of young Archie's disappearance hung even more heavily over proceedings. When his father died, Archie should have been the one to take over the reins of the organisation, not his uncle, and Maxwell would have been reduced to the same powerless position Bruce now so reluctantly occupied.

'As long as we have our fifty-fifty veto, nothing can happen that will ruin us, Mum. We'll just have to settle for that,' he said, smiling at her. She didn't reply, but he followed her eye line to where Brady was sitting across the table.

A strange look passed across Ailsa's face.

Daley knocked on the door of Percy Williamson's cottage. He could see a candle flickering in the window, almost obscured by thick snow on the sill. He shivered in the thin morning light, then the door opened a crack, revealing the old man's face.

'Mr Williamson, just checking that everything is OK.'

'Yes, good morning, Chief Inspector. Don't come too close – my wife and I have an awful bug. We've both been very sick over the last few hours. Nasty germ.'

'I was wondering if you'd noticed anything unusual across at the office block?'

'What do you mean, unusual?'

'You know, lots of comings and goings, people you don't know and so on.'

'I stopped recognising who was coming about this place more than twenty years ago. There are so many of them now, how could anyone keep track? Sorry I can't be more helpful.'

'Do you need anything?'

'No, no, you're very kind. We'll battle on here. Never died a winter yet, Mr Daley. Mrs Shannon is very kind, I'm sure she'll see to any needs we have.' Percy stared at Daley, then tossed his head to one side – a nervous twitch, Daley thought. His pallor was grey, his cheeks hollowed. 'If you don't mind, I have to go – call of nature. Please excuse me.' He slammed the door shut; Daley could hear him hurrying along the hall, no doubt to the toilet.

'Doesn't look well, sir,' observed Aitcheson. 'Hope it's not one of these winter bugs that will floor us all. Last thing we need, stranded here.'

Daley hesitated for a moment. 'Better get up the glen and see what we can find. It's light enough now.' There was something about the old caretaker's demeanour that troubled him. He filed the thought away, resolving to talk to Ailsa about it at the first opportunity.

29

Scott stamped his feet to keep warm as he stood in front of the solicitor's office in Kinloch, waiting for John Campbell to arrive. The town's Main Street was barely recognisable under the largest accumulation of snow anyone could remember. Hard-working council staff had managed to dig a pathway up the street, so cars, in single file, could navigate their way through the town.

He watched as an expensive 4x4 made steady progress up the hill, stopping outside the gates to the office. It was an old building, just down the road from Kinloch Police Office and across from the Sheriff Court – in the heart of the town's legal quarter, as Daley put it.

'Morning, DS Scott,' said John Campbell, easing his large frame from the passenger seat. 'Thought it wise to have my good lady take the wheel this morning. She doesn't drink and I'm afraid I rather made up for our shortfall in consumption last night.'

He waded through the deep snow and shook the detective's hand. 'Did you have a decent Hogmanay? Probably on duty so on the bloody wagon, eh?'

'Something like that, Mr Campbell,' said Scott. 'I can't say I'd wouldn't rather be in my scratcher, mark you.'

'Don't worry, we'll get inside and grab a cup of coffee before I dig out old Dryesdale's files. Years since I last looked at them, but very interesting, as I recall. We wanted to archive them at the local museum but the Shannons would have none of it. Blast this snow,' he added as he struggled to push open the front door of the office. 'I've never seen the like, not here at any rate. Only a matter of time until the natives get restless and start worrying about food running out.'

'Is that likely?'

'Well, even though there are two decent supermarkets in the town, people start stockpiling. The last time we had anything like this, I was a young solicitor, just qualified, in fact. Bloody war zone in the town. The amount of assaults and breaches of the peace I dealt with in the weeks after was monumental. Still, I'm sure civility will have improved now we're in the twenty-first century.'

'Doon here? I'm no' so sure,' replied Scott.

'For ever and ever, amen,' said the Reverend Ignatius More, standing at one end of the long boardroom table in the ballroom of Kersivay House. A few echoed his amen, but most simply sighed and got stuck into their breakfast, glad the Minister had finished.

'Well done, Reverend,' said Bruce, smiling up at him. 'I apologise for the lack of respect from some around this table. We really appreciate you taking the time to be with us this morning.'

'That's all right,' replied More. 'I wonder, any chance of me and you having a quick chat once you've eaten? In private, if that's OK?'

'Sure. Needing some funds for the church roof again?'

'No,' replied More, leaning his head closer to Shannon's. 'Mr Casely sent me. I'll meet you on the terrace in about half an hour?'

Bruce watched him walk away, admonishing himself after a few seconds to try and not look so shocked.

Campbell pulled an extending ladder from the loft hatch and climbed up it somewhat unsteadily. 'If I'd known I was going to be as active this morning, I'd have consumed rather less of the amber nectar last night. We have the Shannon papers in a stout old trunk, shouldn't be too hard to find.'

Scott looked around Campbell's office. Stacks of leather-bound books sat in a huge case behind his long oaken desk. All was polished wood, green leather and dark panelling. A laptop on Campbell's desk looked out of place in a space that Torquil Dryesdale of a hundred years before might well have found familiar.

'Ah, here we are,' called Campbell from the loft. 'It's a bit awkward, can you help me down this bloody ladder?' Scott heard something being pushed across the floor above his head then Campbell appeared, a wooden casket at his feet.

After much straining and no little profanity, the two men managed to manoeuvre the box down the ladder and onto the floor of Campbell's office. Scott studied it, noting the brass strips that bound the casket together and the stout lock just under the lid. 'Hope you've got the key, Mr Campbell.'

'Oh, nothing as secure as that in this place, Sergeant. We guard our tea money more closely than our old records. That was one of the reasons we were anxious to hand the damn thing over to the museum, but hey-ho.' He pulled open the lid of the box to reveal old files, many tied together with red ribbon. The smell of must and age filled the room. 'Now, let me see. Old Dryesdale was a conscientious bugger, by all accounts. Not all of this is relevant to the Kersivay House debacle, but most of it is.' He peered through his half-glasses at a couple of old papers, blowing dust off them as he went. 'Now, here we are,' he said, handing a thick file to Scott.

'You, Reverend More – I can hardly believe it,' spluttered Bruce, standing on the frozen terrace of Kersivay House.

'I have my reasons, Bruce. As, no doubt, you do yourself,' replied More with a steely look in his eyes that disconcerted Shannon.

'Yes, well, you've seen how my cousin behaves. The hour my uncle expires we'll be marginalised within this company and who knows where it will all lead.'

'And you don't want to have to go cap in hand to Maxie for your annual dividend, am I right? Listen,' he said in a more relaxed manner. 'There's nothing to worry about. There's been a few little stumbles along the way, but everything will be fine.'

'And what about Casely?'

'Oh, I only know what I've heard. He was off-message, somehow. Too keen on *other business*, if you know what I mean.'

'Women? That doesn't surprise me,' said Shannon, remembering their last meeting in the bar at Notting Hill Gate and the girl with the nice arse.

'I'm here as a safety valve, that's all,' said More. His Australian twang sounded suddenly more pronounced, thought Bruce.

'So you've been here all this time just waiting for this moment?'

'No, not as simple as that, Bruce. As I say, I have my reasons, but nothing you have to worry about.'

'Please tell me that these awful murders have nothing to do with our plan.'

'They don't. We're as surprised as you. It seems your family has its fair share of enemies. But all that's not important. We go ahead today as planned. All you have to do is stick to what we agreed.'

'So nothing changes? What about Maxwell?

'Just you play your part, Bruce. Leave Maxwell to us. Now, if you will excuse me, I have to get back to my wife. She's been . . . Well, she's not herself.'

More left Bruce alone on the terrace, staring down at the long stretch of beach on which his brother had disappeared fifty years before. He couldn't work out whether his shivers were down to the extreme cold or the pounding of his heart.

Scott was looking at a clipping from the *Kinloch Herald*, careful not to tear the fragile old paper. THE MANSION ON THE HILL NEARLY COMPLETE, read the headline. It carried on in smaller typeface: *The people of Blaan set to celebrate with the Shannon family.*

Campbell handed him another newspaper. It described the forcible removal of Nathaniel Stuart and his family from the land upon which Kersivay House was constructed. Scott read on with great interest.

On Thursday last, at Kinloch Sheriff Court, a warrant was issued for the removal of Mr Nathaniel Sinclair Stuart and his family from the land on Kersivay Point, Blaan.

Sheriff McGowan, assisted by his officers and ten constables from Kinloch, travelled to Mr Stuart's steading to effect the order. Unfortunately, they encountered much resistance by Mr Stuart and his extended family, numbering some thirty souls, intent on preventing the warrant from being lawfully executed.

Following what can only be described as the most extreme criminal behaviour and the arrival of a detachment of a company of Argyll and Sutherland Highlanders, peace was eventually restored and the rule of law enforced.

Mr Stuart and ten others were placed under arrest for varying offences including affray, assault on an officer of the court and numerous breaches of the peace and obstruction of constables of the law, as well as wanton utterances of extreme blasphemy and profanity in front of a representative of the Crown.

Mr Nathaniel Stuart will appear in Kinloch on Wednesday next in front of Sheriff A. P. McGowan to answer these charges.

In the opinion of this newspaper, the breakdown of the rule of law is a most serious turn of events. It is to be hoped that Mr Stuart's punishment will be commensurate with the heinous crimes committed.

'Sounds as though the local rag decided who was in the wrong here, eh?' said Scott, handing the paper back to Campbell.

'Not really surprising given that Archibald Shannon was its proprietor at the time. In fact, the family only sold the paper in the seventies.'

Campbell rummaged some more. 'Here's something you may be interested in. It's a transcript from Nathaniel Stuart's court appearance. As I recall, he was sent to Inverary Jail for a period of two years' hard labour.'

'Bugger me, that's kind of steep, is it no'?'

'One can only guess at this distance of time, but I think it would be fair to say that Mr Shannon had more than a little influence over Sheriff McGowan. They couldn't banish Stuart from the area, so it suited them fine to have him turning the wheel up in Inverary while the house was being built, just in case he decided to organise another riot.'

'Turning the wheel?'

'Sounds innocuous, but in reality it broke many a stout heart. The prisoner was forced to turn a crank on a purpose-built machine for hours on end. The prison guard could change the degree of difficulty by means of a gearing system. Restrained brutality, breaking both body and spirit. As far as I'm aware, they subjected Stuart to it relentlessly, but in the end he prevailed, unbowed. Mark of the man, I'd say.'

Scott studied the article, which took up two full pages of the old newspaper, now brown and fragile with age. 'What's this bit here?' he asked, pointing to a passage in the middle of the article underlined in faded blue ink.

'The famous curse, Sergeant. Highlighted by Dryesdale, I assume. By all accounts it haunted him for what was left of his life. Turned from an agnostic into a pillar of the church, no less. And then he was found with his throat cut at the Rat Stone.'

'Yes, Jim mentioned that. Is this where he has them doon for disaster every fifty years? I know all about that.'

'Bit more comprehensive, Sergeant Scott. Here, I'll read it.' Campbell pushed his glasses higher up his nose and cleared his throat. 'When asked if he had anything to say in reply to the sentence, Nathaniel Stuart replied thus: "I curse all you Shannons from now until the end of time. May calamity descend upon you this year and every fifty years in the future, as long as you hold our lands at Kersivay."'

'Aye, I've heard a' that. What's the rest o' it?'

'At the end of days there will be no eyes to see, no mouth to speak, no chest for breath and no finger to point. The many will follow the one consumed by flames after the fall, and death will descend upon you and all who help and aid you, in a deserved hell of fire and destruction, till you and all that come after you shall be left with nothing, not even life itself, and our family be returned to our home."' Campbell looked at Scott with a smile. 'Poetic, really – wouldn't you agree? He was no duffer, old Stuart, when it came to curses, I must say. Of course, after the boy disappeared fifty years ago, the whole thing was resurrected, but people only remember the curse about the fifty years upon fifty. The rest is always forgotten.'

'And what aboot this Stuart? How did he survive? Seems that he left Blaan with very little.'

'Indeed. Though if the stories are true, with his hereditary position as Arch Druid, or whatever he was called, he could always rely on help wherever those traditions prevailed.'

'What? He was a druid? Surely they don't believe in all that stuff anywhere else?'

'Yes, it's very popular in North America to this day, so I'm led to believe. Old myths and traditions have real power through generations of families separated from the "old country", as they would have it. Just look at all the bloody clan gatherings and pipe bands they have across there.'

'Aye, but this mumbo jumbo? Come on, big man.'

'Not as though any of you police officers are involved in any secret societies, eh?'

'Aye, well, that's a different thing all together,' said Scott, clearing his throat and looking uncomfortable.

'Yes, I daresay.' Campbell smiled. 'But don't be carried away with the notion that Nathaniel Stuart was cast to the four winds, penniless and hopeless when he left Blaan. He may well have stumbled upon better times elsewhere. It's almost a certainty, I would say.'

Scott thought for a moment, a frown spreading across his face. 'I'll need tae make a call, Mr Campbell.'

30

Superintendent Symington studied Daley as he donned the bulletproof vest and checked his sidearm. When she'd visited Daley's home, she hadn't cared whether he left his job or not. Now that she'd seen him working here in Blaan, cut off from just about all aid while dealing with a deadly situation, she had made up her mind that such an asset to her new division, to Police Scotland itself, could not be allowed to simply disappear. 'Tell me again, Jim. I want to know how you intend to approach this in detail.'

'I'm reasonably sure that someone has our missing constable, ma'am. I would bet my life on the fact that Maxwell knows more than he's letting on and that he's either involved or pressure is being put on him.'

'Right, so you and five of the unit are going to where Jock reckons he saw this guy.'

'Yes, ma'am. That's about the height of it. Any word from HQ?'

'Worse than yesterday. If this continues across the country, I'm told that the government are going to call a state of emergency. Across the board we're working at less than forty per cent normal operational manpower levels – worse in the rural divisions. Officers simply can't get to work. We're on our own here.'

Daley was about to reply when the phone rang in his pocket. 'Brian, what's happening?' He listened for a few moments. 'Get a copy of this to me on email.' He ended the call.

'Not more problems, I hope?'

'Put it like this, ma'am, things just got a lot worse than yesterday,' said Daley, explaining the nature of Scott's call.

'We really are facing a concerted effort to bring down the family,' said Symington. 'Brockie murdered, Grant killed and mutilated, Bergner sacrificed and burned on the bonfire – this curse, or whatever you'd call it, is being re-enacted to the letter, would you agree?'

'Yes, I would,' replied Daley, checking his weapon. 'The question is, what does the rest of it actually mean?'

'After the fall and all this fire and destruction stuff?

'Yes.'

'It means we're exposed beyond belief, DCI Daley. This is how we'll proceed. I want you to go and check out Jock's lead now, but I can only afford to give you two other officers. I'm taking charge in the mansion, Jim, while you work on the ground, so to speak. I'll need a weapon.'

'Yes, of course, ma'am.'

'If you can't find our missing colleague up this hill, I'm afraid our priorities will have to change.'

'Meaning?'

'It's been made very clear to me that my first duty is to protect the Shannon family.'

'Yes, ma'am,' said Daley, trying not to let his exasperation show.

'But, I'm here on the ground, Jim. I don't care what their surnames are, I intend to for us all to survive this.'

'And this AGM, ma'am – shouldn't we make them postpone it?'

'What does it matter? We're all stuck here, anyway. It's been intimated to our superiors that if we stand in the way of any Shannon International business, they will take legal action against us and the government. You can only imagine the response.'

'The meeting goes ahead.'

'Indeed. Now pass me that sidearm, please.'

Daley looked on as Symington checked and rechecked the weapon. 'Textbook stuff, ma'am. I see you've handled firearms before.'

'I was an inspector in the Territorial Support Group in the Met, Jim. Don't look so surprised, women can fire a gun just as well as men.'

'Oh, yes, of course. I didn't mean . . .'

She smiled. 'You'll find out a lot about me you don't know, DCI Daley. You get going, leave the Shannon AGM to me. And be careful.'

It took Scott three trips to carry the files from Campbell's office to Kinloch Police Office, following which he was tired and hungry. He decided to head to the County Hotel in the hope of getting something hot to eat.

After negotiating the two hundred yards or so of deep snow, he stamped his feet before swinging open the large doors to the hotel.

'Fuck me, if it's no' Guy Fawkes,' shouted Annie from behind the bar.

'How did you get back?' asked Scott.

'Before you. I got a lift fae Duncan Henderson in the tractor. I canna say it was the maist pleasurable trip I've ever had, but jeest as well I came back, the place is going like a fair. I've never seen it this busy on New Year's Day.'

The bar was indeed crowded; Scott noticed that people were being served drinks but no money appeared to be changing hands. 'What's this, very happy hour, or something? A free bar?'

'Naw, nor free. Auld Geordie Kennedy has had some kind o' windfall. He put three hundred behind the bar, aye, an' he says jeest tae gie him a shout when that's done an' he'll put another three hundred up. You'll be after a hair o' the dog yourself?'

'No, you're all right. Just a coffee for me. Have you got anything hot on the go? I'm famished.'

'You're jeest in the nick o' time. We'll run oot o' diesel for the emergency generator in an hour, so I'm told. There no' a pint o' the stuff tae be had in the toon. They've kept what's left for the hospital and yourselves in the emergency services. So get your order in noo or it'll be sandwiches by candlelight.'

'Just a plate o' mince an' tatties for me, Annie.'

'Coming up. I hope you're feeling better after last night?'

'Och, I just got singed, nothing tae worry aboot.'

'No, I mean before that. Dae you no' remember falling your length on the snow? Your eyes were in the back of your heid, man. Fair gibbering you were, tae.'

Scott remembered the vision he'd had, lying in the snow at the back of the Black Wherry, and shuddered. 'We'll just keep that to ourselves, Annie,' he said and made his way to the last empty table, beside a group of old men sitting in the corner of the bar.

'Hey, Hamish, you're friend fae the polis is here,' said an

elderly drinker, surprising Scott, as he could see no sign of the old fisherman.

The table moved, almost spilling a couple of drinks. A hand appeared, then another, clutching at the air. Assisted by his drinking companions, and after no little effort, Hamish was restored to his chair. 'Brian, my auld friend.'

'It's no' even lunchtime, man. You've had a good New Year and no mistake.'

'Och, it's Geordie here. Just an absolute gentleman an' that's a fact.' This brought a murmur of consensus from the others at the table.

One old man was sufficiently moved to rise, unsteadily, to his feet to speak. 'Of all the folk I've known in the toon, Geordie is by far the best.'

'Morris, are you no' the main man, right enough,' replied another drinker with a smile. 'I'm fair chuffed that you like me so much.'

'Aye, I dae that. Lang may your lum reek.'

'Mind you,' said Geordie, taking a sip of his whisky, 'it was only last week you called me the maist thrawn auld bastard you'd ever met.'

'But you weren't buying him drink then,' declared Hamish.

'You've always got too much tae say for yersel, Hamish,' said Morris, still on his feet. 'The way you patter on, you'd think whisky was as big a stranger tae you as bath water.'

Hamish leaned across the table, knocking over two glasses of whisky, and grabbed Morris's jacket. 'Don't you think you're safe standing up there, you bugger. I'll jeest fair loup o'er this table an' gie you the thrashing o' yer life.'

'So you will. If I was as auld as you I'd be back in the hoose wae a blanket o'er my knees, nursing a mug o' cocoa. But if you want tae die wae a drink in your hand, well, you're going the right way aboot it.'

'Noo, boys,' said Geordie. 'Not only is this a new year, I'm getting tae celebrate my guid fortune, noo I'm oot the clutches o' that daughter o' mine.'

'Just you sit back doon, Rocky' said Scott, pulling Hamish back into his seat. 'What was your good fortune, if you don't mind me asking, Geordie?'

'Ach, happened jeest efter Christmas. I was sitting in the hoose, fair lamenting the fact that my daughter and her weans weren't going back up tae Glasgow until after Hogmanay, when I got a knock at the door. Tae cut a long story short, it was two fellas, said they were collecting auld photos o' the area and did I have any?'

'And you did, I take it?'

'Loads, jeest loads. My dear mother was a right wan for photographs. I've got that many o' hers I don't know whoot tae dae wae them. These blokes went through them a' – aye, every one.'

'You'd be glad to get rid o' them, I'm quite sure,' replied Scott.

'That's the strange thing. They were only interested in five photos. But bugger me, they weren't short in paying for them, right enough. They gied me three grand . . .' He hesitated, as though he'd said something wrong. 'But you good folk'll not be interested in a' that.'

'Three grand for five auld photos. What were they of, Bonnie Prince Charlie, Lord Lucan?'

'No, jeest my mother when she worked at Kersivay Hoose in Blaan.'

'You never telt me that,' said Hamish rising from the table

again, his fists bunched into tight balls. 'So you got three grand and jeest thought you'd make your way intae my hoose when you knew fine I had similar pictures, since oor mothers worked together. Well, if you got any mair dosh for them, I'm wanting my share, right noo, you thieving swine!' He took a swing at his drinking companion, then tipped backwards and was caught by Scott, who guided him safely back into his chair.

'Enough's a feast for you, my boy,' said Scott beckoning for Annie to come over. 'These two men that bought the photos off you, Geordie, what did they look like?'

The detective's heart sank as the old man described the butchered journalists Grant and Brockie.

The path up the glen was steep and deep with snow. Daley and two of the Support Unit struggled along in the general direction Jock had described. The silence was punctuated only by the distant lap of the sea on the shore far below and the police officers' heavy footfall and occasional oaths when the snow was deeper than expected.

Daley was carrying a sidearm while his colleagues both carried semi-automatic weapons, slung over their shoulders. Symington had made it clear that they couldn't risk being unprepared. Daley felt enormous, with a bulletproof vest on under his ski jacket.

'Sir,' whispered the cop immediately behind him as they neared a copse of trees. 'Can you smell that? I'm sure it's cigarette smoke.'

Daley sniffed the air; sure enough, the pungent smell of tobacco was obvious. He peered into the trees and saw a thin thread of blue smoke spiral into the air.

All three police officers sank to their knees. Daley turned to them. 'I want us going in from different angles. Side each for you, I'll take the straight route.' He could feel his heart thumping in his chest as he released the safety catch on his handgun and moved forwards towards the smoke. As directed the other officers disappeared into the trees on either side of him.

According to Jock, there was a clearing just after the first line of trees and sure enough, as Daley slid his way forwards, he could see the woods opening out in front of him. Almost bent double, he crouched behind the large trunk of a fir tree, peering ahead through the pine needles.

The sudden fall of snow from the branch of a tree made him jump. He glanced back but there was nothing behind him. He looked left and right for any sign of his colleagues but they were obviously staying well out of sight, awaiting his command.

Something caught his eye; another puff of blue smoke drifted through the trees. Daley eased himself up and squinted further into the clearing. He caught his breath when he made out a figure sitting on a log, their back to the detective, a cigarette dangling from their outstretched fingertips.

Again, Daley looked left and right – no sign of the Support Unit officers. He reached for the handset in his pocket. They were all wearing earpieces, so voice contact, as long as he was quiet, was possible.

'Alpha One calling Sierra Uniform One and Two. Make your way slowly into the clearing using due caution. Suspect spotted straight ahead of me. Over.' He listened for the blip response indicating the men had heard his message, but there was silence. 'Sierra Uniform One and Two, please respond, over.' Again Daley's pleas went unanswered.

He sighed. Should he try to move forwards and attempt to engage the smoking figure? He reckoned he had no alternative. Daley left the relative security of the tree trunk and half ran, half waded through the thick snow. He was only feet away from the figure on the log when he stopped.

'I am an armed police officer. Please stand slowly with your hands in the air.' The figure didn't move. Daley took two steps closer.

On the edge of his hearing, he could make something out. In the beginning it was barely perceptible, soon it became a whine. The wind was getting up and the branches of the trees began to wave in the breeze, divesting themselves of their heavy white burden. All around him, snow began to fall in heavy clumps, thudding dully as it landed. A bird flapped into the air and Daley jumped. He could see the figure properly now. Puffs of blue smoke still rose into the cold air.

'One last time – turn around!'

Slowly the figure, draped in a black cloak, stood and turned to face Daley. His gasp of recognition was stopped in his throat as he felt a crushing pain on the back of his head. He struggled for a few heartbeats, trying to remain conscious, as the familiar face swam in front of him. Then another blow hit him hard on the head, as the whine through the trees grew louder.

31

People began to take their seats around the long boardroom table in the ballroom of Kersivay House. Ailsa sat at one end, her son Bruce to her right, her granddaughter Nadia, accompanied by Mrs Watkins, to her left.

At the other end of the table sat Maxwell. To his right, where normally Lars Bergner would have been seated, the grey figure of COO Lynton sat, meticulously polishing his glasses with a grey cloth. Across from him was Brady, staring at an iPad and seemingly entirely at ease.

Bruce looked on as various members of the extended family took their seats. They were, in the main, minority share holders, but their stake in the family business had made them rich – and in most cases spoiled and disinterested. They were there to nod and vote and do what they were told by either of the power bases that protected their interests. They attended the AGM only because, as per the company constitution, they stood to lose their shares if absent.

He studied his mother. She was composed, with a benign look on her face – as hard to read as ever.

As the board of Shannon International settled into their seats, a stream of accountants, lawyers, advisors and mere bag carriers entered the room, mainly taking position behind the central players. His mother's accountant and corporate lawyer sat behind her, not part of the meeting but able to whisper in her ear as it progressed.

At the other end of the table, Maxwell's people arrived, clustering around him, much greater in number than his mother's advisors.

Bruce watched as they jostled for position behind his cousin, who was already wearing his self-satisfied grin. A dark-haired girl sat down near Brady. She was pretty, with deep brown eyes. Something about her was familiar, but he couldn't work out what it was. He had to avert his gaze when she caught his eye and smiled. It was then that it dawned on him: she was the girl with the nice backside he'd seen in the bar in Notting Hill only two days earlier. She was the woman he'd seen leaving the bar with Trenton Casely. This could be no coincidence.

Suddenly the reality of how deeply he was involved – exposed, even – hit home.

Scott stared at his computer screen. Though it was New Year's Day, he had decided to call the local librarian, at home, in the hope that she might be able to throw some light on the history of Kersivay House – and why old images of the place were suddenly in such demand.

The thought had churned over in his mind as he waited for her to answer the phone. Why would someone go to all the trouble of paying journalists to look for old photographs of the building and those who occupied it so long ago? Moreover, why then would those same journalists end up dead?

As it turned out, the librarian had been very helpful. She told Scott that Grant and Brockie had visited her at the library a few days before Christmas, asking about Kersivay House and whether she knew anything of its history or had any old photographs.

'Funny,' she had said. 'We used to have a display on the Shannons and their affiliation with the area on display in the old library when I started working there. Apparently they complained so the whole thing was stuck in the attic. When I spoke to the journalists, I told them that it must have been disposed of at some point. I certainly didn't see hide nor hair of it when we moved to our new building.'

'And?'

'Well, they asked if I had any images on file or the computer and I said no. They seemed to lose all interest after that. It was only a couple of days later when I was going through boxes, still unopened after our move, that I found it.'

'What, the display?'

'Yes, dusty and a bit sorry-looking, but intact. I took pictures of it all and filed them digitally. I had intended to pass it on to the journalists after the holidays. I called the number they left, but never got a reply.'

Scott was staring at those images now. The old house on the hill in sepia print. People in old clothes, from around the thirties, Scott thought; some smart and prosperous, others dressed in the threads of service.

For the time, Scott reckoned, the photography was good, obviously the work of a professional, though everything seemed very stiff and posed. As he went through the images and text about how the house came into being and what wonderful, benevolent and successful people the Shannons were, he stopped at one image. A little boy had been caught on the edge of a group of people, all standing stiffly and looking solemnly into the lens. The young lad must have thought himself out of shot, for unlike the others, he was looking to the side, a little away from the main party. It was the expression on the boy's face that caught his eye: a waspish, disgruntled glare, so at odds with his age. 'Auld before your time,' Scott mused aloud. There was something really familiar about that face, he thought, and the expression on it. He took his phone from his pocket and snapped a picture.

He flicked through more photographs to see if he could see the young boy again. As he clicked open another folder of images, he stopped. His throat began to constrict and he could feel the sweat on his brow. There, wearing a little camel coat with a velvet collar, was another little boy. Scott didn't have to wonder about the familiarity of that face – he'd seen it before. It was young Archie Shannon, the photo obviously taken not long before his disappearance.

Scott gripped the desk in front of him, his fingers going white at their tips, desperately trying to force away the blackness at the corner of his eyes and remain conscious. He took deep breaths, telling himself he was safely ensconced in Kinloch Police Office, but still the ringing in his ears began.

'Fuck this, no, no!' he shouted, slamming his fist down into the desk. 'I'm not giving intae this.'

'I would like to bring the Annual General Meeting to order,' shouted Maxwell, banging a wooden gavel. The general buzz died down to a whisper, as the Acting Chairman of Shannon International cleared his throat and consulted the notes in front of him. 'As you know, it is with a heavy heart that I chair today's proceedings. I would much rather my father, our Chairman, were here. Sadly, as we all know, his condition remains the same, though every effort is being made to care for him.'

Bruce could only smile at the murmur of agreement that echoed around the table. Of one thing he was sure: if he could get away with it, Maxwell would happily strangle his own father in order to have the full reins of power. The hypocrisy was staggering. Still, this was the little world in which they found themselves, and in Bruce's experience, hypocrisy was always the order of the day.

'As you are also aware, beside me now should be our CEO Lars Bergner. I don't need to tell you about his disappearance, nor the events surrounding it. Our thoughts are with his wife and children as we earnestly hope for his safe return. I am aware that some of you believe that this meeting should not proceed under these circumstances. However, I think you are wrong. Lars is a professional to his fingertips,' said Maxwell, raising a few eyebrows at his use of the present tense, not to mention any talk of fingers. 'He would want us to carry on in a professional manner. We have a global business to run, which is bigger than any one of us.' There was a murmur of general agreement. 'Besides,' he continued. 'We're stuck here in Blaan, what else have we got to do?' Despite the circumstances, many members of the board of Shannon International began to laugh. 'All agreed?' Maxwell looked around the table for detractors. 'Good, let us proceed.'

Scott had bettered the vision, fought it away. He was now drinking a cup of strong coffee, his hands shaking, trying to compose himself.

It's good news, he thought. Maybe I'm getting the better of this, maybe the booze is losing. Then he remembered the amount of whisky he'd consumed on Hogmanay. He sighed and looked at the wall, then decided to look for more images of the little boy with the scowl who was so strangely familiar. There were no more pictures of him in the library files so he decided to delve into the old casket of papers Campbell had given him.

He turned over press cutting after press cutting referring to the Kersivay House case. Torquil Dryesdale, in one way or another, appeared to have been obsessed by it all. He had archived just about every snippet of information there was available.

Under the piles of newspapers, Scott found more old photographs. One image showed some low cottages and outbuildings; judging by the surrounding landscape, it was the site on which Kersivay House now stood. He found a tattered sepia photograph that had been torn in two and glued back together. It showed a broad, thickset man in a leather apron, standing beside a sturdy plough horse. He had a shock of dark, wiry hair and eyed the camera with a steady gaze. When Scott turned the photograph over, he found the name *Nathaniel Stuart* scribbled across the back in faded ink.

He ploughed on, until he came to another picture of Stuart. Older now, his face was lined, with streaks of white through his hair. He still looked broad and strong, standing beside two young children on a pier in front of a steamship. As Scott peered at the photograph, he realised that the boy in the image was the same young lad he'd seen scowling at the stiff, posed subjects of the old picture taken at Kersivay House. What was it about that child that was so familiar? The scrawled writing, this time bolder and less faded, read,

Nathaniel Stuart leaves Kinloch. There was no mention of the children, who looked too young to be Stuart's offspring. Beside the boy, a little girl clutched a rag doll to her chest.

Brady spoke up in his loud New York drawl. 'I have the figures for the last year of trading by our global holding company. If you open the folder in front of you, you'll be able to follow what's going on quite easily. You can see that our turnover is down by 1.3 per cent since this meeting last year. This may seem insignificant, until you factor in the numbers we're talking about,' he said, as assorted board members nodded in solemn approval. 'As a business, we aren't out of trouble yet, though I'm pleased to say that Shannon International has weathered the recent financial storm better than most.'

'I see this is correct only until Monday last, Charles,' said Ailsa.

'Yes, that's true, but we always have the same cut-off date prior to our AGMs here. You must understand that, such is the complex nature of these accounts, we have to have statements fully prepared and checked well in advance.'

'May I ask about trading in the last ten days? Particularly in the days after Christmas?'

Brady looked across the table towards Maxwell, who took the hint and interrupted the little exchange. 'Of course we can get you those figures, Aunt Ailsa, but not today. I'll send them to you as soon as they're prepared.'

'Oh, good, I'm sure it'll make for most interesting reading.'

Bruce looked between his mother, Brady and Maxwell with interest. Brady did his job and did it well; he was part of

Shannon International's leadership, but not of it. Most importantly, he had always been Ailsa's man, but now Bruce sensed a change.

The dark-haired girl leaned into Maxwell, listened to what he had to say, then quietly left the meeting. Bruce watched her go, admiring her as she went.

'Now, ladies and gents, if you could take a look, we'll go through what's been making us all rich this year,' said Brady, as a large screen slid silently from the ceiling, almost filling the entire wall at the far end of the ballroom.

Bruce was convinced that he saw a nervous look pass between Brady and Maxwell. When he looked to see if his mother had picked up on this, he noted that she looked as serene and untroubled as ever.

There was no doubt about it, the next few hours were going to be amongst the most testing of his life, but he was ready. Suddenly, Bruce wished that the glass in front of him was full of whisky instead of mineral water.

Scott busied himself reading the rest of the history of the Shannon family that had come from the library. Much was made of their long connection to Blaan and the philanthropic work they had been responsible for over the years. He wasn't surprised to note that the police office in which he was currently ensconced, as well as the Sheriff Court down the road, had both been built by previous Shannons and gifted to the town.

It was only when he read about Blaan itself that he encountered the history of the Rat Stone – or Stane, as it was termed in the old document. He squinted through his glasses and read.

The Rat Stane occupies an oaken copse nestling in a valley known locally as the Vale of the Druids. Its origins appear to be ancient, possibly prehistoric, dating back to the hunter-gatherer period. One of many theories about the stone is that it was a meeting place or site of governance, as in the Teutonic Rathaus. But, this is not universally agreed upon.

In James VI's treatise on witches and the supernatural, the monument is mentioned in connection with the druidic tradition. Indeed, the literal translation of its location is 'valley of the magicians', as many considered this ancient order to be. Time has obscured their true nature but stories of human sacrifice abound in local myth and legend and the construction of the stone itself would appear to lend credence to this hypothesis. It is probably also the case that they saw themselves as guardians of tradition and of their surroundings. There is little doubt that they acted positively to protect and nurture their landscape, keeping the balance between ancient people and their impact on their environment.

Of current inhabitants of Blaan, none are more intimately connected with its ancient past than the Sinclair Stuarts. Local legend tells us that they dominated the area from their base at the top of Kersivay cliff, fending off all-comers, including, it is said, the Romans. It was only the arrival of the Scotti, or Scots, from across the North Channel that brought about the end of their power in the region. The druids were routed, forced to the margins of society, until their extinction at the hands of the families who settled the village thereafter.

Most notable of these families were the Shannons, who now have significant land holdings in and around Blaan, stretching as far as Kinloch. Legend has it that they learned how to work metal from the Sinclair Stuarts and were skilled blacksmiths.

The worshippers of Blaan still talk of 'going to the stane' when they attend the Kirk in the village. Here again, the Shannon family appear to have usurped the Sinclair Stuarts as hereditary ministers of the parish. From the infamous Bloody Minister to the present day, it is a Reverend Shannon who calls the faithful to prayer in Blaan.

Scott read the passage over again. So, not only had Nathaniel Stuart lost the family's ancient home to the Shannon family but, over hundreds of years, the incomers had taken almost everything from them.

The little boy in the coat with the velvet collar sprung to mind. This time though, Scott was untroubled by the mental picture. He rifled through the papers that Campbell had given him; there he was again. For the first time, DS Scott saw something unutterably sad in young Archie Shannon's expression – sad and, like the boy with the scowl, oddly familiar.

32

Daley was kneeling on what felt like pebbles. He had just regained consciousness and was desperately trying to orientate himself. He was cold, shivering uncontrollably. His hands were tied behind his back and he realised, as he tried to move, that he was tethered to something. Through his stinging nostrils, the smell of the sea was strong.

'Let me out of here,' he shouted, his voice weak with cold, but still echoing around the dark space. 'I'm a police officer,' he called again, in no real hope that his pleas would make any difference.

He was surprised when he heard a groan in response. Somewhere behind him there was a faint voice.

'Sir, it's me, Sandy Whitlock – PC Whitlock.' The man's voice was strained. 'I, I came with you to . . .' He let out a blood-curdling scream and fell silent.

Daley could hear footsteps crunching behind him. He felt his spine tingle, waiting for the blow, the kick, the sharp knife in his back. He remembered the horrific sight of Colin Grant, eviscerated, his lungs thrust over his shoulders in bloody agony as his life drained away.

'Who are you?' he asked, as calmly as he could. There was no reply, though the footsteps had stopped. His captor was now studying him as he kneeled forwards, trussed up on the pebble floor. Daley tried desperately to think through the fog in his brain. His head was pounding, no doubt caused by the blows that had rendered him unconscious.

A seagull's distant cry sounded a pitiful lament – for lost souls, or for those about to be lost. Daley thought of his young son, so new to this world. He felt tears welling up in his eyes; his throat ached. He clenched his teeth to banish them. He had to remain strong – if not for himself then for his fellow captives.

'I am a police officer,' he repeated. 'If you harm me or any of my colleagues, you will be caught and you'll never be free again for the rest of your life. Whatever it is that you're trying to achieve, whatever twisted purpose you have in mind, it has to end here.'

Silence.

He was shivering so badly, he could barely make the words form in his mouth. 'I want you to think about what you are doing. Think very hard.'

The person crunched closer to him, stopping at his back. Daley looked at the ground before him in the gloom. A dim light shone from somewhere up ahead.

'I know where we are. We've been investigating the death of Colin Grant, your sea cave is no secret . . .' He stopped suddenly, involuntarily, sharply drawing the cold air into his lungs. A soft hand ran slowly down the length of his back.

DCI Jim Daley closed his eyes and waited for the agony to begin.

'Jock Munro? It's me, Sergeant Brian Scott. I hope I'm not disturbing you,' he said, looking at the old photograph of

Nathaniel Stuart on the pier at Kinloch with the two young children.

'And how's the head this morning?' boomed Jock, his voice just as loud and resonant over the phone. 'I've seen police officers at some capers in my time, but never jumping through the flames of a bonfire. You're obviously a one-off, Brian.'

'You're no' the first person tae mention that, my friend.' Scott raised his eyebrows. 'I'm glad the phones are still working.'

'The phones will be the last thing to go here. As I said to you last night, we in Blaan have the Shannons to thank for such connectivity. They tell me that we even have broadband here – not that I have use for such a thing.'

'I need to pick your brains about something,' said Scott. 'Do you know anything about what happened to Nathaniel Stuart when he left the area?'

'Bits and pieces, Brian. The old man had faced humiliation, as I mentioned to you. He had relations over in Ireland – Donegal, I think I'm right in saying. He left Blaan sometime in the thirties. I'm not sure of the exact date.'

'I have a photograph here of him with two young children. It was taken the day he left Kinloch, or so it says on the back. Dae you know who they are?'

'That will be his grandchildren, Brian. His daughter's children. She was married, then suffered some kind of breakdown. Some people said she was wrong in the head, but you know how it goes in small communities. Anyhow, he was like a father to the children, so it is said.'

'So none of them ever came back?'

'Well, if you listen to the fishwives in this village, you might believe that Nathaniel Stuart did pay one visit back to

Blaan . . . It was a black day in the village when young Archie Shannon went missing.'

'Archie Shannon? Where did that come fae?' said Scott, slightly discomforted by mention of the little boy who kept appearing in his head.

'There are many in the village that would swear they saw Nathaniel Stuart around that time – back here in Blaan.'

'What, you mean that he took the wean?'

'So the gossips would have it, Brian.'

'But he must have been an old man.'

'He didn't die until the seventies, in a hospital in Dublin. Somehow, the *Kinloch Herald* got a hold of the story – a minor miracle in itself, I assure you. He was in his nineties.'

'And what do you think, Jock?'

'Though old Nathaniel was forced into hard times, he had no shortage of allies. He was the keeper of great secrets, again, if you believe the tittle tattle. True or not, he commanded a lot of respect in certain quarters, aye, and not just in Kinloch.'

'What secrets? And I thought he was damn near destitute.'

'There are many greater things than money, Sergeant Scott. Nathaniel Stuart is credited by many as being the last holder of a great office.'

'Not you too, Jock. Mair mumbo-jumbo.'

Scott was slightly put out when he heard Jock's laugh bellow through the earpiece. 'Many will tell you that Nathaniel Stuart was the last druid. Google that – I think that is the correct expression – and see how you get on, Brian. Now, if you'll forgive me, I must get out for my constitutional before the snow comes on again.'

Scott said goodbye and ended the call, staring into the commanding eyes of Nathaniel Stuart in the old photograph.

In Blaan, Jock Munro looked out of his window and sighed, still holding the telephone. He put it back onto the table and walked across to the bureau upon which sat his old typewriter. He opened a slim drawer and fumbled under some sheets of paper, removing a small photograph.

He sighed deeply as he looked at the tall, broad-shouldered man and the two children, standing in front of the steamship on the pier at Kinloch.

Superintendent Symington awoke with a start. It was the same dream she always had, the kind that didn't end with sleep. The boy was in slow motion, a look of horror on his face as he was propelled towards the windscreen.

She'd been dozing, sitting in her room in Kersivay House with DC Dunn and Inspector Aitcheson from the Support Unit.

'Are you OK, ma'am?' asked Dunn.

'Fine. Just a bad dream.' Symington took a deep breath and tried yet again to banish that face. She'd hoped moving to a new job might make a difference.

There had been no contact with Daley and his party for over two hours and the superintendent was beginning to worry.

'Definitely no way we can get anyone from Kinloch at the moment, ma'am, and you are aware of the situation as regards Division,' said Dunn. 'The road between here and Kinloch is blocked, though my information is that they will be able to make it through with snowploughs in the next hour or so, as long as we don't get another heavy snowfall.'

'What do the weather people say?' asked Symington.

'I talked to the Met Office at Prestwick, ma'am. They're finding it hard to give an exact forecast.'

'Oh, very helpful.'

'One thing they're pretty certain of is that there will be more snow.'

Symington looked at the bank of the screens in front of her, showing various parts of Kersivay House on CCTV. 'We have four missing officers and one of the richest families in the world to protect. Bloody brilliant.'

'We could try and get some cops from Kinloch by boat, ma'am,' suggested Dunn.

'If we hear nothing from Daley in the next hour, we might have to consider that.' Symington walked to the window and looked out over the bay. 'How far is the place Colin Grant was found from here, DC Dunn?'

'Three or four miles across the hills, ma'am. The way things are underfoot, I don't think a tractor or a 4x4 would make it. Has to be by air or sea.' Dunn stopped suddenly. 'Ma'am, you don't think . . .'

'I have to think everything, Mary. But if it's hard for us to move about, then it's equally hard for everyone else.'

'Once they're at sea ma'am, there's no problem,' remarked Aitcheson, unfolding a map of south Kintyre. 'Look at this – little coves, inlets, secluded beaches. If you have local knowledge you could easily hide away.'

'Do your rounds, Inspector. We may need to consolidate things in the house if Daley doesn't turn up soon.'

'Yes, ma'am.'

Symington looked at her young colleague. DC Dunn was wringing her hands, staring out at the heavy sky above the grey sea.

'I know how you feel, Mary,' she said.

'Sorry, ma'am?'

'You don't need to say anything, I'm not being judgemental. These things happen.'

'How did you find out?'

'I'm a detective, Mary. Underneath all this braid, I mean. It wasn't hard. The way you and DCI Daley look at each other is proof enough.'

'Sorry, ma'am. I . . . I don't know what to say. We've tried so hard to make sure it doesn't affect our work.'

'Take my advice, Mary. Not as your boss, as someone who knows the score. Don't have regrets, don't let what "seems right" make any decisions for you. Regardless of what anyone says, it's your life.'

'Thank you, ma'am.'

'Not the kind of advice I should be giving you, as your superior officer. I should be threatening you with hell and damnation, instant dismissal, but I know that won't work. When I'm old and buggered with no one to talk to, do you think Police Scotland will send somebody round to keep me company?'

'Do you think he'll be OK?'

'Of course he will,' replied Symington, with much more confidence than she felt.

The Shannon International AGM at Kersivay House was becoming unruly. A number of the smaller investors were arguing about a proposal to dilute the shareholding of the company in order to bring other non-family members onto the board. Maxwell was doing his best to quell their doubts but decided to lay the issue aside in favour of the most pressing item on his agenda.

'We have to accept the fact that, as a company, we have a shortage of board-level expertise in certain sectors, notably nanotechnology and robotics. These are areas we cannot hope to avoid given the structure of the organisation. We need strong, independent leadership, not the hobbled executive we have now, which has to defer to the board whenever a decision is made.'

'You mean we should let you do what you want,' said Bruce.

'Who else?'

Ailsa had been uncharacteristically silent during the course of proceedings. In fact, she had seemed distracted, spending much of her time poring over an electronic tablet with one of her advisors.

'I would like your input before we put this motion to the vote, Aunt Ailsa,' said Maxwell impatiently.

'It's the same as last year's motion – and the previous three years, if I'm not much mistaken.'

'That I be invested with full executive authority over global operations, in line with my position as Executive Chairman? Yes, it is.'

'Acting Executive Chairman, darling,' said Ailsa with a smile.

'I propose we vote.'

'Seconded,' said Lynton, at his side.

'All those in favour of awarding full executive powers to our current *Acting* Chairman, Maxwell Shannon, please raise your hands,' Lynton said, looking down both sides of the long boardroom table.

It was at this point the Shannon AGM normally split along partisan lines. Sure enough, those normally in Ailsa's camp remained resolutely unmoving.

'Motion failed,' said Lynton, making sure he had counted twice before making the decision. 'Two votes short of a majority.'

'Hang on.' Brady turned to face Ailsa. 'I'm sorry, Mrs Shannon. We can't go on the way we are. We need leadership and Maxwell's the only leader on offer right now.' He raised his hand to vote for the motion.

'You're still one vote short.' Nadia leaned forwards and looked at Maxwell. 'You can't do anything unless you have a majority,' she said with a nervous, if somewhat triumphant, smile.

'Ah, dear Nadia,' said Maxwell. 'But we aren't finished, are we?' He looked down towards Ailsa's end of the table.

Slowly, Bruce Shannon raised his hand.

33

Daley was reeling. He'd taken another hefty blow to the head, which had spiralled him into unconsciousness. This time, as he came round, he found his thoughts and memories even more difficult to grasp. The only thing that seemed to matter to him was the biting cold and he found himself struggling to breathe.

He had to use his experience, remember the lessons that so many years in the job had taught him. *As soon as you lose your heid, son, you've lost the lot.* The words of his first sergeant were like a salve. He had repeated them to himself many times over the years, but they were more important now than ever before. He had to fight the darkness in whichever form it presented itself.

'You're back with us, Mr Daley.' The voice was slow and quiet. 'It's hard seeing such a strong man brought down like this. But you're not the first and you won't be the last. Men like you have been falling for hundreds – thousands – of years.'

Daley was still struggling to control his breathing, to make sense of his circumstances, but something was telling him that to recognise this voice was important – that it could save him.

'You . . . you shouldn't do this. You don't have to,' he said, trying anything to strike up some kind of dialogue with his tormentor.

'Ah, but I do. I must admit, I didn't expect you to fly into my little trap. I'm pleased to see you though, really pleased. The stronger the heart, the greater the sacrifice.'

'What?'

'It's like giving, Mr Daley. The more you give, the greater will be your return in the afterlife. Is that not what you Christians believe?'

'Us Christians – what are you on about?' Inside his throbbing head, something told him he knew this person, he recognised those smooth tones. But he was so cold and broken, so confused.

'Tonight we take you to the stone.' The voice was near him, almost whispering into his ear. 'You will give us immortality as we send you to the void.'

Bruce didn't look at his mother or daughter as he rushed from the ballroom and down the long sweep of the stairwell. He had to get out and into the fresh air. He felt as though the ballroom was about to swallow him whole. He could feel the anger and hatred in the atmosphere. He had let them down, but how could they know the real reason for his actions?

He needed a smoke, he needed a drink.

Finally he was at the huge front door. It hadn't changed since he was a child. He'd been warned never to open it, never to go out alone, thoughts of his older brother never far away. His mother, father, Percy – every adult he could remember – warned of the danger of turning the big brass handle that he had to stand on tiptoes to reach. Even doing this now sent a pang of fear through his heart, the memory still strong. Through this door, his older brother had left Kersivay House, never to return. As he looked down at the handle, he felt as though he'd done the same thing: left his family, left his life.

Banishing these thoughts, he pulled it open and walked outside, fumbling for his cigarettes.

'I want you to get here as soon as you can, DS Scott. What's the latest with the road?' asked Superintendent Symington.

'They're having bother getting up the brae. Trying tae get some snowblower up tae move the stuff. It could be hours yet. Apparently it's drifted tae over twenty feet in some places, ma'am,' replied Scott, playing with an unlit cigarette he was desperate to smoke.

'Well, we have no air support, everything is snowbound in Glasgow. There's only one alternative . . .'

'It's OK, ma'am. Every time I'm here, it's only a matter of time until I'm on a boat. I'll see if I can get a hold o' Newell. It might be a terrifying experience, but it's fast, and we need tae find Jimmy – I mean DCI Daley, ma'am.'

'I'm worried, Brian,' she said, surprising Scott with her familiarity. 'We've had no contact with him or his party. I can't afford to lose anyone else from here. We're already well below the number of men the Chief Constable demanded we use to protect that Shannons. If I go looking for Daley in this snow, leaving a skeleton presence here at the house, I could be placing everyone at risk. Get here as quickly as you can, by any means possible, with as many men as they can spare in Kinloch. And make sure anyone who's permitted to carry a firearm does so.'

'Could they not just be stuck in the snow? DCI Daley, I mean, ma'am.'

'Anything is possible. But after what's happened here over the last few days, we can't take any chances. I'm not willing to risk the lives of my officers. Even if they are just lost in the snow, how long do you think they'll last? Do you expect them to build a bloody igloo or something? We have to search.'

'Yes, ma'am,' said Scott putting down the phone. Guns and boats, he thought, that's how I'll remember this place. Guns and boats.

He looked at his desk. The photograph of Nathaniel Stuart and the two young children sat amidst old paper clippings, sepia images and other detritus from the old casket of papers from the solicitors. He stared at the young boy's face but, try as he might, he couldn't make the connection. He picked the photograph up and thrust it into the inside pocket of his jacket. Beneath lay an old newspaper from the sixties. Another young face stared up at him, from a photograph taken decades later. This time Scott was ready. He grabbed onto the desk and closed his eyes. 'This is no' going tae happen again,' he said, as he heard the familiar whine in his ears and felt his chest contract. He held his breath then let it out slowly. 'Right, Jimmy, I'm on my way – don't know how, but I'm coming, mate.'

Bruce was fumbling in his pockets for his lighter when he heard the large front door creak open again.

'Well done, mate,' said More. 'You did what you had to do.'

'I'm not proud of it. I wish to fuck I'd never become involved with this nonsense. I can't believe I've helped give my cousin control of the company.'

'Listen, Bruce, you know the score. Stick to the plan and your cousin won't be smiling soon, trust me.'

At he flicked at his lighter, Bruce spotted something at the bottom of the steps, almost obscured by snow. He stepped down to examine what turned out to be a box covered with a thick layer of black duct tape. He picked it up and shook it, then turned it over. *Ailsa Shannon, c/o Kersivay House,* read a note covered in polythene and taped to the underside of the box.

'What's that?' asked More.

'Don't know. It's addressed to my mother,' said Bruce, still examining the parcel.

'Bloody hell. The way things are going here, it could be anything from a late Christmas present to a parcel bomb. I'd give it to your security boys to open, if I were you.'

'Good thinking,' said Bruce. 'Then they can give it to her. I'm certainly the last person she wants to see bearing gifts right now.'

Scott had managed to round up three other officers from the town. It left Kinloch woefully undermanned, but these were exceptional circumstances. They collected weapons and body armour and drove through the snow down Kinloch's Main Street to the pier, where Newell's RIB was normally berthed. Scott had tried to phone the retired sea captain, but got no reply. He cursed when he saw Newell's place at the pontoons empty.

Scott looked around; the pier, deep in snow, appeared deserted. He called Campbell's home number, deciding that he would have to ask the local lifeboat, of which Campbell was coxswain, to take him to Blaan. After all, the life of his colleague could very well be at stake.

'DS Brian Scott here from Kinloch Police,' he said, when a woman picked up the phone. 'Is Mr Campbell there?'

'Hello, Sergeant. No, I'm afraid my husband is off on a mercy mission. The hospital were running out of certain vital medicines and he's taken the lifeboat across to Ayr to get them. They left about an hour ago.'

Sure enough, when Scott looked across to the far pier he saw that the large orange-and-blue lifeboat was nowhere to be seen. 'Fuck, he's away, right enough . . . I mean, oh, you're quite right, Mrs Campbell,' he said, wincing at his oath.

He looked around; a few fishing boats were moored at the quayside, their tackle, rigging and superstructure covered in thick snow. There was not a soul to be seen.

'Sir, do you hear that?' asked McKinven, a young constable, standing stiffly in a flak jacket.

Scott cocked his head to the side. Sure enough there was singing and what sounded like a harmonica coming from further up the pier. He ended the call to Mrs Campbell. 'Come on, lads.'

They walked along the snowy quayside until Scott stopped and looked over the edge of the pier where the singing was loudest. The vessel was a fishing boat, but small and old-fashioned, made of wood, unlike the larger, more sturdy modern craft.

'I wish I was in Carrickfergus,' sang a rough chorus made up of three or four voices.

'You down there!' shouted Scott to the singers, who were out of sight somewhere aboard the small boat. 'It's the police. I need to talk to whoever's in charge.'

'You better get yourself oot there,' said a slurred voice that Scott recognised. Eventually after much coughing, swearing and stumbling, a man in an old flat cap poked his head out of the wheelhouse.

'Can I help yous?' the fisherman slurred.

'Aye, you can. I'm commandeering this boat, in the name of . . . in the name of Her Majesty,' said Scott, rather unsure under what authority he was about to take the vessel.

'Noo, you'll find that the law o' the sea and the law o' the land are two very different things. For instance, I can stand at the heid o' this pier and consume as much whisky as I can throw doon my throat, in broad daylight. The minute I step ontae the road, you boys have the right tae huckle me away up the brae tae the cells.'

'And your point is?'

'Jeest an illustration o' how you've nae powers tae order me tae gie you the time o' day, never mind command o' my boat.' The old fisherman crossed his arms, happy with his response.

'What about being drunk in charge o' a fishing vessel?' asked Scott, now even more unsure of himself.

'No such charge. The Royal Navy could maybe get me on that but no' a landlubber like yourself. If I was you I'd get up tae the Douglas Arms. When I was in there a wee while ago – jeest for one, you understand – there was a wile carry-on. Aye, fair brewing it was. Peter Mackintosh had jeest called Tommy Witherspoon a cheat at golf, so you can jeest imagine whoot was aboot tae kick off. Dae yourself a favour and nip it in the bud. If you don't mind, I've a date wae a nice bottle o' malt and some good friends o' mine.' He turned as if to head below, but stopped in his tracks at Scott's bellow.

'Don't move or I'll shoot!'

Constable McKinven sidled over to Scott, who was now wielding his pistol. 'Sergeant, I don't think that's in force standing orders.'

'I daresay, it's no'. But if you can tell me the right piece of legislation we need tae quote tae take this tub oot tae Blaan, then be my guest,' replied Scott, from the corner of his mouth.

'Eh, no, we never covered that at the police college.'

'Right, well, at gunpoint it'll have tae be then. Desperate times call for desperate measures. Superintendent Donald used tae say that all the time.'

'Look what happened to him.'

Another head appeared around the wheelhouse door. 'Noo, Dougie, Dougie Dougie,' said Hamish, looking none too steady on his feet. 'I've been fortunate tae have my ain vessel commandeered by the Constabulary and let me tell you, I made mair money oot it than a whole week at the fishing. Aye, a week o' proud shoals tae. If you ask me, you're looking a gift horse in the mouth if you turn this man doon.'

'Oh, you reckon?' said the fisherman.

'I do that. In any case, I know that bugger wae the gun well enough. He means whoot he says, he'll likely shoot you in a couple o' minutes if you don't bend tae his will.' He leaned towards the other man. 'Between you and me, he's fair nasty wae a drink and it looks as though he's carrying a cairtful, right now. Jeest smile and take him where he wants tae go. I've few enough friends left tae contemplate losing another.' He winked up at Scott.

The deal was done. The two other passengers clambered unsteadily up the ladder to make way for the police officers, who made their way, equally unsteadily, onto the small fishing boat.

'Get me tae Blaan and don't spare the horses,' said Scott, anxious to get underway.

'Sergeant,' said McKinven, tapping him on the shoulder. 'These old blokes are both drunk.'

'And?'

'Do you think they should be taking the boat out? We can't condone this.'

'Oh, shut up or I'll shoot you and a'.'

As the little vessel chugged out into the loch, Scott's phone rang.

'Yes, ma'am, I'm on my way.' He listened for a moment. 'Well, Mr Newell and the lifeboat were unavailable. We might be a wee bit longer than we thought.' Scott grimaced as the skipper staggered at the wheel.

34

The AGM was about to reconvene. When Bruce took his seat, he was surprised to be greeted by a pleasant smile from his mother, though his daughter Nadia looked sullen and resentful.

As others began to gather around the huge table, Ailsa spoke. 'Part of a boardroom coup, darling. I knew there was something afoot this year but I didn't think you were going to be part of it. Well done. You're normally as transparent as that window. I didn't think the little plan you mentioned the other day would involve siding with your cousin against me. Perhaps you are a Shannon, after all.'

Bruce was about to reply when a tall security guard walked up to his mother and handed her the parcel he had found on the front steps. Bruce noticed that the box hadn't been opened, so guessed that they had scanned it in some way to check for anything untoward. Rather than look at the contents of the package, his mother took it off the table and left it at her feet.

'I wonder what it is?' said Nadia.

'Oh, most probably some jam or a knitted jumper from one of the villagers. I always get a few things from the ladies of my own vintage. Fewer of us every year, of course,' said Ailsa, looking suddenly rueful.

Bruce was puzzled by how well his mother appeared to be taking Maxwell's victory. He was now solely in charge of everything, the outright boss of a massive organisation. It was something Ailsa had been trying to avoid for a long time. Bruce supposed that she had given up, tired of the constant battle against her nephew. She couldn't know that Maxwell's delight at his success was going to be temporary – very temporary.

'Hi,' he said, as the dark-haired girl walked past him to attend to his cousin. 'Remember me?'

She stopped and looked at him for a few moments. 'From where, exactly?' she said with a smile.

'The Churchill. You know, in Notting Hill Gate, the night before Hogmanay. Goodness, I must be getting old. Only had eyes for Trenton, I suppose.'

'I'm sorry,' she said, walking away. 'You must have me confused with someone else.'

Bruce thought for a moment. If there was one thing he could do, it was remember a pretty face; even more, it was remember a cute backside. Her blatant lie made him uneasy. He took the phone from his pocket and dialled Casely's number. Again, it went straight to voicemail.

He looked back at his mother. As the room came to order, she sat, smiling and seemingly unperturbed.

Bruce Shannon was confused.

There was no thought in Daley's head but the cold and pain in his knees and back. Being trussed up like this for hours was unbearable torture.

He couldn't think straight, couldn't work out whether this was caused by the blow to his head or if he'd been drugged.

He recalled setting out from Kersivay House, traipsing through the snow towards the glen, but then nothing made sense. He knew that there was something he couldn't get a hold of; a detail that remained out of reach. Intermittent moans from behind told him that he wasn't alone in this cold, harsh space; his colleagues were still with him.

Suddenly someone cried out, a cry of great pain, and Daley was gripped by rough, strong hands. His bonds were untied and he was dragged to his feet; the pain that shot up his legs and back almost made him pass out.

'Where are you taking me?' he asked. His throat was so dry that his words were barely audible. Thoughts of Colin Grant filled his head as a mug full of some stinking brown liquid was thrust in his face and his head was jerked back by the hair. Someone held his nose, his jaw was forced open and the musty, bitter drink was poured into his mouth. Though he coughed and spluttered, he couldn't resist the swallow reflex, gulping in air in between mouthfuls of the foul drink.

Suddenly, he felt weak, his body losing sensation from the legs up. He slumped into a pair of strong arms and was dragged out of the cave and onto the rocky shore beyond.

Daley was aware of the screech of gulls, the crunch of pebbles and then the rough springy grass of the machair under his feet. Before him was an old van coughing clouds of acrid fumes into the cold air. As his captors forced him into the back of the van, he tried to push back, to fight against them, but he was too weak and they pushed him inside easily.

Before long, the van pulled away and struggled up the path from the shore onto a narrow road, turning quickly onto a forestry track, where a thick canopy of branches sheltered the road from the worst of the snow. Up ahead, a copse of tall oak trees, their bare branches clothed in winter threads, were still beneath a pearlescent sky. A long, dark stone stood out against the white.

Scott shivered in the wheelhouse of the old fishing boat. He'd been forced to travel aboard a number of different craft since his first trip to Kinloch, but this seemed the slowest of all.

'Can you no' gie it a bit o' welly?' said Scott to the skipper, whom everyone seemed to know as Binder.

'How much fuckin' welly dae you think we've got? We'll get a good twelve knots oot o' her wae a fair wind. No' as much the day, whoot wae the metera . . . the metcorolig . . . wae the current weather conditions,' he replied, with a distinct slur.

'You'll no' beat Newell's RIB in a standing start, that's for sure, my man.'

'Och, RIBs. Aye, they'll go fast, nae bother. You jeest try riding oot a heavy sea on one o' them, then you'll know a' aboot it. You could sail tae America in this vessel wae a sound mind.'

'If you'd twenty years tae spare.'

Their conversation was interrupted by Constable McKinven poking his head through a hatch at the rear of the wheelhouse. 'Sergeant Scott, bit of an issue below.'

'What kind of issue?'

'Erm . . . there seems to be rather a lot of water coming in through the side of the boat. That kind of issue.'

Binder turned and faced the young policeman with a scowl. 'There's no' a vessel afloat that doesna take some water noo and again. Mind, this is a craft made fae the finest timber, the way boats are supposed tae be made. When it's cauld like this, the wood contracts and you'll always get a wee bit seepage. If you'd a brain in your heid you'd be getting a couple o' buckets and bailing oot fae time tae time.'

'The old boy down there is telling us we'll all end up in a cold watery grave.'

'Och, wid you listen tae it? The younger generation fair scunner me.'

'Constable Dow took his whisky off him. He was worried the old boy was getting the worse for wear.'

'Well, noo, there's your answer. Gie the man back his whisky and you'll restore his equilib . . . his equiri . . . his peace o' mind.'

'Do as he says, son,' said Scott. 'Hamish hasn't died a winter yet. And get a bucket and start getting rid o' some o' that water.' He eyed Binder. 'How long until we get tae Blaan?'

The old man squinted into the distance, then stood on tip toes, looking at the lie of the land through the grubby wheelhouse window. 'Dae you know, I'm no' right sure. Nothing looks right wae a' this snow lying aboot and that's a fact.'

35

Superintendent Symington stood with DC Dunn at the back of Kersivay House, looking along the glen to where Daley and his party had gone to investigate the encampment seen by Jock.

'We'll give DS Scott a few minutes and then we'll have to go ourselves,' said Symington. 'I'll leave Aitcheson in charge here.'

'Just you and I, ma'am?'

'Yes, that's all we can spare. I'm really worried about Daley, as no doubt you are, too. I've only been in command here for a few days, I'm not about to lose one of my senior officers – even if he's decided to quit the job.'

'He hasn't – I mean, I don't think he'll leave ma'am.'

Symington smiled and looked at the younger woman. There was no doubt she was beautiful, an openness in her innocent face. 'It was my job to encourage him to stay. I see you've succeeded where I failed.'

'I hope so. DCI Daley is too good a detective to be lost to the job, if you don't mind me saying, ma'am.'

'I need to know I can rely on you out there, Mary.'

'You can, ma'am. No question.'

There was something about the steely look in Dunn's eyes that left Symington in no doubt she meant it. 'No time like the present. Let's get kitted up. I'll call DS Scott before we leave.'

Ailsa cleared her throat and, unusually for a Shannon International board meeting, stood up to speak.

'Before we get this session underway, I would like to congratulate my nephew, Maxwell Shannon, on gaining control over this company. This is something that he has coveted, as we all know, for a very long time. It must be a great triumph to him that he has now succeeded.' This was greeted with mumbled expressions of congratulation, the muted nature of which spoke volumes as to the real mood of the room now that the reality of Maxwell's Shannon's victory had sunk in. It was clear that even some of those who had voted for him weren't entirely at peace with themselves. As for Maxwell, he was leaning back in his big leather chair, his hands behind his head, a large smile plastered across his face.

'Thank you, Aunt Ailsa. I know that we will be able to put these years of bickering behind us now that there is only one pair of hands on the tiller.' His expression was one of smug arrogance as he sneered down the table at the older woman.

'Indeed, Maxwell. If I had a glass of champagne, I would happily raise it in your direction. I think you're right. In fact, if I had been thinking properly, I would probably have voted for your accession myself.' She glanced at her son Bruce, who stared back in disbelief. 'I realise now that we need strong, united leadership, someone able to make quick decisions, like never before. Someone to accept the buck when it stops at his desk. Especially in the light of recent events,' she said, gesturing to the huge screen on the wall, which now flickered into life. 'We all know that the basis of the company's rise to its current eminence began when my husband gained a range of mineral rights in the sixties, across much of what was then communist Russia as well as their neighbours in China. It was an absolute coup and the foundation of all we've done since.'

'The gift that keeps on giving,' said Maxwell.

'Interesting that you use the present tense, Maxwell. May I draw your attention to this joint statement from the Russian Federation and the People's Republic of China. It's in your inbox now, my dear.'

Maxwell flung himself forwards in his chair, grabbing for his iPad. 'And when was this statement made, may I ask?'

'Oh, about an hour ago. Just about the time you were being anointed as king of the castle,' she said with a bright smile. 'The Chinese aren't really bothered about when we celebrate our New Year. Nor are the Russians, by the looks of things.'

Brady was also poring over his tablet, his face white. Bruce, who despite the dire circumstances was beginning to enjoy himself, studied the American carefully. Normally he had a laid-back attitude to proceedings; now, Bruce could see that his hands were shaking, an uneasy look spreading across his face.

'How long have you known about this, Ailsa?' said Brady, as Maxwell leaned back to talk once more to the dark-haired girl.

Ailsa watched her leave the room, then smiled broadly. 'Oh, Charles, my team monitor the situation in the east all the time. I suppose I've carried on where my dear husband left off. As you can see, in one fell swoop they have rescinded our rights across both nations.'

'We're fucking ruined,' whispered Maxwell, his hand cupped in front of his mouth.

Daley was lying on his back on the cold floor of the van. His feet and hands were tied but he couldn't have moved anyway, such was the effect of the drug he'd been given.

He saw his tiny son, his face so real that he almost called out to him. He saw a ruined figure lying in a filthy stairwell in a pool of dark blood; he saw Brian Scott falling as gunshots ripped through his body, dashing red blood onto the white sand. He felt Mary's mouth working hard as he cradled her head in his hands – but when she looked up, he saw only hatred in the slanted cornflower-blue eyes of his wife, Liz. He watched a woman with a grey flecks through her dark hair as she placed coals on a fire, bending down over the low grate. Then he saw her again, her hair much greyer, as she cried for the gaunt man in the hospital bed, wired up to a company of machines that flashed, bleeped and wailed as his life drained away. He heard himself shout, but the vision had already melted away.

He saw a line of white crosses, in rank and file, march up the prow of a hill. The wind whipped his face as he walked past each one; name after name, etched in cold, white stone.

The hill was steep and he tired as he reached the top. Old gnarled hands twisted up from the dark earth, writhing and grasping at a small child, wide-eyed in their midst. As a root wrapped itself around his leg, the boy screamed. He was slowly dragged backwards to a black stone, its darkness blending into the shadows around it. A figure dressed in white rose slowly from the stone. The woman was beautiful and in her hand she carried a bright blade, which flashed in an unseen light.

The little boy struggled in vain, the long roots gripping him tighter as he was offered up to the woman. She leaned forwards and sliced at the boy's back, a slather of dark crimson blood splattering up her robe and onto her face.

Before she slashed again, she paused, staring straight into Dalcy's face.

'You! Stop!' he shouted.

And then he was back, trussed up in the back of the dirty van. Now though, he'd remembered. He knew who his tormentor was.

'Where dae you want tae berth, officer?' asked Binder as they rounded a long jut of land. 'There's an auld jetty in the lea o' the castle rock. If we have enough water under the keel I'll set you doon there.'

'What's the alternative?' asked Scott.

'If I canna get in tae the wee castle jetty, it's going tae be a long wade through the surf.'

'In this cold? Just you get us doon at the place you're talking aboot and maybe I can forget the long list o' crimes and misdemeanours you've committed on the way here.'

Ignoring this, the skipper raised his binoculars to his eyes and stared into the distance. 'That's it there,' he said, pointing to a line of boulders jutting out into the bay that, to Scott at least, looked as though they'd been dumped there rather than placed to form part of any meaningful construction.

'And how are we going tae get off this tub and ontae the quay?'

Binder looked at him with a flat expression. 'Yous'll need tae jump.'

'Not this again,' said Scott, remembering the last time he'd had to jump off a boat.

At his back, Hamish appeared. 'Well, it's a while since I last landed at the auld castle pier, Binder, and that's a fact.'

'Well, I hope you remember how tae get off the boat,' said Scott.

'Ach, yes. Easy as downing a wee sensation,' replied Hamish. 'You've got tae remember that time's course and the sea have eroded a good part o' the structure. Bits of the thing are noo broken off and oor friend here canna get as close as he'd like.'

'Great news.'

'It just means a wee jump. Don't worry, I'll keep you right.'

'And how long is it since you last flung yourself intae mid-air, Hamish?'

'No' long ago at all. Seems like yesterday, in fact. By my reckoning it was when I was crewing for auld Colly Morrans. Bastard of a skipper he was, tae. Never had such poor rations aboard a boat. Is that no' right, Binder?'

'Aye, Hamish. Auld bugger, he was.'

'And what year was that?' asked Scott. 'Or is it a state secret?'

'I'm thinking nineteen fifty-seven,' said Hamish. 'But it might have been fifty-eight. I've been wrong once before but I don't often speak aboot it.'

'Brilliant. It'll be right fresh in your mind then,' said Scott, watching as the soft swell broke against the dilapidated jetty ahead.

Symington and Dunn waded through the deep snow. Both were dressed in thick ski jackets, waterproof trousers and boots, but the cold still made their bones ache.

Symington looked back the way they had come. 'There's been another fall, but I would say these are definitely what's left of their footprints from earlier.' She pointed to marks in the snow that led up past their current position and further up the hill.

'Yes, ma'am,' replied DC Dunn. 'This is certainly where they looked to be at on the map.'

'Good. I'll try DS Scott again. There should be a path that leads away from those trees, back into the village,' she said, pointing ahead. 'He can take the other end and search for Daley from that direction.'

'Good thinking, ma'am.'

'Thank the North Yorkshire Girl Guides, not me.' She noted the expression of Dunn's face. 'Where I come from, the guides was just about the only thing to do.'

Before they plodded on, Symington called Scott. 'They're here,' she said, pointing at a distant boat below the loom of the promontory. 'DS Scott says that once they disembark he'll get his bearings and hit this from the other end. Funny, he doesn't sound like his cheery self.'

'Ma'am, look,' said Dunn, pointing up the snowy rise. A figure, muffled in thick winter clothes and a balaclava, was striding down through the snow towards them.

'That's not Daley, is it?' asked Symington.

'Hello, ladies,' boomed the familiar voice of Jock Munro. 'Bit later on the go today, it's all that whisky I've been enjoying recently. Still, I made it up through the drifts.'

'We're looking for DCI Daley and two other officers, Mr Munro,' said Symington. 'I don't suppose you've seen anything?'

'It's funny that you say that,' he said, taking off the balaclava, his grey hair sticking up in clumps. 'There are footprints, half covered by the most recent snowfall, but there all the same. A few folk by the looks of things, plus they've cleared the old forestry track that leads back down the other side of the hill. Some kind of vehicle has been there – within the last few hours I would say.'

Symington looked along the wooded ridge, concern etched on her face. 'Where does this track lead, Mr Munro?'

'Down to the outskirts of the village. As you can see, the Forestry Commission have been busy over the last thirty years around here. They have tracks and paths all over the hillsides. Great scars on the landscape, if you ask me, to say nothing of these close ranks of fir trees that blot out the sun, meaning nothing can live in amongst them. When folk see trees they think . . .'

'I'm sure the environmental issues you raise are valid,' interrupted Symington. 'But I have to find my men. Can you help us, Jock?'

'Yes, yes, of course. Stupid of me to keep blethering on. If we go back down the hill again, we can cut up a farm lane and join the forestry track about half a mile that way,' he said, pointing further along the ridge. 'That vehicle will certainly have left its mark, so it should be quite easy to follow.'

'Good, we'd better make a start. DS Scott is coming from the other end. Maybe you can help me with directions for him?'

'Not a problem – though we better get a move on. It'll start to get dark shortly.'

Symington looked at Mary and sighed. It was only mid afternoon but of course, this was Scotland. She hadn't thought of that.

36

Scott watched Hamish as he threw himself off the fishing boat and across three feet of water to the rabble of boulders that comprised the ancient jetty. He landed squarely on two feet, bending his knees to soften the impact. Not bad for a drunk man in his seventies, Scott thought.

The three constables he'd brought from Kinloch now stood behind Hamish, all gathered on the jetty, waiting for the detective, the last of their number, to jump off the boat.

Admittedly, their skipper had done a better job than Scott had thought possible in getting them close to the pier. Still, there was something about the gap between boat and hard stone that made him flinch. He thought of his friend and gathered his courage. If an old man like Hamish could do this, then so could he.

'C'mon now, sergeant, let's be having you,' Binder said, trying to galvanise the policeman into action. 'A wee child could get o'er that gap. And if you don't mind, I'd like tae get back to Kinloch before dark. Up and at 'em man.'

'Aye, all right, hold your horses,' said Scott, as he stepped over the side of the fishing boat. 'We're no' all born tae this kind o' stuff, you know.'

'Och, it's like a millpond. You couldna wish for better conditions tae land here. Jeest step o'er wae a wee bit gusto and you'll be safe as hooses.'

Sure enough, the sea was so calm it hardly felt as though they were afloat at all. The swell was gentle and the vessel rose and fell very little at its temporary mooring.

'Right, here goes,' said Scott, taking a deep breath and bending his knees. As he did so, though, he heard a distant whine. His chest tightened and he felt unsteady, perched on the edge of the vessel.

'Get a move on, man,' shouted Hamish, holding out his hand towards Scott.

No, not now, not now, he thought, as the whine grew louder. He was beginning to breathe more heavily, but he'd managed to stop the visions before and he was determined to do so now. He knew he had to help find his friend. He closed his eyes and gritted his teeth, grabbing onto the rail until his knuckles went white. Sure enough, the noise began to subside and he felt his breathing return to normal.

'Come on, Sergeant,' shouted one of the cops, trying to encourage him. Scott held up his hand to indicate he'd heard then looked up from the gap onto the jetty, ready to make the jump. He caught his breath when he saw someone strolling down the quay towards his colleagues and Hamish.

'Look,' he said, pointing beyond the small group. 'Who's that?'

Everything seemed to slow down; the noise of the water lapping against the side of the boat, the rush of the breeze and the sound of seabirds disappeared. There, standing with his arms folded, a broad, mocking smile on his face, stood a man Scott had known for almost thirty years.

'Come on, Sergeant Scott,' he said. 'Make the bloody jump. What's the worst that can happen – end up dead, like me?'

Scott's world went black to the sound of John Donald's mocking laugh echoing around the small bay. The laugh of a man who had been dead for months.

The Shannon International AGM at Kersivay House had descended into chaos with the revelation that huge mineral contracts in China and Russia, the very foundation of the company, had been lost. Some of the board members were arguing amongst themselves; others looked deep in thought, no doubt trying to calculate the impact this would have on their lives. A few looked around the room, pale and confused, trying to make sense of it all.

Maxwell was furious. He glared at his aunt at the other end of the table. The reality of his position began to dawn on him: he was now fully responsible for an organisation that was being challenged on all fronts – challenges that could well bring the whole company down.

He pushed himself up from his chair and strode the length of the long boardroom table, Ailsa watching his progress with a faint smile.

'You old bitch!' he shouted, pushing his niece out of the way and banging his hand on the table. 'You've brought us to our knees, just because you knew you were going to lose.'

'How can you possibly think that decisions made in Beijing and Moscow have anything to do with me?'

'But you knew about it. If you'd told me, I could have done something about it, not just sit back and watch as it all went tits up.'

‘By greasing a few palms, Maxie? Or perhaps something more creative?’

‘What do you mean?’

‘Oh, I don’t know . . . How about a portfolio of blue chip companies around the world that don’t show up on any of our accounts but whom we own and run by proxy?’

Maxwell’s face lost all of its colour. ‘What the fuck are you on about now?’

Ailsa continued as though she hadn’t heard him. ‘Just imagine that one, or maybe more, of these companies got into trouble. We could lose millions every hour in markets all around the world – billions, even. I wouldn’t like to be the man in charge when that little secret comes out. The buck stops here – or in this case, with you, I think I’m right in saying? I certainly have no knowledge of these dealings. Something I can prove quite conclusively.’

Maxwell leaned forwards on the table with both arms outstretched, his head bowed, like a boxer on the ropes.

Without warning, he lunged across the table, sending laptops, tablets, papers, cups of coffee and bottles of water flying. He grabbed Ailsa by the arm and pulled her forwards in her chair, making her cry out in pain. ‘You fucking old bitch! I could go to prison for this shit.’ His face was bright red, in contrast with his flaxen hair, which flopped over a forehead displaying a bulging vein.

‘You’re hurting her, let her go!’ said Nadia, battering Maxwell’s arm with her fists.

Bruce rushed round to the back of his mother’s chair and made a dive at his cousin. But before his fist made contact with Maxwell’s face, the new chairman of Shannon International arched his back in agony as he received a sharp punch in the kidneys from Brady, standing behind him.

'That's enough, you little prick,' shouted Brady as Maxwell sank to his knees, clutching his back. 'You – we've – played the game and lost. Do you think attacking an old woman will make this all go away?'

Bruce leaned over his stricken cousin. 'I'll give you thirty seconds to leave this room or I swear I'll pick you up off this floor and throw you off that fucking balcony.'

Slowly, Maxwell got to his feet, still reeling at the pain in his back. He looked at them one by one. 'This isn't over,' he said quietly, then walked out of the ballroom.

Scott was being helped up from the cold stone of the jetty, the young cops he'd brought with him from Kinloch staring at him with a mixture of concern and surprise.

'Sorry, lads. You know how it is – taking a trip on the sea makes me fair dizzy.'

'This happened when we were stuck at the brae with the Shannons, too,' said the young constable. 'I was driving, I found you in the snow. You weren't talking sense, just like now. What's wrong with you, Sergeant Scott?'

'Och, but you know fine what's up wae the sergeant,' said Hamish. 'I canna blame him, neither. How would you dae if you'd been shot in the line o' duty and near died? Aye, and then near got burned tae death on a bonfire. Can you no' make sense o' whoot effect that has on a man? Doesna make him a bad person, or a bad polisman, come tae that.'

'Aye, just a turn,' said Scott. 'There's nothing tae be worried aboot. Besides, it's no' me we should be fretting over – we've got tae find the Chief Inspector and the rest o' the boys. We'll get off this bloody jetty and give Symington a phone. I'll be fine.'

Scott watched the three policemen make their way down the jetty and turned to the older man. 'Thanks for that, Hamish. I'm obliged tae you, man.'

'Fine if I wisna lying through my teeth, Brian. Did you know whoot you were shouting oot?'

'No, I kind o' blacked oot, sorry.'

'You were shouting tae John Donald tae leave you alone. I've had a few drams mysel' today, Brian, but I'm no' seeing the deid come back tae life.'

Scott shook his head. 'I don't want you tae tell anyone aboot this, OK?'

'No, you have my word on that. But, I tell you, I've seen plenty o' folk wae the heebie jeebies. Fuck me, Kinloch's full o' them. I used tae work wae an auld fisherman that widna go tae the wee toilet in the boat because he thought there was a monster living in the pan. Used tae shite o'er the side o' the boat – in a' weathers, tae.'

'And what are you saying?'

'You've got a worse case o' it than him.'

'Oh, thanks for that, buddy.'

'I'll have your back, until we can find Jim Daley. But you've got tae get help.'

Scott watched the old man walk up the uneven pile of rocks that comprised the old quay. He knew Hamish was right, but first he had to find his friend. He shivered as he looked around the bay. The big house stood on the high cliff in the distance, dark and unyielding in the white landscape. Something about it made him think of the stone. He remembered the vision he'd had of Jim Daley being trodden into the dirt as his back was slashed by the man in black; he thought of little Archie Shannon with his dark hair and pleading eyes; the rugged face of Nathaniel Stuart, standing on the pier with the young children. It was as though the past, present and future, things that had happened and others that never would, had coalesced in his mind.

He pulled the phone from his pocket and dialled Symington's number. 'Ma'am, we've just landed. Have you managed to come up with anything?' He listened, his heart sinking when the answer came back in the negative. 'I have an idea, just a notion, ma'am. I'm going tae this Rat Stone.' He didn't wait for her reply.

He'd listened to Jim Daley for years, banging on about his gut feelings and his instinct. To save his friend's life, Scott was going to take a leaf from Daley's book.

As Daley shivered, the pain in his head got worse. He clenched his teeth in an effort to banish the throbbing from his skull, so acute that he could see it pulsing in his vision.

Mercifully, the narcotic effect of whatever he'd been forced to drink was starting to fade. He was still trussed up in the back of the freezing van and, by the look of the light coming through the filthy back window, it was already getting dark.

He held his breath and tried to listen for anything that could give him an idea of where he was, or at least if he was alone or not. He could hear a scraping noise, low and slow, like steel on steel. It took him back to when his father used to sharpen the big carving knife for the Sunday roast.

Someone was sharpening a blade. *The greater the sacrifice, the greater the reward*. His captor's words echoed in his head.

He heard footsteps and the back doors of the van were thrown open by two figures dressed entirely in black. He was pulled out of the vehicle by his legs. Again, his head battered off the cold metal floor and he cried out in pain.

He landed heavily on the ground, the impact and the shock of the cold snow winding him. He struggled to control his breathing.

'Why are you doing this to me?' he said breathlessly. 'You of all people.'

He heard the snow crumple underfoot as his tormentor walked towards him.

'You need help. You and whoever is aiding you in this need help.'

There was no reply.

'I remember now. I know who you are.'

37

More looked through almost every stitch of his wife's clothes. Finding nothing to help him, he moved onto her make-up case, handbag and personal files containing her passport, birth certificate, qualifications and driving licence. He found nothing.

There was no sign that she was anyone other than the woman he had met five years before at a retreat on the island of Iona, the nun who had been so abused by her fellow sisters that she had given up her calling and looked for another life. The tall, dark-haired beauty who had made him remember that he was flesh and blood, that his life wasn't all about his parish and the scores he had to settle.

He had been flattered by her attentions. He'd always kept himself trim and fit, but he couldn't keep age at bay; the greying hair, fading eyesight, the lines on his forehead and shadows under his eyes, the aches and pains he felt merely getting out of bed in the morning. He was getting old and he was pleased that someone still in possession of her youth and vitality could possibly wish to spend the rest of her life with him.

But, like him, she appeared to have a secret.

He remembered finding her in the dark church, wrapped in that cloak, and shivered. He thought back to their first few days together: the passion with which she made love; the way she liked to hurt him, the mixture of pain and pleasure bringing him to a climax like he had never experienced before.

He had seen her as a damaged woman – broken, just as he had been. He thought he could make her well, bring her back to life.

Exhausted, he sat on the old Chesterfield sofa and stared into the flames of the roaring fire. Suddenly he felt the pain of being small and alone, the pain of being taken away from a life he had barely known. He had spent so long trying to remember, lying under the stars in the Northern Territory, grabbing onto any little detail that brought him back to who he really was. The grey skies, the warm house, his mother's eyes.

His adoptive father always punished him in the same room. Punish wasn't even the right word, for usually he had done nothing to merit the beatings he was forced to endure. It was as though the rough man, stinking of alcohol and sheep shit, flayed him with the old leather belt just because he liked it. He could feel the pain anew, the agony each time the belt made contact with his back, opening old wounds and making new ones. All the time he was forced to lean on the old bureau, his hands grasping the dark wood, desperately trying not to cry, knowing that if he did the beating would only gain intensity.

He remembered the little brass plaque on the old piece of furniture: *Property of Shannon Agricultural (Australia) Ltd.*

Like many other children, he'd been taken thousands of miles from the orphanage to be a slave on the other side of the world, all in the name of charity and good deeds.

His phone rang. 'Yes, mate,' he said, looking up at the old clock on the wall. 'What's Plan B?' He listened for a while, then ended the call.

Yes, he wanted revenge – but at any price? The hatred of a faceless organisation was one thing, the death of an old woman something else entirely. He had to think.

And where – and who – was his wife?

Daley squirmed as she pushed her face into his. Someone unseen was holding him down as the woman straddled him. A fire blazed, sending sparks into the darkness. He was naked from the waist up and the cold stone made his back ache. He'd been forced to drink something else and this time, instead of being rendered unconscious, he felt only a strange calm, as though the man pinioned to the dark artefact was someone else.

'Jim Daley.' Veronica was silhouetted by the fire that crackled behind her. 'The greater the sacrifice, the greater the reward.'

Her hair covered his face as she slid her fingernails down his neck and onto his chest. She arched her back and screamed, 'You will give me your last!'

He was aware of voices, people crowding round; they began to chant. Veronica appeared to be in a trance. She swung her head back, staring up into the black sky with her arms outstretched.

Bruce leaned forwards, his head in his hands, in his mother's room in Kersivay House. 'I had to do something – the plan was simple. Why wasn't I kept up to speed about the Chinese and the Russians?'

'You could have told me what you were doing,' replied Ailsa. She was speaking to her son but her attention was focused on her granddaughter Nadia, who was gazing out of the huge window into the darkness. The electricity was still down and the back-up generators supplied power only to certain parts of the large mansion, so Ailsa's room was lit by dim, battery-powered LED bulbs, installed in the house as a failsafe.

'What did you think you would achieve, Bruce?'

'The plan was simple, Mother. Let Maxwell gain control of the company then leave him holding the baby when something nasty was uncovered. He wouldn't be the first businessman to go down, would he? We'd get rid of the bastard then carry on as my father wanted.'

'As your father wanted – how wonderful.'

'That's what you've always worked for, isn't it?'

'How would you know what I want, Bruce? You and I haven't been close since before you went to Cambridge.' She ran her hand along the parcel that she'd been given in the ballroom. 'I wonder what this is.'

'Never mind the bloody present. How much do you know about all of this?'

'Darling, I've known for two years that Maxwell and his cohorts had set up these shadow companies. He made the same mistake as you.'

'Which is?'

'Thinking I'm a sad old woman, living in the past, trying to keep the spirit of your *wonderful* father and my lost son alive.'

'What do you mean by that?'

'You and your father are so similar. The same love of the *good* things in life: the wine, the women, the music, even the drugs.'

'Only he was a success and I'm a nothing. Is that what you mean?'

'I know you are aware of your own shortcomings, darling. But your father was no better. He found his inspiration at the bottom of a glass, a white line on the table, or between the thighs of his latest tart.'

'Come on, Mum. You can't take away what he did for this company – you mentioned it yourself at the meeting.'

'Don't be so bloody stupid,' said Alisa, a flash of anger in her voice. 'Do you really think your washed-up father made all those mineral deals, all the banking and oil agreements? This company was heading for ruin until I took control.'

'What?' Bruce was incredulous.

'Can you imagine? Your poor mother running this great business edifice. A mere woman. Impossible, isn't it? Especially when you consider that I'm not even one of your precious Shannons.'

'What are you saying? I don't understand.'

'Again you fail to grasp the obvious. Until your stupid uncle descended into dementia, I was the one running this company.'

'What, even before my father died?'

'Of course. It was our little understanding. He could stuff lines of coke up his nose and whore about as much as he wanted, as long as he left everything important to me.'

'And you just carried on when my uncle took over? I'm sorry, that's even harder to believe.'

'Oh, it took him a few weeks to grasp the reality of things. But, to his credit, he soon came around when he realised that the famous company constitution left behind by Archibald Shannon meant bugger all. Power is power – and the power to reward is the greatest of all. Remember, dear, I have an excellent degree from Oxford, not the miserable third-class efforts you and Maxie managed to attain.'

'At least I wasn't trying – at university, I mean. Maxie worked his arse off.'

'I would remember that, if I were you. What a fitting epitaph for your time on this planet. *At least I wasn't trying.*'

Bruce watched in disbelief as his mother calmly went about opening the parcel that had been left on the steps of Kersivay House earlier in the day. Everything he had been so certain of had suddenly changed. He had always thought of his father as a flawed genius, the man who had turned Shannon International into a truly global company. To discover that his mother was behind it all was bizarre. But rather than stoking any great feelings of pride in his mother's achievements, it kindled a new empathy for his father, who had no doubt been just as crushed and browbeaten as he.

He flinched as his mother stood up, sending the contents of the parcel spilling onto the floor. She looked down, hand to her mouth, all the composure she had shown that day entirely gone.

'What the hell is the matter?' asked Bruce, bending down to pick up the object that had rolled to the floor. It was old fashioned, with a crepe sole. The tan leather was cracked and shrivelled with age, but it was still easily identifiable as a child's right shoe.

It was only when his mother remained silent that significance of what he was holding dawned on him, and he dropped the tiny item of footwear to the floor as though it was red hot.

*

Daley's breathing was growing heavier. Veronica was swaying above him, her hair brushing his bare chest. He tried to think through the haze of the drugs, but lost his way in the flickering flames and the heat of her flesh.

'Why?' he managed to say.

'The end for you and all those who aid the Shannons.'

She looked down at him, green eyes blazing in her face, red lips parted. 'In this way, we create new power – a power that will save our planet, not destroy it. Now!'

Something was placed around Daley's neck and roughly tightened. As he struggled for breath she leaned over him, her face nearly touching his.

As Jim Daley choked, she placed her lips on his, drawing the last breath from his body.

38

'This way,' said Hamish as they struggled through another drift. It was completely dark now, the winter afternoon fading quickly under the snow-laden sky.

'How do you know so much about Blaan?' asked DS Scott, trudging at the back of the little group.

'Och, as I said to you before, my mother used tae work at the big hoose. And in them days, before a' this jetting off tae Spain and the like, folk used tae take holidays nearer home. Much better if you ask me. We used tae jump ontae the bus tae Blaan wae oor buckets and spades. My faither had an auld army tent we stayed in on the shore. Limpets for tea and jeest blue sky and sea, that's what he used tae say.'

'Idyllic stuff, Hamish. You're right, the old days were the best, nae doubt about it.'

'Well, the limpets wirna too clever, but you're right apart fae that.'

'Sergeant, what's that noise?' shouted a cop up ahead.

The little group stopped and Scott listened carefully. Sure enough, from somewhere up ahead came a low chant. Scott flashed his torch at the young policeman. 'I can hear folk humming, like monks or something. Is that what you heard?'

'Yes, Sergeant. And I thought I heard someone cry out before that.'

'That's the Rat Stone,' said Hamish with a shiver. 'It's jeest o'er that hill.'

'Right, come on. We need tae be quick,' said Scott.

'Yous'll no' mind too much if I jeest stay here,' said Hamish. 'I heard too much aboot that place when I was a boy tae want tae go rushing up there in the dark.'

The policemen left the old fisherman behind as they struggled up the slope, heading for the Rat Stone.

Daley's vision was beginning to fade. He could only manage to draw in tiny breaths with a high-pitched whine in his throat, so tight was the belt he had around his neck.

Just as he was about to be enveloped by darkness, he heard shouting. The pressure around his neck slackened and he managed to suck in just enough breath to stay conscious.

He heard her scream as a hooded figure tried to pull her off him. 'Leave me, we haven't finished!'

In the light of the fire, a blade flashed red. Daley moved his head to one side as it crashed down. There was a flurry of sparks as steel hit stone, only nicking his left ear.

Veronica squirmed free of the hands trying to drag her away and wrenched hard on the belt around Daley's neck. The shadowy figures were melting into the darkness beyond the fire as she pulled herself up on her knees, the long blade gripped between both hands and held high above her head.

'Now you give your life!' She threw her arms forwards, ready to plunge the knife into Daley's chest.

The faces of his son, of Liz, his mother and father flashed

before his eyes. He felt the warmth of a kiss on his cheek, saw her smile as her face vanished into the blackness.

'Mary,' he whispered, waiting for the pain to hit.

There was a loud crack. Astonished, Veronica looked down at the huge hole that had appeared in her chest, then fell backwards, the blade slipping from her hands and onto the stone.

'Jim – Jim!' Scott rushed to his friend's side, ignoring the woman he had just shot. He placed his fingers on Daley's neck – there was no pulse. Without another thought he began CPR on Daley, alternatively pumping his chest, then trying to re-inflate his lungs. 'Come on, Jimmy, come on, man!' he shouted, massaging Daley's heart. Peering at his friend's face in the firelight, he could see nothing behind his blank stare.

A large security guard placed the tiny shoe into a plastic bag. 'This will have to go to the cops. I'll give it to that superintendent when she gets back. I'd better gather the packaging, too. Has anyone touched anything apart from you, Mrs Shannon?'

'I did. I handled the shoe,' said Bruce. He looked at his mother, sobbing in her high-backed leather chair, Nadia comforting her. 'Mum, don't fret. It's just another sick wind-up, like the bones on the stone.'

She looked up at him. 'No, no, it isn't. It's his shoe.'

'Oh, come on, you can't be certain.'

'Go into the top drawer of that old chest,' she said, pointing to the corner of the room.

Bruce slid the drawer open to find a small box. He lifted it out and handed it to his mother. 'Is this what you wanted?'

'Yes,' she replied, laying it on her lap. With shaking hands, she lifted the lid from the box and angled it towards her son. 'You see, there can be no doubt.'

Bruce stared at the tiny shoe. It was in better condition than the one she had been sent, but there was no doubt they were a pair.

'It was all I had left of him for so long.'

'I'm sorry, I really don't understand why this is all happening.'

Nadia walked back to the window. It had started to snow again; huge, pale flakes drifted in the darkness. 'They're coming for us,' she said quietly.

'Darling, please, this is not the time for one of your little flights of fancy,' said Bruce.

'They are!'

'I'm sorry, Mum. I know this is the last thing you need right now.'

'She's right, Bruce. They are coming.'

Bruce looked at his mother's face; there was something about her expression he didn't understand. As in the boardroom when Maxwell had seemingly won the day, her face was inscrutable.

'What – who – what the bloody hell are you all on about?' He turned quickly at the sound of the door being opened. There, in the flickering gas light, stood Percy, a large bruise on his face.

Just as Scott was beginning to tire, utter despair in his heart at the thought of losing his best friend, Daley turned his head and started to cough. 'Brian, please, get this off my neck.'

'It's no' on your neck, Jim. We took it off. Just try and breathe, my friend.'

Scott pulled off his jacket as the two of the cops cut away Daley's bonds with the knife that, only moments ago, had been about to take his life – a human sacrifice to a cult, a power, that he knew nothing about.

Now that Daley was out of danger, Scott walked around to where Veronica was lying. Her breath was laboured, bubbles of blood forming at the corner of her mouth and trickling down her chin. He leaned down to cover her with another jacket, thinking he could at least keep her warm, when she caught his arm.

Her eyes were focused, blazing with hate and fury. 'Tonight they die. Tonight it's over,' she whispered, her long nails digging into Scott's arm.

'Who dies?'

'The Shannons, all of them . . .' The words caught in her throat and her grip eased. She slumped backwards, her head resting on the black Rat Stone.

'Jim, she's gone.' He turned to Daley, who was trying to sit up, swathed in a large ski jacket and rubbing at his neck. 'You OK, bud? I'll no' lie, I thought you were a gonner, there.'

'I'm OK. Well, at least I will be,' he said, his voice a croak.

'Maist minister's wives arrange the flowers and take the Sunday school,' Scott observed. 'Clearly no' this one.'

'Where are the rest of them?'

'Ran off when they saw us coming, Jim. They must have seen the beams of oor torches as we were coming through the trees.' He looked at his friend, who was shivering and wheezing. 'That was a close one.'

'It's not over, Brian. We have to get back to Kersivay House. I was just the starter. The main meal is still to come.'

*

'Percy! What's happened to you?' cried Ailsa, looking at the old man's face.

'I was kidnapped.'

'Kidnapped, what on earth do you mean?'

'Something's going on here – something big. Your nephew Maxwell is involved, but he's scared, I'll tell you that. They thought I was unconscious but I heard everything. Somebody is trying to take over the company, I'm telling you!'

Ailsa tried to calm the old man down as he ranted on about checking the outbuildings, then being taken prisoner in his own cottage.

'Big Irish boy, a bruiser. I've seen the day when I could have tackled him. Not now, too bloody old. They took one of those useless cops prisoner, too. To keep the rest of them busy looking for him – eyes off the ball. I'm telling you, something's not right.'

'How did you escape?' asked Bruce, wondering if the old man's situation had been something to do with the plan he was involved in.

'They just took off. The big chap got a call and off they went – not a bloody word.'

'Where is Maxwell now?' asked Ailsa, once again composed in front of the old retainer.

'Oh, I don't know. Has the world gone mad? The things I've been through with this family.' He stared at Ailsa, his face suddenly calm. 'Is this it – the end of all this shit?'

'What on earth are you on about?' said Bruce. He looked at his mother, who looked only at the huge snowflakes on the black window, her face a mask.

39

The police officers warmed themselves in front of a roaring fire in Jock Munro's tidy cottage. Scott's men had found the policemen who had been taken with Daley lying drugged in an old van near the Rat Stone. They were being taken care of in the Black Wherry by the local district nurse.

Jock looked around the room. Superintendent Symington was checking her phone and DC Dunn was in the corner with Daley; the huge welt around his neck where he had been strangled was clearly visible. Three younger constables, nursing cups of tea, talked quietly amongst themselves, still bemused by finding their boss about to become a ritual sacrifice and two other colleagues trussed up in an old van. DS Scott was sitting beside Hamish on the old couch, trying not to look envious as the old man sipped at a large dram of whisky.

'Right,' said Symington. 'It would appear that we are now alone. Phone, internet, power – everything is down.' She looked around the room, arms crossed. 'The snow is heavy again, so we must assume that the road to Kinloch is still blocked and the cavalry are not about to come charging over the hill. We must also assume, given what happened to DCI Daley and the threat made by Veronica as she drew her last, that we are facing a formidable foe, intent on doing real harm to the Shannon family. Suggestions, people.'

'I could fair go another dram,' said Hamish, holding his glass out. 'If yous don't mind, I'd rather sit oot this battle wae evil here on Jock's couch wae a fine bottle o' malt. I'm only here as a guide and I think my guiding duties have come tae their natural conclusion.'

'Our advantage is that we now have the element of surprise,' said Daley, his voice a harsh rasp. 'We know where they're going, but they can't know where we are.'

'Och, in this place, Jim – sir,' said Scott, suddenly remembering protocol in front of Symington. 'There'll be eyes everywhere. And in this snow, if we're going tae get back up tae that nightmare hoose, we'd better make it snappy. At least we're armed.'

'Aitcheson is at the house with three colleagues and the Shannon security team. How many of them are there, DC Dunn?'

'Six, ma'am. Though can they be relied on if things get really nasty?'

'Good point. What do you think, Jock?'

The big man was standing with his back to the fire, a mug of steaming tea in his large hand. 'Anyone employed by the Shannons will be top notch. They normally use ex-military as bodyguards. The question is, who can you trust? These are strange days as far as Kersivay House is concerned.'

'Do you think it's this hundred-year curse thing that's brought all this on, big man?' asked Scott.

'It sounds ridiculous, but I do, what with the anniversary and those bones turning up. I've never heard so much talk about Nathaniel Stuart and the history of the village since the wee boy went missing all those years ago. Would you say that it's just coincidence, Superintendent?'

'No,' said Symington. 'As far-fetched as it all seems, I think we're dealing with some kind of cult that means to do the family real harm. We've seen what they can do.' She nodded at Daley. 'These people are organised, significant in number and purposeful. A bloodbath in that mansion house is the last bloody thing I, or any of us, want.'

'We'd better get up there, I suppose,' said Scott, eyeing Hamish with resentment as Jock handed him a half-full bottle of whisky.

'Yes, but not en masse,' said Daley. 'The phones are down but our radios still work on their direct settings. Well, until the batteries run out. I think, instead of marching up there as a group, we should go in twos and threes. One big target is too easy.'

'Agreed,' said Symington. 'DCI Daley, you take DC Dunn and one of the lads. DS Scott, you're with another. Same goes for me.'

'And what am I to do, Superintendent?' boomed Jock. 'Just sit here pouring drinks for my old friend from Kinloch? You'll need someone with a bit of local knowledge up there. Aye, and remember, as far as that family are concerned, nothing is ever as it seems.'

'Meaning?'

'Meaning exactly that. Allies and alliances come and go. You'll never be able to tell friend from foe with any confidence.'

'You're with me, then,' replied Symington. 'But remember, if anything kicks off, you stay out of it and do exactly as I say.

'Your wish is my command, Superintendent.'

The three constables immediately started to get their equipment together and prepare for the long trek up to Kersivay House. Dunn reached out to assist Daley to his feet but he gently brushed away her offer of help.

'Here, Brian,' he said. 'Give me a look at those pictures you took on your phone.'

After a short struggle with the device, Scott managed to bring up the images. 'Ring any bells, Jimmy?'

Daley looked at the boy on the edge of the sepia group photograph, then the children on the pier with Nathaniel Stuart. 'Yes, it does, Bri. Hard to believe, but . . .'

Symington caught Daley by the sleeve and pulled him into the tiny hall. 'Are you sure you're up to this, Jim? DS Scott thought he'd lost you back there at the stone.'

'Yes, ma'am. I'm a bit shaky, that's all. We need all the manpower we can get. These are the people that did away with Grant and Brockie. We know that they're insane and will resort to anything. You need me out there.'

'Indeed, DCI Daley. So what are your suggestions?

'One group through the back door, one through the front. One group to remain in the grounds, scouting about in reserve, until we know what we're facing. Our job is to contain everyone in one space and secure the area until help arrives. This snow can't last for ever.'

'Very good, that's how we'll proceed.'

'I don't want my last case to be a massive fail, ma'am.'

Symington smiled, looking at Dunn as she secured her body armour in the living room. 'We both know that's not true, Jim.'

'What's not true?'

'This isn't your last case.'

*

Maxwell was in the large office annexe with two security guards, the satellite phone to his ear.

'I want you to make sure none of our assets in China and Russia are operable,' he said. 'I don't care how you do it, just get it done. If they are to remove us from the mineral contracts, they sure as hell won't get to commandeer our plants and equipment. Blow the fucking places up if you have to. And what about those transactions I asked you to find out about? Who authorised the payment to those journalists?'

He listened carefully, scribbling notes down on a piece of paper. He paused before writing the last words. 'Are you sure? It can't be. Why . . .' He scribbled *Lars Bergner* in bold letters and underlined it twice.

Nadia Shannon stood on the freezing balcony terrace at Kersivay House, snow falling on the thick coat draped around her shoulders. Having had to deal with unexplained, unannounced and often terrifying hallucinations for most of her life, she was now much better able to deal with the problem of her temporal lobe than had once been the case. It was a battle that had required great resolve – alongside expensive drugs and counselling.

Often now, she could see something playing out in front of her that she knew existed only in her own mind and ignore it. *If it doesn't seem real, it isn't real.* The mantra played out in her head, placed there by the Harley Street psychologist.

As she looked out over Blaan, she knew what she was seeing wasn't real. On the promontory at the end of the long beach stood a castle, its curtain walls and crenulations ablaze with fire as crowds of men fought with each other on the machair below. She knew she was looking at the course her father had taught her how to play golf on, not a raging battlefield.

She kept her breath steady and fought to keep the panic in her heart at bay. *If it doesn't seem real, it isn't real.* She was in control, not the part of her brain that concocted all of this.

She heard footsteps behind her and turned her head away from the carnage, hoping that this interruption would, as was so often the case, break the spell.

At first she thought there was nobody there, until, from behind a wrought-iron table piled with snow, a little boy appeared. He wore a jacket with a velvet collar and tan shoes. He smiled at her from under a mop of dark, wavy hair.

Nadia felt a rush of wind as the little boy stepped closer to her. The sounds of battle had ceased. *If it doesn't seem real, it isn't real.* She moved her lips in time with the silent mantra.

'Can you help me?' asked the little boy. 'I'm lost. I've been lost for a long time. I can't find my way home and I miss my mummy.'

Nadia began to gulp down air, backing away from the child, who walked towards her, a pleading look on his face.

'Please don't go. Everyone runs away. No one will talk to me and I'm lonely.'

She gasped as her back collided with the railings at the end of the terrace.

'Please help me.' Tears started to spill from the boy's eyes.

'No, no – I can't help you. please leave me.' She had to make the child go away. She'd seen the little face before, staring out from so many photographs and the heartbreaking cine films her grandmother played over and over again. The footage was grainy, everyone's movements slightly too quick, flashes of white where the old film was damaged.

‘I can’t help you,’ she sobbed, pulling herself up against the rails, determined to escape the child, his tiny hand held out for her to hold.

She scrambled onto the edge of the railings; behind her was the sheer drop down the cliff and onto the rocks below.

‘I know you,’ said the little boy. ‘I know you.’

She leaned back as her hands fought for purchase on the freezing ironwork.

‘Nadia, no!’ It was her father’s voice. He bounded across the terrace and pulled her down from the railings atop the stone parapet. They landed in a heap in the cold snow as she sobbed into his shoulder.

‘Dad,’ she cried, clutching at her father. ‘I’m so lonely. Why did you leave me?’

Bruce looked down at her, his heart breaking. At that moment he knew that he would swap all the women, drugs, booze and money in the world to help his daughter. Shame welled up in his chest. He had abandoned her, but he would never leave her again.

They sobbed together on the terrace of the big house, high, high above Blaan.

40

Daley tried the back door of Kersivay House, surprised to find it open. He walked into the narrow corridor, noting the various doors and passages leading from it. This was the preserve of servants and underlings; a place that had existed to tend to the Shannon family's every whim for a hundred years.

He heard a shuffling noise and hurried to the door from behind which the sound came and flung it open, much to the surprise of the room's only occupant.

'You? I thought you were missing,' said Percy.

'What exactly is that?' asked Daley.

'A bit of wood. What did you think it was?' replied the old man. 'Honestly, I don't know what's happened to the constabulary. Used to be full of fine, upstanding men. Now it's buggers like you and that useless oaf Pollock, all carrying too much weight. Couldn't catch cold, never mind a crook. If this gets tasty, I'll soon subdue them with this.'

'Put it down, Percy.'

'Indeed I will not. While you've been out on a wild goose chase, I've been held hostage in my own house and Mrs Shannon's been assaulted – not to mention the bloody shoe.

Didn't you see me trying to signal to you when you came to my door earlier?'

'No – what signal?'

'I was narrowing my eyes. Like this,' he said, giving a demonstration.

'I thought that was your normal expression, sorry. Who kept you in the house – and why?'

'Big Irish bruiser. Something to do with Maxwell, that little snake.'

'Give the cosh to DC Dunn, Percy.'

'To this girl? What use will she be when those hoods come back? Better making herself useful and getting the kettle on.'

Dunn stepped from behind Daley and with one swift movement caught Percy's wrist and sent the cosh clattering to the flagstone floor.

'What did you do that for, you stupid bitch?' Percy hissed, rubbing his wrist.

'To disarm you – and teach you some manners,' said Dunn, picking up the weapon.

'I hope you'll be as brave against that big Irish boy. He's not an old man like me, you know.'

'Right, Percy, come on, enough of this. You've been here a long time. What do you think is going on?'

'It's a reckoning, Mr Daley. Nathaniel Stuart, back from the grave, to claim what is rightly his. If there's a Shannon left alive by tomorrow, I'll be surprised.'

The attic was dark, illuminated by only a couple of flickering candles. A dim glow was cast on the clutter: an old rocking horse, a rusty bike with perished tyres, a faded couch from which the horsehair stuffing was escaping, crockery, boxes and a brass coal scuttle. All items that had been discarded over the years by those who occupied Kersivay House.

Sitting cross-legged on the bare floorboards was a man, draped in the folds of an old cloak, the hood pulled down over his face. The little radio in his hand buzzed.

'Is everything in place?' He listened to the tinny voice in silence. 'Good, then we can proceed.'

The voice on the radio spoke again.

'Of course her loss is regrettable. Don't you think I know that – me of all people? She has given herself to a greater cause; a sacrifice that any of us would be proud to make.' He paused, controlled himself and spoke again, his voice harder. 'There are police in the house. They must be dealt with first – in any way. Leave the Shannons to me, we have arrangements in place. We will put the final part of our plan into place an hour from now. After this is finished you will need to be ready to defend our cause. The world will again know our name.'

He placed the radio back into the folds of his cloak and picked up something from the floor in front of him. In his little coat with the velvet collar, Archibald Shannon peered out of the black-and-white photograph, a large toy plane in his arms, a shy smile on his face. He was standing on the terrace of Kersivay House, fifty years ago.

The man looked at the picture for a few moments than spat on it before he ripped it in two.

'Listen, son,' said Scott to the young cop, standing between the snow-covered bushes in the grounds of Kersivay House.

'As soon as you got detailed with me, you should have known that we'd be the ones oot in the cold. Story of my fucking life, my boy.' The long hike up to the mansion had not improved his humour.

'DCI Daley was nearly killed, remember, Sergeant,' he replied, stamping his feet to keep warm.

'Indeed. Only oor Jimmy could bounce back and lead the charge,' said Scott under his breath. 'Anyway, we'll stand here for a few minutes, then move tae the back. Noo that lassie's lying dead in the district nurse's garage, the wind will be oot their sails, mark my words. All we have tae do is keep things secure until those useless buggers up in Glasgow can get someone doon here tae get these Shannons up the road and out of oor way. The only thing we'll catch the night is pneumonia, trust me.'

'What's that, sergeant?' The cop was pointing to the side of the house, where Scott could just about make out movement in the luminous glow of the snow.

'We'd better check it out, son,' he replied. 'DS Scott tae all stations. Movement on the left hand side o' the hoose. We're attending, over.'

'Roger. Keep me informed, Brian,' came the reply from Symington, now ensconced in the mansion. 'And use your bloody ear buds or whoever it is will hear the radio a mile off.'

'Already in, ma'am.'

'Liar. Good luck. Symington out.'

Scott cursed as he pulled the earpiece from his pocket. 'I don't know what it is when you get a bit o' braid on your bunnet. Seems you're able tae see through walls. The last bugger was just the same.'

They sneaked around the back of the bushes, along a wall and onto the gravel path, their movement silenced by the snow.

'There, sergeant, just on the path. Two, maybe three of them.'

'Right, wait and I'll call this in. DS Scott to all stations. About to intercept three individuals at the west side of the house, over. May require assistance.'

'Symington to DCI Daley. Did you get that, Jim?'

'Roger, ma'am. Myself and DC Dunn attending.'

Daley and Dunn rushed out of the back door of the mansion, under a stone canopy where riders had once dismounted from their horses, then onto the path that led round to Scott's location.

'Stay behind me, Mary,' Daley said, his voice as rough as sandpaper.

Scott reached the area where they had last seen their quarry. He bent down and passed his hand over the snow. Sure enough, there were fresh, deep prints. 'They were here,' he whispered to his companion. 'But where the fuck are they now?'

'Sergeant!' called out the young cop, before Scott heard a sickening thud and the young man toppled onto him. He struggled to get out from under the constable's limp body but was caught on the chin with a boot. Stars flashed through his vision.

Another kick to his stomach winded him and sent the gun spinning from his hand. He heaved himself onto all fours, desperately trying to get up to face his foe, gasping for breath as the young cop groaned on the ground beside him.

His attacker picked something up from the ground. Scott heard the safety catch of his own firearm being clicked off.

A shot rang out in the cold, dark night, echoing around the hillsides high above Blaan.

41

Symington heard the echo of gunfire from her position on the high terrace of the house. She called to two Support Unit cops and rushed through the ballroom, where the Shannon family were already beginning to gather for safety. She spoke briefly to Inspector Aitcheson, whom she left to guard the family alongside one of his men and two of the Shannons' own security detail.

'Symington to DS Scott. Who discharged a weapon? Over.' There was no response as she hurried towards the large spiral stairwell. Because of the loss of power, the lift wasn't operational, but emergency lights had been installed along the corridors and on the stairs, so the way ahead was clear if somewhat dim. Soon she and her little party of officers were on the ground floor of the mansion.

'Which way?' she yelled, as one of the Support Unit cops took the lead. Having carefully studied the layout of the house, he knew the quickest way to the location Scott had last called in.

'Open it constable,' commanded Symington as they reached an old fire door. The officer strained at the release bar and eventually the double doors burst open, a rush of cold air hitting the police officers like a wall.

She raced out onto a set of shallow steps. In the moonlight she saw a man lying in the snow, a group of people looking on.

'What's happening?' she shouted to Daley, who had his handgun pointed at two men standing with their hands on their heads. She instantly recognised Maxwell.

'Ma'am, this man aimed a weapon at DS Scott. They backed down after a warning.'

'This is outrageous,' spat Maxwell. 'Your Chief Constable will hear of this as soon as I can raise him.'

'Why did you allow him to remove the safety catch of the weapon and aim the pistol at my officer's head?' asked Daley.

'It all happened in a fraction of a second. We thought we were under attack.'

'My arse,' shouted Scott. 'We spotted you lurking about the house. What was that, eh?'

'A security check, nothing more. I wish you had just left this to me and my men,' said Maxwell. 'The police have been worse than useless since they arrived.'

As one constable helped Scott to his feet and another tended to his young colleague, still reeling from the blow he had taken to the head, Daley, Symington and Dunn examined the security worker. He'd been hit in the arm by Daley's shot and was groaning in pain.

'You'll live,' said Symington. But we'll need to get you some first aid up in the house. Help me up with him, please, DCI Daley.'

'Stop! Everyone stay just where you are.' The cockney accent of Maxwell's head of security was unmistakable. He stood a few feet away on the path, a machine gun pointed at the group.

'Put the bloody gun down, Barrie,' said Maxwell. 'One of these police officers is likely to blow your fucking head off.'

'Can't oblige, I'm afraid, Mr S,' he replied, grinning at his boss. 'Nev, collect the shooters.'

Another Shannon security man walked over to the nearest of the Support Unit cops. 'Give it here, mate,' he said, taking possession of the constable's automatic rifle.

'Right, now the rest,' shouted Barrie, as he was joined by two other members of the private security detail, all with drawn weapons.

'What in hell's name do you think you're doing, Barrie?' said Maxwell, walking towards his head of security.

'That's far enough, Mr S. We wouldn't want you to get one in the head now, would we?'

Daley groaned as he was frisked and his handgun taken from him.

'Fucking brilliant, Maxwell,' said Scott. 'Good to see you've got guys you can trust.'

'I like you, Mr Scott, so I won't blow your fucking brains out,' said Barrie, walking over to the group of police officers. 'And just to make sure you all behave, I'll be having this pretty thing.' He grabbed Dunn by the hair and pulled her towards him.

'Get your hands off her,' shouted Daley, taking a stride towards Dunn and her captor, his fists clenched.

Barrie pulled back Dunn's head and held his machine gun at her throat. 'Come on, DCI Daley. Wouldn't it be a pity to slot this little piece of tail? I think you've been doing a bit of that already,' he smiled, as his men began to laugh. 'I've got to say, I thought this would have been much more difficult. Don't make policemen like they used to, that's for sure. Not up here in Jockoland, anyway.'

‘Twenty-one, code twenty-one.’ Symington, who was standing out of sight behind Daley, spoke quickly into her radio. She was about to say more when she was pistol-whipped by Barrie, knocking her to the ground.

‘That wasn’t very clever now, was it?’ he said, his firearm thrust back into Dunn’s neck. ‘The only reason I don’t off this girl right now is that I’ve taken a bit of fancy for her. It’s going to be a long cold night and I’ll need a bit of warming up.’

‘My inspector will have heard that call. You forget, we’re not the only police officers here,’ said Symington, rolling onto her hands and knees and spitting blood into the snow.

‘Let’s see about that. Nev, give the lads a shout, would you?’

‘Everything secured in the ballroom, over?’ said Nev into his radio.

‘All good up here. Cops disarmed and subdued.’

‘Now, ladies and gents, if you don’t mind, let’s get out of the cold. There’s someone coming to see you all.’ He dragged Dunn by the hair, making her cry out, as they and the rest of the group, under the watchful eyes of the armed security guards, made their way back across the snow into Kersivay House.

More looked at the his wife, lying pale and lifeless in the improvised mortuary in the Blaan district nurse’s garage. The nurse looked on, wringing her hands in concern.

‘I’m sorry you have to see her like this, Reverend More. It’s all we could do, what with the snow and all. Once the road’s clear we’ll get her to the undertaker in Kinloch.’

'What? Oh, yes,' said More. 'I'm obliged to you, Mrs Pirrie. I know you've done your best. She's at rest now.'

'Yes, indeed. I can't believe this has happened.'

'Nor me, Lena, nor me.' He stroked a loose strand of hair from his wife's forehead. 'Who did this? I mean, who fired the shot that killed her?'

'Oh, I don't know for sure, Reverend More. I heard the police officers talking when they brought her in. I think it was the Detective Sergeant, the one who was caught up on the bonfire.'

More sighed. 'Yes, I know who he is. Could you give me a moment?'

'Certainly. Just come through when you're ready.' She padded off, leaving More alone.

'I don't know what you were doing. I don't even know who you really are. It seems we were on opposite sides, but I'm not even sure of that. But I promise you, I'll pay back those that killed you. That bloody family has had a good go at ruining my life and now they've ended yours. Revenge is all there's left.' He kissed the cold forehead of his wife and left the garage.

42

There was gasp of dismay when the police officers, along with Maxwell, were led into the ballroom at Kersivay House, hands on heads. Superintendent Symington staggered, a livid bruise already blooming on her face where she had been hit with the pistol. Daley was pale and exhausted, still recovering from his ordeal at the Rat Stone. He blinked in the bright light of the ballroom, one of the few areas of the main house supplied with energy from the generators. The room was filled with the Shannon family and their staff, including some villagers who had been hired to attend to the party during their time in the house. A young woman sobbed as she watched the policemen being marched forwards.

'Right, people,' said Barrie. 'I want you cops where we can keep an eye on you – sit there.' He pointed to the middle of the long boardroom table. 'Make yourselves comfortable while I get acquainted with Mary here – that's your name, isn't it, darling?'

'Wait,' said Symington, her voice weak but determined. 'If any harm comes to my officers, you will be brought to justice, I promise you that. The road to Kinloch will be clear soon and my officers will be here shortly, not to mention our colleagues from Glasgow. They won't take kindly to one of their own being harmed. Whatever you intend to do, give it up before things get serious.'

'Things are just about as serious as they can get. Just relax – after all, it's the start of a new year. The last one for most of you, I shouldn't wonder.' He laughed as he dragged the struggling Dunn from the room.

'I'm sorry, Mr Daley. I really am,' said Ailsa, sitting in her usual place at the head of the table. She appeared calm, though tired, with large shadows under her eyes. 'Superintendent, are you all right? I demand that somebody attends to this woman.' She looked around the room at the security guards, who were now holding the family hostage rather than protecting them.

'Yes, do as my aunt says,' shouted Maxwell. 'You men still have a chance to get yourselves out of this. We'll make you all rich if you let us go and help us get out of here. I promise—' But his words were cut short by a blow to the head; he cowered into his chair, hands over his head for protection.

Bruce spoke up. 'OK, guys. Take it easy. We're all here for a reason, so let's not get carried away. You're not going to massacre us, so what's the deal, eh?' He was holding his daughter Nadia close and felt her flinch as Nev barked a reply.

'You're very confident. I'm not sure I would be if I were you. Now shut up, the lot of you!' he shouted.

As the room hushed, the large doors burst open and a cloaked figure stepped into the crowded ballroom.

Jock Munro was standing in one of the mansion's long corridors, debating what to do. Despite his assurances to the contrary, he'd followed Symington out of the building and watched from the shadows as she and her team were taken prisoner by the Shannon security detail. He decided that he really had only one option – to try and get to the village and seek help. He'd counted ten security men so far, but there were plenty of stout farmers in Blaan with access to guns. He was about to search for a quiet route out of the house when he heard voices.

'Now, don't be shy. I tell you what, you play the game and I'll make sure you get out of this little mess alive.'

Jock peered around the corner. The brawny security guard he'd seen earlier had unzipped Dunn's ski jacket and was pushing her up against a wall, groping her through her thick jersey as she struggled to get free.

'Come on. What's a little ride? Or would you prefer some of this,' he said, forcing her to her knees with one hand, while unbuttoning his trousers with the other. 'No biting, now.' He held her nose with his large hand, so that she was forced to gulp air in through her open mouth. He laughed as Dunn squirmed.

'Leave me alone, you bastard,' she said, then screamed as he caught her by her auburn hair and forced her head back.

Suddenly she felt his body go limp. He slumped forwards and slid down the wall. Dunn fought to push him off her and onto the floor. She was shocked to see Jock in the corridor, the machine gun Barrie had left on the floor clasped in his big hands.

'You'd better take charge of this,' he whispered. 'I hate the bloody things. We have to get out of the house and down to the village to get help. There are ten security guards – well, nine now,' he continued, looking at the limp figure on the floor. 'We have to be quick.'

'Is he dead?' said Dunn.

'I gave him a fair dunt on the head, I must admit. Come on, lassie, this one's mates will come looking for him soon.' He pointed down the dim corridor to a back stairwell. 'We'll get down to the ground floor this way, but then we'll have to work out how to get out of this bloody place.'

Dunn took the lead, the gun slung over her shoulder, as they made their way down the narrow staircase.

They were on the last flight of stairs when someone called out from the floor below. 'Stay exactly where you are and put the gun down.'

'Bastard!' said Jock.

More stood at the bottom of the long driveway that led up to Kersivay House. The moon's eerie light was diffused through the clouds, lending a weak luminescence to the snow.

He looked around, making sure he was alone. As he stared into the bay a large object appeared from behind the long promontory where once the castle had stood. Even in the strange light, it was clearly a vessel, long and sleek.

More ducked into the shadows as he took his first step on the driveway towards the house. Though the road had had been kept relatively clear of snow, he chose to plough his way through the accumulations on the verge. Here he could stay out of sight as he climbed the winding path to the mansion.

He knew that the death of his young wife should have been his driving force, but it wasn't. She had been part of something he didn't understand.

With every step, he felt the pain of the belt as it hit his back and legs, the kicks to his stomach and punches in the face. The brass plaque – *Property of Shannon Agricultural*

(Australia) Ltd. – shone out at him from the bureau. He had been as much of a possession as the old piece of furniture.

The plan to wrest control of the company from the Shannons had excited him. It was all he had worked towards for years. Install Maxwell as boss, force him to transfer funds into his associates' bank accounts, then leave him to take the fall as his company disintegrated. He'd told himself – prayed – that he was doing the right thing. Now he was sure of it.

He turned to face the sea. The large ship was motionless now, about a mile out in the bay. Someone had come to Blaan to see the Shannons. But why?

He couldn't wait to find out; he hurried on through the deep snow.

Daley had an ache in his heart as he watched the figure under the hooded cloak; by size, shape and demeanour, it was obviously a man. He recalled the shock of seeing Veronica sitting on the log in similar attire, casually smoking a cigarette.

The robed man said nothing, nor did he move. Suddenly, the huge screen at the end of the ballroom began to unroll across nearly the whole length of the wall. There were choked sobs as those in the room tried to muffle their fear, not wanting to draw the attention of the guards. Everyone looked scared – apart from Ailsa, who merely raised an eyebrow.

Symington's face had swollen, her right eye puffy and bruised. Bruce held his daughter as she hid her face in his chest. Daley leaned forwards, catching Scott's eye. His grizzled detective sergeant – his friend – looked determined, but Daley could see something behind his eyes, a flash of fear, something he'd never associated with the man he'd come to rely on. Almost imperceptibly, Scott nodded to him; it was time they tried something. Daley's response was equally subtle: a shake of the head only those watching very closely could possibly register.

The huge screen was now completely unfurled. Members of the family and staff alike recoiled as the man in the cloak walked past them, awaiting the blow that would send them into oblivion.

Having reached the screen, the man in the cloak stopped. An image flickered into life, illuminating the large dark room. He pointed at the screen.

Everyone in the ballroom at Kersivay House watched as a picture began to form.

43

Neither Dunn nor Jock could see the man in the shadows. 'Stay exactly where you are,' he said gruffly. 'Put the weapon on the ground.'

Slowly, Dunn leaned down and placed the machine gun on the floor.

'Now put your hands on your head and turn around – both of you!'

Jock and Dunn did as they were told. They heard footsteps as the man walked towards them and retrieved the weapon. 'You can turn back round now – but no funny business, mind.'

'Percy!' said Dunn, shocked to see the old caretaker hefting the weapon awkwardly on his shoulder.

'I would have thought you'd have known better than to be involved with this shit, Jock,' said Percy.

'And just what do you mean by that?' asked the big man, struggling to keep his voice low.

'What have the Shannons done to you?'

'Nothing – not directly, anyway,' said Jock.

'So why are you part of this . . . this plot?'

'What do you mean?' asked Dunn.

'I know everyone's imprisoned in the ballroom – including your boyfriend with the gut,' declared Percy. 'You must be in on it, otherwise you'd be up there with the rest of them. What did they give you to betray your own folk, Jock – money?'

'You've always been a stupid bugger, Percy. Put the gun down and listen to what I've got to say.'

'And have you and this bitch overpower me? Not likely. She knows these marital arts, you know. She nearly broke my bloody wrist earlier on.'

'You mean martial arts.'

'Whatever they're called, she's a bloody danger as well as being a temptress. Has that big oaf that's meant to be in charge by the balls. I hope you haven't fallen for her charms, Jock. You're too old for that shit.'

'We've escaped. We're trying to get to the village to get help,' said Dunn.

'And the band played 'Believe It if You Like'. Do you think I came down in the last shower? I've seen some things in this house over the years, but these goings-on take the biscuit. I hope you haven't harmed Mrs Shannon – you'll pay if you have!' he said, his voice suddenly raised.

'You've been a faithful retainer all these years, *Percy*,' said Jock.

'And what's that supposed to mean?'

'Och, I've always known who you really are. Now put the gun down.'

Dunn looked on in amazement as the caretaker lowered the weapon and shrugged his shoulders. 'You're wrong – whatever you think is wrong.'

'What does it matter now?' replied Jock. 'We've more important issues to consider, I think you'll agree. The people up in that ballroom are in real danger, including your precious Ailsa Shannon. You have to help us.'

'I will,' said Percy. 'But on one condition.'

'Which is?'

'Just you keep your suspicions to yourself.'

Dunn, now thoroughly confused, was about to ask what they were talking about when a distant crack echoed down the stairwell.

'What was that?' asked Percy, concern etched on his face.

'A gunshot,' replied Jock.

FOR EVERY ACTION, THERE IS AN EQUAL AND OPPOSITE REACTION. The words were emblazoned across the huge screen.

'This must stop now! What do you think you're doing?' shouted Daley, getting to his feet. A security guard marched over to him and forced him back into his chair with the butt of his weapon.

'Sit down, there's a good chap. Everyone shut up and watch the man!' he shouted.

An image of an emaciated child swaddled in a dirty blanket filled the screen. Flies swarmed around the child's mouth, nose and eyes, which stared out of a gaunt, skeletal face. In the background a woman sobbed as a exhausted doctor in a white coat shook his head.

The picture faded, to be replaced with stark black writing on a white screen: *As a direct result of corporate actions taken by Shannon International in the developing world, more than twenty thousand children have lost their lives.*

The next display was different: a nameless UK high street, late at night. In a doorway sat a bearded man covered by an old sleeping bag. He patted a little dog by his side, its coat patchy where great sores had taken hold. The man looked at the camera, the desperate plea behind his eyes easy to discern.

Again the image faded. *Over eight thousand people have been made effectively homeless in the UK alone after being evicted from Shannon International properties or having loans and mortgages foreclosed by banks and other lending institutions controlled by the company.*

Now they saw an aerial shot of the ocean. Amidst the blue and green of the waves, a brown slick spread into the distance. Hundreds of fish lay dead on the surface, their silver bodies bobbing amidst the oil. A seabird, its plumage a black gloss, was dying, poisoned while trying to clean itself and fly away. It flapped its heavy wings in vain.

The shot panned to a huge tanker. Brown filth spilled from the scuppers as the crew flushed out unwanted fuel. Though the flag was one of convenience, the word *SHANNON*, emblazoned along the side of the vessel, displayed the real inconvenient truth. *Vessels, industrial plants and factories owned by Shannon International across the globe pump thousands of tonnes of toxic chemicals into our skies and seas every day, as though it is their right to destroy our world.*

A teenage girl stood on a dimly lit street corner. Her blonde hair straggled down her back, as the camera drew level with her. As she turned to face the lens, she pulled down her skimpy red top to reveal tiny breasts, like pimples on her skinny rib cage. She stuck her tongue into the corner of her mouth as she gestured with her hand. *As a direct result of economic activity by Shannon International, hundreds of thousands, worldwide, find themselves in poverty, forced into crime and prostitution in order to survive.*

The wrinkled face of the woman spoke of old age and exhaustion. She sat on rough grass outside a hut in a shanty town. Around her, dogs barked, barefoot children played in the red dust and others went about their business. *This woman has yet to celebrate her fiftieth birthday. On average, employees of Shannon International in Africa have a life expectancy of fifty-one.*

'Enough!' roared Ailsa, getting to her feet, her face reflecting the glow of the screen. She stood her ground as the screen went blank and the cloaked figure walked slowly towards her.

'We can use this side exit,' whispered Percy. 'I'm the only bugger who knows it's here, I dare say.'

'Isn't it locked?' asked Jock.

'Yes, of course it is. I've made sure every door has been secured, what with all this shit going on in the last few days.'

'Congratulations,' said Dunn. 'Doesn't appear to have worked though, does it?'

'Never mind that,' said Jock. 'How do you propose we get through? We can't break it down. The noise would attract attention.'

'I'm not that wandered,' replied Percy indignantly. 'Might like the odd dram now and again, but my mind's all there. Here's the keys.' He pulled a huge bunch from his pocket, each bearing a small wooden tag. 'Now where is the bastard? I can hardly see in this light.'

'Come on, man,' pleaded Jock. They were at the end on a corridor and the only way forwards was through the old oak door.

As Percy continued to fumble with the set of keys and mutter under his breath, Dunn held out her hand.

'I think this is it,' said Percy, trying to fit the old mortise key into the lock with shaking hands.

'Please, we need to hurry,' said Dunn.

'Got, it!'

'Aye, but we'll have to get out of here quick. They're all over the place . . .' Jock stopped. Percy was leaning against the door, clutching his chest.

'I . . . I have a pain,' he said in a weak voice, as the door slid open and he fell out into the pale moonlight.

Dunn leaned over him. 'Percy, Percy, try to keep calm.'

Jock bent down stiffly. 'Can you hear me, Percy? Listen, we have to try to get to the village and get help. You understand, don't you? We have to save everybody – we have to save Ailsa.'

Percy's voice was barely a whisper. 'Do what you have to, Jock,' he said, his thin fingers clutching the big man's sleeve. 'Save her, please. She's all I've got left of . . .'

'I will. We have to go.' Jock tried to stand, but Percy, with the last of his strength, grasped his arm more tightly.

'Promise not to tell anyone about us, Jock. My name . . .'

'I promise, Lachie. You have my word.'

Percy looked up at Jock, tears welling in his eyes. 'I should have kept her safe. I've let her down,' he whispered, as the light left his eyes.

Dunn straddled the old man and breathed air into his mouth, then started the rhythmic pumping of his chest as she had been trained.

Jock stared down and placed his big hand on her shoulder 'Come on, lassie. He was an old man. All this excitement was too much for him, but had a good innings. We have to go – if we get into the shadows, we might have a chance.'

Reluctantly Dunn stood up, drawing the small radio from her pocket. The security guards, confident she had been subdued, hadn't bothered to remove it. 'DC Dunn to all stations receiving. I'm OK and have managed to leave the building. The old man, Percy, is dead, his heart gave out. I couldn't save him. I am going for help, over.' She stared at the device, hoping that someone had heard what she had to say, even though she knew they wouldn't be able to reply.

The pair hurried away, leaving Percy's body behind. His blue eyes stared across the land that had once been his home.

44

Bruce got up and stood in the way of the cloaked figure as he made his way to Ailsa, still standing boldly at the end of the long table. A security guard stepped forwards, ready to pull Bruce back into his seat, but the man raised his hand, the folds of his cloak falling loosely over his bare arm.

'She's my mother, you bastard. Lay one finger on her and I'll kill you. I don't know how, but I will.'

At Bruce's side, his daughter Nadia also stood, her chin jutting out bravely. 'She's my grandmother, don't dare harm her,' she said through her sobs.

The man in the cloak paused for a split second then slowly removed his hood. 'I know who she is,' said Brady in his New York drawl. 'And now you know who I am.'

Despite himself, Bruce stepped backwards, gripping the table to remain upright. Gasps around the room were soon replaced by cries of bewilderment. By revealing his identity, Brady had shifted the emotion in the large room; the fear of the unknown was becoming contempt for the familiar.

As though sensing this, Brady swung round, his handgun raised. 'Who would like to be first?' he said, a large smile plastered across his face. 'Lynton? Or what about you, Maxwell? Yes, I think I'd like you to be with me at this difficult time.' He nodded to a security guard, who pulled the cowering Maxwell from his chair at the other end of the room and marched him towards Brady.

Maxwell was visibly shaking as he was deposited in a chair in front of Brady, who pressed his gun tight against the back of Maxwell's head.

'Now. Let's play a little game. Who wants to save Maxie's life – any takers?'

Maxwell snivelled; keeping his head still, he looked around the table, wide eyes staring.

'Oh, come on. Don't be shy, guys. This is your new chairman, the guy you look up to. Can nobody think of anything that will save him?' He paused for a minute, waiting for a reply. 'Nothing, eh? I want to ask you a question before I blow your brains out, Maxie. I had a nice little plan brewing – scupper the associate companies, cause some panic, then get you elected as chairman.' He leaned his head into Maxwell's. 'But you were ahead of me, weren't you?'

'I don't know what you mean,' replied Maxwell in a quivering voice.

'The Chinese and Russian mineral deals falling through. Do you think I'm stupid? I know you've set up a shadow company to take over the contracts.' He gestured round the table with the handgun. 'You saw the misery your family has caused – is causing – around the world. Aren't you ashamed? Aren't all of you ashamed? You sit in the lap of luxury, not lifting a finger, while people die – while the planet dies around you. All because you were born with the name Shannon. Or married one,' he said, looking pointedly at Ailsa.

'I promise,' whimpered Maxwell. 'I didn't have anything to do with the mineral deals falling through. Nothing at all.'

'You lying bastard,' shouted Brady, forcing the gun into his head.

'He's not lying.' Ailsa's voice was calm and clear. 'I'm responsible for that. What an executive board. All your schemes and plans, what a parcel of rogues. You're by far the most impressive, Charles. But you've paid a heavy price too, haven't you?'

'Meaning?'

'Your daughter. Veronica.'

Daley was taking everything in, looking round the room for any chance to seize control of the situation. In his ear bud he heard Dunn's voice and had to stop himself from crying out with relief. One of the security team caught his eye and patted his machine gun. Daley stared back, showing no emotion.

It was as though a huge weight had been lifted from his shoulders now that he knew she was safe. Despite the scene playing out in front of him, despite nearly dying on the Rat Stone, despite it all, he knew one thing was true. He loved Mary and he wanted to be with her.

Daley saw Scott lean forwards and widen his eyes, as if trying to draw his attention to something. He followed his DS's eye line and spotted one of the guards lighting a cigarette, his weapon hanging loosely by its webbing strap at his side. He moved his head a fraction, to show Scott he understood.

Daley coughed, then Scott fell backwards in his chair. The guard dropped his cigarette and fumbled with his gun. He was too slow though. Daley dived from his chair, catching the man in a rugby tackle as he watched Scott roll back to his feet with the fluidity of a gymnast. He too dived at the security guard and the pair wrestled the weapon out of his hands.

It had taken split seconds to disarm the guard. Daley heard screams as those in the room realised what was happening and rushed from their places around the table. In the ensuing chaos, he twisted round with the gun and brought down an onrushing security man with a short burst of automatic fire, which caught him in the arm. He turned quickly again, keeping low, as another charged towards him. Between them, Scott was still wrestling with the first guard. Despite the risk of hitting his friend, Daley raised the weapon, ready to fire. The man knew he was beaten and held up his hands by way of submission. Scott quickly stripped him of his weapons as Symington did the same to the guard Daley had shot down.

Daley looked round. They had gained the upper hand, but it had been too easy. Something wasn't right. He looked across at Brady and could see that he was equally unnerved.

People had rushed for the large doors, but a bottleneck was forming, as though unable to leave the room for some reason. Amidst the fleeing bodies, Symington appeared at his side, her right eye now almost closed where she had been pistol-whipped earlier. 'Brady has Ailsa and her party at the end of the room – we have to consolidate!' she shouted, as the screams of those unable to get out of the ballroom at Kersivay House grew louder.

Daley saw Brady, his cloak now stained with blood, with two security guards, holding a small group of people hostage at the far end of the room, amongst them Ailsa, Bruce, Maxwell and Nadia, as well as Inspector Aitcheson and the constable from the Support Unit.

Brady spotted Daley and called out. 'Stop what you're doing or I kill them all!' The guard at his side fired a long burst of ammunition into the ceiling, bringing a terrified hush on the room.

Daley was about to speak when Symington stood and walked towards the table. Though she was slight, her back was straight and her head high as she spoke to Brady. 'We seem to have reached an impasse. Why don't you give this up? You're going nowhere from here. My officers are armed.'

'You think you have the advantage? I have the cream of the crop here – the top Shannon elite, not to mention two of your men. You surrender or they die, one by one.'

Ailsa stepped forwards. 'Why are you doing this, Charles? In the years I've known you, haven't we always got on well? You've even been on my side – I admire you.'

'Isn't all the misery this family has caused reason enough? Don't you have any shame?'

'I'm not a Shannon, remember.'

'Oh, that's right. I should have thought more about that. Let me tell you an interesting little tale,' he said, holding up his hand when he saw the old woman was about to interrupt. 'No, trust me, you'll want to hear this, Ailsa.'

'What now?' whispered Scott, now at Daley's side. 'And how the hell can nobody get oot o' here? Something's no' right, Jimmy.'

Ignatius More stood behind the huge doors of the ballroom. He'd managed to place the thick metal bar between the handles just before the screaming and gun fire had started.

He was breathing heavily and, despite the cold of the night, could feel perspiration running down his nose.

He hated being in this house, hated being anywhere near the Shannon family. Each time he saw a member of the family, he felt anew every one of the hundreds of lashes he'd had to endure over the years. They'd taken him from the orphanage where he'd been deposited as a little boy and sailed him across the world to be a slave on one of the huge farms Shannon Agricultural owned in the Northern Territory. He often wondered how many other children had suffered the same fate. Taken from the UK to a strange land, to be battered and cowed until they were broken, by brutal sheep farmers who cared more about their animals than the children under their care.

He had loved his adoptive mother, though. He remembered seeing her for the last time, her face swollen and bruised where his father had battered her. He'd told the doctors she'd been in a road traffic accident. Whether they believed it or not made little difference. It was the seventies in the Northern Territory, where men were men and their word was their word. More had managed to escape, to build a new life, some months before. She hadn't.

He'd made it to her bedside just in time. As he held her hand the old woman whispered to him, 'I love you, son.'

She held on for a few more hours, but spoke no more.

He saw to her funeral, which his adoptive father did not attend. Despite his better judgement, and even though he was free of the man who had brutalised him for so long, he made his way back to the farmhouse one final time.

The old man was in the yard. He'd grown deaf over the years but he was still fit, a life on the farm leaving his shoulders broad and his forearms thick. He was bent over a piece of machinery as the boy he had beaten throughout his childhood crept up behind him and hit him over and over again with a heavy shovel.

Then More walked back into the hell that had once been his home and looked at the bureau: *Property of Shannon Agricultural (Australia) Ltd.*

He removed the tiny brass plate before setting fire to the old piece of furniture and then walked up to a nearby rise to watch the property blaze. He'd thrown what was left of the man he called his father into the house as the flames began to lick at the sides of the white wooden building.

Now, More pulled the brass plate from his pocket. He'd carried it everywhere with him since that day, and it felt familiar in his hand as he rubbed it for the last time.

He remembered the face of his wife – too young and too beautiful to die – and flung the brass plate on the ground. Picking up the first jerry can, he sloshed petrol down the long corridor outside the ballroom.

Daley watched Brady. He couldn't be sure he hadn't played a direct role in any part of the horror he had faced at the Rat Stone, but for some reason he doubted it. Brady seemed too focused, too determined, to be part of the insane cult – yet here he was in robes, clearly at the heart of whatever was being perpetrated against the Shannons.

'I want you all to listen!' shouted Brady. 'I was brought up in rural Ireland. Our life there was quiet, we lived on a small farm on the west coast. Big skies, green hills, rain. Hey, it was Ireland, right.' He chuckled mirthlessly. 'But I remember, every night I would wake up, my heart beating in my chest. I could never work out why.

'One summer – oh, I'd have been about twelve years old – a man came to call. He was old. A big man, with broad shoulders and huge hands. He took me away from my folks to his cottage up in the hills. We fished, we hunted, we talked. He told me how he'd been watching over me for a long time, how he had plans for me. I was clever at school and he wanted me to be cleverer.' Brady walked slowly down the room. Behind him, the guns of the remaining security guards were trained on Daley, Scott and Symington, who returned the compliment with the weapons they had recovered.

'When I finished up in the village school, he came back. My folks packed my bags and said goodbye. I went with the big guy. First to Boston, where I went to high school, then to New York. I was a clever kid and he encouraged me to be the best at everything I did. I ended up at Harvard. And the rest, you know. Well, most of it.'

Daley was listening carefully when he smelled something, a sharp, pungent smell. He turned towards the main group, still huddled around the door, now convinced he was smelling petrol. Quietly, he tried to attract Scott's attention as Brady carried on with his story.

'To cut a long story short, the old man was dying. He was over ninety. He asked me to go to his house. I was working on Wall Street at the time – still wet between the ears but I knew who was who. I couldn't believe it when I walked into that room. There was my boss from the trading floor; an old college professor; the CEO of one of the biggest banks in the city; even a Senator. That was the night I became one of the brotherhood. That's when I became a member of the Society of the Golden Bough.'

‘A druid. Well, well, such a surprise,’ said Ailsa.

‘It’s taken me a long way. I don’t concern myself with all that sacrifice bullshit. That’s in place as the opium of the stupid – the foot soldiers. Keeps them working hard, fighting for the cause.’

‘The cause? To kill, maim and commit all manner of perversion?’ shouted Symington. ‘Your followers nearly killed DCI Daley. We know what they’ve been responsible for in the last few days. There’s nothing noble or glamorous about a collection of deranged sadists.’

‘There’s nothing noble or glamorous about a company that kills and maims thousands, ruins our planet and everything that lives in it, motivated by pure greed. Someone needs to hold the corporate world to account. Someone needs to champion our world. It has been our duty, our privilege, for millennia.’

‘And leaping about in cloaks killing people in the most cruel and degrading way possible is *championing the planet*? I never had you down for a psychopath, Charles,’ said Ailsa, the disgust plain in her voice.

‘There are many things that even you don’t know about me, Mrs Shannon,’ replied Brady, with a smile.

45

Dunn scrabbled and slipped through the drifts, trying to stay off the cleared pathway, which was slick beneath a fresh layer of snow. She'd already fallen and grazed both knees. They ached as she pushed on, her chest burning as she gasped for breath in the cold air. She'd left Jock behind; despite being fit for his years, he couldn't keep up. He had urged her to push on to the first cottage, where its occupant, Tom Fletcher, would raise the village in order to save the Shannons.

As Dunn struggled on, she realised that she didn't give a damn about the rich family or their clifftop mansion. She was doing it for one person only: Jim Daley. She'd nearly lost him to the Rat Stone, she wasn't ever going to let that happen again. She repeated this to herself, whimpering, as she forced herself to push onwards as fast as she could.

Up ahead, she saw a tiny light. She lengthened her stride and hurried towards the flickering candle flame.

'I need to talk to you,' shouted Daley, interrupting Brady's story.

'You do, Mr Daley? Be my guest, we've got all night. Well, some of us have,' he said, looking at his captives.

'If you intend to set fire to the house, I'll have to stop you. You must realise that.'

'Who mentioned burning down the house? I've got a much better plan than that.'

'Can't you smell the petrol, Brady?'

He sniffed the air and shrugged his shoulders. 'Sure, I can smell it. What do you intend to do about it? I tell you what, fix the problem, if there is one, and you can have Nadia. Don't fix it, or fuck me about, and you can have her back with her throat cut. You got me?'

Daley looked at Scott. 'One wrong move, aim for him, Brian,' he said, making sure Brady could hear. 'As far as I know, there's only one way down from here, and it's through those doors.'

'Don't you think the bastard's at it, Jimmy?' asked Scott. 'Who else would be trying tae torch the place?'

'Oh, and if you're not back in twenty minutes . . .' Brady looked at Nadia and raised his gun to her temple.

Daley took his machine gun and elbowed his way through the crowd of people. The closer he got to the huge doors, the stronger the smell of petrol became. He tugged at the large brass handle, but the doors wouldn't budge.

'Is this the only way out?'

After a mumble amongst what remained of the Shannon AGM, an old woman spoke. 'The only alternative is via the balcony terrace. There's a service path. It was used to string lights along the front of the building. But you'd need a harness – in this weather you could never keep your feet. It's only about six inches wide, tight up against the wall.'

Daley tried the doors again. He considered trying to break them down with fire from his machine gun, almost instantly dismissing the idea for fear he ignited the fuel.

'If you make it to the far end of the service pathway, there's a window with a catch on the outside of the frame. I used to watch Percy laying the light cables along it when I was a boy. From there you can access the corridor,' said another man, who looked like he could have been Bruce Shannon in another twenty years.

'It's a suicide mission,' said another woman. 'In this cold, in the dark, it's impossible.'

'Time's ticking on, Daley,' shouted Brady.

He forced his way back to Scott's side. 'The doors are stuck fast – barricaded in some way. The only way past it is along a service pathway on the outer wall of the building . . .'

Brady spoke before Daley could finish. 'Be my guest. One way or another, I have no intention of being fried – certainly not in this company.' He pointed to the French windows that led onto the balcony terrace.

More had learned as a young man to do things properly or not at all. If he completed any task less than perfectly he would be punished with a beating. As he wound his way down the long corridor with the third can of petrol he knew that there was no escape for the family he despised. He pictured their death throes in the flames that would engulf them and their precious house. Die in the fire or jump. It had a symmetry that pleased him.

He reached into his pocket for the big brass lighter that had belonged to his wife; he'd borrowed it to light candles in the Kirk during the power outage.

He knew that the Shannons and their captors were now imprisoned in the ballroom, victims of their own security measures. In the nineties the old doors had been strengthened with steel plates; the ballroom was like a massive panic room, where the family could gather to wait for help. But he would make sure help was out of reach. To ensure success, he'd disabled the sprinkler system, controlled from a panel in the caretaker's office in the basement. He wasn't sure if would have worked considering the power cut but, with the emergency generators still running, he didn't want to take the risk.

Old Percy had been so keen to show him all round the house. He felt a pang of guilt about deceiving the old man; after all, he had wasted his life at the beck and call of the family. More had stepped over his lifeless body on he way into the mansion.

The Shannons' demise would be recompense; not just for the horrors he'd experienced as a child, not just for the death of his troubled wife, but for the thousands of others who had suffered at their hands.

He thought of his adoptive mother, her frail attempts to protect him from the beatings, always in vain. He could see her smiling face, battered and bruised, trying to make him feel better as she tended the wounds on his back with cotton wool and the disinfectant that stung him so.

He remembered the day the boss had come to call. He'd arrived in a big truck, the name *Shannon Agricultural* showing proudly on the side through a layer red dust.

'Is the boy any good?' asked the man who, if anything, looked even rougher and more unkind than the man he was forced to call Father.

'Oh, you know, mate. Needs a kick up the arse every day to keep him right.'

'Here, let me save you the job today.' The stranger chased him around the truck then administered a kick to the young Ignatius More's stomach. He could still feel the pain as he curled up in the dirt, the two men laughing at his agony. 'That'll teach the little bastard.'

Eventually, the man drove off. *Shannon Agricultural.*

More flicked his thumb across the wheel of the lighter.

Daley was on the terrace. With his torch he could make out the service pathway – no more than a ledge, now covered with snow. About thirty feet along it, he could see a long window, with a catch showing proud of its frame. Along the wall were iron brackets, no doubt in place to string the harness and the lights he'd been told about.

He looked down. Under the jut of the big balcony he could make out the lower floors, then nothing save the cliff and the luminous crash of the waves far below. His chest tightened – he had no head for heights.

He walked back into the ballroom. At one end were Brady and his captives; at the other, Scott and Symington. He had his machine gun levelled at Brady, with his guards and the captive policemen, while Symington had hers pointed at the guards they had disarmed. The rest of the Shannon party were still crowded around the door.

'I'll have to go for it. There's a ledge along the front of the building that leads to an window. I can't see another way. If that fuel is ignited we'll all have to jump for it, and trust me, that isn't a pleasant prospect. Either way . . .'

'Did you see anything? I mean, any sight o' someone through they windows, Jimmy?' said Scott, keeping his eyes trained on Brady.

'Nothing.'

'Could it no' just be some kind o' leak or something? They've been using petrol generators.'

'No, it's coming from behind the door. We have to be quick.'

'I'll do it,' said Symington.

'What?' asked Daley and Scott in unison.

'I'll climb along this pathway. It makes sense.'

'How so?' said Scott. 'I'm no' intae throwing wee lassies off the side o' tall buildings. I'll have tae dae it. Eh, begging your pardon, ma'am.'

'Are you a climber, DS Scott?'

'No, I've climbed oot o' a few scrapes in my time but no' what you'd call actually real climbing. Something wrong wae the folk that dae that, if you ask me. I'll gie it a try, though.'

'I'll go, and that's final,' said Daley.

'May I remind you gentlemen of the command structure here. You're not built for it, DCI Daley, and DS Scott shakes like a leaf most of the time. I'm a climber, it's one of my hobbies. I'm doing it – end of discussion.'

She walked forwards, the bruise on her face a horrible dark colour in the light of the ballroom. 'I warn you, Mr Brady. My officers have orders to shoot you dead if they think any harm is about to come to any of your hostages. I'm going to stop us getting burned to death. Do you understand?'

'Good luck,' said Brady. 'You'll need it.'

'You seem very calm, if you don't mind me saying. You'll burn with the rest of us.'

'I have faith and my faith can move mountains,' he said with a smile. 'I'd get moving if I were you.'

More cursed the lighter as he threw it down the passageway. No spark came from the flywheel when he had tried to ignite the flame. The flint was exhausted.

He tried the doors, all of which seemed to be locked. Then he remembered; as he'd slipped in the back door over Percy's body, he'd noticed a candle burning on a tall table. It was two floors below. He ran to the spiral staircase and began winding his way down to the lower floors of the building. Soon the Shannons and their magnificent mansion on the clifftop would be cinders and his soul would be at rest.

Superintendent Carrie Symington looked over the stone wall that protected the side of the balcony terrace. Sure enough, she could make out a little step onto a narrow ledge that ran all the way to the window, its catch protruding in the light of her torch. At about head height, iron bars jutted a few inches out from the wall. These had once been used to string lights along the wall, but would serve as decent hand holds.

Her bare hands were already stiffening in the bitter cold, but she stepped up and over the thick stone parapet and tentatively placed her foot on the ledge.

'Be careful, ma'am,' said Daley. He was standing with his back to the parapet, holding a torch in one hand and his weapon in the other. He glanced at his Superintendent and then back in through the French windows to Brady, still inside the ballroom with his captives. He could see Scott from the corner of his eye, his gun trained on the erstwhile Shannon finance director.

'Has she fallen yet?' Brady shouted from inside the ballroom.

Symington slid her foot along, pushing the snow from the ledge. It was difficult, but in a way it helped her. The snow had insulated the surface of the ledge from forming ice, so once she slid it from the next section, she could glide forwards, her body flat against the cold stone of Kersivay House.

Daley looked down as the white snow displaced from the ledge tumbled into the darkness. There was one thing he now knew about his new boss – she had guts.

More reached the bottom of the long spiral staircase, his knees aching with the effort. He turned left and headed down the passageway that led to the rear of the house. The corridors became narrower here, less well decorated, the carpeting thin and utilitarian in the places intended for the family's lackeys.

He leapt down a short flight of stone steps and into the small vestibule at the back door. Sure enough, the large candle was still flickering in its sconce on the table.

Carefully, he pulled it free of the holder. At one point, the flame flickered alarmingly, forcing him to stop in his tracks until it steadied. Old houses were filled with drafts; he would have to be careful. Slowly, he made his way along the passageway, up the short set of steps and along a narrow corridor. He turned a corner and there before him, at the very end of the passage, he could see the first curl of the spiral staircase. He walked forwards, as quickly as he dared.

46

Symington was about halfway along the narrow ledge, the wavering beam of Daley's torch her only light. The machine gun hung off her back by its webbing strap. She stopped, trying to control her breathing and master her fear, the way she had been taught to do when climbing the crags and peaks in the north of England. This though, was another discipline entirely.

Again, she edged forwards, sliding snow off the ledge with the side of her boot as she went.

For some reason, something in the periphery of her vision made her glance below her feet. She had broken the first and most simple rule – don't look down. But she could see what had prompted the reflex action. There, about two floors down and to her right, she saw a flickering flame pass one of the long windows on the spiral stairwell.

They're coming, she thought, the notion making her catch her breath. She felt herself slowly falling back from the stone wall. She tried to gain purchase on the slick surface, but with no success.

Desperately, she groped above her head.

'Carrie!' shouted Daley, as he watched her slip into the darkness.

*

More had two floors left to climb.

'Steady mate, she'll be right,' he muttered under his breath as he paused yet again, the flame guttering in the draft from one of the tall windows.

All he had to do was keep the flame alive. Soon this tiny speck of light would become an inferno that would consume those he most despised.

Just as she lost hope, her hand grasped one of the bars protruding from wall above her head. She cried out as her feet slipped on the ledge, but managed to steady herself.

On the balcony behind her, Daley breathed a sigh of relief. He had fully expected to see the slight figure of the superintendent falling through the darkness onto the rocks and breaking waves below.

Symington hurried along, the thought that someone was climbing the stairs driving her on. In a few more steps she reached the long window and grabbed onto the catch. At first it wouldn't turn, but as she applied all of her strength the handle gave and she pulled the window open with a dull crack. The stench of petrol assaulted her senses.

She placed her right foot on the sill then flung herself through the window and onto a wide window ledge in the dimly lit passageway.

More hesitated as he reached the top step. He was sure he'd heard something, but there was no way anyone could have escaped the ballroom. Those security doors would have withstood a tank being driven at them.

As he stepped across the landing, the flame guttered unexpectedly and he looked up. Standing before him in the dim light of the emergency LED bulbs stood the policewoman who had visited he and his wife when they had discovered the tiny skeleton on the Rat Stone.

'Stay where you are, Reverend More,' said Symington. She was pointing an automatic weapon at him with a determined look on her face.

'Well, never thought I'd be seeing you again,' said More, edging forwards. He noted that her face was bruised, her right eye swollen, the gun shaking in her hands.

'Not another step!' shouted Symington. 'I will fire. I know you're trying to ignite the corridor. No matter what you feel about the Shannons, leave this to us.'

'Oh, it's not just those bastards I'm worried about. What about your mate – DS Scott? I heard what happened to my wife at the Stone. No matter what she did, she didn't need to die.'

'We tried to find you. We have a situation here, please don't make matters worse. You can walk away from this, you have my word.'

'Situation? That's a bit of a euphemism, Superintendent. Some of the richest and most powerful people in the world are imprisoned by bloody nutters, while I get ready to roast the lot of you. I don't think "situation" even begins to cover it.'

'This is your last warning, sir. I will fire if you come any closer.'

'You know, being a man of the cloth gives you an advantage over other folks. I don't mean having a hotline to the man upstairs, either. I don't know what my wife was involved in, but I know she wanted to wipe out the Shannons as much as I do.' He took another step nearer to the police officer. 'You learn to see the truth in people's eyes. You could no more shoot me than float down those stairs, Superintendent.' He lunged forwards, the large candle held out at his side.

Carrie Symington didn't hesitate. She fired a short burst at More's legs. He wasn't in possession of a weapon as such, but if that fuel was ignited he would take many lives, as surely as if he lined people up against the wall and shot them.

The candle rolled across the floor, its flame now a line of harmless grey smoke.

'Guess I was wrong about you,' said More weakly. Blood was pouring from the wounds in his legs.

Symington looked down at him and considered trying to stem the flow of blood with some improvised tourniquet. Then she noticed the damp stain spreading across his belly.

As though he'd read her thoughts, he looked down and placed his hand over the wound. 'Don't worry, Ma,' he said, as his eyes lost focus.

Daley heard the gutter of gunfire. He looked across at Brady, who was still holding Nadia around the neck. What was left of his security team kept their weapons trained on the captives. 'Looks like your boss has been successful,' called Brady. 'Unless she wasn't the one doing the firing, that is.'

Daley rushed to the doors, again trying to push them open. 'Superintendent, can you hear me?' he shouted. There was no reply and he was about to shout again when he heard movement from behind the huge doors. 'Ma'am, is that you?'

'Listen, Jim,' said Symington, dispensing with all formality. 'I'm going to free the doors but this whole place is soaking in petrol. Everyone is going to have to take it really easy, OK?'

Daley turned to the people now crowded around him. He could see Scott standing in front of the group, his weapon pointed at Brady and his captives at the far end of the room.

'Listen, everybody, when the doors open, you're all going to have to leave this room in as orderly a fashion as you can muster. As you can smell, the place is dripping in petrol, so the least spark will set the whole thing ablaze. Do you understand?'

He looked around. Old, young, fat, thin, beautiful, ugly – they all had one thing in common: they wanted to get as far away from the ballroom of Kersivay House as possible.

'OK, ma'am. Go for it. Brian, back up towards me as they leave the room.' Scott nodded his head as something metallic clanged from the hallway and the doors swung open.

Before he could say anything, Daley was pushed back by a wall of people, all desperate to get away from Brady and his henchmen. Daley cursed as he was forced out of the room in the melee.

He felt himself falling and desperately tried to regain his footing. He managed to stay upright and forced his way back into the room towards Scott.

'Jimmy,' called Scott. 'Get out of here, man!'

'I have to stay, Brian.'

It was as though the crowd was being sucked from the room. Soon they had all vanished and Daley heard the large doors close with a bang.

Symington watched the figure of DCI Jim Daley disappear behind the heavy steel doors. As they slammed shut, she saw sparks dance in the gloom. 'Quickly, everyone out of the corridor!' she shouted as, with a muffled thud, the petrol caught fire.

47

Dunn was making her way back along the road towards Kersivay House. She had managed to raise the alarm and hoped fervently that the arrival of a band of brawny farmers with shotguns might sway things in their favour. She had no idea what was happening up at the mansion and the worry made her heart race.

She saw a tall figure standing on the road and as she approached realised that it was Jock, breathing heavily as he stared out into the bay.

'Sorry, my dear. I gave up. The years have taken their toll, right enough.'

'Don't worry. Your friend is spreading the word. Hopefully we'll get some help soon,' she replied, staring at the loom of the mansion in the distance. Low lights emanated from the distant windows, but she didn't know what was happening behind the high stone façade.

'I'm not sure that's good news,' said Jock, nodding towards the bay.

Dunn followed his line of vision. As the pale moon shone through low cloud, she could make out a dark shape. A large vessel was sitting at anchor, no more than a mile off Blaan's shore. Even to the untrained eye, it had low, sleek lines and looked like the expensive vessels owned by the super-rich, normally harboured in more exotic climes in the Mediterranean or Caribbean.

'Somehow, I don't think it's the Royal Navy,' observed Jock.

Daley watched as Ailsa calmly took her seat at the head of the long table, as though she was taking her place at another board meeting, not facing a foe bent on destroying the whole family.

'Who said you could sit down?' asked Brady, levelling his weapon at the old woman.

'I don't need your permission to sit down in my own house, Charles.'

Daley could hear the fire blazing beyond the thick doors. 'Never mind that, we have to get out of here somehow. Those doors won't hold back that fire for long.'

'How could you be part of this?' said Brady, ignoring Daley. 'You're only a Shannon by marriage. It's as though you've become one of them. I know how much you've influenced the running of this company in the last fifty years. You're the real boss.'

'What the hell do you mean?' asked Maxwell. 'My father ran this organisation for years while Ailsa and Bruce sat back and enjoyed the spoils.'

'You really are a stupid little fuck, Maxie. So full of yourself you can't see what's right in front of your eyes.'

'Now, now,' said Ailsa wearily. 'What does it matter who did what and when? It's all in the past. We spend far too much time in this family looking backwards. I'm as guilty of it as anyone.'

'You don't have to worry about that any more, there isn't any future for you to look forward to. We're going to die here. It will be the end of this company and all it stands for,' said Brady.

Ailsa hesitated, her hands held in front of her face, as though in prayer. 'I always find that one's perception of the realities of life differs somewhat from what's really happening. Don't you agree, Charles?'

'What do you mean?'

'Meaning that I know much more than you think.'

'Don't try and manoeuvre me the way you do with your stupid nephew or your pickled son. I know what you're all about. I've made it my business to find out.'

'Oh yes, breaking into pensioners' houses to steal old photographs and butchering the journalists sent to investigate what was going on.'

Brady hesitated, put off his stride. 'How do you know about all of that? The old man – I bet you don't know who he really is.'

'Percy, you mean? I think I can guess what you've found there. But what about your mentor?'

'What about him?'

'Oh, a mystery benefactor selects a child he sees promise in and inculcates him into the ways of an ancient brotherhood. I know what influence the Society of the Golden Bough has had over the years. Governments, crime, business; all ready to *serve and prosper* – isn't that what you say? All ready to jump to each other's assistance when things get tough.'

'I would have had a very different life if it hadn't been for the Brotherhood, have no doubt about it. Our world is in free fall because of institutions like this. We are here to save it.'

Aitcheson and the other two captive police officers looked on as this exchange took place. Bruce held his daughter, utterly taken aback by his mother – by everything, in fact. He'd always known that he had been kept in the dark, away from what really went on with the company. Now he was beginning to realise how little he knew about everything else in life.

'Why don't you tell him, Ailsa?' asked Daley. 'Tell him who you really are and the real reason you became involved with the Shannon family.'

'Why, DCI Daley, how clever of you. You'll indulge me for a few more moments. Those doors are designed to hold back a fire – could hold back a small army, in fact. Time enough for me to tell my short tale.'

'What is this?' asked Brady, looking between the big policeman and the old woman.

'Like you, I was groomed to serve a greater purpose. You didn't know that?' Ailsa said quietly. 'I was beautiful, once – clever, too. I know that's hard to imagine now. Well, the beautiful part, at least.'

'We've all got a past, Ailsa. Who the fuck cares? Pretty girl with brains marries the heir to a mega business. It's happened since the dawn of time.'

'I was brought up to despise the Shannon family. We had lost everything at their hands. Our livelihood, our home – all long before I was born, but the hatred was passed down to me.'

Bruce gaped in amazement. He looked to his cousin Maxwell, whose face bore a similar expression.

'My grandfather spotted my potential. He made sure, through his influential friends, that I had the best education money could buy and moved in all the right circles. Oh, no, not rural Ireland for me, but Oxford and all that went with it. That's where I met my future husband – engineered, of course.'

'Mother, what the hell are you saying? That you were coerced into marrying Father?'

'Well, that's partially true, darling. More accurate to say he was coerced into marrying me. Men are so stupid – a quality passed down in spades to you, I'm sad to say.'

'I don't understand. You married my father and it was arranged by somebody else?'

'Oh, yes. All very clever. But my grandfather was a clever man, you know.'

'And who was he?' asked Bruce, now thoroughly bewildered.

'Nathaniel Stuart,' said Daley. 'Ailsa is Nathaniel's granddaughter.'

Brady looked as though the scales had fallen from his eyes. He glared at the old woman. 'Nathaniel Stuart was your grandfather?' He could hardly make the words form in his mouth.

'Odd, isn't it. For all those years, until Maxie's old man went gaga, it was Nathaniel Stuart's granddaughter running the great Shannon empire.'

In the distance, through the tall doors to the terrace, a thudding noise could be heard, growing louder.

'A chopper!' shouted Aitcheson. 'I knew we would get reinforcements.'

Brady ran over to the French windows and looked out beyond the snow-covered terrace. Sure enough, a helicopter was flying over the bay towards the mansion, lights flashing on its undercarriage.

'I urge you to give yourself up, Mr Brady. Whatever you were trying to achieve here, it's not going to happen now,' said Daley, the relief in his voice plain.

'Don't be ridiculous, Mr Daley,' said Ailsa. 'The helicopter is coming for me. But he's right, please give yourself up, Charles.'

'Look around the room, Ailsa. It doesn't matter if you have a whole fleet of helicopters outside. You're in this room and you're not leaving. Not alive, anyway. They can take away your body in a bag.' The intent in Brady's voice was plain.

'Oh, really,' she replied, examining her fingernails. 'Neville, if you please.'

Slowly, the security guards who had been taking their orders from Brady turned their guns on him.

'Put the gun down,' said Nev.

In a heartbeat, Brady swung round and caught Nadia by the sleeve, pulling her towards him. 'I'm not finished yet,' he roared.

48

Daley looked on dumbfounded. 'Are you people all mad? All that matters is that we get out of here alive. Mrs Shannon, tell us about the helicopter.'

'As I said, Mr Daley, that's *my* escape route. The job here is done, the threat to the company about to be removed.'

'Your brother is dead,' said Daley.

'What?'

'Percy – or whatever his real name was. He died earlier. I'm so sorry. His heart gave out. He was trying to save my officer's life – all of our lives, come to that.'

Bruce looked at his mother as she sat heavily in her seat, the blood draining from her face. 'Your brother? My uncle? This just gets more weird.'

'You don't know the half of it,' said Brady, still struggling with Nadia. 'Trust me.'

Scott and Symington fled down the spiral staircase. When they were two floors below the ballroom, and the conflagration, Symington stopped, breathing heavily.

'What are we going to dae now, ma'am?'

'It's not exactly how we envisaged things panning out, DS Scott.'

'Aye, well, that's oor Jimmy for you. Nae half measures and that's a fact.'

'Those heavy doors will keep the blaze at bay for a while, but I'm not sure what else we can do,' she said, a note of panic in her voice. 'But it's my job to save everyone in that room and that's what I intend to do.'

'Aye, good luck wae that, ma'am. The only thing I can think of is if they shin doon the front o' the hoose somehow.'

'I'm not sure that "shin doon" is going to be an option. What's that noise?'

They listened as a distant thud became louder.

'Sounds like a helicopter, ma'am,' said Scott, hope in his eyes.

Ailsa smiled weakly at Brady. 'As you get older, the utter futility of life strikes you more and more. So many deaths – and now my brother. Let my granddaughter go, Charles, and I'll save you from this.'

'And then?'

'And then we'll have to see. It's a chance you must take. I'm pragmatic, of course. Nathaniel Stuart made sure of that. I'm sure he did the same for you.'

From behind, the great doors shook, as if something had exploded. The roar and crackle of the fire was much louder now, held back only by the heavy doors and thick walls of Kersivay House.

'We have to be quick. Please, Mrs Shannon. For the sake of your family, please!' pleaded Daley.

As the thud of the rotor blades grew louder, the lights of the aircraft swept into the room through the large French windows. 'Well, can you live with our agreement, Charles?' asked Ailsa. 'You needn't suffer.'

He grunted and loosened his grip on Nadia, letting his gun fall to the floor.

'Thank you,' said Ailsa. 'A good decision.' She picked up the radio and spoke into it. The helicopter took a wide arc of the bay, its incredibly bright search light penetrating the gloom as it hovered a few hundred yards from Kersivay House.

'What now?' shouted Daley above the din, coughing at the acrid smoke that was now billowing from under the steel doors.

'We should leave – if this little charade is over. Is it over, Charles?'

He stepped towards her, slowly, the hem of his cloak brushing the floor. Two security guards kept their weapons pointed at his back.

'You know, don't you?' he said, looking straight into the old woman's face.

'Yes. I've known for a long time.'

'Doesn't it make a difference?'

'Remember pragmatism,' she replied.

'What do you know?' shouted Bruce.

Brady turned to face him. 'I'm Archibald Shannon.' He looked back at his mother and nodded. She smiled back in return.

It was as though time had stopped. Despite the roar of the raging fire and the thud from the helicopter, everything seemed to slow. Those in the room stared at each other as though mesmerised. 'Mother, is this true?' asked Bruce in disbelief. 'I . . . I can't believe it!'

'Again, you've failed to grasp the essentials, Bruce.' She turned to Brady, her eldest son, and reached out to touch his face. 'There really was no need for the bones and that shoe. All very melodramatic but I'm not spooked very easily.

Bruce stared at the unlikely pair. He could see it now; the resemblance to his father in Charles's face. 'You've grieved for my brother for years, we all have, and now it's as if you don't give a damn.'

'I grieved for the little boy I lost. The little boy my grandfather couldn't bear to see turn into all he despised – a Shannon. That child was lost a long time ago.' She held Brady's gaze. 'And he's not coming back.'

Brady stared into his mother's face. 'He saved me from turning into of *them*. But it was too late for you; you're a Shannon now, through and through. All these terrible things, it was you in charge all along.' He looked at Bruce – the man who'd been his friend, his long-lost brother. 'I would never have harmed her,' he said, nodding at Nadia, who cowered in her father's embrace. I had a daughter, too.'

'What do you mean?' said Bruce. 'What daughter?'

'Veronica More, my dear. Mr Daley's tormentor, so I'm led to believe. She even had the same problems that your poor Nadia still suffers from. All in the genes, I'm afraid. My other granddaughter.'

Bruce thought of the Australian minister's young wife. The same dark hair, green eyes – the same lost look. He almost cried out.

Ailsa spoke calmly into the radio again and the helicopter slowly turned to circle the bay, gaining height as it did so. 'We have to get to the roof,' Ailsa said calmly. There is a helipad there. We'll be out of this house in minutes.'

‘But how do we get to the roof from here?’ The panic in Maxwell’s voice was plain.

‘You must remember, Maxie, there’s not an inch of this house I don’t know.’

‘So this has all been a charade, Mrs Shannon?’ asked Daley. ‘Let me tell you now, it’s been a deadly one.’

‘I had to deal with what confronted me, Mr Daley. I’ve done my best. I’m sorry for those who lost their lives.’

Charles Brady – Archibald Shannon – looked back at his mother, his brother his niece and his cousin. He nodded his head, then, without warning, ran out across the balcony towards the edge of the parapet, onto which he clambered unsteadily in the snow.

‘Charles, or whoever you bloody well are, what on earth are you doing?’ shouted Maxwell. ‘Come back in, for fuck’s sake. We need to get out of here.’

Brady paused. In the distance, the rock thrust out into the promontory under the pale moonlight. The rock where once the Shannons had served the king in his castle, fought with swords, been strong and brave. The long beach was a silver strip, shining in the gloom.

He stepped out into the darkness, his arms outstretched, and fell. His cloak billowed out behind him as he plummeted down the side of the mansion, past the cliff and onto the dark rocks below.

49

Daley looked on in disbelief. More smoke was escaping under the doors now, making breathing difficult.

'He was my first son,' said Ailsa. 'I loved him. My grandfather couldn't go through with his plan. Couldn't watch my child slowly become a Shannon the way . . . the way I did. The day he took him away, it was already too late.' Ailsa looked out into the distance. The noise from the helicopter was at its loudest now, directly above the house.

'Don't you feel anything?' shouted Bruce above the din. 'What kind of monster are you?'

'I'm the head of the family. The Shannon family,' she said, almost to herself.

'Can we just get out of here!' said Maxwell.

'Archibald Shannon, my son, died fifty years ago.'

'No he didn't!' shouted Bruce. 'That was him, Brady. Don't you care at all?'

'Grow up, Bruce. Be a man and stand up for what's yours for once in your life. If you want to be my heir you'll have to toughen up.'

'No, Mother, I don't want to be your heir. I can't stand it any longer. Do what you have to save us. But then it's over.'

'Your choice,' said Ailsa. 'You have the next few minutes to reconsider. But son or no son, if you decide to go, there's no coming back.'

'I have no doubt about that, Mother.'

'Now, shall we?' She looked around the ballroom. 'Goodbye, brother,' she whispered.

Dunn could see the flames leaping from broken windows. The top half of the mansion was ablaze.

She and Jock had seen the helicopter hover above the house and then disappear across the bay to the sleek vessel moored there. She prayed that Daley was safe, but fear held her heart in its icy grip.

As they neared the building, she could see a crowd of people streaming towards them down the steep drive.

'What's happened?' she shouted, grabbing an elderly woman who was about to slip on the slick surface. After hearing what the old lady had to say, Dunn elbowed her way through the throng towards the house. She could see Scott and Symington standing below the mansion, staring up at the flames.

'Sergeant, ma'am, where's . . .' She didn't manage to get the rest of the words out. The look on Scott's face was enough to make her scream in despair.

'Look!' shouted Jock, pointing back down the drive. Far below, flashing lights could be seen, making their way through the village and towards the long driveway. 'The road must be clear,' he said, his deep voice resonant in the night air.

Scott looked at Symington. 'Too late for oor boys,' he said grimly.

Symington passed her hand across her face, trying to hide her strain from her colleagues. She'd been flung headlong into a nightmare that seemed to have no end. She looked about, desperate to do something, say anything, to mitigate the terrible situation, but no words came.

From behind, she heard a shout. As she and Scott stared into the darkness, four figures made their way from the back of the mansion.

'Jimmy!' shouted Scott, running towards his friend. Daley, Aitcheson and the two Support Unit cops – one the missing constable Booth – staggered along the path towards them.

'How the fuck did you get out of there, man?'

Daley stopped and bent down, his hands on his knees, coughing. 'Long story, Bri,' he said, gasping for breath. 'There was an old service stairway behind the ballroom at the rear of the building. Ailsa knew about it all along. We got onto the roof and were taken off by the helicopter.'

Dunn looked up. She didn't care about protocol any more, about the fact that Daley was her boss or their superintendent was looking on. She rushed towards him and jumped into his arms. 'I love you, Jim,' she whispered.

He didn't hesitate. 'I love you too, Mary.'

'Good to see a close-knit working unit,' smiled Jock.

'I've known him for years and he's never been that close-knit wae me,' said Scott.

'Bugger off,' said Symington with a smile.

Out in the bay, the helicopter was landing on the Shannon cruiser. A blue flash heralded the arrival of the emergency services at the bottom of the long driveway. Jock looked back at the mansion. The top floors were now ablaze and the roof was beginning to catch fire. 'It's been here for a hundred years but I don't think it'll make another hundred.'

He produced a black-and-white photograph from his pocket. Two young children stood on a pier beside a tall, powerfully built man. 'Poor Percy – or Lachie, as I first knew him.'

'You mean he's the boy in the photo? I knew I recognised him,' said Scott. 'I racked my brains trying tae work that out.'

'Aye, he is that. We played together as boys. How he thought I wouldn't recognise him when he came back as an adult, I don't know.'

'I don't suppose you know who the wee lassie is, then?' asked Scott.

'It's Ailsa Shannon,' said Daley, still holding Dunn. 'The woman who was sent to destroy the Shannons but became one of them. Everyone concentrated on the wee boy and forgot the little girl. We all made the same mistake. Even Brady. His body is at the bottom of the cliff under the house. I'll fill you in later, ma'am. He jumped, by the way, but there's so much more to it than that.'

'I'm sure we can put the details of all this to bed over the next few days, people,' said Symington, aware that not only police officers were present.

'It's a strange world, right enough,' said Jock. 'I kept my distance from the family, it was obvious that they wanted no truck with me. I left them alone and they left me alone. But in the end, the Stuarts never really left the land at Kersivay.'

'Wait, I'm confused,' said Scott. 'If you knew a' this, how come you never said anything?'

'Nobody asked me.'

Scott's reply was drowned out by sirens as the emergency services reached the top of the long drive.

As ambulances, police cars and fire engines finally made it to the top of the hill, Kersivay House burned.

On a rise beyond the house, out of sight, a figure looked on, the flames and flashing lights dancing on a dark cloak.

The wind whistled through the tall, old trees that stood sentinel around the Rat Stone. The serenade began; it could never end.

50

Back in the village, paramedics checked Daley and the other officers who had been trapped in the ballroom for problems caused by smoke inhalation, but passed them fit to travel back to Kinloch.

'I'll wind this up, here,' said Symington. 'Privilege of the new girl,' she added with a smile. 'It's been a rough few days. I want you all to get a rest and we'll meet tomorrow evening at the office for a debrief.'

Daley tarried at Symington's side. 'I want to thank you, ma'am.'

'Really, what for?'

'That climb you made. It was one of the bravest things I've ever seen.'

'Get away with you, Jim,' she said, smiling, a slight flush on her cheeks. 'Listen, you and I have to talk over the next few days. I hear you've changed your mind about retiring. Am I right?'

Daley smiled and looked across at Dunn, who was brushing dirt from DS Scott's jacket. 'I've kind of made a promise. It's difficult though, ma'am. I know you're aware of how things are.'

'Nothing is insurmountable, Jim. This is the twenty-first century. Shit happens.' She looked up into his face. 'We're this job, it doesn't need to be us. We'll sort something out. I'm just pleased you've changed your mind. If the division's going to be this challenging, I'll need my best senior officer with me.'

'Well, I wouldn't bet against it being challenging, ma'am.'

'Please, no one can hear you. It's Carrie.'

'Yes, Carrie,' replied Daley awkwardly.

'Now, get a lift home. I'll see you tomorrow.'

'Wherever home is,' said Daley, his gaze back on Mary.

Pollock was driving the police car carefully along the road back to Kinloch. Great white walls of snow lined the route, but the road itself appeared to be safely navigable.

'We'll drop you off at Machrie, dear, then we'll get back to Kinloch,' said Scott, turning round from the front seat to face Daley and Dunn in the back of the car.

Daley looked out into the darkness and sighed. 'Drop me at Mary's house, too, please, Willie.'

Dunn looked at him in the darkness. 'Are you sure?'

'It's not going to be easy. Not in the beginning, anyway. But I'm sure. Are you?'

'I couldn't be surer,' she replied, squeezing Daley's hand.

They were dropped off at Dunn's neat little cottage on the outskirts of Machrie. As a pale dawn broke over a white world, Daley waited at the door as she twisted her key in the lock.

'Come in,' she said, pushing open the door and turning on the hall light. 'Welcome home.'

Daley didn't hesitate as he walked into his new life.

*

She flung her head back as her motion eased. He cried out as he climaxed, then took a deep breath of the cold air of the little bedroom.

'I love you, Jim Daley,' she whispered, curled up by his side.

They stayed silent for a few moments, as their breathing eased, then Daley spoke. 'I'll have to go and see Liz later. Tell her how things are.'

'I know it won't be easy,' she said. 'I know how you feel about your little boy. I'm sorry I've made things so difficult.'

'Couples divorce every day. It's better he's brought up by two parents who are happy apart than the reverse. Liz will soon move on, no doubt about that.'

'I'll have to tell Angus, too,' she said. 'I know it's not the same, but . . .' Her voice tailed off as she drifted off to sleep.

Bright sun shone through the flimsy curtains as he awoke in the double bed; not his own, but where he felt truly at home. The arty black-and-white photos hung on the wall beside the straw hat with the red bow, pinned to the side of the bed.

He could hear her moving around in the kitchen, but was surprised when she walked into the room dressed in jeans and a thick purple jumper, her auburn hair in a single pleat that hung over her right shoulder.

'Here, have some coffee. I wasn't sure you were awake, but I made it anyway.' She gave him a thin smile.

'What's wrong? Have you changed your mind already?' said Daley, only half in jest.

'I'm off to tell Angus. We had plans, you know. Holidays, stuff like that. I'm dreading it. I hope his parents aren't about.'

'Yes, I know,' said Daley, sipping his coffee. 'Be careful. The roads might be clear but they're still treacherous. Keep the foot off the floor.'

'Yes, sir,' she said laughing. Then she was suddenly serious. 'You've been married for such a long time – and now there's wee Jim to think of, too.'

'Don't call him wee Jim,' said Daley, anxious to brighten the mood. 'Makes him sound like a circus act.'

'OK. Jimmy Junior then.' She bent over to kiss him.

'You're going now? No time for . . .'

'No!' She punched him playfully in the stomach and he spilled some coffee on the sheets.

They kissed, then she walked to the door. She turned back and looked at him. 'I love you so much, Jim Daley. I've never felt like this in my life before. It's . . . it's like the day you're going on a special holiday. You know, one you've been looking forward to all your life. Do I sound stupid?'

'No. No, you don't. I love you too. Being apart from you – seeing you every day, seeing you with him – it's broken my heart, over and over again.

'Ditto, love, ditto,' she said jokingly. 'I won't be long – about an hour or so, once I get to their farm and back. I shouldn't think what I have to say will take long, but it has to be face to face. He deserves that, at least.'

'Yeah, he does,' replied Daley, already dreading the thought of telling Liz much the same thing.

'See you later,' she shouted, leaving the room. 'Have a snooze. I'll pick you up when I come back.'

He heard her pause in the hall. The bedroom door swung open again. 'And don't think you can go back on your promise. You're withdrawing your resignation, right?'

'Yes, I'm withdrawing my resignation. I've already

spoken to Carrie about it. I'll sort it out over the next few days.'

'Oh, Carrie, now, is it? I'll have to watch her.' She grinned.

'Very funny. I don't sleep with every pretty colleague I work with, you know. You're the first and you'll be the last.'

'Too right, Jimmy boy,' she said, aping Scott's voice. Her face softened, tears in her ice-blue eyes. 'It's you for ever, Jim Daley. Please never forget that.'

Before he could reply, she was gone. He heard her footsteps hurrying down the hall, then the door opened for a second and slammed shut.

He turned over in the bed. He could smell her perfume on the pillow as he drifted back off to sleep.

As Mary drove back to Machrie, she slipped a CD into the car stereo. She wasn't sure if she'd always been keen on eighties music, or if she'd been trying to fit in with Daley's tastes then come to enjoy it.

She hummed along tunelessly to the A-ha track as she felt the car slip slightly on the icy road surface. Better take it easy, she thought.

Mary felt guilty about Angus. He'd looked so pleased to see her, embracing her on the threshold of the big, warm farmhouse. When she took him aside and told him the bad news he'd looked crushed.

She knew that there was no point in prolonging the agony, so made her excuses and left immediately. She tried to banish the image of him sitting on the couch, tears welling, from her mind. She had cared for him, but not as much as he had for her; and certainly nothing like the feelings she had for Jim Daley.

As the next track played, she laughed. 'No, I'm not going to cry again,' she said, as though in reply to the song.

Without warning, the car slid and her view of the world tilted as the steering wheel dragged itself roughly from her grip.

Daley awoke with a jolt and looked at his watch. Shit, she had been gone for more than two hours. Obviously her conversation with Angus was more difficult than she'd imagined.

He pulled himself stiffly from the bed, rubbed his throat where he'd almost been strangled on the Rat Stone, and stumbled through to the kitchen in his T-shirt and boxer shorts, wincing as he trod on a discarded earring in his bare feet.

Waiting for the kettle to boil, he made his way into the small living room. He hadn't been in the house for a few months and was impressed to see that she'd bought a stereo system that played old-fashioned vinyl records. Very trendy now, he mused.

He thumbed through her small collection of albums, smiling at the silhouette of a man's head in a trilby hat; it was so familiar, he had the album himself.

He switched on the stereo, carefully removed the record from its sleeve and placed it on the turntable. He listened to the satisfying thud and click as the needle connected with the plastic and a mournful voice sang of praying for the light.

A Note from the Author

Those of you who have knowledge of Kintyre may recognise that Blaan is my fictitious version of the village of Southend – originally St Blaan – located on the southern tip of the peninsula. This settlement has such a rich history it is impossible to do it justice here, but I will do my best to give you a brief insight.

There does exist a real Rat Stone, or Stane, as it is referred to locally. It can be found on the shore at Pennyseorach, two miles or so from the centre of Southend. While its origin and age are uncertain, it has long been associated with fertility. Indeed, well within living memory, local farmers would place metal pins in its carved stone bowl as a traditional offering to guarantee a good harvest.

The great saint of the old Celtic Church Saint Columba has long been associated with the area. Tradition has it that what is now Southend was his first stopping-off point when he left his native Ireland on a mission to spread the gospel throughout Scotland. You can see Saint Columba's footprints near the local graveyard, where he allegedly made his mark. The two prints – carved into the stone – are more likely to be remnants of the old 'Fealty Foot' whereby the new king-in-waiting would place his foot on the stone and take his vows of kingship in the manner of his forebears. You can still stand in them today.

Indeed, it is reckoned that the Kintyre peninsula was the first part of the country settled by the Scoti tribe (who eventually gave Scotland its name), when they made their way across the North Channel. The real 'red yins'' presence is still felt in modern Scotland by the reluctance of some to have only those with dark hair as a first foot (the first visitor to a house in the hours after the bells of Hogmanay). Going back in time, to welcome a red-haired member of the Scoti tribe into your home would have been to court mayhem and death, as they slowly displaced the indigenous population.

As a child, like many from Campbeltown and the surrounding area, we would flock to the beautiful beach at Southend to enjoy the long hot summer days of the seventies, days that we don't seem to get any more. As we sat under the shadow of Dunaverty Rock, upon which the old castle used to stand, we had little idea that one of the great massacres in the history of these islands took place right where we were building sandcastles or kicking footballs about.

In 1647, after being trapped in Dunaverty Castle, with the water supply poisoned, 300 or so souls – mostly MacDonalds – were allegedly persuaded to surrender by General David Leslie of the Covenanter Army who promised them good terms. However, at the insistence of the Reverend Naves (or Nevoy), chaplain to Archibald Campbell, 1st Marquess of Argyll, all but a few were cut down, the slaughter only ending when Leslie himself, ankle-deep in blood, could no longer stomach it.

That massacre dwarfs the more well-known horror perpetrated against the MacDonalds of Glencoe in 1692, and marked the beginning of the dominance of the Campbells in the area, leading to the change of name of the settlement of Kinlochkilkerran to Campbeltown.

To find out more about these episodes, seek out the wonderful autobiographical books of Angus MacVicar (*Salt in My Porridge and Rocks in My Scotch*, now sadly out of print but available online), or those of local historians such as Angus Martin (*Kintyre: The Hidden Past*, The Grimsay Press, 2014).

The Druids

As noted in the epigraph to this book, Julius Caesar was the first to draw the attention of the wider world to the existence of the Druids, who dominated spiritual affairs in the islands now known as Great Britain and Ireland during the Iron Age.

The Druids were men of learning and healing, who after many years of rigorous training gained the power both to nurture and to destroy. They led armies into battle, and even the kings or chiefs of the day were wise enough to bend the knee to these spiritual leaders. Using a mixture of superstition and terrifying cruelty, they maintained a grip on this primitive society. Though the Romans – no strangers to bloodletting themselves – did their best to eradicate them, they did not believe that they ever really succeeded.

Somewhat incongruously, the Druids were fervent guardians of their environment, with more than a little in common with those of a green persuasion today. Using herbs, plants and lichens to heal, they were medics, feared and respected in equal measure.

Saint Columba, with his commanding presence and affinity with nature, had more than a whiff of the Druid about him, despite his dedication to spreading the Christian message.

The next time you put up your Christmas tree, it is worth remembering that the glittering baubles you are hanging on the branches are an ancient throwback to the Druids, who were in the habit of hanging the severed heads of their enemies on oak trees during times of celebration.

Who knows when, or indeed if, their influence ever really came to an end.

D.A.M.
Gartocharn
March 2016

Acknowledgements

As always, thanks to my family – Fiona, Rachel and Sian; Hugh Andrew, editors Alison Rae and Julie Fergusson, cover designer Chris Hannah, and all at Polygon who work so hard to bring Daley et al to the page; to my agent, Anne Williams, at the Kate Hordern Literary Agency, for continued help, support and a listening ear. And to the late, great Angus MacVicar, who remains an inspiration after all these years. You may spot a couple of familiar names I've used in 'my' Blaan by way of a tiny tribute. I fervently hope that some enterprising publisher will rediscover his work, especially his autobiographies and wonderful children's books, which remain as fresh and beguiling as ever, and bring them back into print. Finally, to the good people of Kintyre, and all of those who have enjoyed the books: to one and all, my heartfelt thanks. I urge you to take in the world of D.C.I. Daley and visit Kintyre for yourself. You won't be disappointed, I promise.

The D.C.I. Daley Thriller series

Book 1: *Whisky from Small Glasses*
ISBN 978 1 84697 321 5

When the body of a young woman is washed up on an idyllic beach on the west coast of Scotland, D.C.I. Jim Daley is despatched from Glasgow to lead the investigation. Far from home, and his troubled marriage, it seems that Daley's biggest obstacle will be managing the difficult local police chief; but when the prime suspect is gruesomely murdered, the inquiry begins to stall.

As the body count rises, Daley uncovers a network of secrets and corruption in the close-knit community of Kinloch, thrusting him and his loved ones into the centre of a case more deadly than he had ever imagined.

Book 2: *The Last Witness*
ISBN 978 1 84697 288 1

James Machie was a man with a genius for violence, his criminal empire spreading beyond Glasgow into the UK and mainland Europe. Fortunately, James Machie is dead, murdered in the back of a prison ambulance following his trial and conviction. But now, five years later, he is apparently back from the grave, set on avenging himself on those who brought him down. Top of his list is his previous associate, Frank MacDougall, who unbeknownst to D.C.I. Jim Daley, is living under protection on his lochside patch, the small Scottish town of Kinloch. Daley knows that, having been the key to Machie's conviction, his old friend and colleague D.S. Scott is almost as big a target. And nothing, not even death, has ever stood in James Machie's way . . .

Book 3: *Dark Suits and Sad Songs*
ISBN 978 1 84697 315 4

After a senior Edinburgh civil servant spectacularly takes his own life in Kinloch harbour, D.C.I. Jim Daley comes face to face with the murky world of politics. To add to his woes, two local drug dealers lie dead, ritually assassinated. It's clear that dark forces are at work in the town, and with his marriage hanging on by a thread, and his sidekick D.S. Scott wrestling with his own demons, Daley's world is in meltdown.

When strange lights appear in the sky over Kinloch, it becomes clear that the townsfolk are not the only people at risk. The fate of nations is at stake.

Book 4: *The Rat Stone Serenade*
ISBN 978 1 84697 340 6

It's December, and the Shannon family are returning home to their clifftop mansion near Kinloch for their annual AGM. Shannon International is one of the world's biggest private companies, with tendrils reaching around the globe in computing, banking and mineral resourcing, and it has brought untold wealth and privilege to the family. However, a century ago Archibald Shannon stole the land upon which he built their home – and his descendants have been cursed ever since.

When heavy snow cuts off Kintyre, D.C.I. Jim Daley and D.S. Brian Scott are assigned to protect their illustrious visitors. As an ancient society emerges from the blizzards, and its creation, the Rat Stone, reveals grisly secrets, ghosts of the past begin to haunt the Shannons. As the curse decrees, death is coming – but for whom and from what?

Book 5: *Well of the Winds*
ISBN 978 1 84697 368 0

Malcolm McCauley is the only postman on the island of Barsay, just off the coast of Kintyre, part of D.C.I. Jim Daley's rural patch. When he tries to deliver a parcel to the Bremners' farm he finds no one at home. A kettle is whistling on the stove, breakfast is on the table, but of the Bremners – three generations of them – there is no sign.

While investigating the family's disappearance, D.C.I. Daley uncovers links to Kintyre's wartime past and secrets so astonishing they have profound implications for present-day Europe. But people in very high places are determined that these secrets stay in the shadows for ever – at any cost.

Denzil Meyrick eBooks

All of the D.C.I. Daley thrillers are available as eBook editions, along with an eBook-only novella and the two short stories below.

Dalintober Moon: A D.C.I. Daley Story
When a body is found in a whisky barrel buried on Dalintober beach, it appears that a notorious local crime, committed over a century ago, has finally been solved. D.C.I. Daley discovers that, despite the passage of time, the legacy of murder still resonates within the community, and as he tries to make sense of the case, the tortured screams of a man who died long ago echo across Kinloch.

Two One Three: A Constable Jim Daley Short Story (Prequel)
Glasgow, 1986. Only a few months into his new job, Constable Jim Daley is walking the beat. When he is called to investigate a break-in, he finds a young woman lying dead in her squalid flat. But how and why did she die?

In a race against time, Daley is seconded to the CID to help catch a possible serial killer, under the guidance of his new friend, D.C. Brian Scott. But the police are not the only ones searching for the killer . . . Jim Daley tackles his first serious crime on the mean streets of Glasgow, in an investigation that will change his life for ever.

Empty Nets and Promises: A Kinloch Novella

It's July 1968, and redoubtable fishing-boat skipper Sandy Hoynes has his daughter's wedding to pay for – but where are all the fish? He and the crew of the *Girl Maggie* come to the conclusion that a new-fangled supersonic jet which is being tested in the skies over Kinloch is scaring off the herring.

First mate Hamish, who we first met in the D.C.I. Daley novels, comes up with a cunning plan to bring the laws of nature back into balance. But as the wily crew go about their work, little do they know that they face the forces of law and order in the shape of a vindictive Fishery Officer, an Exciseman who suspects Hoynes of smuggling illicit whisky, and the local police sergeant who is about to become Hoynes' son-in-law.

Meyrick takes us back to the halcyon days of light-hearted Scottish fiction, following in the footsteps of Compton Mackenzie and Neil Munro, with hilarious encounters involving ghostly pipers, the US Navy and even some Russian trawlermen.

And here is a taster from the fifth book in the series, *Well of the Winds.*

Kinloch, 1945

The spring evening had given way to a night illuminated by a full moon, intermittently obscured by dark scudding clouds. Elsewhere, a bright night like this was dreaded: cities, towns and villages picked out in the moonlight, prey to waves of enemy bombers, or worse still, the terrifying whine of the new super weapon: the doodlebug. Not so here on Scotland's distant west coast – here, there was a safe haven.

Out on the loch, the man could see a dozen grey warships looming, framed by the roofs and spires of Kinloch and the hills beyond that cocooned the town. Crouched behind a boulder down on the causeway, he watched the breeze tugging at the rough grass that gave way to the rocky shoreline and the sea hissing and sighing.

In the distance he heard the stuttering engine of a car making its way along the narrow coast road from Kinloch which skirted the lochside before disappearing into the hills. The headlights cast a weak golden beam, sweeping across the field behind him. The engine stopped with a shudder and the lights flickered out as the vehicle came to a halt in the little lay-by beside the gate to the causeway. The man held his breath as the car door opened and then slammed shut.

It was time.

He'd always known this moment would come, but a sudden chill in his bones compelled him to draw tighter the scarf around his neck. He reached into the deep pocket of his gabardine raincoat, feeling the reassuring heft of the knife. He closed his fist over the wooden handle and waited, heart pounding.

He saw the beam of a torch flash across the waves and gasped as a creature – most likely a rat – scurried away from the light. He breathed in the cool air, tainted by the stench of rotting seaweed. The footsteps were getting closer now, scuffing across the rocks in his direction. He heard a man clear his throat.

'Hello . . . are you there?' The voice was deep and resonant with no hint of trepidation. For a heartbeat, he wondered how the end of existence could creep up so suddenly – unbidden and unannounced. Was there no primeval instinct at work, protecting flesh, bone and breath? How could the path of one's life come to a sudden dead end without even the tiniest hint?

He stepped out from behind the boulder, shielding his eyes from the glare of the torch now directed straight into his face.

'What in hell's name are you doing here?' Though the question was brusque, the voice was calm, almost uninterested. He watched as the man turned the beam of the torch back along the way he'd come and firmly pulled down his trilby when a gust of wind threatened to send it spinning into the waves.

Ignoring the remark, he rushed him from behind. He hooked his left arm around the man's stout neck and snaked his right arm across the man's waist. Up and twist, right under the ribcage, as he'd been taught – plunged into him again and again. There was only fleeting resistance as the long sharp blade did its job. The man had been completely unprepared for the attack – just as they'd said he would be. His victim tensed, then went limp. A gurgle – almost a plea – came from the depth of his throat, as his life drained away. Aided by his assailant, who took his weight, the dying man sank to the ground.

He dragged the body behind the boulder that had been his hiding place, almost losing his balance when a deep sigh – the last sign of life – issued from the victim's gaping mouth. Leaving the corpse propped up behind the boulder, he stood up straight and took deep gulping breaths.

He waited, with only the thud of his heart in his ears and the restless surf for company.

It had been as easy as they'd predicted.

In what must only have been minutes, but seemed like hours, he heard another car making its way slowly along the narrow road towards him

His job was done. The greater good had prevailed – the greater good must always prevail.